Praise for *Roseghetto*

'*Roseghetto* is a remarkable, at times confronting, story. It is a tale that needs to be told, with both tenderness and honesty. Only a writer of Kirsty Jagger's calibre could write this story. *Roseghetto* is in her blood and in her bones.' – **Tony Birch**

'Kirsty Jagger has produced something profound in *Roseghetto*, a gritty, urban story about the underprivileged existing in plain sight. Jagger inhabits the landscape of poverty, oppression and injustice with a light hand and a deeply authentic touch. The veracity of this book is never in doubt, as Jagger explores a childhood of deprivation and hardship, while never losing the sparkle of hope.' – **Michelle Johnston**

'Disturbing and moving, *Roseghetto* is a clear-eyed exploration of growing up under the unyielding threat of violence and economic powerlessness in Sydney's poorer western suburbs of the 1980s and 90s. And yet Kirsty Jagger writes with enough love and understanding to make her story a chronicle of just about every decade in the darker side of Australian life. Her protagonist Shayla is beautifully drawn, a heartbreaking but ultimately powerful lightning rod for the way self-determination can grow from even the cruellest beginnings.' – **Venero Armanno**

'Courageous, deeply moving and beautifully written, *Roseghetto* is a glorious paean to the power of stories, and to the power of speaking the truth. It's impossible not to love the brilliant and determined Shayla – and impossible to finish reading *Roseghetto* and remain unchanged. A powerful and important debut.' – **Kathryn Heyman**

Kirsty Jagger is a journalist by trade. In 2019, she won the inaugural Heyman Mentorship Award for a writer from a background of social or economic disadvantage. *Roseghetto* is partly inspired by Kirsty's experience of growing up in the housing commission estates of Sydney's western suburbs. This is her first novel.

Roseghetto

KIRSTY JAGGER

UQP

First published 2023 by University of Queensland Press
PO Box 6042, St Lucia, Queensland 4067 Australia

University of Queensland Press (UQP) acknowledges the Traditional Owners and their
custodianship of the lands on which UQP operates. We pay our respects to their Ancestors and
their descendants, who continue cultural and spiritual connections to Country. We recognise
their valuable contributions to Australian and global society.

uqp.com.au
reception@uqp.com.au

Cover design by Amy Daoud
Typeset in 12/16 pt Bembo Std Regular by Post Pre-press Group, Brisbane
Printed in Australia by McPherson's Printing Group

  UQP is assisted by the Australian Government
through the Australia Council, its arts funding and
advisory body.

A catalogue record for this book is available from the National Library of Australia.

ISBN 978 0 7022 6604 1 (pbk)
ISBN 978 0 7022 6740 6 (epdf)
ISBN 978 0 7022 6722 2 (epub)

UQP uses papers that are natural, renewable and recyclable products made from wood grown
in well-managed forests and other controlled sources. The logging and manufacturing processes
conform to the environmental regulations of the country of origin.

MIX
Paper | Supporting
responsible forestry
FSC® C001695

For the gutter kids

This book is about breaking the cycle of violence. It contains depictions of violence perpetrated against women, children and animals. It also deals with the very real consequences of repeated and sustained trauma, including substance abuse, self-harm, suicidal ideation and revictimisation. I believe these are critical issues that we need to discuss and examine. I also recognise that survivors of domestic, family and/or intimate partner violence may find some of the content triggering. But please remember: this is a story about *breaking* the cycle, not being broken by it. It's about strength, resilience and, ultimately, triumph. There's lots of hope, love and light among the darkness.

Prologue

I haven't been back in sixteen years, so I take the scenic route via Dickens Road, Ambarvale. Nothing's changed. It's still as scabby as ever. Illegally dumped household items pollute the street, so poor and pathetic that even Mum and Rob, problem hoarders, wouldn't give them a second glance. Stray cats dart in front of my car, broken glass crunches beneath the tyres, people watch from their front steps as I drive past. Dozens of dilapidated houses, accommodating hundreds of public-housing tenants, are squished together in claustrophobic cul-de-sacs, despite being surrounded by vast, empty reserves. The reserves are littered with rusted shopping trolleys turned upside down, wheels in the air. The yellow and brown of dead grass and leaf litter is occasionally interrupted by big black garbage bags; filled, tied and dumped on the side of the road. Some houses look vacant. Others resemble junkyards. Neighbours share walls and driveways. Tattered tarps, sun-bleached shade cloth and rotten bamboo roller blinds blow in the breeze, hanging precariously from the gutters of those who want a little privacy.

I pause at the intersection of Dickens Road and Copperfield Drive. This is different. New, privately owned homes have been built on the corner of Cleopatra Drive. They have fresh concrete façades and glassed-in second-storey balconies. Windows are fitted with the same blinds or shutters throughout. Newly laid lawns are green and boarded by hedges that sparkle with water sprinkled from professionally installed irrigation systems. Front steps and verandahs are tiled. Some even have paths right up to their front doors.

I reach for my Spirax reporter pad on the passenger seat and jot down some notes. *Urban planning and development; the wins, the*

1

fails, the casualties. Injuries sustained, lives lost, futures destroyed. Most of the stories go unreported – to police, by the media – until something like the Rosemeadow riot thrusts issues into the public spotlight.

I was only a week into my cadetship with the Australian Broadcasting Corporation when street violence erupted in the suburb in 2009. Police and media reports said the brawl started in Macbeth Way, between two warring families, over the alleged sexual assault of a fifteen-year-old girl, before it spilt out onto Copperfield Drive. Twenty fought with knives, baseball bats and a rifle, while around eighty others looked on. Two men were shot, four – including the sixteen-year-old accused shooter – were stabbed, one was glassed and others were bashed with baseball bats. The riot squad rolled in, and so did the politicians.

'We will not tolerate neighbourhood terrorism,' New South Wales housing minister of the day, David Borger, said of the Rosemeadow riot. 'It's a community that needs rebuilding.'

As it turns out, he meant from scratch. A mother of fifteen, with four sons allegedly involved in the brawl, was among those evicted. And Rosemeadow Estate was ordered demolished.

'While the high unemployment, low income and large numbers of children are a problem, perhaps the single most pressing issue is the disaster created in the 1970s when the state government implemented the American Radburn design for public housing,' the *Sydney Morning Herald* read.

They quoted Philip Cox, the architect who introduced the design – characterised by homes built back-to-front on narrow dead-end streets connected by poorly lit laneways – to New South Wales decades earlier. He declared it an 'urban design experiment that failed'.

The car behind me beeps and brings me back to 2018. I wave an apology and turn left into Rosemeadow proper. Macduff Way, Malcolm Way and Macbeth Way are the first to greet me. Police know them as 'the 3Ms'. I know them as the characters of a Shakespearean tragedy. In my research for this assignment, I've read that thirty townhouses in Macbeth Way have been torn down and replaced with a mix of public and private housing, including accommodation for the elderly and a community centre. Macduff Way and Malcom Way, however, look as though they've only received a fresh lick of paint.

Directly opposite them, first on the right, is Westminster Way. I pull in, park on the street and remember a time when I wanted to tear this place down, down to the ground, and bury it. Now someone's done it for me. There's not a house left standing. All that's left is the street sign. And me. I step out of the car, turn around and look back the way I came.

1

Mummy's asleep. She makes the pop-pop-pop noise that comes out of her mouth when she's very tired. I whisper and tap her on the shoulder, softly.

'Mummy. Mummy.'

She jumps out of her sleep, throws the covers off and puts her hand to the long, sharp knife on her bedside table. She holds her breath for a second, then breathes out loud when she sees me.

'Oh, thank Bowie!' Her hand moves away from the knife and over her heart, like I gave her a big fright. 'What's wrong? What's going on?'

'I had an accident.'

Mummy's shoulders fall. 'Not again.'

'I didn't mean to.'

Mummy drops her hands into her lap. I trace the lines in her palms, the ones Nanna says she can read. Nanna's told me they say Mummy will have one child, a long life and live alone. Mummy always says, 'Yeh, you'd like that, wouldn't you?' and pulls her hands away.

'I don't know why you keep doing this, Shayla.'

'It wasn't my fault.' I hold Mummy's fingers.

She rolls her eyes and nods.

'I had a nightmare.'

Mummy stands up. 'Yeh, well, you never tell me what the nightmare is.'

'I can't remember.'

Mummy walks across the hall and turns on the bathroom light.

'I don't remember, Mummy. I promise.'

'If this keeps happening, you're going to have to start wearing nappies again. You know that, don't you?'

'No, Mummy, no.'

'Well, I don't know what else to do, Shayla. What am I meant to do? It's every bloody night. What happened to being a big girl now, huh? Don't cry. There's no point crying, Shayla.'

I try to stop crying, or to cry quieter. I look down at the bathroom floor, so Mummy can't see my tears. My arms hang heavy by my sides. Cold, wet Barbie pyjama pants stick to my legs.

Mummy turns the taps on and pulls my shirt up over my head.

'Ooh, that hurt.' I hold my nose.

'Sorry,' Mummy says. 'I'm just trying to be quick about this. I'm tired, okay?'

The bathroom mirror starts to fog up. I look at Mummy's messy dark-red hair and the black make-up marks under her eyes.

'I won't wake you up anymore.'

'What are you going to do if you wet the bed then, huh?'

'I won't wet the bed.'

'And if you do?'

'I'll clean it up.'

'No, you won't,' Mummy says. 'You're not to get in the bath alone, in case you slip and fall, okay? And you're not allowed to take the sheets down the stairs, in case you trip and fall down those too, understood?'

I hold on to Mummy's shoulders while she pulls the wet pants down my legs and over my feet. She holds my hand as I step into the tub.

'You okay to wash yourself while I sort this mess out?'

'Yes.'

I wet a fresh flannel and rub soap into it. Mummy picks up my dirty pyjamas.

'Hey,' Mummy says from the doorway. 'I'm sorry too. I don't mean to be grumpy. I'm just tired, that's all. You know I love you, right?'

'I love you too, Mummy.'

Mummy smiles a soft, small smile at me. I try to smile softly back.

I hear Mummy pull the bed out from the wall, open and close the linen press, take the wet sheets downstairs and start the washing machine. Soon she brings a fresh set of pyjamas.

'You done?'

I nod.

Mummy wraps a fluffy pink towel around me, lifts me out of the bath and puts me down on a fluffy bathmat.

'Mummy?'

'Yes, Shayla?' Mummy's green eyes look tired, her full lips thin.

'Can I sleep with you tonight?'

Mummy's unhappy with me. She says I haven't been myself lately. I've said and done things that upset her.

'She's been agitated when she comes home from his place,' Mummy says. 'She uses bad language. Tells me I'm not her mother. She won't eat. She wets the bed.'

I peek around the corner. Mummy pulls out a chair and sits down at the head of the dining table with a fresh cup of coffee.

'I took her to a paediatrician on Tuesday. They said they couldn't find anything wrong with her and suggested I contact you.'

'Really? They suggested you contact the Department of Community Services?'

I can't see the face of the woman asking, just the back of her head. She has short dark-brown hair. It's wavy and there's a lot on top. She pulls pen and paper from her handbag.

'Yeh. They gave me your number. I called as soon as I got home. Thanks for coming out so fast.'

'We like to action these kinds of referrals as quickly as possible.'

'Yeh, when you said Thursday, initially I thought you meant next week.'

'Do you mind if I take some notes while we talk?'

'That's fine,' Mummy says.

'And are you comfortable with me talking to Shayla today?'

'Sure. Do you want me to grab her now?'

I hide around the corner and hold my breath.

'I might just ask you a few questions first, if you don't mind?'

'Sure.'

I let out the breath and sit down on the lounge to listen. It's a big lounge. Grey and a little bit scratchy, with red and white lines in it. It's made of three parts. The middle part is a corner piece. That's my seat.

'How old are you, Lauren?'

'Twenty-four, turning twenty-five in March.'

'What do you do for work?'

'Sales and admin. I work part-time in a music shop. They also run classes for kids after school.'

'How old is Shayla?'

'She turned three on the twenty-first of January.'

'Does she go to day care or preschool?'

'She goes to Puff 'n' Billie Preschool in Macquarie Fields.'

'How often?'

'Two days a week. Mondays and Wednesdays.'

'While you're at work?'

'Yes. My parents mind her on Fridays.'

'At their house?'

'Sometimes.'

'Other times?'

'Sometimes they mind her here.'

'And how long ago did you notice changes in Shayla's behaviour?'

'I'd say just after Christmas last year.'

'December 1990?'

'I think so, yeh.'

Papers shuffle. 'So, you noticed these changes a few weeks after your divorce was finalised?'

'Yeh, that sounds about right.'

'You were separated from your husband for some time before this?'

'Yes.'

'And Shayla lived with you?'

'Yes. We had a unit at Mount Druitt.'

'And there were no changes in her behaviour when you moved there?'

'None that I noticed.'

'What about when you moved to this house?'

'She's a bit scared of our neighbours,' Mummy says. 'To be honest, I'm a bit scared of them too.'

'Why's that?'

'They fight a lot. The woman next door had a fight with her husband, or whatever he is – partner – last week, and she threw her bloody lounge through the front window!'

'I did notice it was boarded up.'

'We've got shared walls on each side, so we can hear everything,' Mummy says. 'Glenfield isn't a very nice place to raise a small child, you know? Well, not this part of it, anyway. I mean, it's better here than where we were at Mount Druitt, but there's still always police and ambulance in the street for stuff – domestics, suicides. The other night there was an overdose.'

Mummy makes her voice small, so I have to listen harder.

'The guy on the other side of us was just released from prison,' she says. 'I don't know what he was in for, and I don't want to know, but it's just not a good situation for a young single mother and her toddler to be in. It would've been nice to be a little bit closer to my mum and dad in Punchbowl, so I could have some extra support, but it's all we could get at the time.'

'Have you put in for a transfer?'

'I have.'

'But when you moved to this house, there were no changes in her behaviour?'

'No.'

'At the time of your separation, you agreed to joint legal and physical custody?'

'Yes.'

'Why did you separate?'

'Because he's an evil prick.' Mummy sort of laughs.

'Can you be more specific?'

There's the flick-flick-flick of a cigarette lighter. 'He was violent.'

'Towards you or Shayla?'

'Towards me.'

'Can you describe the violence?'

'Like, what he did?'

'Yes, please.'

I hear Mummy suck on her smoke.

'Was the violence verbal, physical, sexual?'

'All ...' Mummy's voice cuts out. 'All of those.'

'Was he violent towards other people?'

'Yes.' Mummy sniffs. 'And animals.'

'But never towards Shayla?'

'No.'

'And she has access with her father?'

'Every second weekend.'

'Is anyone at the house with them when she's there?'

'I don't know. His parents might visit. I'd have to ask Shayla.'

'She doesn't talk about what happens when she visits?'

'Not really, no. I think she knows I don't like to talk about him.'

'Does anyone else live here with you?'

'No.'

'Does anyone else stay?'

'Sometimes my parents.'

'Where do they sleep when they stay?'

'They take my bed and I sleep down here on the lounge.'

'Tell me about Shayla's bedwetting.'

'It doesn't happen when she sleeps in bed with me. It only happens when she's in her own bed,' Mummy tells the stranger.

My face burns.

'She says she has nightmares. And she must, because even when she sleeps in my bed she thrashes around and murmurs in her sleep. And she feels clammy, like she's having a cold sweat. But she says she doesn't know what the nightmares are about. Wakes up and can't remember.'

I quietly go back upstairs.

When they call me, I'm sitting on the top step looking at *The Poky Little Puppy*. It's my new favourite Little Golden Book. Poppy gave it to me for my birthday. Mummy stands at the bottom of the stairs with the woman whose face I couldn't see before.

'Hi Shayla. My name's Joan. I'm a district officer with the Department of Community Services. It's nice to meet you. Mummy's told me so much about you.'

I close the book and stand up. 'She told you I wet the bed.'

Joan smiles. She's older than Mummy. The skin around her eyes is crinkled and her neck is a bit wobbly, like the flabby skin under Nanna's arms.

'I didn't mean to embarrass you, Shayla. I'm just trying to find out why it's happening,' Mummy says.

She's in her black Rolling Stones T-shirt. The one with the big red mouth on it and a tongue poking out. Her hair is pulled back in a high pony with a thick black velvet scrunchie. It's so long it hangs halfway down her back. She looks like a Barbie doll.

'I've told you, it's an accident!'

Mummy's eyes get big and her cheeks turn pink. 'I'll just get her lunch,' she tells Joan, turning away and walking fast towards the kitchen.

Joan watches me closely as I come down the stairs. 'Did you want to keep it a secret, Shayla?'

'It's private.'

'I understand,' Joan says.

We sit down at the dining table.

'I won't be a sec,' Mummy calls from the kitchen.

'Can I have a look at your book?' Joan holds her hand out. 'Oh, my grandkids have this one too. Would you like me to read it to you while we wait?'

'Yes.'

Joan turns the pages. Mummy puts a cheese and Vegemite sandwich in front of me. I shake my head.

'But you haven't eaten all day.' Mummy drops back into her seat at the head of the table.

'I feel yucky in the tummy.'

'Maybe your tummy feels yucky because you're hungry,' Joan says.

'I'm not hungry.'

'Do you feel worried about anything?' Joan puts her hand on the table. There are lots of gold rings on her fingers. 'Mummy tells me you've been having nightmares.'

I stare at the sandwich. White, yellow and black-brown.

'You know, sometimes when we keep secrets they give us nightmares, or they make us feel yucky in our tummy. And that's how we know it's a bad secret,' Joan says. 'Do you know the difference between a good secret and a bad secret, Shayla?'

I shake my head.

'If Mummy buys Nanny a birthday present and she tells you to keep it a secret, so it's a surprise when she gives it to her, that's a good secret. Do you know why it's a good secret?'

I shake my head. The cheese in the sandwich looks sweaty.

'Because it's only a secret for a short time. Soon everyone will know what Mummy bought Nanny for her birthday, so it won't be a secret anymore. And it's going to make everyone happy when they find out, because Mummy has done a nice thing for Nanny. No-one is getting hurt. No-one has done anything wrong.'

I nod at the sandwich. The bread looks a bit dry and hard.

'A bad secret is when someone has done something wrong or naughty and they don't want anyone to find out about it, ever, because they would get in big trouble if anyone else knew,' Joan says. 'Can you think of an example of a bad secret, Shayla?'

'What does that mean, that word?'

'Example? It means ...' Joan looks to Mummy sitting across from her. 'Alright, let me give you an example then. So, if someone is hurting you – let's say someone pushes you over at preschool, or they bully you – and they tell you not to tell anyone, that's a bad secret. Do you understand?'

I nod.

'They might say that if you tell on them, no-one will believe you. They might say that if you tell, they'll hurt you again, maybe worse than they already have. They might say that if you tell, they'll hurt someone in your family or a friend. They might even offer to give you something, like a present, if you don't tell on them. That means it's a bad secret.'

A fly lands on the sandwich and rubs its legs together. Mummy tuts, shoos it away, then takes the plate into the kitchen. Joan puts her head on the table, in place of the plate, in front of my face. I look into her dark-brown eyes.

'And you should never keep a bad secret, Shayla. Only bad people ask you to keep bad secrets.'

2

Mummy sits on the lounge and cries into her ashtray, arms wrapped around her tummy. Her head hangs over the coffee table, hair almost touching the floor.

'Mummy?'

Mummy's head pops up. The white parts of her eyes have turned red. Black make-up runs down her cheeks. It kind of makes her look like the four men on the front of her KISS T-shirt, who have their faces painted to look scary.

She wipes the tears away and pushes hair back off her wet face. 'You're meant to be in bed, Shayla. What are you doing up? Did you have another accident?'

I shake my head. The Valentine's Day card I made Mummy at preschool is on the coffee table next to the ashtray. 'Don't you like it?'

'What?'

'The card I made you?'

'Oh, honey, I love it.'

'Are you sick?'

'No, honey, no.'

'Why are you crying?'

'The card … it just reminded me … it just made me think … Oh God, Shayla.' Mummy's lips turn down. 'I'm just *so* lonely.' She drops her head into her hands. Her shoulders shake.

'What's wrong, Mummy?'

'I don't have anyone. I don't have anyone to love me. I'm all alone.'

'I'm here.' I pat Mummy's head. 'I love you.'

'I know, honey. It's just that I wish I had someone to talk to.'

I sit down next to her. 'I can talk to you.'

'I mean like a grown-up. I miss having adult conversations, adult company, an *actual* valentine. Instead, I'll be spending Valentine's Day alone. Forever.'

'Not alone.' I hold Mummy's hand.

'You know what I mean.' Mummy squeezes my hand before she takes hers back to light a cigarette. She sucks her cheeks in, blows grey-blue smoke out of her mouth, watches it disappear.

'When I was a little girl, all I wanted was to marry a nice man and have a family. I wanted seven kids, one for every day of the week, and to live in a two-storey house with a white picket fence,' Mummy says.

She pulls tissues out of the box with the cover that we picked out at Frank Whiddon retirement village. Sometimes they have fêtes and the old people sell things they've made: doorstops painted with wattle and bottlebrush, key rings made from gumnuts, knitted baby booties in soft pink, blue or white. The cover makes the tissue box look like a tiny bed with a white fitted sheet and lacy cover on top.

'And now' – Mummy flicks her cigarette hand out to the side – 'well, now Nanna's probably right when she reads my palms and tells me I'm going to grow old and die alone. This' – Mummy shakes her head at the lounge room – 'this is not what I imagined my life would be like at this age. But here I am.' Mummy taps her cigarette on the ashtray. 'A divorced, single mother, living in this hellhole before I even hit twenty-five.'

Mummy moves her hand up her throat, catching tears on the way up to her chin. She wipes them on her black jeans.

'It's my fault. I married the wrong man. I let the one I really wanted get away. Anyway, I shouldn't be telling you all of this. You're just a child. See?' She points the red-hot end of the cigarette at me. 'This is why I need an adult to talk to.'

'Where is he?'

'Who?'

'The one you wanted.'

Mummy smiles, but she looks sad. 'Rob,' she says. 'Last I heard he was living with his mother at Ingleburn.'

'Where's that?'

'It's not far from here, but I don't know if he's with someone else now.'

'Like a girlfriend?'

'Or a wife. He might even have kids by now. Although, I guess he wouldn't be living at home with his mother if he had a wife and kids. So maybe he's alone too.'

'Maybe we should send him a Valentine's Day card then.'

Mummy's eyebrows move up. 'That's not a bad idea, Shayla. I can put our phone number in the card and then, if he calls, that's up to him.'

He calls. Every night. And they talk for ages. Mummy says they have lots to catch up on. She wraps the curly blue telephone cord around her finger and her green eyes light up like a Christmas tree. Her laughs are small and soft on the phone – not like when we watch Red Symons and Ossie Ostrich on *Hey Hey It's Saturday* together and she laughs until she snorts – but I've never seen her look so happy. And when they get off the phone, she puts on Deborah Conway and we dance under the shiny disco ball in our lounge room to 'It's Only the Beginning'.

'Do me a favour?' Mummy asks. 'Don't mention Rob to your grandparents just yet.'

'Is this a bad secret?'

'No, of course not,' Mummy says. 'They just don't need to know about him yet.'

'When they find out will they be happy?'

'Probably not.' Mummy's eyes shine. 'But I'm happy, Shayla.' She takes my hands and squeezes. 'And we'll tell them soon. I promise. It's just so new, there's really nothing to tell them at the moment. We're just friends. I'm allowed to have friends, aren't I?'

I nod.

'I don't need their permission to talk to a friend, do I?'

I shake my head.

'So, it's not a secret.' She takes a puff of her cigarette. 'It's just none of their business.'

Sometimes he visits her at work. I know when he has, because on the way home from preschool she listens to 'Top of the World', by a band she's said is called the Carpenters. And when the song's over, she tells me about it.

'He popped in after his shift. He's working as a garbo now, so he finishes early. I made us coffee. We listened to music. Talked.' She looks at me in the rear-view mirror. 'And now he wants to come over.'

'When?'

'Whenever, really. But I said no, not yet.' Mummy blows smoke out the car window.

'Why?'

'I don't want him to see where we're living.' Mummy turns right into Kikori Place.

'Why?'

'Well, it's not very nice, is it?'

I look out the window. Big houses. Some tall, some short, all spread far apart. They have big front yards, lots of room to play. There's sunshine all around them. Mummy keeps driving. Our part of Kikori Place is hidden right up the back. It gets darker as Mummy drives. The street gets skinnier. The front yards get smaller. The houses are stuck together.

'Goblin City.'

'What?'

'It looks like Goblin City.'

'From *Labyrinth*?'

I nod.

'Yeh, I guess it does. All brown and beige. Run-down and dirty. Tiny little places clumped together in windy little streets. Bunch of weirdos for neighbours. Oh, look, more cops today.' Mummy points

17

up Dobu Place. 'See why I can't bring him here? He lives in a nice privately owned home with his mother. He remembers me living in an even nicer house with my parents. I don't want him to see me living like this.'

Mummy parks on the side of the street and hops out of the car. Her hair shines in the sun like Nanna's dark ruby earrings. She opens the driveway gates, so short she could step over them. Every house is the same shape and colour, has the same fence, letterbox and carport. Ours looks a bit nicer because Nanna hung white lace curtains in the windows instead of old sheets. All our furniture is inside the house, not on the front lawn. And our garden is neat and tidy because Poppy comes to mow every second weekend.

'You could go somewhere else,' I tell Mummy when she gets back in the car. 'Somewhere nice. Like the shops.'

'What do you mean?'

'With Rob.'

'Like a date?' I watch Mummy's face in the mirror. Her lips turn down, eyebrows move up. 'Maybe we could go out for dinner and a movie or something. You'd have to stay at your grandparents though.'

'I like staying with Nanna and Poppy.'

'Okay.' Mummy nods. 'I'll ask him.'

She pulls into the driveway, parks the car.

'Mummy?'

'Yes, Shayla?'

'Does he love you?'

Mummy sits back, takes a deep breath, looks away. 'I don't know, honey. He used to. When we were kids. We were engaged to get married at sixteen.' She looks at me in the rear-view mirror. 'Did you know that?'

I shake my head. 'What happened?'

She turns her head back towards the house. 'Your grandparents happened.'

'What does that mean?'

Mummy lifts her shoulders, then drops them. 'They just didn't like him.'

'Why?'

'I don't think they like anyone.'

'They like me.'

Mummy spins around in her seat. 'They *love* you.'

'They like you too.'

'Yeh. Sometimes.'

'Why didn't they like him?'

'I don't know.' Mummy starts to look sad. 'I really don't know.'

I point at the movie we've borrowed from Video Ezy. *Snow White and the Seven Dwarfs*. We've watched this one before. Mummy likes it. She likes all the fairy tales. 'The prince always finds the princess, and sometimes she doesn't have a nice castle.'

'How'd you get so smart, huh?' Mummy pushes the car door open with her foot. 'Must be all those books you read.'

Nanna and Poppy live on James Street. Their house has a brick fence around it. It's so tall Mummy can't even see over it in her black high heels. She opens the gate and I step inside.

The front yard is Nanna's garden. The backyard is Poppy's. Nanna loves flowers. Real ones outside, fake ones inside. She's taught me the names of all her flowers and which ones can be grown by slip. Flowerbeds run along three sides of short, soft, very green grass. There are petunias, pansies and pigface, of all different colours. Purple bougainvillea climbs the fences, full of thorns and bees. Pink azaleas and camellias have been planted in the corners. Dark-red roses, the colour of Mummy's hair, bloom by the front door. They're Nanna's favourites. She has geraniums the same colour too.

The gate to the garden clicks shut. The white lace curtain in the window by the front door falls back into place and, before Mummy has a chance to knock, Nanna opens the door, tea towel in hand, short hair in light-blue curlers, slippers on for pottering around. I wrap my arms around her. She pulls me close and fluffs my hair, smelling like Tabu perfume. It's her favourite. She sprays it on her wrists and neck, dabs a bit behind each ear.

'Lauren,' Nanna says. 'You look very nice today.'

'Thank you.'

Nanna frowns. '*Why* do you look so nice today?'

'I'm going out tonight.'

'Oh. Who with?

'A friend.'

'A *male* friend?' Nanna raises her eyebrows with her voice.

'Yes, actually, Mum – a *male* friend.'

'Well, you better come in then. We wouldn't want you to be late, now, would we?'

Mummy holds the screen door open. I follow Nanna. It's warm and busy and noisy inside. *Mother and Son* plays on the television. The oven timer dings. The hum of cars and trucks on Stacey Street comes through the back door.

'Walter,' Nanna calls for Poppy. 'The girls are here.'

Nanna walks through the lounge and dining rooms, into the kitchen. She lights the gas, fills the kettle, puts it on the stove. I sit down at the round wooden table.

'You have time for a coffee before you go, don't you, Lauren?'

'I guess so.'

The chair squeaks when Mummy sits down. Nanna moves a vase of dusty fake flowers, straightens the white doily in the middle of the table and puts a plate of four vanilla butterfly cupcakes down. There's white powder on top, jam and cream inside, and a little silver ball between the wings.

'There's more for after dinner.' Nanna pats my head. 'Here, use a dessert fork.'

The kettle starts to whistle.

'Walter!'

'Yes, Doris, I heard you.' Poppy comes through the back door with a basket of fruit and veggies from his garden. 'Lauren, you look …'

'Nice?'

'Like you're dressed for a funeral.'

'Do we have to do this every time we see each other, Dad?'

'I don't know. Do you have to wear so much black all the time?'

'Yes.'

'Then I guess we do.'

Mummy rolls her eyes.

Poppy's wearing yellow and blue. His favourite colours. Blue shorts with a crease down the front of each leg. White singlet under a yellow shirt with a collar and a penguin on the pocket. Poppy has lots of shirts like this one, in all different colours.

Nanna puts two cups of tea on the table. 'She's got a date.'

'It's not a date.'

'Hello, Shayla.' Poppy kisses my forehead. His face smells like the Brut Original aftershave Mummy bought him for Christmas. It came in a pack with a green spray can for under his arms too. 'What book have you got today?'

I show him *Where's Spot?*

'Very nice,' he says. 'How about we read it together later?'

I nod.

'I've hired us a movie to watch tonight too.'

'What movie?'

'*Oliver*,' Poppy says. 'It's set in England.'

'Still pining for the mother country.' Nanna sets down two cups of coffee.

'And Nanna's made your favourite, pea and ham soup.'

'It smells delicious,' Mummy says.

'She's a good cook, your mother.'

Nanna sits down, puts a tea towel over her lap. 'I'll do a roast for Mother's Day tomorrow,' she says. 'And hot apple pie with custard and ice cream.'

Poppy stirs sugar into his tea. The teaspoon clinks around the sides of the cup. 'Do you really think you should be dating right now?' he asks.

Mummy picks the wings off her butterfly cupcake and eats them. 'He's just a friend, Dad. And it's just dinner and a movie.'

'It's obviously more than that if you've shipped Shayla off for the night.'

Mummy frowns at Poppy and pulls a lighter black denim jacket over her dress. 'Don't talk like that in front of Shayla. I haven't shipped her off anywhere. She's spending the night with her grandparents. I haven't gone out since Richard and I separated. I think I deserve one night to myself, don't you?'

'But it's not to yourself,' Nanna says.

'*I* need this.' Mummy points at her chest. 'A friend. Adult conversation that isn't with my parents. A movie suitable for mature audiences. A night of having the house to myself, of having my bed to myself, of not having to wake up and change wet sheets, of being able to sleep through. Hell, maybe even sleep in.'

'Well, she doesn't wet the bed here.'

'Yes, I know that, Mum. Thank you. I'm aware.'

'And I thought you were having that seen to, anyway?'

'I told you weeks ago that the woman who came to see us called and said there was nothing she could do to help.'

Mummy's green eyes stare into Nanna's green eyes. One of my eyes is green, like theirs. The other is blue, like Daddy's. Poppy's eyes are brown, but Mummy says I got his curls.

Nanna looks away, stirs her coffee. 'I don't remember that.'

'That's because you don't listen to me.'

'I do listen to you, Lauren. I just don't remember you telling me that.'

Mummy slides down the chair and crosses her arms. 'Well, I did.'

'Well, can you tell me again, please? Why can't she help you?'

'Because when she came to visit us, Shayla didn't say anything that would prompt them to get involved.'

'So, it's still happening? The bedwetting?'

Mummy nods. 'But she did say it might just be a phase and Shayla will probably grow out of it.'

'Well, that wasn't much help, was it?'

Mummy tucks her hair behind big, dangly earrings. 'To be honest, I don't even know why the paediatrician suggested I contact them. I thought DoCs looked after at-risk kids. Put them in foster homes and stuff. What were they going to do about bedwetting if a specialist can't even figure it out?'

'I guess they deal with all kinds of stuff. Maybe he thought they'd be able to help somehow.'

'Well, they don't seem concerned. I guess that's a good thing, right? Means this kind of thing isn't unusual?'

'She'll grow out of it,' Nanna says. 'It can't last forever.'

Poppy clears his throat, sits up straight, leans forward. 'So, this man, he isn't coming to your house?'

Mummy closes her eyes, breathes out loudly. 'No, Dad. He doesn't even know where we live. I'm meeting him at a little Chinese restaurant.'

'So, who is he?' Nanna asks.

'Who?'

'Don't play dumb,' Nanna says. 'The man you're going out with tonight. Who is he?'

'Why do you need to know?'

'Why won't you tell us?' Nanna asks.

'Because it's none of your business.'

'It absolutely *is* our business,' Nanna says. 'As soon as you asked us to mind Shayla for the night it became our business.'

'Shayla stays here all the time.'

'With you.' Nanna points at Mummy. 'She stays here with you. This is the first night you're leaving her alone.'

Mummy pulls her head back into her neck. 'And, what, I'm not entitled to any privacy?'

'No, you're not,' Nanna says. 'You're her mother. What if there's some sort of emergency and we need to know how to contact you?'

'Fine!' Mummy throws her arms up, then slaps her hands back down on the table. 'I'm going out with Rob.'

'Rob?' Poppy sips his tea.

I sip mine too.

Nanna frowns. 'Tell me it's not that Rob from around the corner.'

'Yes, Mum, it's that Rob.'

Nanna looks angry.

'And he doesn't live around the corner anymore.'

Nanna drops her cup onto the saucer. 'You never learn, do you, Lauren?'

'Who's Rob?' Poppy asks.

'That young lout she dated in high school.'

Poppy tuts, shakes his head. 'How long has this been going on?'

'We've been talking since February. He's dropped in to see me a couple of times at work. That's all.'

'That's very unprofessional,' Nanna says.

'What is?'

'Having a male caller visit you at work.'

'See, this is why I don't tell either of you anything.'

'No,' Nanna says. 'You didn't tell us because you know you're being stupid.'

'You don't even know why you don't like him, do you?'

'He's no good for you,' Nanna says. 'He wasn't then and he isn't now. All he did was distract you. Distract you from school. Distract you from fulfilling your potential.'

'*You* wouldn't let me fulfil my potential.'

'What? Your dream of becoming the next Chris Stein?' Nanna asks. 'Oh, grow up and move on, Lauren. It was never going to happen. He would have distracted you from that too. Just like he's distracting you from your work now.'

'Who's Chris?' I ask.

Mummy, Nanna and Poppy look at me, eyes and mouths wide open, then at each other.

'Chris Stein?' Mummy asks.

I nod.

'He's the guitarist for Blondie, my favourite band,' Mummy says.

24

'We sing along to them in the car sometimes. You know "One Way or Another"?'

'I like that one.'

'Well, that's who Chris Stein is.'

Nanna dabs the corners of her mouth with the tea towel and lays it back across her lap, lips pressed into a tight circle. 'He brings out the worst in you, Lauren.' Nanna picks up her fork, eyes on the cupcake. 'He always has, always will.'

'I'm not exactly sure why you think you're such a good judge of character, anyway. Either of you.'

'Oh, really? And why is that?'

'I didn't want to marry Richard, but you forced me into that. And look how it turned out.'

'That had nothing to do with your father or me.'

'You knew I hated him and that I didn't want to get married.'

'You're the one who went and got herself pregnant.' Nanna digs her fork into the cupcake. 'So, you couldn't have hated him that much.'

'You've got no idea what you're talking about!'

'Oh, what are you going to tell us next? That it was the immaculate conception?'

Mummy and Nanna argue. They shout over each other, voices loud. I put my hands over my ears.

'You're upsetting Shayla.' Poppy reaches for my arm. 'It's okay, sweetheart. Everything's alright.' He turns back to Mummy. 'Lauren, lower your voice. Lauren!'

Mummy crosses her arms, looks away. 'I'm not a child anymore. You can't tell me what to do or who to see.'

'That's right. You're not a child,' Nanna says. 'You *have* a child. So perhaps you should stop behaving like a sixteen-year-old girl.'

Poppy scoops two eggs out of the hot saucepan onto my favourite orange egg-cup saucer. I eat mine the same way he does: white parts first on the end pieces of the toast, orange part second, mopped up with the middle bread soldiers. He doesn't cut his crusts off. I snack on mine at the end. Poppy says the crusts keep my hair curly, like Shirley Temple.

'Did you like the movie last night?' Poppy asks.

I nod, mouth full of food.

'Who did you like best? Oliver Twist?'

I shake my head, swallow before I speak, hand over my mouth, like Poppy's taught me. 'Dodger.'

'The naughty one?' Nanna raises her eyebrows.

'I like him too,' Poppy says. 'After breakfast do you want to watch *Looney Tunes*?'

'Yes.'

'What's the name of that skunk that falls in love with the cat?' Nanna asks.

'Pepé Le Pew,' Poppy says.

'I like that one,' Nanna says.

'I'm a Bugs Bunny fan, myself.' Poppy makes the teeth. 'What's up, doc?'

'What about you, Shayla?'

'Wile E Coyote.'

'Not the Road Runner?' Nanna asks.

'No.'

'I think we're going to have to keep an eye on you.' Nanna winks. 'Walter, she likes the villains.'

'That's fine, as long as they're on the TV screen or in the pages of your books,' Poppy says. 'It's the real-life villains you have to stay away from.'

'A lesson I wish her mother had learnt,' Nanna says.

Poppy looks over his newspaper at her and shakes his head.

'What's a villain?'

'The bad guy,' Poppy says.

'The bad guy in *Oliver* made me feel yucky in the tummy.'

'Bill Sikes? Well, he's not real, so you don't need to worry about him,' Poppy says.

'He's not real,' Nanna says. 'But there *are* men like Bill Sikes in the world. And when you get that feeling, you should always listen to it, heed its warning.'

In the middle of Nanna's front lawn there's a lacy-looking table. It reminds me of a doily, round and white, but the seats are very heavy. On top is a cane basket. Inside are Nanna's clippers, a kneeling pad and two pairs of gardening gloves. Next to the basket are two watering cans: one big one and one little one. Nanna stands in front of a green bush full of white flowers. 'I wasn't sure these would bloom in time for Mother's Day this year,' she says.

'How do you say it?'

'Chrysanthemums,' Nanna says. 'Chry-san-the-mums.'

I shake my head.

'It's a hard one to say. Easier to call them Mother's Day flowers.'

Nanna snips long stems and hands them to me. I pull the leaves off the bottom and put them in the basket. Some of the petals have opened, others are still shut tight. Nanna points with her clippers to the closed ones. 'These ones are called buds,' she says.

'They're pretty.'

'How about we put one in a pot today and try to strike it? Then you can take it home with you and start your very own garden.'

'Yes, please.'

'See that little red plastic pot over there? Fill that up with some dirt and then bring it back. Here's a spade. Try to get the dirt from under a plant so I don't have to look at a big hole.'

I dig up some of the dirt from under the blue hydrangeas. It's wet and soft. 'Yuck!'

'What?'

'Worms!'

'Worms are good,' Nanna says. 'They mean healthy soil and plants. Worms are why we have nice flowers to give to Mummy today. We do not like snails.'

'But they're cute.'

'Snails? Snails are cute?'

I nod.

'And that's why you should never judge a book by its cover. Do you know what that means?'

I shake my head, watching for worms, careful not to cut into their wriggly bodies with the sharp spade.

'It's an old saying,' Nanna says. 'It means some things that look good can be bad, just like some things that look bad can be good. Worms may look ugly, but they feed our plants, make them healthy, keep them pretty. Snails may look cute, but they eat our plants, make them sick, sometimes even kill them.'

I put some worms in my flowerpot and Nanna sticks a stem in the soil.

'So, do you like Rob?' she asks.

I push the soil down around the stem.

'Have you met him yet?'

'No.'

'Well, at least she hasn't involved you in her silly business.' Nanna stands up and brushes her hands over her knees.

'Do you like Rob, Nanna?'

She holds her lower back while she looks at her rosebush. Some of the leaves have holes in them. Others are turning yellow, their edges crispy.

'Mummy said you don't like him.'

Nanna pushes her lips together. She picks the sick leaves off the rosebush, follows a shiny, silver line to a big fat snail.

'Why not?'

'It's complicated,' Nanna says. 'And you heard too much yesterday. We shouldn't be having adult conversations like that in front of you. You'll grow up too fast.'

I sit on the foam mat, look up at Nanna and wait. Leaves crunch in her hand. A dog barks. The kettle whistles. A car blows its horn.

Nanna lets out a long, loud breath. 'Okay,' she says. 'Let me put it this way. See this rose? I grew this from a tiny slip and it's beautiful. My favourite.' She frowns at the snail and picks it off the rosebush by its shell. Its soft, slimy body hides inside. 'It's taken years. Lots of time and energy and love and care. And when you've put that kind of effort into growing something beautiful, the last thing you want is something or someone coming into your garden and destroying it.'

Nanna throws the snail over the tall brick fence. I hear its shell crack on the concrete.

3

Stray cats sunbaking in the middle of the street run away. His big black car rolls down the road, parks in front of the house. The bedsheet on the window across the street opens a little bit at the side. I watch from my bedroom above the carport. He takes his black sunglasses off, puts them on top of his head and looks around. He has light-brown hair. A beard. His sleeves are rolled up to his elbows. The street is empty now, only black tyre marks and speed bumps. He tucks his shirt into his jeans, taps his back pocket and walks towards the house. The sheet curtain across the street closes.

I stop at the top of the stairs. The front door is already open. His hand is on Mummy's bum. It's a hairy hand and there's a gold ring on his pinkie finger. The hand squeezes. I drop my book. Mummy spins around as I bend to pick it up. She straightens her black jumper. On one side of the zipper it says 'AC', on the other it has 'DC'.

'Shayla, come down here. There's someone I want you to meet.' Mummy takes my book so I can shake hands. 'This is my friend, Rob.'

'Oh, is that all I am?' Rob asks. 'A friend?'

Mummy rolls her eyes at him. 'Rob, this is my daughter, Shayla.'

I hold my hand out, making it firm, not floppy, like Poppy's taught me. Rob squeezes my hand tight, squishing my fingers together. It hurts. I pull my hand away and take a step back.

'How ya going?' Rob asks.

'Good.' I point at the tattoo inside of his arm. 'What does that say?'

'"Such is life."'

'What's that mean?'

He shrugs. 'It is what it is, I guess.'

He sniffs, and the hair under his crooked nose twitches with his lip. One of his front teeth is chipped. His moustache grows into his beard and his beard grows into his hair and his hair has grown to his shoulders. It's like he's wearing a hair helmet.

'You're very hairy.'

Rob pulls his head back into his neck, like a turtle.

'Shayla, don't be rude! You say sorry, right now.'

Mummy's voice is sharp. It stings my eyes. I look down at my feet. My face feels hot.

'It's okay. She's right. I'm hairy.' Rob throws his arms out, grabs Mummy around the tummy and tickles her. 'Real men are supposed to be hairy, aren't they?'

'My daddy's not hairy. Mummy calls him "Baldy".'

Rob slaps his leg. 'I rest my case.'

Mummy laughs her little telephone laugh, slaps him on the arm. 'Coffee?'

'Sounds good.'

Rob follows Mummy towards the kitchen. He isn't much taller than her. He pulls a wallet out of his back pocket and puts it on the dining table. It has velcro like my Barbie joggers.

'Let me know if I should put the heater on,' Mummy says. 'This house gets so cold in winter. June wasn't too bad, but July's been a bit chilly.'

Rob's shirt is black, blue and white. It looks warm. I touch the sleeve to feel the fabric. He looks down at me.

'I have winter pyjamas like this, but mine have Barbies on them,' I say.

He raises his eyebrows, sticks his hands in his pockets. 'This ain't no pyjama top.'

'Sit down,' Mummy calls from the kitchen. 'Make yourself comfortable. I'll be there in a tick. Just putting lunch on while I wait for the kettle to boil.'

Rob grabs the back of the dining chair and pulls it out. I sit down across from him, but he looks away.

'Do you like books?' I ask.

'When they make movies outta them.'

'Shayla, show Rob what you're reading.' Mummy pokes her head out of the kitchen, hands Rob a book.

'*The Complete Adventures of Blinky Bill*,' Rob reads from the cover.

'He's a koala bear.'

'Yeh, I remember him.'

'He's on TV too.'

Rob flicks through the pages. 'You can read this?'

I shake my head.

'Preschool says she's advanced for her age when it comes to reading, but that book is written for slightly older kids,' Mummy says.

'Yeh, there's lotsa words in there.'

'She knows some of the words though, don't you, Shayla?'

I nod.

'Dad bought it for her. He says we should read her stories that are beyond her reading level, if the content is appropriate. He's been reading to her since the day she was born.'

Mummy smiles at me, puts her hand on Rob's shoulder. He reaches up, puts his hand on top of hers. They look into each other's eyes.

'Sugar?'

'Three. Thanks.'

Mummy comes back with two cups of coffee and *The Very Hungry Caterpillar* tucked under her arm. She puts it down in front of me and taps the cover. 'This one she can read.'

I open the book for Rob. 'It looks like he's eaten holes in the book. See?'

He nods, sniffs, twitches.

'Do you want to sit in the lounge room and read until lunch is ready?' Mummy asks me. 'It won't be long.'

32

I listen to them talk from the lounge room. *Round the Twist* plays on the telly, but it's turned all the way down.

'Where's ya guitar?' I hear Rob ask Mummy.

Mummy lets out a long, deep breath. 'Had to sell it.'

'Why?'

'Needed the money,' Mummy says. 'Things were hard when I left Richard. I thought the money I got from hocking my rings would get us through, but it didn't. It was either sell the guitar to pay rent on a derelict apartment in Mount Druitt or wind up in a women's shelter.'

'Sounds tough.'

'We were living out of cardboard boxes. I was eating baby food. There was nothing left. I thought we were going to have to go back to him. Then this place came up. It's shitty, but at least we've got a roof over our heads.'

'Your folks couldn't help you?'

'You know what they're like,' Mummy says. 'Super conservative. I embarrassed them by having a child out of wedlock, then I disappointed them by getting divorced. I mean, they wouldn't have let us go homeless. They wouldn't have done that to Shayla. I just don't think they realised how bad things were. We weren't talking at the time, so I didn't tell them. I made the mess, I had to clean it up, they said. So, I did.'

'But you loved that guitar.'

'I thought I'd be able to buy it back,' Mummy says. 'But I haven't been able to afford it. I used to go in and look at it, maybe once a week on my lunch break, just so it knew I hadn't forgotten about it. I know that's silly, but anyway. Then a few weeks ago I went in and it was gone. Sold.'

'Ah, shit.'

'Yeh,' Mummy says. 'But I'll get another one someday. And I still get to play sometimes. At the shop. When no-one's around. Pretend I'm tuning things.'

'Yeh, but you were meant to go to Newtown Performing Arts, become the next Chris, ah, Chris, ah …'

'Stein.'

'The next Chris Stein.'

'Yeh, well, my parents made sure that didn't happen. Sent me to secretarial school instead.'

'But you were really good.'

'Yeh, well. It is what it is.'

'Such is life, huh?'

'Such is life.'

Dining chairs slide across the carpet. I open my book. Mummy puts coffee cups in the sink, gets plates out of the cupboard.

'Who wants to watch a movie while we eat?' she calls from the kitchen.

'Me!'

'Do you want to pick a movie then, Shayla?'

'*Milo and Otis!*'

'You okay with that, Rob?'

'Ah, yeh.'

'Stick it on, Shayla.' Mummy carries a big bowl of cocktail frankfurts into the lounge room. 'Come sit down, Rob. Sorry the house is such a mess.'

There's no mess. Mummy's been cleaning for days, while a song called 'Romeo and Juliet' by a band she's told me is called Dire Straits has played over and over. She's cleaned the whole house. Even the windows. Inside and out. Curtains. Cupboards. The fridge. Today she even wiped water out of the bathroom sink after I washed my hands.

'Can you hold this for a sec?' Mummy asks.

Rob takes the bowl in one hand, a stack of plastic cups in the other.

'I'll never buy black furniture again,' Mummy says. 'It collects so much dust.'

The lounge room still smells like Mr Sheen. There's no dust, just the black coffee table with shiny gold edges. Same as the entertainment unit. Mummy bends to wipe the table over again.

Rob stands behind her, holding the frankfurts. She turns around, shakes her head, slaps his arm. He puts the bowl down and follows her back to the kitchen. She brings out a loaf of white bread and a bottle of cola. He brings two small bowls of sauce – one tomato, one barbecue – with teaspoons in them.

I press play on the VHS machine. Rob sits in the middle part of the corner lounge. I look at Mummy. She looks from me to Rob.

'Come sit next to me over here,' Mummy says to him, patting the seat to her left.

'I am sitting next to you.'

'Yeh, but come sit on this side.'

'Why?'

'Well, it's just that that's Shayla's spot,' Mummy says. 'And if you sit next to me here, we'll both be right in front of the television. Best seats in the house.'

Rob raises his eyebrows, wipes his hairy mouth with this hand, pushes up off the lounge.

'Sorry.' Mummy rubs his leg.

Rob does his sniff-twitch. I sit in my spot.

'Shayla, do you want me to make a hot dog for you?' Mummy asks.

'No, thanks. My tummy doesn't feel good.'

Mummy sits between me and Rob, legs crossed towards him. His right hand is between her knees. After a bit, he squeezes her leg, whispers something in her ear. She smiles, shakes her head. He squeezes, whispers, again. She rolls her eyes.

'Rob's just going to help me fix something upstairs. Will you be right down here on your own for a bit?'

I nod.

They leave holding hands, Rob following Mummy up the stairs.

'Shout if you need anything,' Mummy calls.

The movie finishes. Mummy comes downstairs. Rob follows.

'How was it?' Mummy asks.

'Good.'

There's a purple mark on Mummy's neck. A bruise that wasn't there before. Rob buckles his belt, tucks his shirt into his jeans. Did he hurt her? My tummy starts to ache like it did when I saw Bill Sikes hurt Nancy in *Oliver*. But Mummy doesn't look hurt. She looks happy.

'I better get going.' Rob taps his back pocket. 'Better grab my wallet first though.' He taps the other back pocket. 'And my keys.'

Mummy waits at the bottom of the stairs. I stare at the bruise. She pulls her long hair in front of it, like a scarf.

Rob pushes past me on the way to the front door. 'See ya later, kiddo.'

4

'What's wrong with her?' Nanna asks.

'I don't know,' Mummy says. 'She cried all the way home.'

'She's *very* flushed.'

'Her father said she played up holy hell for him all weekend. Wouldn't eat Father's Day lunch with his family. Just kicked and screamed and cried the whole time.'

'Maybe she's not well.'

'Shayla, are you feeling sick? Honey, please stop crying. Tell Mummy what's wrong.'

'Maybe we should give her a cool bath.'

'Just let me get her upstairs first.'

'Should we try to get her temperature down?'

'I don't think she has a temperature,' Mummy says. 'I think she's just hot from all the crying.'

'I'll get a wet flannel for her forehead.'

'Shayla, honey, you have to try to stop crying. You're going to make yourself sick.'

'Here, put her into bed.'

'What about dinner with Dad? He's expecting us soon.'

'Don't worry about it. I'll call him. Father's Day is just another day, Lauren. We'll celebrate next weekend.'

'Thanks, Mum. Shayla, don't cry, baby. You're okay. Please don't cry.'

'Mummy and Nanna are here with you.'

'Can you watch her for a sec? I need to take a Panadol. My head is splitting.'

'Can you get me one too, please?'

'Yep.'

'Ooph. Lauren, she just vomited all over the sheets.'

'Here, Mum, hop out the way. I'll put her in my bed.'

'I'll get another cloth to clean her face. Maybe it's something she ate?'

'I don't think so. I think she's just worked herself up into a tizzy. Shayla, I need to take this shirt off you. Sit up for me for a second, will you?'

'I'd leave her singlet on,' Nanna says. 'Don't want her catching a chill.'

'I *know*, Shayla. I know. We're almost done. Just give me the other hand.'

'Do you think we should take her to the doctor?' Nanna asks.

'Everything will be closed at this time on a Sunday.'

'What about the hospital?'

'I don't think she needs to go to the hospital, do you?'

'I don't know, Lauren. She won't stop crying. But you don't want to be sitting in the emergency department for hours waiting either. Not with her like this.'

'If the vomiting doesn't stop, I'll call the hospital and see what they say, but I think she'll be fine.'

'Shayla, Nanna's just going to put a nice cold cloth on your forehead. It will help you feel better. Okay?'

'Now, close your eyes, honey,' Mummy says. 'Everything's okay. We'll look after you.'

Mummy yawns and rubs her eyes. She stretches up and back. Things crack inside her body.

'What is that?'

'What?'

'That sound.'

'Old bones.'

'Does it hurt?'

'Nah, just sounds like it.'

I point to her shirt. It has a man in a hat on the front. He's playing guitar. 'What does that one say?'

'Santana.'

'Sultana?'

'Almost.' Mummy laughs. 'Want bubbles?'

'Yes, please.'

She squirts pink shampoo under the tap and swishes the water around to make the bubbles bigger. I watch as my yellow rubber ducky is swallowed by white foam.

'Mummy?'

'Yes, Shayla?'

'Daddy told me he's going to burn this house down.'

Mummy's head swings around. 'What?' Her hand is still in the water.

'Daddy told me he's going to burn this house down.'

Mummy stands up straight. She doesn't look tired anymore. Her eyes are wide open. 'Does he know where we live, Shayla?' Water runs off the flannel in Mummy's hand onto the bathroom floor and puddles near her feet.

I nod.

'Oh, Shayla!' Mummy slaps the wet flannel down on the bubbles in the bath. 'Why'd you tell him?'

'I didn't know it was a secret.'

'Shit, Shayla.' Mummy turns in small circles, one hand on her hip, the other on her forehead. 'Fuck,' she whispers.

I've never heard her say the F-word before.

'I'm sorry, Mummy.'

'Don't.' Mummy holds her hand up. 'Just don't speak to me right now, okay? I've got to go make a phone call. Mum!'

'But—'

'Mum!' Mummy puts her head out the door and shouts down the stairs. 'Can you come up here please? I need you to bathe Shayla. I've got to call Housing.'

'Coming!'

Mummy grabs the bathroom sink, and it looks like it's holding her up. Her chin wobbles a bit. Her lips make an ugly, sad shape. She closes her eyes and a tear comes out from under her black eyelashes. It cuts a white line through the make-up on her cheek.

'Mummy.'

Mummy shakes her head at the sink.

'Daddy told me—'

'Yeh, I know what Daddy told you, Shayla.' Mummy frowns at me in the mirror.

I shake my head.

Daddy told me he's going to shoot Rob. I've seen the gun. It's in the bottom of his wardrobe. He said he's allowed to have it because he's a soldier in the army. And that he'll shoot Mummy too, if I ever tell her our secret.

Mummy spins away from the mirror, looks down at me, eyes small and angry. 'I just can't believe you told him where we're living.'

I hang my head, eyes on the floor. My tummy ache moves up into my chest.

'I'm here,' Nanna says. 'Go. Go.'

Mummy pushes past Nanna and runs down the creaky stairs.

'She's in a rush,' Nanna says.

'Mummy's angry with me.'

'I'm sure she's just tired. We didn't get much sleep last night.' Nanna turns the tap off and rolls up her sleeves. 'I need to let some water out, otherwise it'll overflow when you hop in.'

Me and Barbie get undressed. Nanna folds a towel, puts it over the puddle Mummy made on the floor.

'Are you feeling better?' Nanna asks when I'm in the water. 'You weren't well last night. Mummy and I thought we were going to have to take you to the hospital. We slept on either side of you to keep an eye on you through the night.'

'I'm sore in between my legs.'

Nanna reaches for the soap. 'Maybe it's the bubble bath.'

'No, it's the needle.'

'What needle?' Nanna rubs soap into the flannel.

'Daddy's needle.'

'Does Daddy have a needle?

'Yes and he hurts me with it down here.' I point between my legs.

Nanna stops with the soap. She looks at me, hard. Her eyes dig into mine, like her long fingernails dig into my arm when I go to cross the street without holding her hand. 'What does the needle look like, Shayla?'

I pull Barbie's arm out, make it straight. 'It's like that. Sometimes he wraps it up.'

'What with, Shayla? With paper?'

'No, it looks like a balloon.'

The soap slips out of Nanna's hand, down the side of the bath and across the bottom.

'He pulls it off the hair and the needle and throws it in the bin.'

'Where does he put the needle, Shayla?'

I open Barbie's legs and point between them. Nanna's green eyes grow big, like the plants in her garden.

'Nanna, can you ask Mummy to ring Joan, please? Tell her to stop Daddy from hurting me?'

It hurts when I sit down. *Mr Squiggle*, the man from the moon, plays on the telly, but the volume is turned all the way down because I have a headache now too. Joan and Mummy talk in the dining room.

'What do you think of what she said?' Mummy asks.

'In my almost thirty years' experience, children her age don't lie,' Joan says.

'Oh, I believe *her*. I just can't believe *it*. I don't want to believe it, you know?'

'I know.'

'I guess now I know why the paediatrician told me to call you, huh?'

'You didn't suspect?'

'No, not at all. If I had, I would've done something sooner. I wouldn't have just let her go out there with him and let him hurt her like that. I would've stopped it. But who thinks the father of their child is going to … going to do *that* to their own child? To *any* child? He's sick. I fucking hope he rots in hell for this, the filthy bastard.'

I've never heard Mummy swear so much.

'I understand how you feel, but you need to try to remain calm. I know that seems like the last thing in the world you can or want to do right now, but that's what Shayla needs. Children her age take their emotional cues from their parents. The more upset and stressed you are, the more she will be. And she might also feel responsible.'

'Wait. Did you know? Last time you came here and spoke to her, when you asked all those questions, did you know then?'

'It's my job to suspect. But Shayla didn't give me much to go off. Nothing at all, in fact. From everything you said, his violence had never extended to her. She displayed no physical signs of abuse. She didn't say anything incriminating. She was just a kid with a tummy ache, wetting the bed. It happens to some kids in the best of circumstances. All I could do was give her permission to tell someone if she needed to.'

I hear tissues pulled from the box.

'Do you think it's my fault? Do you think he did this to her to get back at me? For leaving him? Divorcing him? Starting to see Rob?'

'I don't know why he did it, Lauren. I don't know him. But what I do know is that Shayla looks like she's in some physical discomfort. Have you taken her to see a doctor?'

'Not yet. To be honest, I didn't know what to do next. And I didn't feel comfortable with people looking at her, you know? I mean, I know they've got to, but I just feel like I don't want anyone to look at her or touch her ever again.' Mummy sniffs and it sounds snotty.

'I understand.'

'I feel like I'm in a nightmare, waiting to wake up. This can't be real, right? It can't be. Who does this? Who does this to their own flesh and blood? To a child? Who does it? I just can't believe it. I can't. I just can't.'

'It's real. I'm so sorry to say that, but it is. You're not going to wake up from this, Lauren. Instead, you're going to wake up *to* it, every day. And it will be that way for quite some time. You are, however, going to have to take her to a doctor. And they are going to have to examine her. Tomorrow.'

Mummy blows her nose. 'Do I just take her to a normal doctor? Or does she need a special doctor?'

'She's going to need a couple of special doctors. Firstly, you need to take her to see a gynaecologist.'

'Oh God.'

'Take her to Springfield Cottage in Penrith. They're a sexual assault service. They specialise in this sort of thing. She'll be in good hands there. Here's a card. Tell them I sent you and that Shayla needs to be seen tomorrow. Any questions and they can call me.'

'Thank you.'

'I also strongly recommend you take her to see a child psychologist. Here's the card of someone good in Liverpool who specialises in this area. She might even be able to help with the bedwetting issue now that we have a probable cause.'

'The bloody bedwetting. All this time I've been so focused on the bloody bedwetting and I missed it. I missed what was causing it. I missed what was happening to my baby girl. And I've been nasty about it. Tired and grumpy and mean. And the whole time she's been going through all this all alone. Oh God. I'm a horrible mother. I'm a horrible person. How didn't I know? She's my child. How didn't I know?' Mummy sounds like she's cry-choking.

'Like you said before, it seems impossible that this kind of thing could happen, especially that a father would do this to his own child. In my experience though, it's always someone you trust with your child. They have the most access to them.'

'Do you think she's going to be okay? What about as she grows up into a woman? Oh God. How am I going to do this, Joan? How am I going to do this on my own?'

'You'll do this because you must. And because there's no-one else who can. We humans have an innate ability to just keep on keeping on. You'll do the same. It's going to be bloody hard and you're going to hate it: hate that it happened, hate all of it. But you have to do this for Shayla and for yourself.'

Mummy sniffs again.

'I can't speak to the long-term impacts of this,' Joan says. 'The child psychologist is going to be better placed to talk to you about that but, in the meantime, I think you need to keep her away from her father. And I think he's going to make that very difficult for you.'

'Yeh, he will. He's an arsehole.'

'Have you spoken to anyone?' Joan makes her voice softer. 'About all the stuff that happened with him before this?'

'No. I haven't told anyone.'

'This is going to be hard on you too. I think you should talk to someone professional as well. The more help you have, the more you'll be able to help your daughter, now and into the future.'

5

I've thought about how to get out if Daddy burns the house down. I'll go into Mummy's bedroom and wake her up. We'll climb out my bedroom window onto the top of the carport. Mummy will slide down the pole to the driveway first. I'll follow and she'll wait to catch me in case I fall.

Mummy's car is parked under the carport. It's yellow. Not just any yellow. She calls it 'yellow glow'. It's the most colourful thing in the whole street.

Today the street is empty and still. Nothing moves except me and Mummy coming out of the house. Not the leaves on the trees, not the birds on their branches, not the sheet curtains in the windows. Even the stray cats hide from the sun.

'Mummy, I'm hot.'

'I know. I can't get over how hot it is already.'

I pull at my shirt with the long sleeves. 'Can I wear something else, please?'

'No, sweetie.'

'Why?'

'Because we're going to be late. What book are you taking?'

'*The Velveteen Rabbit*.' Poppy gave it to me for my fourth birthday.

'I like that one,' Mummy says.

'Me too.'

Mummy pulls the wooden door closed, clips the screen door lock shut. 'How are your ears feeling?'

Mummy took me to get them pierced for my birthday. 'Better.'

'Good.' Mummy opens the back door. 'You almost ripped the

bloody shirt off my back when the lady got the piercing gun stuck in your earlobe.'

Mummy clips me into my car seat. A smoke hangs from her lips. I cough and she pulls back out of the car. There's a bag of my clothes on the back seat.

'Where are we going?'

Mummy stands up straight, between the car and the door. I can't see her face anymore, just her black Guns N' Roses T-shirt.

'Mummy?'

Her arm rests on the car door, cigarette between her fingers. Her nails are short, square, painted a bright pink. They disappear up towards her face. She takes a long puff of her smoke and blows it out, slowly.

'Mummy? Are we going to Nanna's?'

'No, honey.' Mummy drops her cigarette butt, stamps it out on the driveway. 'You have to go see Daddy.'

I shake my head. She slams the back door and slides into the driver's seat. My tummy starts to gurgle like a drain.

Mummy puts her hand behind the seat next to her, looks out the back window and reverses down the short driveway. 'I think we'll have to get you a booster seat soon,' she says.

'Mummy, can we please go to Nanna's?'

'Not today.'

'But I feel yucky in the tummy.'

'I can't keep telling them you're sick, Shayla,' Mummy says. 'I've been telling them that since September. It's almost March.'

'I don't want to see him.'

'I know you don't want to see him, sweetie. But he wants to see you. And his lawyers want him to see you.'

'Why?'

'Because he hasn't seen you for your birthday yet. Because he hasn't seen you since Father's Day. Because I've been telling them you're sick every second weekend and they're wondering what the hell is wrong with you and what I have to do with it.'

'But I am sick, Mummy. I am.'

46

Mummy parks on the side of the road and hops out of the car. I wait for her to open my door, unclip me, take me back inside. But she walks straight past my window and closes the gates. I look down at the red button where my arm and leg straps meet. The one Mummy presses to let me out of the car seat. The one she's told me to never touch. I give it a push. Nothing happens. I try again. Tears drip onto my hands and the buckle. I can't get the red button to go down. I'm not big or strong enough. I pull at the straps buckled into it, try to pull them out. It hurts my hands. I try to pull the straps off my shoulders so I can wiggle up and out of the car seat, but they're too tight. I can't get out.

Mummy hops back in the car. The car starts moving. I throw my head back and scream.

I scream until Mummy points at Cuddles 'n' Mum in Casula.

'Remember when we went there and you saw Humphrey B Bear? You pushed your way up front and climbed on stage with him. Remember that? And we got in trouble.'

'Mummy, please.' My throat is sore. My hair is wet from sweat and tears. It sticks to my face.

She looks at me in the rear-view mirror.

'Please, don't make me go. I don't wanna go.'

'You have to.'

I kick my feet, push wet hair off my hot face. 'Why?'

'Because the man at court said you have to. I don't have sole custody of you yet, Shayla. They've threatened to take you away from me and put you into foster care if I don't do what they say. Do you want to be taken away from Mummy?'

'No!'

'You want to live with Mummy?'

'Yes!'

'What about Daddy? Do you want to live with Daddy?'

'No!'

'Do you want to see Daddy?'

'No, Mummy. Please take me home.'

'Daddy says he didn't hurt you, honey. He says Rob or Poppy has been interfering with you, not him.' Mummy stops at the traffic lights and turns around to look at me. 'Was it one of them, Shayla? Did Poppy or Rob hurt you?'

I shake my head.

'I can see you shaking your head, Shayla, but I need you to use your words. Did Poppy or Rob ever hurt you? Yes or no?'

'No!'

'Did they ever touch you on the bum?'

'No!'

'Did they ever show you their needle? Or touch you with it? Or make you touch it?'

'No!'

'Would you tell me if they did?'

'Yes!'

'So, you didn't lie to Joan?'

'No!'

'Would you tell me if you did?'

'Yes, Mummy, I'd tell. I promise.'

'So, you didn't lie?'

'I didn't lie, Mummy. I didn't lie. Why don't you believe me?'

'I do believe you, honey. I do believe you.'

I'm sorry. Mummy makes the words with her mouth, but they don't come out loud. The lights go green. The car behind beeps and Mummy starts driving again.

'Please don't take me to see Daddy. He knows I told on him. He's gonna be angry. He's gonna hurt me even worse now.'

Mummy puts her sunglasses on. I can't see her eyes in the mirror anymore. She chews her lip.

'No-one is going to be there to help me, Mummy. I can't go. I can't go.'

'I've made sure you won't be left alone with him. Granny's going to be there the whole time.'

'No, Mummy, no.' I wrap my arms around my tummy. 'Please, Mummy. She's no good.'

'What do you mean, Shayla? Why is she no good?'

'She saw. She saw Daddy hurting me. And she yelled at me. I got in trouble.'

Mummy's tyres screech. She stops at the red light and spins around to look at me. She takes her sunnies off and puts them on top of her head. Her face looks tight, maybe because of how stretched her eyes are. 'Why didn't you tell Joan, Shayla? When did this happen?'

'I don't know.'

'Where were you?'

'In the bedroom with Daddy.'

'And, what, she was there the whole time?'

'No. She came home early.'

'And she found you?'

'Yes.'

'Did she help you?'

'When I took the pillow off, she yelled at me to get dressed.'

'What pillow?'

'The one on my face.'

'Fuck.' Mummy turns back to the traffic lights, pushes her fingers through her hair, knocks the sunnies off her head. 'Fuck!' She reaches behind the seat and grabs her glasses off the floor.

The traffic light goes green. Mummy's car stalls. The car behind beeps.

'Okay, okay. Give me a second, for Christ's sake.'

Mummy gets the car going just as the light turns orange, but she goes anyway.

'I can't do this. I can't do this. How can they expect me to do this? To endanger my child like this?' Mummy changes lanes fast.

Someone behind her holds the horn down.

Mummy punches the steering wheel with the side of her fist. 'Fuck!' She changes lanes back. 'I don't know what to do. I don't know what to do.'

49

'Mummy, please.'

'Shayla, I need you to be quiet for a minute.'

'Please take me home.'

'Just one minute, Shayla.'

'Don't make me go.'

'I need to drive.'

'I don't wanna go.'

'I need to think.'

'Please, Mummy, please.'

'Shayla! I said enough!'

I stare at the back of her red head, brown at the top, and feel hot all over my body. Even my eyes burn. I want to kick and scream and pull her hair. I want to hurt her, like she's hurting me. I throw my head sideways. It hits the side of the car seat. My face burns. 'You said you'd always look after me!'

'I will always look after you.'

'Liar!'

'I didn't lie, baby.'

My crying gets bumpy, like I have the hiccups. 'Yes. You. Did. Yes. You. Did.'

'I need you to trust me, honey. I'm not going to let anyone hurt you.'

'You are! You're going to let him hurt me again!'

Mummy's lips make the ugly, sad shape, and tears come from under her sunglasses.

I kick her seat. 'I hate you! I hate you!'

I see the drop-off point. Casula Fruit Market. Mummy turns into the car park. I cry long and loud. Prices are painted on blackboards in bright white, orange and pink. Big wooden boxes have been wheeled out front, full of fruit and veggies. He's already there. His Jeep is parked out front. The same green colour as his army uniform. The windows are so dark I can't see inside.

I can't remember his face properly anymore. Mummy cut him

out of all our photos. When I close my eyes and try to see him, his face is blurry, like I've scrubbed pencil out with a rubber. He's just a bald man in an army uniform.

He jumps down from the car, in army pants and boots, and lights a cigarette. His bald head shines in the sun. His lips are so thin it's like he doesn't have any. There's a tattoo of a spider and a rose on his arm. He's told me it's a 'red-back spider'. Mummy told me he's a 'rock spider'. I don't like any kind of spiders. He takes his mirrored sunglasses off and tucks them into the neck of his T-shirt. Mummy's told me that I have a cleft chin like him, but his cleft is deeper. His eyebrows are blond like my hair.

I look at my hands and turn them over, close them and open them. They feel tingly, like maybe they're made of the black-and-white fuzz that comes up at the end of a video. My feet feel the same.

The back door of the Jeep opens and Granny gets out. Mummy slows the car down.

Beep!

Another man in an army uniform comes around from the other side of the car.

'Who the hell is this guy?'

Beep! Beep! The car behind isn't happy with us.

'Shit!' Mummy looks around. 'I didn't realise he was bringing fucking reinforcements.'

Beep! Beep! Beep!

Daddy leans back on his car, a nasty little smile on his face.

The other man has something black in his hand. He points it at the car. Mummy blinks a few times, leans forward over the steering wheel and scrunches her eyes up. 'Is that a video camera? It is! He's filming me!'

The person behind us holds their horn down. People come out of the fruit market to see what all the noise is about. Mummy lets the car roll forward slowly and turns into a spot. The man in the car behind drives past and yells bad words out the window. Daddy laughs and throws his smoke on the ground. Granny lights up, stands next to the man with the camera. There are a couple of empty spots between Mummy's car and Daddy's car. His arms swing as he marches across them. My body feels tight, like it did when Mummy almost went through the red light on the way here.

'Give me a sec to get her out, will you?' Mummy shouts over the car.

He stops, stands still, feet apart, hands behind his back. She opens the back door on her side, pops the buckle on the child seat and pulls me out of the car. I can't feel my feet and I fall. My hands and arms slap against the hot concrete of the car park. Mummy puts her hands under my arms, picks me up. It always tickles when she picks me up like this, but not today.

'Don't be difficult, please, Shayla.'

'My feet have gone to sleep.' I try to hold on to her while she pulls my pants up, top down, long sleeves over my hands.

'No, they haven't.' Mummy holds my hand up over my head and drag-walks me around the back of the car.

He's tall. Taller than Mummy. There's a small scar above his eyebrow and, on the other side of his face, one just under his eye. Both are thin straight lines of skin, a bit higher and pinker than the rest. His eyes are dark blue. Sharp and clear. The same colour as my blue eye.

He opens his greedy arms and reaches for me. 'Come to Daddy.'

A little bit of sick comes up and I swallow it back down. It burns. My throat stings, my eyes sting. I'm hot and tired and wet and sticky. I hold on to Mummy's leg. My legs shake. Hers do too.

'Come to Daddy, Shayla.'

'No.'

He stands up straight, raises his eyebrows and the scar above folds into the wrinkles across his forehead. He's angry. I hide my face behind Mummy's leg. She touches my head, softly.

'Richard, she doesn't want to go.'

The air smells like mangoes. My face and hands feel like I've just eaten one. Sticky with snot and tears. I wipe my nose on my sleeve and the trail left behind reminds me of the snail Nanna picked off her rosebush and threw over the fence.

'Just give her to me.'

Six lanes of traffic zip past on the Hume Highway. Cars beep and screech. Music goes doof-doof-doof. Shopping trolleys rattle over speed bumps. Car doors open and close. There's a loud boom-boom-boom-boom that I can hear in my ears and feel in my body. Everything is hot and busy and messy. I sink down onto Mummy's white joggers. She bends down and picks me up, maybe to hand me over.

'Come to Daddy.'

He steps closer and I scream.

'No, I don't want to!'

People turn to look; bags of fruit and veggies hang above trolleys, boxes stop halfway into the boots of cars. I hold on to Mummy's shirt like I did when the piercing gun got stuck in my ear.

He puts his hand out, like he wants to push my voice back down. 'Just give her to me, Lauren.' He speaks quietly. 'You're making things worse.'

'No!' I wrap my arms around Mummy's neck, tight. 'Mummy. Please no. Please.'

'Shayla. Stop. Stop! You're choking me.' Mummy pulls my arm away from her neck.

I start to hiccup-cry again. 'Help. Me. Mummy. Please. Help. Me.'

Mummy steps back towards the car and reaches behind her to open the door. 'Hop back in the car.'

She watches him as she puts me down. I hurry into the car and across the back seat.

'I've got all this on video, Lauren. You're going to look so bad in court. They'll take her off you and you'll never see her again.'

I quickly get into my seat and put my arms through the shoulder straps.

'Shayla's told you herself that she doesn't want to go with you. Look how distraught she is. She's been through enough. I'm not going to have her traumatised any further.'

He rubs the back of his bald head and looks around while Mummy buckles me in.

'Wait. I want to kiss her goodbye.'

'You better make it damn quick.'

Mummy steps back. He leans into the back seat. I hold my breath.

'Come with Daddy, Shayla. Daddy loves you.'

I shake my head.

'I may not see you today, but I will be seeing you, darling.'

He walks back towards his Jeep. I wipe my face and close my eyes. It's so hot and sunny that I see red behind my eyelids. I open my mouth to take a big deep breath and someone screams right in my face.

'Like hell you're not coming with us!'

My eyes pop open. Granny is in the car. Her eyes are black and the parts that should be white look yellow. She snatches at my car-seat buckle. I put my hand over the red button. Mummy's hand reaches through the car door. The pretty pink of her nails disappears into Granny's grey-black hair, right at the top of her head. She pulls and Granny lands on her bum in the car park. People stop to watch, but none come to help.

'Take a picture,' Mummy yells at them. 'It'll last longer.'

'You crazy bitch!' Granny screams, hand on her head.

'You want to see crazy?' Mummy bends down, points her finger right in Granny's face. 'You or your bastard son touch my child again and I'll show you fucking crazy.'

Daddy helps Granny up. 'Come on, Ma. She's not worth it. We'll go home and call the lawyers.'

The look on Granny's face gets uglier.

'We've got it all on camera,' Daddy says. 'She's directly disobeyed a court order. That judge is going to fucking crucify her. She'll never see Shayla again. Let's go.' He pulls Granny towards the Jeep.

'Ma, we've got to go.'

She rips her arm away from him and runs up behind Mummy, towards the car. Mummy catches hold of her shirt and swings her around, away from me.

'Get her, Richie! Get Shayla!'

He looks back at his army friend, who still has the video camera pointed at Mummy's car, and puts his hands in his pockets.

'You need to leave,' Mummy says.

Granny spits in Mummy's face, pushes her away. 'Get her!' Granny screams at Daddy.

Daddy looks at the ground, shakes his head. Mummy wipes the spit off her face.

'Well, if you don't do it, I will!' Granny turns towards me.

Mummy steps between us. 'You're not taking my child.'

Granny pushes Mummy hard in the chest and, as she does, Mummy grabs the front of Granny's shirt with her left hand and punches her in the face with the right. There's a loud crunch. Granny bends over, holds her nose. Blood leaks through her fingers.

'That's the last fucking time one of you bastards gets to spit in my face,' Mummy says.

I wake up in Nanna and Poppy's driveway. Mummy unbuckles the car seat. I flop over her shoulder. Nanna holds open the gate. Poppy holds open the door. Mummy wipes her joggers on the faded black door mat that Nanna's told me is made from recycled tyres. Rows of rubber are joined by colourful little bits in between.

'Lauren! Why is she dressed for winter when it's thirty-four degrees out here?' Nanna asks.

'Because I didn't want him ... I didn't want him *looking* at her.'

'Quick. Get her inside before she overheats.'

Mummy lays me on the lounge. It's nice and dark and cool inside. My tired, stingy eyes blink shut. I listen to the whirl of the blades in the pedestal fan. Nanna's hand feels nice and cold against my forehead.

'She's boiling. Lauren, help me get all these clothes off her. Walter, bring the fan closer, would you?'

Mummy starts with my shoes. Nanna starts with my shirt. They leave me in my underwear; singlet rolled up off my tummy and lower back. Poppy sets the fan up so I can feel the air move across my body.

'The police came here looking for you,' Poppy says. 'They just left. You probably drove past them.'

'I didn't see them.'

'But you were expecting them?'

'Yeh, I thought they might come here.'

'Lauren, has she had any water?' Nanna asks. 'Her lips look very dry.'

'No. She wouldn't take anything from me in the car.'

'Walter, can you bring me a cup of water with a straw, please? And some cold compresses? Four. No, five. Help me prop her up, Lauren.'

Mummy pulls me forward. Nanna puts a pillow behind my head.

'They said they have a warrant for your arrest,' Poppy says. 'That you broke his mother's nose.'

'Did I?'

'Don't sound so pleased with yourself.'

'She had it coming.'

Nanna wipes my face and neck, my hands and feet, with one of the wet clothes. 'See how warm that is now?'

'Mhmm.' Mummy sucks on her cigarette.

'That's how hot she was.' Nanna puts the other four flannels on my forehead, tummy and legs.

'They told us to call them when you got here.'

'Don't worry, Dad. I'll call them myself in a minute. Just let me have a smoke first.'

'Here, give that to me,' Nanna says.

A plastic straw scratches at my lips. I open my mouth. It's so dry my tongue feels stuck. Cold water moves down my sore throat, through my hot body and puddles in my upset stomach.

'Before you call them, how about you tell us what the hell is going on,' Poppy says.

'I took Shayla to the drop-off point for visitation.'

'Why would you do that?' Nanna asks.

'She hasn't gone for so long the court ordered it.'

'Why didn't you just tell them she was sick?' Nanna asks.

'Because I've been telling them that for months and the judge said I couldn't defy any more of his orders without being in contempt of court.'

'So, what, you were just going to hand her over?'

'No, Mum. Of course not.'

'So why did you take her there?' Nanna asks.

'I needed it to look like I was trying to comply.'

'Well, according to the police, it *looks* like you beat the crap out of an old lady in a car park,' Poppy says. 'They said they have the whole thing on video.'

'Yeh, some army guy I haven't seen before was there filming the whole time.'

'And when they show that video to the judge presiding over your custody case, how do you think that's going to go for you?' Poppy asks.

'They'll be able to see how much Shayla didn't want to go with him. That's not me stopping her. I took her there. I did what the court told me I had to do. She told him herself that she didn't want to see him.'

'They'll also see her mother behaving like a wild animal in a public place,' Poppy says.

'Richard and his lawyers said I was keeping Shayla from him, that she wanted to see her father and I was stopping her.'

'That's not true,' Nanna says.

'I know. But the judge said I had to take her to see him or I risked jail time and losing her until the custody battle was resolved. He said he'd put her into foster care if I didn't obey.'

'Oh God, you don't want that,' Nanna says.

57

'No, obviously. But I also didn't want to send her out to him. And she didn't want to go either. She screamed and cried the whole way there. She said he was going to hurt her again. She said that Granny knew.'

'*What?*' Nanna almost shouts.

'Yep. She walked in on them one day.'

'And she did nothing?'

'Apparently she yelled at Shayla.'

'So, the bitch *did* have it coming.'

I've never heard Nanna call someone the B-word before.

'And she said that Rob and Poppy had never touched her or hurt her. When we got there, she told Richard she didn't want to go with him. I think he realised his videotaping plan had backfired. It was very clear she was terrified of him and that she didn't want a bar of them. So, there's video evidence of that too, Dad.'

'Sounds like it was all going in your favour,' Poppy says. 'So why didn't you just leave then?'

'I was trying to. Shayla was buckled into her seat. We were about to leave and then suddenly, I don't even know what came over her, but his mother was *in* my car trying to snatch Shayla, so I pulled her out.'

'By her hair,' Poppy says.

'Yes, by her hair. And she pushed me and spat in my face, so I punched her in the nose. Just once. It was self-defence. She tried to take my child, she assaulted me, I did what I had to do to get us out of there safely. There were three of them and one of me.'

'It's going to be their word against yours,' Poppy says. 'And they have evidence.'

'So do I.' Mummy lights another cigarette.

'What?' Nanna asks.

'I recorded the whole thing. From before we left the house, until after we left the fruit market. Everything Shayla said, about not wanting to go, about him hurting her, about that old bitch knowing, about Rob and you, Dad, never touching her. I have it all on tape.

His mate was standing too far away to record what everyone was saying, so I think my version of the story, the one the police can actually hear, will be far more interesting.'

I open my eyes. Mummy lifts the corner of her shirt, pulls a little black box off the side of her pants and pops out a cassette, like the ones she plays in the car.

'I'm sorry, baby. I'm sorry I had to put you through that. I'm sorry that I had to ask you all those horrible questions in the car. But now, hopefully, we have what we need to get that evil prick out of our lives once and for all.'

6

The rain's so heavy it's dragged the grey of the sky down into the streets. Mummy leans over the steering wheel, trying to turn right into Fourth Avenue, Macquarie Fields. A big spray of water shoots up the side of the car as she pulls up outside Puff 'n' Billie Preschool.

I've been back at preschool for a few weeks. Mummy kept me home for a whole month after what happened at Casula Fruit Market. Then one day the owner of the music shop called and said that she had used up all her leave and would have to come back to work, otherwise she wouldn't have a job.

'I'll come around that side and pick you up,' Mummy says. 'I don't want you getting your shoes and stockings wet.'

She pops up the umbrella, throws my Barbie backpack over her shoulder and carries me on her hip. Miss Lisa opens the gate to the garden. Most of it is undercover so we can play outside even when it's raining. Kids dig in the sandpit, making castles and decorating them with leaves and twigs that have fallen from the big gum trees.

'I love your shoes,' Miss Lisa says. 'They're beautiful, just like the little princess wearing them.'

'Thank you,' Mummy says, putting me down. 'Shayla, what do you say?'

I step behind Mummy's leg and hide my face against her jacket. Little spots of rain wet my cheeks. 'Thank you, Miss Lisa.'

'You're most welcome.'

'Probably not the most practical shoes for this weather,' Mummy says. 'But they're her favourite.'

'I can certainly see why.'

'I don't think I've met you before. Lisa, is it? I'm Lauren.'

'I'm new here, started just before Easter,' Miss Lisa says. 'I met Shayla last week. We talked about how much she loves books. Didn't we?'

I nod.

'She's a very good reader.' Miss Lisa leans closer to Mummy, lowers her voice. 'Much more advanced than most of the other children here.'

'I probably have her grandfather to thank for that.'

'That's nice to hear.' Miss Lisa smiles. 'My mother was always of the view that reading was an essential life skill. When she was growing up, and *where* she grew up, girls weren't given the same access to learning. She always said the two most important things a woman needs to be able to do are read and drive; education and escape. She believed books could be just as much of an escape as being able to drive a car, if not more.'

'She sounds like a smart woman.'

'Yes, she was.'

I pull on Mummy's hand.

'Yes, Shayla?'

'I need to go bathroom.'

Miss Lisa bends over, hands on her knees. 'Do you want me to take you so Mummy can go to work?'

I squeeze Mummy's hand tight, shake my head, look at the gold buckles on my shiny red shoes.

'That's okay. I'll take her.'

'Are you sure?'

'Yeh,' Mummy says. 'If I don't take her, she'll hold it in all day.'

The bathroom has eight cubicles, but none of them have a door. Mummy stands where the door should be, back to me. Long hair reaches her bum. There's more brown hair at the top now and the red hair further down doesn't shine like it used to, before I told her the bad secret I was keeping.

'It's okay,' Mummy says. 'No-one can see you.'

I pull my blue dress up, white undies down. I try to do a wee, but not much comes out because I went before we left home. I pull the chain and the toilet flushes.

'I thought you said you had to go. You know you can go without me, don't you, Shayla? That's why we're doing dresses, so when you sit on the toilet no-one can see. The skirt covers your lap. You can't keep holding it all day. It's bad for your insides.'

Miss Lisa waves from a short, kind-of round table, with six straight edges. Colourful plastic chairs are pushed in underneath. Tubes of paint and jars of water are on top.

'Have you made a butterfly before?' Miss Lisa asks.

I look at my shoes, shake my head.

Miss Lisa reaches for my hands, holds them in hers, tries to look into my face. 'Hey,' she says. 'I feel a bit shy too. I'm new here and I don't have many friends yet. Will you be my friend?'

I nod at my shoes.

'What book are you reading this week?

'*Garfield, the Easter Bunny?*'

'Did you get it for Easter?'

'Yes. Poppy bought it for me.'

Miss Lisa folds a big piece of paper in half and smiles. It's a sunny smile. Her cheeks lift. Her eyes sparkle. They're brown, like her hair.

'Mummy says I need to practise.'

'Practise reading?' Miss Lisa writes my name on the piece of paper in black marker and runs her hand down the crease in the middle. She pushes the paper across the table towards me.

'No. Making friends. I don't get to practise anywhere else.'

'You play with other kids here, don't you?' Miss Lisa unfolds another piece of paper. Her legs can't fit under the table, so she sticks them out to one side.

'Not really. I'm not very good at making friends.'

'I think you are.'

Miss Lisa picks up a paintbrush and I copy her.

'Mummy says it's because I'm an only child.'

'I'm an only child too and I make friends all the time,' Miss Lisa says, painting on one side of the line on her paper with dark greens and light greens. 'You just made a friend now.'

'Mummy says teachers don't count.'

'Oh, why not?'

'Because you're a grown-up.' I blob paint on the right side of my paper: splashes of pink, strokes of orange, swirls of yellow. 'All my friends are grown-ups.'

'And she wants you to make friends with children your own age?'

'Yes.' I dab on some blue dots. 'Before I go to big school.'

'Done?'

'Yes.' I dunk my paintbrush in the jar and swish it around, watch the clear water cloud with colour.

Miss Lisa points to my picture. 'May I?'

I nod.

She carefully folds the paper back in half. 'Now, run your hands over it.'

I slowly run my hands over the paper. It feels cool to touch because of the cold, wet paint between the pages. I feel it squish under my palms.

'And open it.'

The paper sticks as if painted with Clag glue. But when it opens, both sides are colourful and the same, like butterfly wings.

'Do you want to add some glitter?'

I put blue glitter on the blue dots.

'Your mum's going to love it.' The rubber bottoms of the metal chair legs squeak across the floorboards as Miss Lisa pushes away from the table. 'Here, let me hang it up to dry for you.'

The bell at the front gate rings.

'Won't be a moment,' Miss Lisa says.

She brings back a little girl with black hair and denim overalls.

'Amanda, this is Shayla. Shayla, this is Amanda. She's new to

63

Puff 'n' Billie and I was hoping you could be her friend for the day and show her around.'

I stand up and hold my hand out to Amanda, like Poppy does when he meets someone new. 'It's nice to meet you.'

Amanda bites her bottom lip and frowns, like maybe she hasn't seen someone shake hands before.

'That's very grown-up of you, Shayla,' Miss Lisa says.

Amanda reaches out, takes my hand and holds it, like Mummy does when we cross the street. I look to Miss Lisa. There's a nice, soft smile on her lips and in her eyes. The doorbell rings again.

'I'll be right back.' Miss Lisa winks at me.

I turn to Amanda and try to do what Mummy told me to do: make friends. 'I like your glasses. They're red like my shoes.'

Amanda looks at my shoes. 'They call me four eyes.'

'Who?'

'At my old preschool.'

'That's not nice.'

Amanda shakes her head.

I squeeze her hand. 'Barbie sometimes wears glasses. But she never has eyes like mine.'

Amanda looks up. 'You have pretty eyes,' she says. 'You don't need glasses like me.'

'Mine don't match like yours. I've never seen a Barbie with one blue eye and one green one, have you?'

Amanda looks at my shoes again and shakes her head. We're still holding hands when Miss Lisa comes back.

'Shayla, would you like to show Amanda our little library?'

The reading nook is in the corner of the classroom, bookcases on all sides except for one corner, so we can get in and out. The floor inside is made of soft coloured squares that have letters on them and fit together like the pieces of a jigsaw puzzle. I let go of Amanda's hand and flop down into a big beanbag. All the air whooshes out and the stuff inside sounds crunchy, like it's full of Coco Pops and milk. 'Come sit next to me. There's enough room for both of us.'

Amanda sits down and my side of the beanbag lifts, like we're on a seesaw. Amanda laughs. I do too. And then we spend the rest of the morning playing *Where's Wally?*

Miss Lisa stands at the front of the line for the bathroom. I stand at the back of the line with Amanda and start to feel yucky in the tummy.

'Why did you let them push in?' Amanda asks.

'I like to go last.'

'Why?'

'I don't want anyone to see me wee.'

The line moves up, but I don't. Two more kids go ahead of us. Amanda crosses her legs. 'I really need to go,' she says.

'I'll just wait for you here then. I don't need to go.'

But I do. And maybe today I can.

Miss Lisa sees me and smiles. All the other teachers have said no to being my door, but I have a good feeling about Miss Lisa. She's my friend. So I hop back in line. Mummy will be very happy if I tell her I made a friend my own age *and* went to the toilet without her being here.

More children line up behind me. The yucky feeling starts to move up to my chest and I want to sneak back into the classroom with the kids who have already gone, like I always do, but I also want to be brave for Mummy too, so I stay.

When I'm next in line, I reach out to tap Miss Lisa on the arm. 'Excuse me, Miss Lisa?'

She turns and smiles. Round pink cheeks move up towards shiny brown eyes. The skin around the corners of her eyes crinkles. 'Yes, Shayla?'

I open my mouth but hear Amanda's voice instead. 'Miss Lisa!'

We both look towards the end cubicle.

Amanda pokes her head out. She looks upset, sounds like she might cry. 'Help!'

'Coming.' Miss Lisa leaves the line.

And so do I.

*

Naptime makes me worry because I'm full of wee and I don't want to have a bad dream and wet the bed in front of everyone.

'Come on, Shayla. Into bed.'

'I don't want to sleep. I'm not tired.'

'I know you don't like naptime, so I brought you a book from the nook.' Miss Lisa hands me *The Trapdoor* and winks. 'Have you seen the TV show?'

'Yes.'

'Who's your favourite?'

'Berk.'

'Me too. Are you happy to just have a little lay down with your book while the teachers eat their lunch?'

'Yes, Miss Lisa.'

The bed is made from the same scratchy fabric used in sack races, pulled over a frame with four short legs. There's no pillow and no blanket. It's full of sand from the pit in the playground. Ceiling fans swoosh, grey with dust. Paintings flutter like leaves in the wind. I peel some Blu Tack off the wall and chew it like Nanna's gum while I read my book.

The doorbell rings. There are footsteps on the floorboards, knocks on the door. Miss Lisa's voice is light and sing-songy. 'Hi, how can I help you?'

'I've come to collect my daughter.'

It's a man's voice and I feel like I know it, but I can't remember where from.

'And who, may I ask, is your daughter?'

'Shayla.'

I suck my breath in, almost swallow the Blu Tack.

'This is my first day here.' The smile has left Miss Lisa's voice. 'I'm not sure I've actually met Shayla.'

My mouth feels dry, my body cold.

'Let me just check she's here.'

I stand up, spit out my fake gum.

'She's here,' he says.

My legs feel empty.

'I'll be right back. Just one moment.'

The front door is closed, chained and bolted. Miss Lisa comes into the classroom and looks at me – eyebrow up, head to one side – like she's asking me a question without using her words. I shake my head. She puts a finger over her lips and turns towards the staff room. The sound of teachers talking and laughing stops.

The next voice I hear is Miss Mary's. She's an older lady and the boss of everyone else. Her grey hair is always pulled back into a neat bun. Mummy says she's 'elegant'.

'Good afternoon, I understand you're looking for Shayla?'

'I am.'

'And you are?'

'I'm her father, Richard.'

'Well, I'm sorry to say, Shayla isn't in today.'

'I know she's in there.'

'Any other Wednesday and you'd be right,' Miss Mary says. 'But Lauren called this morning to say Shayla wasn't feeling well and that she was going to keep her at home today. Another gluey ear infection. I'm sure you know how badly she suffers with them.'

'Shayla!' He bangs on the screen door. 'Shayla!'

Miss Lisa comes in again and takes me by the hand into the staff room. I haven't been in here before, but I don't get much of a chance to look around. Miss Lisa stands me near a bunch of boxes stacked against the wall and pulls a curtain across so I'm hidden.

'Richard.' Miss Mary uses her you're-in-big-trouble voice. 'Shayla is not here.'

'I've been watching this place all day, lady. I saw her get dropped off this morning. She's wearing a blue dress and red shoes.'

I step back, body pressed against the boxes, so my shoes don't poke out from behind the curtain.

'I'm afraid you're mistaken,' Miss Mary says. I hear a wobble in her voice and my legs start to shake.

'Shayla!'

'He's going to wake all the kids up.'

'And scare them.'

'He's scaring *me*.'

'You don't think she'll let him in, do you?'

'Ladies,' Miss Lisa says. 'Don't forget we have company.'

I look down at my shiny red shoes. They're my favourite because they remind me of Dorothy's magic shoes in *The Wizard of Oz*. I close my eyes, click my heels together and whisper, so soft even I can't hear, 'There's no place like home. There's no place like home. There's no place like home.' But they don't work. They're not magic.

'Shayla!'

'Please lower your voice,' Miss Mary says. 'Shayla isn't here, but I do have other children inside and your shouting is going to upset them.'

He rattles the front door and I start to shiver all over, like I'm very cold.

'Richard, if you don't leave, I will call the police.'

'I know my daughter is inside. And I know, legally, in the absence of a court order, you don't have the power to refuse a parent from collecting their child. So, how about *I* call the police?'

I feel yucky, all the way up to my throat.

'I've never seen you before in my life – Richard, was it? You've not given me your surname. You've not presented any form of photo identification. I honestly have no idea who you are,' Miss Mary says. 'What I do know is that you are behaving in a disorderly fashion, like perhaps you are drunk or under the influence of drugs, and even if I knew for sure you were the father of a child here, I would not be able to let them leave with you in this state because I have a duty of care.'

I need to wee, really badly. My stomach is so full, it hurts to touch.

'You don't get to take away my parental rights, only a court can do that.'

'And I'm sure they will,' Miss Mary says. 'In the meantime, if you would like to call the police, there's a payphone around the corner. Or if you'd like to wait across the road, the police will be here in a few minutes anyway. I hope, for your sake, you can pass the drug or alcohol test when they arrive, since it appears that you drove yourself here.'

The door slams shut and I let out a little bit of wee.

'Where is she?' Miss Mary asks.

No-one says anything. Maybe they point.

'Move all the other children into the back room,' Miss Mary says. 'No-one is to be in the front room. No-one is to go outside.'

Chairs scrape across the floor, feet shuffle out the door, tyres screech outside.

'I think he's leaving,' Miss Lisa says.

The curtain is pulled back. Cool air hits my hot, wet face. I blink and squint into the bright light. My hands are between my legs to try to hold in the wee. Both teachers have wide eyes and tight jaws. Their lips are pressed into thin lines, foreheads creased.

Miss Mary has the phone against her ear. She puts her hand over the mouthpiece. 'Miss Lisa is going to take you to the bathroom while I call your Mummy, okay? Hello, Lauren? Hi, it's Mary from Puff 'n' Billie Preschool. Yes, she's fine, but we have had a bit of an incident down here and I need you to come and get Shayla immediately.'

I walk to the bathroom with Miss Lisa, hands still between my legs. No-one else is around. She grabs my backpack out of the storage cube on the way.

'Can you be my door, please?'

'Absolutely.'

A little bit more wee comes out as I let go of myself. 'Oh no!'

'Don't worry. I'll get the spare undies out of your bag.' Miss Lisa puts my backpack over her chest and unzips it. 'Don't be upset. It's not your fault.' She pulls out a plastic bag, a fresh pair of undies, and passes them back.

*

Mummy stands in the corner, head down. Brown-red hair hides her face, but I can tell she's upset.

'I'm sorry, Lauren. I wish I didn't have to do this, but Shayla can't come back here,' Miss Mary says. 'Legally, we can't refuse him, because you don't have a court order granting sole custody yet. We can't protect her from him. And her being here puts all the other children, and staff, at risk.'

'Is there somewhere else?' Mummy asks. 'I can't take her to work. I'm going to lose my job.'

'Nowhere safe,' Miss Mary says. 'Not until this court case is done and dusted. The same rules apply everywhere, so you're going to have the same issue wherever you go.'

Miss Mary and Mummy keep talking while Miss Lisa puts my bag on my back.

'Will I get to see you again?'

'Oh, I don't think so, honey.'

'What about Amanda?'

Miss Lisa sucks her lip into her mouth and shakes her head.

'Can you say bye-bye to her for me?'

'Of course I can.'

I look around the classroom, at the cosy book nook and sandy beds, dusty ceiling fans, Blu Tack chewing gum and toilets without doors. Miss Lisa grabs my butterfly painting off the wire line where it was drying.

'Don't forget this.'

'That's okay. You keep it.'

'Oh, but why?'

'For being my friend.'

Miss Lisa holds my butterfly to her chest.

'Shayla?'

'Yes, Mummy?'

'We've got to go. Now, please.'

Mummy's already out the door. I run after her.

'Hey, Shayla,' Miss Lisa calls.

My shoes squeak to a stop on the floorboards.

'You're really good at making friends. You'll do great at big school.'

7

Keeping Up Appearances plays on the TV. 'The Bouquet Residence, Lady of the House speaking.' I look from the telly to Nanna. She kind of looks like Hyacinth Bucket. She's the same size. Even her hair is the same shape. Today she's wearing a bright blue knitted cardigan. All the pockets of Nanna's cardigans have the same smelly stuff in them that's inside the middle of Mummy's cigarettes, but Nanna says she doesn't smoke, that she hasn't touched one in more than twenty years, and that the tobacco in her pockets must be from way back then. When she says that Mummy and Poppy roll their eyes.

I've spent a lot of time at Nanna and Poppy's since I got 'kicked out' of preschool. That's what Mummy calls it. She says I got kicked out of preschool and she lost her job because of *him*. She doesn't say his name anymore. No-one does. Not even me.

Mummy drives me here on the days she has to go to court and reads me a short story before she leaves. Today it was *Funnybones*. Nanna and Poppy drive me back in the afternoon. In between we watch *Murder, She Wrote* and *Fawlty Towers*. Mummy said today was the last day of court, that they would hand down their 'verdict', but she didn't look happy about it. She looked tired and worried. And when she kissed me goodbye, she promised to call from a payphone when it was all over and done with. But we haven't heard from her yet.

A car door slams outside. Nanna looks across the lounge room at Poppy. Poppy listens for a moment and, hearing nothing else, shakes his head at Nanna. He goes back to his book. She goes back to her knitting. I sit between them and build a village out of Nanna's poker cards. I bend two so they can stand up against each other. Those are the walls. One card is carefully put on top. That's the roof. I do this all around the edge of the rug, until the phone rings. The springs in the lounge squeak as Nanna gets up. She groans, holds her lower back, bad like Mummy's, and steps into the dining room to pick up the phone on the kitchen bench. I stand up ready to talk to Mummy.

'Hello. Oh, hi, Lela.'

Lela lives across the road. She always wears the same types of dresses – soft, stretchy, floral – that fit around the top and fan out at the bottom. They have square necks, T-shirt sleeves and skirts that Nanna says are 'too short for a woman her age'. I go to sit back down, but the look on Nanna's face holds me still.

'Okay. Thanks. Bye.' Nanna hangs up.

Poppy glances up from his book.

'He's out the front,' Nanna whisper-shouts at him, swooping back into the lounge room to scoop me up with her claws, like a magpie.

Poppy turns the knob on the front of the telly and the screen goes black. He chains the front door. The sliding back door is latched. So is the kitchen window. All the blinds are drawn. Nanna takes me upstairs as downstairs becomes quiet and still and dark.

She sets me down in her bedroom, everything in its place. The queen bed is made with a quilted floral bedspread. It has a ruffled lace skirt that touches the floor. I run my hand over it and feel the little bumps of fluff-balls. There's a lacy bed doll in the middle of the mattress. Nanna's long dressing table is covered with what she calls 'Bohemia crystal'. Every second weekend, we carefully move it all onto the bed, dust each piece and then put them back exactly where they were. The vase, perfume bottle, jewellery box and ring holder go on a crystal tray in the middle. White ceramic jewellery boxes, painted with pink flowers on top and gold trim around the edges of the lids, are placed on opposite ends of the long white doily. Afterwards we go across Stacey Street, through Stevens

Reserve – where there's always an old Chinese man and woman doing what Poppy says is called 'Tai Chi' – to Bankstown Square. When we get there, I sit on the tall stools at the milk bar on level one, next to a big fruit market. I always order hot chips with extra chicken salt and a vanilla milkshake that comes in a fancy tall glass with a stretchy-neck pink straw. Not today though.

Nanna steps in small circles, looks around the room.

'What are you looking for, Nanna?'

The front gate to Nanna's garden slams shut, like it's been blown by a strong wind in a big storm. We both jump. Nanna's eyes lock on me and sharpen. I hear a man shout out the front of the house and I know the voice. It's the one that got me kicked out of preschool. I turn towards it and Nanna grabs me. Her long nails dig into my arm, leaving little dents in the skin. She opens her wardrobe.

'Get in,' she says.

I step inside, and the buckles on her black sandals, lined up under racks of clothes, poke me in the feet, then the shins, then the bottom. Her normally cuddly knits hang all about me, itchy and scratchy. They smell like the tobacco she says she doesn't smoke and Tabu. I look up at her as she closes the door on me in the dark, dark wardrobe.

'And don't come out, no matter what you hear.'

Nanna's marble cake has sunk in the middle.

'I don't know why you turned the oven off.'

'I didn't know how long he was going to be there. I didn't want it to burn and set the bloody fire alarm off. I thought the idea was to pretend we weren't home. Fire alarms don't go off when people aren't home, Doris.'

'Sometimes they do.'

'If their house has gone up in flames, they do. I just didn't think it wise to give a valid excuse to the man who already wanted to bash our bloody door down.'

'The oven has a timer, Walter.'

'Well, I wasn't really thinking about that at the time, was I, Doris?'

'Weren't really thinking at all, obviously.'

I sit in the back seat, marble cake on my lap. Nanna has filled the dip in the middle with so much pink icing the cake looks just as it should. She's in the front passenger seat holding a container of bubble and squeak.

'I *was* thinking,' Poppy says. 'I was thinking, what the bloody hell do I do if he gets in? I'm an old man. What good am I going to be? How am I going to protect my wife and my granddaughter from anyone, let alone a trained soldier less than half my age? I didn't know if I could call the police. What if he had won sole custody? What if he was there to take her away? What if I called the police and they came and just handed Shayla over? I was hiding in the laundry holding a fry pan. A bloody frying pan.'

'Anyway,' Nanna says, waving her hand, 'it worked, didn't it? He left. Maybe he thought we'd already taken her home. I think the fact that the phone kept ringing out made it more convincing.'

'How did Lauren sound when you spoke to her?'

'Relieved that she finally got through to us. She said she was about to head over to make sure we were all alright.'

'We're lucky he left when he did.'

'Well, she has sole custody now, so hopefully we never have to see or speak or think of him again.'

'I don't think we've seen the end of him yet.'

Nanna shakes her head, looks out the window. 'I don't want to talk about it,' she says. 'I never want to speak about any of this ever again.'

'You can't just pretend like this never happened.'

'I'm not in denial, Walter.'

'What is it then?'

'She's young. She's *so* young. Maybe she'll forget.'

'Doris ...'

'No, don't *Doris* me. Did you read the psychologist's report? About all the issues she'll have as an adult?'

'They didn't say she would definitely have them.'

'Self-harm. Drug and alcohol abuse. Sexual permissiveness. Physical and sexual re-victimisation. Mental illnesses. Post-traumatic stress disorder. Isn't that what soldiers get when they come back from war?'

'They said *some* survivors experience those issues.'

'He's ruined her. He's damaged her for life. She'll never get to be the person she was meant to be because of him. The best version of herself. Now we'll never see who she could have been, who she should have been.'

Nanna starts to cry. Poppy opens his mouth to say something. I can see him in the rear-view mirror. But nothing comes out. A man sings on the radio about what a wonderful world it is, and Nanna turns it off.

I close my eyes.

After a while Poppy speaks. 'People have hardships. We lived through the Great Depression, World War II. I came here on a boat via India during Partition. People were split in two on the street.'

'We weren't children.'

'I grew up in an orphanage and no-one ever came for me.'

'It's different. Those things were character building. This, this is character breaking.'

'I don't know if that's true.'

'I don't want it to be true,' Nanna says. 'I don't want any of this to be true.'

'None of us do.'

'But if we don't talk about it, if we pretend like it never happened, maybe she'll forget about it.'

'Doris ...'

'No, think about it. How far back can you remember? How old are you in your first childhood memory?'

Poppy is quiet for a minute. 'I don't know,' he says. 'But I'm a bloody old man. I can't remember what I did last week anymore.'

'Mine is from when I was around four or five.'

'So, it's already too late.'

'Maybe not. And maybe helping her forget will give her a chance to grow up the way she was meant to.'

'Or you're wrong and it will do more damage than good,' Poppy says. 'I'm no psychologist, but I imagine suppressing memories probably isn't a good thing. Isn't that how people end up with multiple personalities, like Sally Field in *Sybil*? And all of this assumes that he just disappears out of her life and she never thinks of him again, but I have a feeling he's going to hang around like a bad smell for a while.'

'We shouldn't be talking about this in front of her.'

'No, we shouldn't,' Poppy says. 'But it's okay, she's asleep.'

I keep my eyes closed all the way home.

When I open them again Kikori Place is full of sirens and flashing lights, blue-and-white check tape, police and an ambulance. The street has never looked so busy. People have come out from behind their bedsheet curtains. They stand on their front steps and front lawns. Some even stand on the road. Nanna and Poppy look at each other as a policeman steps in front of the car and holds his hand up. Poppy stops the car and rolls the window down.

'Evening, sir.'

'Hello, officer. Everything okay?'

'Far from it, I'm afraid. We've got a suspected homicide on our hands. Do you live here?'

'No, we're just dropping our granddaughter home to her mother.'

The officer dips his head, looks though the window at me.

'She lives down there.' Poppy points down the road.

'What number?'

'Four.'

'Wait here a moment.'

Poppy parks the car.

77

'Has someone died?' I ask.

'Everything's fine, sweetheart,' Poppy says.

There are so many people out, but I can't see Mummy. 'Where's Mummy?' My heart starts a nervous flutter. 'Has he done it?' Butterflies explode in my chest, deep-dive down into my tummy. 'Has he burnt the house down?' I don't see any fire engines. 'Is she murdered?'

Poppy bites his lip, looks to Nanna. She turns away and puts her elbow on the windowsill, hand holding her head like she has one of her migraines. I look for the police officer. He points at our car. A bald man in a black suit turns, nods, pats him on the back. He starts a slow jog back. The butterflies swirl up and down, around and around, like they want to get out. I hold my stomach, hunch forward and squish the marble cake. 'Did he shoot Mummy?' I look up through my hair. 'He told me he would if I told on him. It's my fault. It's my fault she's dead.'

'Sir?'

Poppy jumps. 'Yes?'

'Please follow me,' the police officer says.

'In the car?'

'In the car.'

The policeman walks down the street, tells people to move out of the way. They take their time. He waves us forward. Poppy slowly rolls towards the house. It's still there. It hasn't been burnt down. And the lights are on inside.

Mummy opens the door before I can get out of the car. 'Oh, thank Bowie, you're okay!' She swings me up into her arms and holds me tight. I can feel the beat of her heart, the warmth of her skin, her breath on my face. The pink icing on my shirt squishes onto her black Led Zeppelin T-shirt, but she doesn't seem to care.

'She's shaking,' Mummy says.

'She thought you'd been murdered,' Nanna says, heading for the kitchen.

Poppy puts my bags on the lounge and lets out a deep breath. 'It's been a big day.'

I look into Mummy's face. She doesn't seem hurt or sad, just worried and tired. I put my head in the nook between her neck and shoulder. Her hair smells burnt from the dryer.

'Have you eaten?' Nanna asks.

'Not yet.'

'Should I put this in the oven and warm it up then?'

'What is it?'

'Bubble and squeak.'

'Yes, please. Is there enough for Rob too?'

'Is Rob coming?'

'He's already here.'

'Where?'

'Upstairs. He's just in the bathroom.'

'Oh, I didn't see his car.'

'It's not here. I picked him up this morning. We caught the train in together.'

'He went to court with you?'

'Not *into* the court, but he waited for me. And lucky Rob was there, because it ended up being just us and *him* at St James Station and, by the look on his face, he would've thrown me under an oncoming train if I wasn't there with someone.'

'You should have told your father. He could have gone with you.'

'I'm glad I didn't. It was better Dad was at home with you two.'

'Well, how's Rob going to get home?'

'We can give him a lift,' Poppy says.

Rob's blue joggers come down the stairs. He's in the same clothes he wore when I first met him.

'Walter.'

'Rob.'

They shake hands.

'Doris.'

Nanna nods.

Rob shoves his hands in his back pockets. 'Did you hear what happened up the street?'

'The policeman said there'd been a murder.'

'Some bloke comes home, finds his missus in bed with his mate, and splits her head open with a shovel!' Rob smiles and rocks back on his heels. 'Talk about pushing up daisies, huh?'

'What happened to the friend?' Nanna asks.

'No idea,' Mummy says.

'Best not to get involved. The people who live here are nuts.' Rob points at the side of his head, moves his hand in circles. 'That's why we didn't go out there.'

'How did you find out what was going on?'

'Just put the bins out,' Rob says. 'Everyone on the street was talking 'bout it.'

'Oh, so there was a little involvement then,' Nanna says.

Rob puts his hands on his hips, does his sniff-twitch.

Mummy sits in the corner piece of the lounge, holds me on her lap. I wrap my arms around her neck, kiss her cheek. 'I'm glad you're not dead.'

'Gee, thanks,' Mummy says. 'Me too.'

'Okay, dinner's almost ready.' Nanna waves a big metal spoon. 'Maybe give it another ten minutes just to make sure it's heated the whole way through.'

'Rob, do you need a lift home?' Poppy asks.

'Actually, I'm thinking, with everything that's going on, maybe I should stay here tonight, keep everyone safe.'

'They should be safe with all those police up the street,' Nanna says, picking up her handbag.

'What do you think, Lozza?' Rob asks.

'Is that okay with you, Shayla?' Mummy asks.

I nod into her shoulder. She bounces me on her knee.

'Your father could always stay,' Nanna says.

'No, that's okay. You've both done enough today. Go home and rest. Rob will take care of us.'

8

Mummy, Nanna and Poppy take me to Glenfield Public School to buy a uniform. Mummy says now the court has given her sole custody and an AVO, I can go to big school.

'What does that mean?'

'Sole custody?'

'And the other one.'

'Sole custody means you never have to go visit him ever again. It means I can keep you safe with me, always.' Mummy crouches down and pulls me in for a hug. 'And AVO stands for Apprehended Violence Order. It means he can't come near you at home or at school. So, if you ever see him here you need to go and tell a teacher straight away.'

'What if he tries to grab me?'

'Then you scream as loud as you can, you kick as hard as you can and you run as fast as you can to the nearest teacher, okay?' Mummy holds the tops of my arms tight. I can feel her nails dig in. 'You are never to leave here with him under any circumstances. If for some reason I can't come to get you, Nanna or Poppy will come instead. But you never ever leave with anyone else. Do you understand me?'

'Yes.'

'Promise?' Mummy holds her pinkie out.

I hook mine around hers and we press our thumbs together. 'Promise.'

Mummy gives me a kiss and stands up. Nanna's black knee-length skirt pushes in between us.

'Do you really have to do that here?' Nanna asks in a low voice.

'What?'

Nanna looks around the dark uniform shop. 'Air all our dirty laundry.'

A lady folds clothes in the corner.

'She can't hear me,' Mummy says.

The lady looks over. Mummy and Nanna give small tight smiles. The lady smiles back, showing her teeth.

'We shouldn't be discussing this in front of Shayla,' Nanna says. 'We've talked about this.'

'Doris ...' Poppy's holding my book, flicking through the pages of *Oh, the Places You'll Go!* by Dr Seuss. He gives Nanna a very small shake of the head.

'I can't just pretend it never happened, Mum. What if he shows up here one day? She has to know what to do.'

'And now she does, so can we please stop talking about it?'

'Shayla,' Poppy calls. 'Come over here. I want to tell you something.'

'Yes, Poppy?'

'Guess what I did the other day.'

'What?'

'I set up a bank account for you to celebrate the start of school. It's with St George Bank and it's called a Happy Dragon account. You get your very own bank book, and I've put a little something in there to get you started.'

'Money?'

'Yes. Fifty dollars.'

'Wow, that's a lot!'

'And we'll keep adding to it as we go, so that when you leave school you've got a nice little nest egg there, for whatever the next chapter in your life story is. How does that sound?'

'That sounds good.'

The uniform shop lady comes over. 'Hi there,' she says. 'You look like you could use some help. What can I do for you today?'

'My granddaughter is starting kindergarten here next year, so we need to get her uniforms.'

'New or used?'

'New, please.'

The lady turns and walks towards a rack of green-and-yellow clothes.

Poppy turns back to Nanna and Mummy. 'Let's focus on why we're here and stop the squabbling, shall we?'

'You'll find her sizes here,' the lady says. 'Just gimme a shout if you need anything else.'

'Thank you, much appreciated.'

I stand next to Poppy and look at the clothes. 'I don't like them.'

'Why?'

'They're yucky colours.'

'Green and gold,' Poppy says. 'The national colours of Australia.'

'Do I have to wear them every day?'

Mummy looks at a piece of paper in her hand. 'Yes, and your sports shirt is yellow too.'

'Nothing wrong with yellow,' Poppy says. 'One of my favourite colours.'

But today he's in a blue penguin polo, tucked into long grey pants with a sharp crease down the front of each leg.

'You'll look like a little sprig of wattle.' Nanna holds a green jumper up to my body. 'Did you know that wattle is our floral emblem?'

I shake my head.

'She'll grow into these.' Nanna hands one to Mummy and grabs another.

The little picture on front in yellow thread makes me think of the gold brooches Nanna wears when she and Poppy go to Bankstown Sports Club for dinner. 'What's this?'

'That's the school logo,' Poppy says.

'What does it say?'

Poppy looks at it, face scrunched up. He puts his glasses on, and they smooth out his face. 'Strive to achieve.' He takes his glasses off again. 'Do you know what that means? It means you should always try your hardest at everything you do. You should always try to be the best you can. Especially at school.'

I sit on the floor with a bunch of other kids. We all wear the same ugly green-and-yellow clothes from the school uniform shop. Mummy, Nanna and Poppy stand at the back of the classroom with the other parents and grandparents. The lady at the front of the room has brown hair. It's short like the heels on her white shoes. She wears a red-striped dress with two rows of buttons down the front.

'Welcome to your first day of big school. My name is Mrs Holmes. Can everyone say, "Good morning, Mrs Holmes"?'

'Good morning, Mrs Holmes,' everyone says, slowly.

'Raise your hand if you're six years old.'

She puts her hand up, high above her head. No other hands go up.

'Raise your hand if you're five years old,' she says.

I put my hand up and so does almost everyone else.

'Hands down.'

Everyone puts their hands down.

'Put your hand up if you're four years old.'

One girl puts her hand up.

'Thank you. Hands down.'

She turns and writes on the chalkboard. 'The name of our class is K1. I'm going to be your teacher for the year and this is going to be our classroom every day. So, when you arrive in the morning, you come to this room. When you come back from recess, you come to this room. When you come back from lunch, you come to this room. Does everyone understand?'

'Yes, Mrs Holmes,' everyone says.

'If you ever get lost, you just find the nearest teacher and tell them you're in class K1 or you're trying to find Mrs Holmes, okay?'

'Yes, Mrs Holmes.'

'Good.' She puts the chalk down. 'If you need to go to the toilet, we're lucky enough to have one at the back of our room here, so you just raise your hand, like this, and ask. Mums and dads will pick you up from this room at the end of the day. You're not to leave with anyone other than your own mum or dad. Are there any questions?'

Mums *or* dads? I look back at Mummy. She shakes her head and points to her shirt, black with a shiny silver guitar on front. I turn back to Mrs Holmes.

'Wonderful! Now, move around so we're sitting in a circle.'

Everyone moves into place. The four-year-old girl sits next to me. She smells like wee. I hope people don't think it's me.

'Everyone was asked to bring something with them today. A toy or a book or something you want to share with us. We're going to go around the circle and tell everyone our name, our birthday and a little bit about the thing we brought with us today.'

Everyone sits on the floor, legs crossed. I'm the only one with my knees together, not apart; legs in an M-shape, feet either side of my bum, so no-one can see up the skirt of my school dress.

Mrs Holmes points and smiles. 'Let's start with you,' she says. 'What's your name?'

'My name's Shayla.'

'Let's all say, "Good morning, Shayla."'

'Good morning, Shayla,' everyone says.

'When's your birthday, Shayla?'

'I just turned five last week.'

'Happy birthday,' Mrs Holmes says.

'Thank you.'

'And what did you bring with you today?'

'I brought *Barbie: A picnic surprise*.' I hold the Little Golden Book up for everyone to see.

'Tell us what you like about your book.'

'I like reading. And I like Barbie.'

'What do you like about Barbie?'

'I like her hair and her clothes, and I like that she does everything.'

'Like what?'

'She's been a doctor and a teacher. She's been to the moon.' I wave my arms around. 'She does everything.'

'That's great, Shayla,' Mrs Holmes says. 'Thank you for sharing. Let's go around the circle now. You're next.'

She points at the girl who smells like wee. Her hands are empty. She doesn't speak. Mrs Holmes bends down on one knee in front of her. 'Hello there, do you want to tell us your name and your birthday?'

The little girl shakes her head. Her brown hair looks dirty and sticks to her head.

'That's okay,' Mrs Holmes says. 'You just let us know when you're ready.' She nods at the next in line.

'Hi, I'm Ashleigh.'

'Good morning, Ashleigh.'

The light-green carpet under wee girl starts to turn dark green. The dark green starts to spread towards Ashleigh.

'I turn six in …' Ashleigh stops. Everyone looks at the wet patch.

Mrs Holmes takes wee girl by the hand towards the toilet at the back of the room. 'That's okay,' she says. 'You all keep going.'

In winter, wee girl's hands turn purple. So do her legs. Everyone has the sniffles, but wee girl seems the sickest. She has a cough too and it sounds like there's a big baby rattle inside her chest. Me and the other girls wear jumpers over our dresses and thick dark-green stockings underneath, but she's still in her summer uniform. She looks hot and sweaty, but she shivers and her teeth chatter, like she's cold. Even on the days she doesn't wee on the classroom floor it smells like maybe she's slept in a wet bed and hasn't showered or washed her school uniform.

She doesn't speak in class.

'Shayla?'

'Here.'

'Bethany?'

Not even to answer roll call.

At lunch she sits by herself, but I never see her with a lunchbox or food order.

I get to place a lunch order every Monday. Mummy puts a few gold coins in a brown paper bag, writes my name on it and, later that day, just before the bell rings for lunch, the same bag comes to my classroom, in a metal shopping basket, with a hot ham-and-pineapple McCain Pizza Single inside. Gold and silver coins jingle at the bottom of the bag like Christmas bells. Mummy calls it 'change' and says it's mine to spend on whatever I want for the rest of the week. Sometimes I put it in my Dollarmites account with the Commonwealth Bank of Australia and Poppy says he'll 'match it' by putting the same amount in my Happy Dragon account. But most of the time I spend it on Bubble O'Bill ice cream because I like the gum-ball nose.

The only time I ever see wee girl eat is when Mummy comes to help with reading on Wednesdays. Reading is after lunch. Mummy comes early to eat with me. She brings hot chips and potato scallops from the takeaway shop down the road. And she always buys extra for wee girl.

'At least she has something warm in her stomach now,' Mummy says.

How the Birds Got Their Colours is open on the big reading stand. Mrs Holmes read it to us today, using a long wooden ruler to point at the words. Now we're learning about different types of families.

The boy sitting next to me is called Banjo. He has brown hair, short and curly, and he wears glasses, round ones without frames. Banjo tells Mrs Holmes he needs two family trees because he's adopted. She nods, touches a tissue to her red nose, gives him a second piece of paper.

'What does "adopted" mean?'

'That the people I live with are not my real parents.'

'Why do you live with them then?'

'They're my godparents.'

'What are godparents?'

'They're the people your real parents choose for you to go live with when they're not around anymore.'

'Where did your real parents go?'

'To heaven.'

'So, you have two family trees?' I look at the birthmark on Banjo's cheek. It's brown like his eyes. Mummy calls it a 'beauty spot'.

'Yes, one for my birth parents and one for my adoptive parents.'

He picks up a pencil with his left hand and starts to scribble names. I pick up a pencil with my right hand and do the same. I write my name, Mummy's name, Nanna's and Poppy's, and then I stop. The sharp tips of lead pencils tap and scratch across the wooden desktops. Ashleigh gets up to use the pencil sharpener on the side of Mrs Holmes's desk. It whirls as she turns the handle. Paper rustles around the room. Pencil cases are zipped open and closed. I look at the books across from my desk. They're in plastic sleeves that clip shut across the top, hung on hangers, like the clothes inside Nanna's wardrobe. Banjo's almost finished his second family tree. Everyone's still scribbling but me.

'How are you going, Shayla?' Mrs Holmes crouches down by my desk. Skin peels off under her nostrils. She smells like the eucalyptus drops I never buy from the canteen.

'I'm done.' I fold my hands over the piece of paper.

Mrs Holmes tugs at the paper, crunches a eucalyptus drop between her teeth and frowns. 'What about your daddy and his side of the family?'

'I don't see them anymore.'

'I know. That's okay. We've got a few students in our class who don't see their mummies or daddies, but we can still write their names down, can't we?'

I shake my head. Nanna's told me not to talk about him anymore, that it upsets Mummy: 'He and his family are dead to us. *This* is your family now. Mummy and Poppy and I. Forget the others. Forget everything about them. Forget they ever even existed.'

'What's your daddy's name?'

Plastic sleeves on the book rack have been pushed apart so I can see the cover of *Possum Magic*. I like Grandma Poss. In the book she makes little Hush invisible to keep her safe from all the big scary animals in the bush.

'Tell me and we can write it down together,' Mrs Holmes says.

'He's dead! They're all dead! And I'm not allowed to talk about it.'

Classmates turn to stare. Mrs Holmes tells them to pack up for the day – it's almost home time.

'You can still put their names,' Banjo says. He shows me the names of his dead parents – and their parents.

I put my hands over my ears and close my eyes. Tears squeeze out. The school bell rings. Chair legs clink against each other as they're pushed away from desks. Mums and dads collect their kids. Classmates say goodbye. It all sounds fuzzy through my sweaty palms, and I stay like that until Mummy squats down next to me and pulls my hands away from my ears.

'Shayla?' There's a heart on her black T-shirt with a big sword through the middle of it. She's worn this one before. It says 'Bon Jovi'. 'What's wrong with her?'

'I'm afraid I might have upset her,' Mrs Holmes says.

Mummy stands up. 'What happened?'

'We were working on family trees, and I didn't realise her father had passed.'

'Passed?'

'I'm sorry,' Mrs Holmes says. 'I've been off sick for a couple of weeks, so I didn't know.'

'Shayla, you pack up, okay? I'm just going to talk to Mrs Holmes over here for a minute.'

Mummy and Mrs Holmes stand in front of the chalkboard where all the letters of the alphabet, both big and little, have been written out in coloured chalk. I stuff a chocolate Space Food Stick in my mouth, grab my reading book out from under the desk and put it in

89

my backpack. There's a grey plastic shopping bag at the bottom, full of green school stockings that I was meant to give to wee girl. I take them over to Mummy.

'Oh, haven't you given those to Bethany yet?' Mummy asks.

'I haven't seen her.'

'Actually, I haven't seen her for a while either.' Mummy looks from me to Mrs Holmes. 'Usually I see her before reading on Wednesdays.'

Mrs Holmes's eyes look watery. 'Oh dear, I'm so sorry to tell you this.'

'What's wrong?' Mummy asks.

'Bethany's no longer with us.'

Mummy's eyebrows jump up. 'As in …'

'I'm afraid so.' Mrs Holmes bows her head.

'Ohmigod!' Mummy breathes the word out.

Mrs Holmes nods. 'Pneumonia.'

I pull on Mummy's hand. 'Does Bethany go to a different school now?'

Mummy crouches down, tucks a curl behind my ear and kisses my forehead. Her eyes look like they're full of tears and I feel bad that I've made her sad again because I lied about the family tree and forgot about the stockings.

'Yes, honey. Bethany goes to a different school now.'

9

Someone shouts. A man. The sound of his voice makes me feel yucky in the tummy.

I put *The Complete Adventures of Snugglepot and Cuddlepie* down and turn off the tap. I stare at the bathroom window, hold my breath and try to tune in with my listening ears, but I can't make out the words.

The man shouts again. Glass shatters.

I stand up and water pours off my body, back into the bath, loud like a waterfall. I wait for it to stop so I can hear what's going on. Heavy footsteps pound up the stairs, past the bathroom, into Mummy's bedroom. It's Rob. He always digs his heels into the floor. The sliding doors of Mummy's wardrobe, where Rob keeps a wooden baseball bat hidden, rattle as they hit the frame. He's been staying with us three nights a week because that's how many nights Mummy said he can stay without the neighbours dobbing her in to Housing.

Angry feet stomp back down the stairs. I hear the front screen door screech open and Rob shout, 'What the fuck's your problem, mate?'

I step out of the bathtub and wrap a towel around my body, quietly open the bathroom door and stick my head out. Water drip-drops from my wet hair onto the carpet. I can hear Mummy screaming into the telephone downstairs, 'Please come quick. I have a child in the house. He's dangerous. He might be armed. We have an AVO.'

I run downstairs in my towel, just as Mummy locks the security door behind her. The telephone receiver dangles down the wall, swinging side to side. I hang it up. *The Ferals* is playing on the TV. I turn it off. There's an empty beer bottle on the dining table, next to Mummy's cigarette, still smoking away in the ashtray. I stub it out.

I can hear Rob and another man shout, Mummy scream, sirens in the distance. I pull the white lace curtains back to see what's going on. Something comes flying towards the window and I quickly cover my eyes with my forearm, just as the glass shatters.

Everything gets louder. I lower my arm and glass tinkles off my body onto the floor. Blood trickles from my shoulder down my chest and soaks into the white towel, still wrapped around me. I look out the broken window, curtain taken down by a rock, and see *him*. Mummy and Rob follow Daddy's gaze and, as their heads turn, he starts to run at full speed towards me. His arms pump, veins bulging.

'Shayla!' Mummy screams. 'Run!'

His right hand comes up. I notice it's gloved. And there's a huge metal spike poking out the side, like a knife. All three of them are running towards me now, but I'm frozen to the spot. I haven't seen him since Casula Fruit Market. I'd forgotten what he looked like. Mummy said we didn't have to worry about him anymore because she has full custody and the AVO.

Daddy's hand-spike catches the sun and shines. Rob pulls out an old footy move: launches his body forward, into the air, and crash-tackles Daddy to the ground. He and Mummy drag Daddy by the legs back across the lawn, full of bindies, away from the window. I stumble back, step on broken glass. Blood soaks into the dark-blue carpet, spreads to the curtains.

When I look up again, Rob is on his back by the driveway. His car has been destroyed. Every window has been smashed. Side mirrors have been ripped off and thrown across the street. The roof is dented, a sandstone rock still on top, and Daddy is standing over Rob, silver spike shining in the sun. He leans in, gets a little closer to Rob, makes sure his spike is within stabbing range. Mummy, who must have fallen over, jumps up from behind her car and runs over to them. She throws a punch and her fist connects with his temple. His head spins towards me, spit slung out the side of his mouth. His eyes focus on me before he turns back to Mummy. He raises the spike. Mummy stands her ground. And he brings his fist down.

As soon as the police arrive, the street is full of people. Most of them are neighbours. They stand around, watch, whisper. Where were they all before? Across the street, Susan Parker, who Mummy calls Nosey Parker, sets up a camping chair on her front lawn. She pops a can of Pepsi Max in the drink holder, opens a bag of barbecue-flavoured Samboy potato chips and makes herself comfortable. Daddy sits in the gutter, hands cuffed behind his back, head hung low. An ambulance arrives; no lights or sirens. A female police officer walks towards me, alone.

'I can't move,' I tell her.

'I'm going to pick you up and sit you on the lounge, okay?'

I nod, and the tear that had been blurring my vision finally rolls down my cheek. She steps through the window. Broken glass grinds beneath her big black police boots. One arm behind my knees, the other behind my back, she picks me up and carries me to the lounge.

'I'm Senior Constable Perkins.' She squats down in front of me. 'What's your name?'

'Shayla.'

Senior Constable Perkins looks at the bottom of my feet, then speaks into a radio on her shoulder. 'Can I get an ambo in here, please?'

A muffled male voice comes back across the radio, but I don't understand it.

I start to shake. My teeth start to chatter. 'I'm cold.'

'I'm Joel,' an ambulance officer says in a cheery voice as he comes crunching through the window. 'And you're in shock.'

'Joel, this is Shayla,' Senior Constable Perkins says.

Joel sets a first-aid kit on the coffee table and pulls out a package that says 'Space Blanket'. It's silver like the aluminium foil that

Mummy wraps my sandwiches in for school. Joel drapes the blanket over my shoulders and wraps it around my body.

'Can I leave this with you for the moment?' Senior Constable Perkins asks Joel.

'Yep, all good.'

Senior Constable Perkins heads back out the broken window. Joel unscrews the cap off a bottle of Mount Franklin Spring Water.

'You got it?' Joel asks.

But my hands are shaking so much I miss my mouth. Joel puts his finger under the bottle to stop it from spilling everywhere while I drink.

'There we go.' He takes the bottle back. 'Now, let's have a look at those feet.'

My whole body aches. Joel says it's because all my muscles tensed up, but I'll feel better in a few days. He tweezes all the broken glass out of my feet, bandages them and sticks a bandaid on the small nick on my shoulder.

When he's done, I take slow steps out the front door in soft slippers. It's starting to get dark. Senior Constable Perkins is loading Daddy into the back of a police truck. The mozzies have come out and the neighbours are starting to head inside. It's almost time for *Home and Away*.

Senior Constable Perkins slams the back of the police truck closed and taps the side of it twice. 'Show's over, folks.'

Nosey Parker scrunches up her empty packet of potato chips, picks up her camping chair and disappears inside. Rob stands on the road, in front of his car, wearing short shorts and thongs. Blood from his nose has dried in dark patches on the front of his blue singlet. A short female police officer takes notes in a small notebook.

'I tripped over one of these.' Rob kicks at one of the smaller sandstone rocks. 'Ended up on my back, over there by Lozza's car. He was standing over me. He was going to stab me. He would have if Lozza hadn't punched him.'

Mummy stands behind her car, at the end of the driveway, blood from a split lip, now fat and purple, on her Iron Maiden T-shirt, an ice pack on her hand. She talks to a male police officer. 'I thought he was going to stab me but luckily he stabbed the car instead. Look.' Mummy points to a hole in the boot of her car. 'That icepick thing, or whatever it is, went straight through. It's lucky you guys got here when you did, otherwise one of us could have ended up dead.'

Senior Constable Perkins takes her police cap off, wipes her forehead with the back of her hand, and pushes blonde hair off her face. She looks from me to Mummy. 'Do you have somewhere safe to stay?' she asks.

10

Nanna and Poppy say we can stay with them until we get a transfer from Kikori Place, but not Rob. Mummy and Rob want to stay together, so his mother, Mildred, says we can all stay at her house. She lives in a nice cul-de-sac in Ingleburn, where the air smells like freshly cut grass on the weekends, and on hot days kids run around under sprinklers on their front lawns.

'It shouldn't be too much longer,' Mummy tells Mildred. 'I put in for a transfer basically as soon as we moved in, but I've been calling Housing every day, sometimes twice a day, since that woman was murdered up the street.'

Mummy's black T-shirt has the word 'Queen' printed on it. I thought the Queen was a woman, but underneath the word is a man in white pants and a yellow jacket. He has a black moustache and his fist is in the air. Mummy told me his name is Freddie Mercury.

'Ah, yes,' Mildred says. 'I remember seeing that on the news. How long ago was that now?'

'He killed her in August 1992,' Mummy says.

'So, two years this month and still no movement?' Mildred looks up from her brown leather armchair by the front window. Almost everything in this house is brown leather or wood. The only colour comes from the heavy floral drapes that cover the windows.

Mummy shakes her head at her feet.

'Even after your own home was attacked?'

'No.'

'That's the disadvantage of relying on the system to support you.' Mildred takes a big gulp of her drink. 'They just put you where they put you and then you can't ever get out.'

'I guess beggars can't be choosers,' Mummy says.

'You know, there's that old saying, "Nothing in this world is free." One way or another, you pay.'

Mummy's eyes grow small and angry, but Mildred keeps talking into her glass.

'And you certainly get what you pay for. Just like that last place you ended up in. Nasty neck of the woods down there.'

'I didn't have a lot of choice at the time.' Mummy folds her arms. 'I had to take what I could get, or I would have ended up in a shelter or on the street with a two-year-old.'

Mildred leans in to whisper. 'The secret is to not divorce them, but to outlive them, and to make sure they're insured up the wazoo. It was Husband Number Two's life insurance that paid for this house.'

'Good things come to those who wait, huh?'

'That they do.' Mildred raises her almost-empty glass as if to toast, then pours herself another drink from the cardboard box on the table by her armchair. Mummy calls it 'rotgut', says that Mildred's an 'alcoholic'.

'Yeh, well, hanging around for him to drop off the perch wasn't really an option for me. Only the good die young. That bastard will probably live forever.'

Rob comes into the lounge room, gives Mummy a kiss on the lips and sits down to tie up his shoes. The same blue joggers with white laces and soles he wears everywhere. 'Hair looks nice,' he says.

'Ugh, I need to get it done.' Mummy wraps a strand around her finger. 'Desperately.'

'Really?' Mildred relaxes back into her chair. 'I just assumed you were growing it out.'

Mummy gives a tight smile. It's the smile she uses when she's annoyed but can't say anything. I haven't seen her smile any other kind of smile at Mildred. Mildred fluffs her poodle hair, fresh from the hairdressers. It still smells like perm and hairspray. Short, tight grey curls.

'No, I just haven't had a lot of time or money for myself – looking after Shayla and getting her settled in to school has been more important,' Mummy says. 'You know, I basically haven't slept through the night in, like, four years. I'm up all night to keep watch while Shayla sleeps, then I come home and sleep during the day while she's at school. I've been on high alert since I left him. I don't even know how I managed it when I was still working. It hasn't been easy. In fact, it's been really bloody hard.'

'Yes, I can see the past couple of years haven't been kind.'

'Gee, thanks,' Mummy says.

'Oh, you know what I mean.' Mildred waves her arm in a half-circle. 'Hopefully, now that you're living with us you'll have time to take better care of yourself.'

Mummy smiles her small, tight, annoyed smile again. Mildred brings her glass to her lips, eyes never leaving Mummy's.

'How old are you these days, anyway?' Mildred asks.

'I turned twenty-eight earlier this year.'

'Oh, I thought you were a couple of years older than Robbie.'

Mummy's told me Rob is two years older than her.

'Because I've looked so haggard?' Mummy sort of laughs, but when she looks to Rob her eyes are watery. He keeps his head down, reties his laces, foot over knee.

'No, of course not.' Mildred waves her hand like she's shooing a fly. 'You've just done so much in such a short amount of time. You've been married.'

'And divorced,' Mummy says.

'And divorced.' Mildred raises her glass again. 'Started a family. Moved around. All I'm saying is that you've lived a very grown-up life, while Robbie's just been here at home with me. No marriage, no divorce, no kids.'

'Gee, Ma. Thanks for making me sound like such a loser.'

'*Loser*?' Mildred sits forward in her chair. 'No. What have you failed at? Nothing.'

Mummy looks to the ceiling, blinks back her tears.

'I'm just saying, you've lived a whole life that Robbie hasn't even had the chance to experience yet. Compared to you, my son is a' – Mildred rolls her hand in small circles, as if trying to find the right words – 'a clean slate. There's no history, no baggage. He's got everything to offer. Everything's still on the table.'

'You're saying that I'm damaged goods?'

'That's not what I'm saying at all.'

Rob stands up, taps his back pocket.

'Robbie, did you hear me say that?'

Rob shakes his head like he can't believe what's going on.

'No.' Mildred points at Mummy. 'You said that. Not me.'

'I just need to get my wallet,' Rob says. 'Then we'll leave, yeh?'

Mummy nods. Rob disappears. Mildred takes another sip of her drink.

'But also, let's be honest here, Lauren. Only one of you is coming into this relationship with a six-year-old child from a different partner, yes? So, you see my point. I'm not saying it's a good thing or a bad thing. I myself brought two children into my second marriage. I'm just saying that having a school-aged daughter made you seem older to me, that's all.'

Mummy flicks faded red waves over her shoulder and changes the subject. 'I think twenty-eight is going to be a good year for me.'

Mildred rolls her eyes into her glass.

'I think the tide has turned. I think things are finally going to go my way.'

'Well, you know what thought did,' Mildred says in a sing-songy voice.

Nanna would answer that with, 'Thought his bum was hanging out of bed and got out to push it back in', but Mummy ignores her. She puts one hand on her hip and rubs her tummy with the other. Mildred's eyes move up from Mummy's tummy. Mummy looks down her nose, waits for Mildred's cloudy brown eyes to meet her bright-green ones. They lock, like they're having a staring competition. The grandfather clock ticks in the corner.

'Did Rob tell you I've asked for a three-bedroom place this time?' Mummy asks in a happy voice.

'No, he did not.' Mildred raises her eyebrows as she lifts her glass. 'But don't go getting your hopes up just yet.' She throws her head back, finishes her drink. 'I know how badly you've been disappointed in the past.'

When the front door closes behind Mummy and Rob, I'm left alone with Mildred. The lounge room is dark and smoky. The heavy floral drapes are drawn to avoid glare on the TV. The red–hot tips of Mildred's incense and cigarettes glow in the dark.

She spends most of her days in front of the telly. Her favourite show is *The Bold and the Beautiful*. She watches it with her two dogs. They're chihuahuas. The white one is called Jessie. She's the girl. The black one is called James. He's the boy. Mildred's told me they're named after Jesse James, an outlaw from the Wild West in America. They settle by her feet.

'What year are you in now?' Mildred asks.

'Year 1.'

'How are you enjoying it?'

'I like it.'

'Your mother's told me you're top of your class for reading.'

I nod into the pages of *Selby Speaks*, open on the floor in front of me.

'Good work.' She raises her glass. 'Keep it up.'

'I will.'

Mildred leans forward, elbow on the arm of her chair, hand under her chin, finger over her lip. She looks at me through round thick-framed glasses, connected to a gold chain that hangs around the back of her wrinkly neck. Her eyes look a little bit wonky, a little bit mean. So does her smile. 'Do you want to know something?' she asks.

'I don't know.'

'Of course you do!' Mildred slaps her knee. 'Loves school. Enjoys learning. Top of her class. Always reading. I don't think I've once seen you without your nose buried in a book. You want to know *everything*, I'm sure of it.'

I shrug my shoulders. There's something about the way she looks at me that makes me feel yucky in the tummy.

'In fact, you're so smart, maybe you already know, right?'

'Maybe.'

'Can I ask you a question then? Because I noticed something today. I noticed that Robbie didn't say hello to you.'

I look away, turn the page of my book.

'Or goodbye.'

I shrug again.

'So, can I ask you a question?'

'Yes.'

'It's rude not to look people in the eye when they're talking to you, Shayla.'

I look up. The red drink in her glass has made two little devil horns above her lip, towards the corners of her mouth. I watch them move as she talks.

'Did you know that your daddy went to high school with my Robbie?'

I close my eyes, shake my head. Nanna told me not to talk about him. It upsets Mummy. Forget him. Forget everything about him. Forget he ever even existed.

'Mhmm.' Mildred sits back, eyebrows raised. 'He did. Do you have anyone who is mean to you at school, Shayla?'

'No.'

'That's lucky for you,' Mildred says. 'Unfortunately, Robbie wasn't that lucky. Back in the day he had a lisp. Do you know what a lisp is?'

'No.'

'It's hard to explain. Some words just come out funny.'

'What do they sound like?'

'It's like some words are slurred or slobbery or something.'

'Why?'

'He was tongue-tied as a child. See this little bit of skin?' Mildred sits forward, lifts her tongue to the roof of her mouth and points underneath, where it's spit-shiny and full of blue squiggly veins. 'It's too tight for some people and they cut it.'

'Like, with scissors?'

'Yeh, scissors, or a knife. One of those special surgical knives. What are they called? Oh, I don't know. I've had too much to drink.' Mildred pours herself another. 'Oh, it's right on the tip of my tongue. It's going to bother me all day if I don't think of it.'

She stares at the TV, frowns. I stay quiet, wait for her to find the word. After a minute, she shakes her head and waves the thought away with her glass.

'Anyway, at the time, I thought he'd grow out of it. It's kind of cute when they're little, but as they get older, not so much. People start to wonder if there's something wrong with them up here.' Mildred taps the side of her head. 'We ended up having the tongue-tie release done when he was in Year 6 and I thought that would be the end of it, but he'd already learnt to talk that way, so he had to unlearn it. I got a speech therapist to help him, but it takes time and he was starting high school. Some of the kids gave him a hard time, you know, as kids do. Well, *you* don't know that, personally, because no-one at school is mean to you.'

'I understand.' Kids at school used to pick on wee girl for not speaking.

'But no-one gave him as hard a time as your father.' Mildred narrows her eyes at me, taps a chipped yellow fingernail on her glass. 'No, your father was particularly cruel to my Robbie. Used to beat him up in the boys' bathroom and everything. Even flushed his head down the toilet once when it was full of piss. He was bigger than Robbie. There were a couple years' difference between them. I think your father dropped out and joined the army just as your mother was starting high school, so she mustn't have met him until afterwards. But he certainly made the first two years of high school pure hell for my poor Robbie.'

The dog next door barks. Jessie and James raise their heads. Mildred pulls the drape back with a wooden back scratcher and looks out the window. Dust-light streams through the window, hitting like a spotlight at the school carols night. The chihuahuas sneeze and paw at their eyes.

'Just the postman.' Mildred lets the curtain fall back into place.

'I'm sorry for what happened to Rob.'

'Don't apologise for what other people have done,' Mildred says. 'You're a good kid. And from what I can make out – although your mother must have sworn Robbie to secrecy, because getting information out of him is like getting blood from a stone – I think he might have been a bit of a bully to you too.'

'I'm not allowed to talk about him.'

The last of the red rotgut dribbles out of the silver bag in the cardboard box into a half-full glass. It sounds like someone doing a wee.

'They think they're protecting you, but this little game of denial they're playing is dangerous.' Mildred shakes her head into her glass. 'Not right now, but one day it will be – because you might be able to escape him, but you'll never be able to escape yourself. He's part of you. *Half* of you. And there'll be lots of reminders. In fact, you've only got to look in the mirror to see it for yourself – one green eye from her, one blue eye from him.'

I pull my knees up to my chin, wrap my arms around them, close my eyes.

'And from what I can tell he's done more than just contribute DNA to shape you as a person.' Mildred lights a cigarette, takes a deep, wheezy breath, then coughs. 'Ah, how differently things could have turned out if your grandparents had just minded their own business. Robbie and Lauren were engaged in high school, did you know that?'

I open my eyes and nod.

'Your grandparents didn't think my Robbie was good enough for their little girl back then. Look how that turned out. And now here you are.' Mildred holds her arms out to me, drink in one hand, smoke in the other. 'Child of his long-lost love and high school tormentor. You even look like him a bit. All the best parts, don't worry. Lucky for you he wasn't ugly on the outside. But it must be hard for Robbie, seeing you, especially now that they're trying to be a family, but she keeps losing all the—' Mildred sits up straight, wine splashing out of her glass, and inadvertently kicks James, making him jump out of his sleep. 'Scalpels!'

'What?'

'They're the surgical knives that I couldn't remember the name of before.' Mildred smiles with dark-yellow teeth. 'Scalpels! That's the word I was looking for. Oh, thank goodness, that was going to bother me all day.'

James moves to his dog bed and flops down with a sleepy-grumpy huff, head on his tan paws. His black beady eyes and eyebrow whiskers twitch from me to Mildred.

'No, I meant, what is Mummy losing?'

'Hmmm?' Mildred's eyes are wide.

'You said they're trying to be a family, but Mummy keeps losing something. What is she losing? Maybe I can help her find it.'

'Oh, don't listen to me.' Mildred waves her arm. 'I'm drunk. In fact, best we keep this conversation between the two of us. Is that okay with you?'

'Is it a bad secret?'

Mildred looks to the ceiling for a moment, eyebrows up, lips down. 'Nah.' She shakes her head. 'More of an uncomfortable truth.'

'What does that mean?'

'It means people already know the truth, so it's not a secret, it's just not a nice thing to talk about. It might upset people, so you keep it to yourself to be polite.'

'Like how I'm not allowed to talk about him?'

'Who?'

'*Him.*'

'I think there's probably more to that than just being polite, but

I've probably said too much. How about we have an early lunch so I can soak this up a bit.' Mildred holds up an empty glass.

I nod.

'Rice?'

11

Mum cuts potatoes in Mildred's kitchen. A cigarette hangs from her lips. The smoke spirals towards the ceiling. 'Eighteen months. Can you believe it?' She looks at me across the breakfast bench. 'It's a long time to be living with your boyfriend's mother.'

I look out the back door. Cars buzz by on Harold Street, Ingleburn. 'It feels longer.'

'Tell me about it,' Mum huffs. 'But I thought that you and Rob would be a bit closer by now.'

The knife hits the chopping board with a loud thwack. Mum's black T-shirt has blue eyes printed on it under the words 'Bette Davis Eyes', like the Kim Carnes song I've heard her sing in the car. Mum's missing her sound system. It's in storage while we wait for Housing to find us a home of our own. These days, when she's upset, I find her chain-smoking in the car with the windows wound up and the stereo on full blast. She says it's the only place she can get 'some damn privacy around here'.

'I've just noticed you two don't seem to talk very much, that's all,' Mum continues. 'It's really important to me that you get along, you know?'

'I know.'

'So I was hoping you might make a little extra effort for me.'

'I will.'

Mum raises her eyebrows.

I slump in the wooden stool. 'You mean now?'

'Actually, now that you've mentioned it, that sounds great.' Mum smiles.

I roll my eyes.

'Don't be like that,' Mum says. 'Just give it a go until I call you for lunch. It won't be long.'

I inch down from the chair then push it back in. I dog-ear the corner of the page I'm up to and put *The Baby-Sitters Club* in my school bag. I scan my homework – look, cover, write, check. I pull out rubbish, pile it on the bench, put it in the bin. I move my book to a different area of the backpack. Then I zip up the compartments. All of them. A couple get stuck on paper, so they have to be reopened, rearranged and closed again.

'Oh, no rush.' Mum puts one hand on her hip. '*Please*, take your time.'

'I'm going, I'm going.' I drag my feet along the carpet.

'Thanks!' Mum calls after me in the sing-songy voice she uses when she's asked me to do something I don't want to do.

I look back over my shoulder and shake my head, stalling just a little longer. Mum sweeps her long hair up into a high pony and waves me goodbye. Her eyes are bright. Her smile is cheeky. Her neck is covered in purple bruises. She calls them 'lovebites' and blushes. Nanna calls them 'hickeys' and curls her top lip.

Rob puts them there. Right now, he's in the lounge room with his mother. It's dark, except for the glow of the television and the end of Mildred's cigarette. There are ceramic chickens on top of the entertainment unit that I can't reach to dust. They're painted brown and beige, the same colours as everything else in this house.

Rob watches *Rex Hunt's Fishing Adventure*, beer in one hand, remote control in the other. His blue Bonds singlet is stained light purple in some places, maybe from the chlorine in the pool. He scratches the Southern Cross tattoo on his shoulder. Mildred sits in her brown armchair by the window. She raises her glass of goon at me, hello. I turn my lips up into a small smile and sit down on the lounge-room floor in my usual M-shape: knees together, legs out to the sides. There are hard little holes dotted throughout the thick beige carpet beneath me, where lit cigarettes have been dropped, melting the synthetic fibres.

A man with a beard and a baseball cap reels something in off the back of a boat.

'What kind of fish is that?' I ask.

'Listen to the show and you'll find out.' Rob points the remote control at the TV. The bright-blue volume bar on the screen gets longer.

I pretend to be interested, wait for the next catch to come up on screen. 'That's a big fish! What's the biggest fish you've caught? And did you eat it or throw it back?' I ask.

Mildred sits in the dark corner behind Rob. She watches over her glass. Grey incense and cigarette smoke waft around her.

I try again. 'I don't really like to eat fish like that. I do like fish fingers though. With tomato sauce. Do you like fish fingers?'

Rob takes a swig of beer and stares at the television.

'Mum's making us lunch now. Hot chips and fried eggs. I can see if we have fish fingers too if you like?'

'Just don't shut up, do ya?'

His words sting like a slap. My cheeks burn and my eyes prickle with tears. I unfold my legs, ready to leave, just as I catch an ugly twinkle in Mildred's eyes. They tighten at the sides like she's smiling behind her glass, but not in a sympathetic way. I get the sense that she and Rob would love to see me run off crying, but Pop's told me that I should never give in to bullies, so I blink back my tears and focus on the television. I stretch my legs out in front of me, cross them at the ankles, lean back on my palms and stay put until lunch is ready.

Rob's older brother, Peter, knows that his wife doesn't like him drinking, but he enjoys making her uncomfortable. I can tell because he gets the same nasty glint in his eye as his mother when he pours a fresh drink, throws it back. Tracey stays silent, and somehow Peter becomes bigger. His voice grows louder, his arm movements wider. She watches him out of the corner of her eye, and every time he touches her or makes any kind of movement towards her, I see her flinch around the eyes. It makes me feel a bit sick in the stomach.

'There's blood on your shorts, Lauren.' Mildred's voice rings out from the head of the table and interrupts the story of how Peter ran over his wife's foot with a lawnmower, removing her little toe. Accidentally.

Peter's head swivels towards Mum's faded black denim shorts with the acid wash and fringing. There's a stain on her butt, like maybe she sat in something. Mum stops in her tracks, back to the dining room, washing basket in hand. Her knuckles turn white, her shoulders tremble, and her waist-length hair ripples like water down her back. I hold my breath and wait for her to whip on Mildred, but she doesn't even look back. She just straightens her shoulders, hoists her head a little higher and marches on. Pop's probably taught her not to give in to bullies either. No-one at the table moves or speaks until they hear Rob's bedroom door shut.

'Don't be slamming doors in my house, missy!' Mildred shouts after her.

Rob stands, leaves the table, follows Mum.

'That time of the month, huh?'

'No.' Mildred peers at Peter over her glass.

'Oh.'

Mildred waves her hand. 'Sometimes Mother Nature knows best.'

I look at Tracey, and she looks away, fixes her eyes on a plate of sticky brown chicken wings – the plate she pushed away, still full of food, when they started to laugh at the lawnmower accident.

Peter pushes it back in front of her. 'You haven't touched your food.'

She picks up her knife and fork. The handles are brown, wooden. So are the salt and pepper shakers. Peter catches me watching them over my glass of Coca-Cola and the side of his mouth lifts. He throws his arm over the back of Tracey's dining chair and the evil sparkle in his eye sharpens. Tracey shrinks into her seat, shovelling chicken wings into her mouth.

★

The house is dark and quiet. I turn on my bedroom light and the flick of the switch is ear-piercing. Mum hasn't left Rob's bedroom. I haven't left mine. Peter and Tracey left hours ago. Mildred's been in front of the telly since. There's been the muffled drone of *Funniest Home Videos*. The frequent flick of a cigarette lighter. The periodic pouring of rotgut into an empty glass. Mildred's rattling cough.

Rob's bedroom door quietly opens and closes. There are footsteps on the carpet. Floorboards creak beneath. I hope it's Mum. I know it's not when I hear a gush instead of a tinkle in the toilet next to my room. It's always louder when Rob does a wee, probably because he stands up, but also because Mum closes the door, like a lady. I wait by my bedroom door, hoping to catch Rob on his way down the hallway to the kitchen, but he heads back the way he came.

'Hey.'

He turns around.

'Is Mum okay?' I ask from the doorway.

'Yeh.'

'What's wrong with her?'

He walks towards me, speaking quietly. 'She's just not feeling well.'

'Is she going to be okay? She was bleeding.'

'She'll be fine.'

'Does she need to go to the doctor?'

'I'm taking her tomorrow.'

I step back into my room as he reaches for the door handle. 'Wait. Can I go see her?'

'She's asleep. You can see her tomorrow. Go to bed.' He pulls the door across after him, the way he does when he doesn't want me listening, but it doesn't latch. My inflatable blue bubble armchair squeaks beneath me as I sit back down with *Orbit*, the school magazine. I tilt my right ear towards the gap between the door and the frame to hear what's going on. Rob moves up the hallway, towards his bedroom, but makes a pitstop in the lounge room first.

'Oh, hello. How nice of you to join us,' Mildred says in a

110

sickly-sweet voice that suddenly turns sour. 'Oh wait, everyone's already gone.'

An empty glass is slammed down on a wooden table.

'Try and keep your voice down. Lozza's asleep.'

The telly is turned low, probably by Rob's hand, not Mildred's. They shout at each other in whispers. I strain my ears trying to listen, but the words are drowned out by my breathing and the beat of my heart. After a few minutes, Mildred's voice becomes louder, drunk and mean.

'If you don't like it, Robbie, leave and take them with you. Oh, that's right, you don't have anywhere to go, do you? Her parents won't let you stay with them, will they? No. I've taken them in. Your new-found family. I've done you a favour, letting you stay here, all together.'

Rob doesn't say anything. He's probably looking at his feet, hands on hips, shaking his head at the floor, like he always does when his mother scolds him.

The brown leather lounge squeaks as she stands up. 'You're all living here rent-free, using my utilities, eating my food, and you haven't left yet, so it can't be all that bad. And tell me, Robbie, what other options do you have? None.'

'Lozza's bought some groceries.' Rob's voice sounds weak. 'Shayla's been helping with the housework, hasn't she?'

'You're not listening, Robbie. You're missing the point. This is *my* house. It's not yours and it's *certainly* not hers. So, my house, my rules. If you don't like it, there's the front door. Don't let it hit you on the way out.'

I imagine her leaning forward, towards Rob, pointing nastily at the front door, empty glass in her hand.

'Don't you think you've had enough?' Rob asks.

'Yeh, I have,' Mildred says. 'But not of this.'

My ears follow the sound of Mildred's cough towards the kitchen. The seals on the fridge door peel apart and there's the clunk of a full glass bottle on the kitchen bench.

'Jessie. James. Dinner.'

Kibble is poured into stainless-steel food bowls. The chihuahuas' nails tap across the tiles. Mildred's cough rattles through the house.

'Might wanna get that cough of yours checked out,' Rob says, mostly to himself, heading in the opposite direction, back towards his bedroom.

Mum gets up early, sits out the back, has her breakfast of 'caffeine and nicotine'. I eat my Froot Loops while she asks me about school, then she heads to the bathroom to blow-wave her hair and put on her make-up. I get dressed, pack my bag and watch *Agro's Cartoon Connection* before she takes me to school.

Mildred sleeps in most mornings. Mum says she's 'sleeping it off'.

'Sleeping what off?'

'A hangover.'

'What's a hangover?'

'It's when you wake up feeling sick after a big night of drinking.'

And that's basically every night for Mildred. Too drunk to stand under the shower in the evenings, she washes in the mornings. Her bedroom has an ensuite. The pipes in the roof clunk when the water is turned on and off, like an alarm clock. This gives Mum time to jump in the car and head out for the day or hide in Rob's bedroom. It only takes Mildred an hour or so to settle down in front of the telly for the midday movie and at that point she's usually already cracked open the cask wine and had one or two drinks. For the rest of the day, she moves between the lounge room and the kitchen, or the lounge room and her ensuite, the horrible cough she has giving away her location and direction.

The layout of the house allows them to avoid each other. Mildred's brown leather armchair is by the window, near the front door. She faces the television, housed in the middle of a three-piece dark-wood entertainment unit. Behind the wall the entertainment unit is on, a hallway runs from Mildred's bedroom at the very front of the house, past Rob's on the right, the bathroom and my bedroom on the left, to the kitchen by the back door. That means Mum can go to the bathroom, pop in to visit me, grab something to eat from the kitchen and duck outside for a smoke, all without having to interact with Mildred. They haven't spoken in more than a week now.

Mum and Rob haven't talked much either. They still talk. Just not as much. Not in the same way. He talks to Mum. She stares off into space. The love bites on her neck have faded. Instead of giving her hickeys, he gathers items from the shed and the garage. Fishing rods and reels. A camp stove and a gas bottle. A blow-up bed. He buys a four-man tent that's on special at Kmart and packs everything in his four-wheel drive.

'You have a sleeping bag, don't you?'

'Yes. Why?'

'We're going away for a few days.'

'Where to?'

No answer.

The blue swimmer crab screams. Froth pours from its shell. Mum puts a lid on the saucepan. Its claws tap at the metal sides and top.

'It sounds like it's in pain.'

'Nah,' Rob says. 'He'll be right.'

Bonnie Vale Campground is nestled between Bundeena and Maianbar in the Royal National Park. Campers are set up on a sandy patch of grass between the beach and the bush.

It's early evening, but the sun is still high in the sky. The campground manager arrives as the green-and-purple tent goes up. He doesn't collect any fees for the day, says he'll be back tomorrow.

'Should've cooked them both.' Rob rams a tent peg into the ground with the heel of his steel-capped work boots.

'And what if she was pregnant?' Mum asks.

She and Rob have a double blow-up mattress in the back room of the tent. The area zips shut. I'm to sleep on the floor in the front room of the tent. Rob's already joked that if someone breaks in, they'll get me first.

'It wouldn't have even crossed your mind if we hadn't caught them in the act,' he says.

'Well, we did.' Mum throws a pillow on top of my green sleeping bag with the same kind of energy she uses to slam the phone down in Nanna's ear after an argument about how she's 'living in sin'.

I step away, follow Deeban Spit until I can see the sand flats of Maianbar to my left. It's low tide and I wonder where all the water went. Tiny soldier crabs scurry sideways, away from me, on transparent legs. I tread lightly, barefoot, watching where I step, careful not to squish them. I can't hear Mum and Rob bicker anymore. I can't hear the crab being boiled alive. But there is a soft rumble that seems a long way off, like a plane high in the sky or a storm in the distance. Whatever it is scares the soldier crabs away. They disappear into little holes in the still-wet sand. All of them. I shade my eyes and squint into the sun. The sand on the horizon moves. It changes colour and shape. Water sweeps across the rippled tidal sand flats, filling soldier crab holes, rolling and waving towards me. I turn back. Bonnie Vale Campground looks a lot further away than I'd like it to be and I'm not sure how far the water comes up here, so I run. Fast. So fast that, if this was the cross-country championships at school – and the logs that line the campground were the finish line – I'd win the gold medal for sure.

'You'll need a tetanus shot.' Rob digs a massive splinter out of my foot with a rusty fishing hook. Blood drips on the sandy grass beneath. 'Lozza, can you grab the rotgut?'

'Why did you bring this?'

Rob squirts some of it over my foot. It stings.

'I'm not drinking that shit,' Mum says.

But she does. And it's the first time I've ever seen her drunk.

'You're an arsehole,' she says, later, while we're eating dinner.

I look up to see who she's calling an arsehole. She stares at the crab claws in her hands or the ground beneath them, I'm not sure.

'Don't start,' Rob says.

He sits on the Esky next to her, elbows on his knees, wearing his blue footy shorts and thongs with thick foam soles.

I put lemon and salt on my crab. I've never had crab before. It's pretty tasty.

'Don't tell me what to do,' Mum says, louder.

'Keep your voice down, Loz. You're drunk.'

'I'm not drunk.' Mum sways slightly in her seat, bath towel wrapped around her shoulders.

Campers have set their fishing rods up along the edge of the water. I watch the rods bend, pulled by the current or a bite, as the sun starts to set.

'You're an arsehole,' Mum says again.

Rob huffs and looks over at her. 'How am I an arsehole?'

'What you said in the clinic.' Mum's head drops a bit, like she can't hold it up. Her long hair, wavy from a day in salt water, falls past her knees like a waterfall.

'What are you talking about?' Rob spits out a bit of shell and throws an empty claw into a shopping bag of scraps.

'Cracking jokes, while I was miscarrying.'

Rob holds his head with his hands and stares at the ground. 'I didn't know what to say.'

'How about sorry?' Mum's voice becomes higher pitched, kind of screechy. 'I'd just lost a child. Your child. Our baby boy or girl died inside me and you're there cracking jokes.'

I start to feel sick in my stomach.

'I *am* sorry.' Rob keeps his voice low.

'And then that bitch of a mother of yours, pointing out the blood on my shorts in front of everyone ...'

Tears make everything start to look shimmery, like the tide when it was coming in.

'I spoke to her about that.'

'Oh, you *spoke* to her about it, did you?' Mum stands, sways.

The towel falls off her shoulders. She wobbles in a black string bikini, hand on her hip. 'And what did you say?'

Cold tears run down my sunburnt face, salty like the crab. A sob bubbles up in my throat and escapes out of my mouth. The sound surprises Mum and Rob, who look at me like they'd forgotten I was here.

'Now look what you've done.' Mum glares at Rob.

Then she vomits on her feet.

12

When Mum said we were moving to Rosemeadow, I took the name literally. The same way I understood brown snakes, red-back spiders and blue-tongue lizards, my nine-year-old mind imagined rolling meadows, blooming with roses.

'Westminster Way,' I'd told Pop. 'That's the name of our new street.'

'Like Westminster Abbey.'

'What's that?'

'A big, beautiful church in London.' He picked a book from the shelf and flicked through the pages, pointing out a building that looked like a castle. 'It's where all the kings and queens, princes and princesses of England get married.'

Today is moving day, and I'm dressed for the occasion – my dress is a soft yellow and the frilly skirt is layered like petals – but I haven't seen anything like Westminster Abbey yet.

Rob drives the moving truck ahead of us. He lost his job as a garbo around the same time Mum lost the baby, but he recently started a new job as a removalist. Mum follows the truck. Cigarette in hand, she taps her thumbs on the steering wheel in time with the beat of Boney M's greatest hits.

'I'm so glad we don't have to live with that old bitch anymore,' Mum shouts over the instrumental. 'Karen Moregold – you know, the celebrity astrologer we watch on TV – she was right. Last week she said there would be a change of scenery and a new door would open, that it was a time for movement and new beginnings for Pisces.'

Mum's dressed up too. Her black straight-bodied dress has splits up the sides to just above the knee. An iron-on red skull and crossbones has been applied to the middle of the chest. She's thrown the dress on over a white T-shirt and accessorised with platform sandals with a cane sole. She's even had her hair done. It's back to being dark red and shiny from her roots down. She dances in her seat, blows smoke out the window like a trumpet. But when the cassette pops out of the player, Mum's tune changes too. She's been a bit moody since Bonnie Vale, a bit up and down.

'I always wanted to be a mother, you know?' Mum says. 'When I was your age, I used to babysit the kids next door.' She flicks the sunnies down from the top of her head and pushes them up her nose, but I can still hear the tears in her voice. 'All I wanted was to be a wife and a mother, live in a nice little house with a white picket fence and just be happy.'

I fold the corner of the page I'm up to and slide *Rowan of Rin* down between the seat and console, unsure of what to say, but willing to listen.

'I guess it just wasn't meant to be that way for me.'

'I'm sorry.'

Worry ripples across Mum's forehead. 'Why are *you* sorry?'

'That it's just me.' I turn away, look at the road ahead. 'That you didn't get everything you wanted.'

'Don't be sorry.' Mum waves my apology away. 'It's not your fault. It's mine. I married the wrong man. Maybe I had to, though.'

'Had to what?'

'Marry the wrong man. Otherwise I wouldn't have had you.' Mum reaches over, holds my hand, squeezes. 'I'm glad I had you. You know that, right? I know it hasn't always been easy for us, but I always wanted you. I picked your name out *years* before you were born.'

'How?'

'There was this Blondie song called "Shayla" that came out in 1979, and as soon as I heard it I thought to myself – one day, when I have a daughter, that's what I'm going to name her.'

'Why?'

'It was a beautiful song, an unusual name, and I loved Debbie

Harry.' Mum pushes the sunnies back off her face and the tone of her voice changes again. 'You don't want to blend in with some boring name that everyone else has. No, you want to stand out.'

'Well, I don't know anyone else named Shayla.'

'See? One of a kind!'

'There's gotta be at least one other out there somewhere, though, or there probably wouldn't be a song called "Shayla" to start with.'

'Maybe it was written for you.'

'I don't think so. I didn't even exist when it was written.'

'Maybe it was kismet.'

'What does that mean?'

'Meant to be.'

'I don't think that's how it works.'

It's not what Mum wants to hear. She believes in fate, karma, destiny. She reads her horoscope religiously, looks for signs from the universe, waits for the stars and planets to align. She knows when Mercury is in retrograde, if the moon is waxing or waning. She collects tarot cards and dream dictionaries, books on astrology and numerology, even though she's never read them – she's more into television: shows on paranormal activity and psychic mediums, past-life regression and reincarnation.

The excitement drains from her voice and her mood swings back like a pendulum. 'How do you feel about your last name?' she asks. 'We can change it, if you like.'

'To what?'

'Well, when I divorced your father, I went back to using my maiden name. You could use it too.'

'What's a maiden name?'

'The name you have before you get married.'

'Are you going to marry Rob?'

'Maybe. If he asks. Again.'

'And then you'd take his last name?'

'Yes.' Mum reaches for the fresh pack of cigarettes in the console and hands it to me to open.

'What if you have kids?' I hand her a cigarette.

Mum nods at her handbag by my feet. 'And the lighter.'

I hand her a black Bic lighter.

'If we have kids, they'll take his last name, whether we're married or not.' Mum sticks the cigarette in her mouth. Her eyes dart between the road and the flame.

'And then I'd be the odd one out?'

She exhales and hands me back the lighter. 'Well, if we got married, you could take his last name then too.'

I close the box of cigarettes and hold it in my lap. 'I dunno. Feels a bit weird.'

'Why don't you start off with something small first? Like, try calling him Dad?'

'Because he's not.'

Mum's left eyebrow spikes. There's one short sharp exhale through her nose. 'Well, in all reality, Shayla, how much of a dad has your biological father been to you anyway?' She snatches the cigarette box out of my lap and throws it into the console. 'Rob even risked his life to save yours at Kikori Place. His car was destroyed and everything. I'd like for us to try and be a family. This is a chance at a fresh start.'

'I haven't called anyone that for a really long time. It feels weird.'

'All I'm asking is that you try.'

'Okay. I'm sorry. I'll try.'

Mum drops the sunnies from her head to her face again and presses her lips into a tight, thin line. She drives past Macarthur Square, turns right at the roundabout outside Campbelltown Hospital, follows the moving truck past Thomas Reddall High School and at the end of the road turns left onto Copperfield Drive. I look out the car window, waiting for yellow grass to become rolling meadows, for weeds to become roses.

There are large empty reserves, some with footpaths to … I can't see where. There are narrow laneways between houses that have their back gates heavily chained and padlocked. Fences

120

that face the road have been spray-painted with swirly words that I can't make out because some of the wooden palings are missing. Garbage bags and shopping trolleys have been dumped along the side of the road.

The moving truck blinkers right. Mum turns the music down and pulls into Westminster Way. Children playing in the street stop, part ways, watch us arrive. They're tanned, skinny, barefoot. The boys are shirtless. Toddlers wobble around, bellies bulging over nappies. Their parents watch too, drinking around a dirt-stained outdoor setting.

I look down at my dress and wipe sweaty palms over the peplums. 'Mum?'

But she's watching a man with a hooknose pick like a crow through the council clean-up left on our front lawn. He's thin and has tattoos. Lots of them. Baggy old clothes hang off his tall, slightly hunched body. Long brown hair is pulled back into a low ponytail. He smiles and the few teeth he has left are black and yellow.

'Here we are,' Mum says.

Rob rolls the back of the truck up. Everything we own is neatly boxed up inside. Thick black marker on the side of each box says what room it should be delivered to. A lot of them haven't been opened since Kikori Place.

Mum hops out of the car and opens the back door. Proper, practical moving clothes are folded in a neat pile on the back seat. Rob pulls a red trolley with two fat black wheels out from the back of the truck and loads it up with cardboard boxes. I try to imagine calling him Dad. I don't even refer to my actual father as Dad. Neither does Mum or Nanna or Pop. We all try to avoid having to refer to him at all. When I have to, I say, 'my father', and they say, 'your father'. We never use the word 'Dad'.

'Hey,' Mum says, reaching between the front seats to hand me the keys. 'These two are for the front doors. Go get changed. Bathroom is down the hallway, second on the right.'

I step out of the car, and dead grass crunches beneath my jelly sandals, silver and sparkly. There are no rolling green meadows here, no marble abbeys – just a bindi stabbing me in the big toe.

'Oi,' Rob shouts. He's got his hands on his hips, work shirt tucked over a small 'beer belly' – that's what Pop calls it – into the waistband of his black footy shorts with the yellow stripes down the side. Today he's swapped the blue Dunlop joggers for his steel-capped work boots. White footy socks poke out the top. 'I'm not your little black boy.'

'Sorry, what?'

'I'm not your slave. You can get your own boxes out.'

'I just need to get changed.'

'Well, don't just stand there. Hurry up. Don't know why you wore that stupid shit in the first place.'

The ache in my chest deepens, weighed down by the tone of his voice. He always sounds angry when he talks to me. Most of the time he just ignores me, and I've started to prefer it that way. I'm not sure why he doesn't like me, what I've done wrong or how I can fix it. I scuff up the driveway. Is he angry with me about what my father did to his car? Should I apologise? Does he want me to call him Dad? Is he offended I haven't yet? Is that what Mum was trying to tell me in the car?

The house is an L-shape. I stand just inside the front door at the corner of the L. Ahead of me is an empty kitchen, dining and lounge room. To the right is a hallway. Five doors open off it. I step into the bathroom, peer into the mirrored medicine cabinet over the sink and silently mouth the word. *Dad.* I watch my mouth move in the mirror. 'Dad.' It moves the way it's meant to, but when the word comes out loud it sounds wrong. 'Dad.' I try to make it sound more natural. 'Dad.'

Floorboards creak in the hallway and my whole body flushes with hot embarrassment at the thought that anyone, particularly Rob, might've heard me practise the word, but it only lasts long enough for me to realise it must be Mum. I would've heard Rob's heavy step coming.

122

My change of clothes slips off the sink. Patterned tights, a matching T-shirt and thick white slouch socks land next to my Barbie joggers. I crouch down to scoop them off the floor as the footsteps come to a stop in the open doorway.

'Sorry, Mum. It feels a bit weird right now, but it'll get better. I'll keep trying. I promise.'

'Don't.'

Another wave of embarrassment floods my body, but this one is icy. Cold sweat prickles in my armpits. I look up into Rob's face. His lip is curled like he's disgusted by me and the thought of me calling him Dad.

'Don't,' he repeats. His voice is low, firm, threatening. He looks down at me, brow heavy, eyes warning.

A spark of temper flares inside me. That sneaky bastard – that's what Nanna calls him, compares him to Scar in *The Lion King* – he snuck up on me! Heat rises in my body, brings me to my feet. He tries to stare me down the way he does with Mildred's dogs, making them look away first. He says that's how a dog knows 'who's boss'. I stare back because I'm not a dog, he's not my father and he's not the boss of me. He seems surprised. Maybe he expected me to cry. My legs shake, and I don't know if it's because I'm scared or angry or both, I just hope he can't see.

'Shayla, are you ready?' Mum's hand lands on the handle of the screen door before it screech-crunches open.

I raise my eyebrows at him, knowing she'll see him first, ask him what he's doing. His eyes narrow and there's a nasty glint in them, but he looks away first and continues down the hall with his normal, heavy-heeled step.

Rob sits down to watch *The Crocodile Hunter* with Steve Irwin. He cracks open a longneck of VB and puts his dirty boots up on Mum's clean coffee table. 'Ah, fuck, I forgot to take the bins out.' He looks to me. 'Do it, will ya?'

'Which one is it this week?'

'Dunno. Not a retard, are ya? Use your eyes. Figure it out.'

The red-lidded bin rumbles down the pebblecrete driveway behind me. A couple of kids sit in the gutter on the edge of our front lawn: a boy holding a scratched-up old football and a girl playing with some string wrapped around her fingers. She holds her hands out to him. He puts his finger in the middle of the yarn. She lets go, and he's caught. They laugh as I pull up by the council clean-up. There's a shopping trolley among the mess, full of clothes. It looks like they've been there for a long time, fabric turned stiff by rain, dirt and sun.

The boy turns to look at me first.

'Hi, I'm Shayla.'

'Hey, I'm Sean.' He points at the girl next to him. 'And this is Charlie.'

'Hi,' Charlie says. 'When'd you get here?'

'Just today,' Sean says to her. 'Saw the moving truck.'

'Yep. First day.'

'So you haven't seen the ghost yet?' Charlie asks.

'What ghost?'

'Oh, yeh,' Sean says. 'Your house is haunted.'

'Haunted? By who?'

'The old fella that lived there before you.'

'Died in the house,' Charlie says.

'On the dunny.'

'Heart attack.'

'Stank real bad when they found him.'

'Because he'd been on the toilet?' I ask.

'Nah. 'Cause it took a few weeks to find him,' Sean says.

'We noticed he hadn't put his bins out for a couple of weeks,' Charlie says. 'Sometimes we used them as cricket stumps, you know?'

'Then the neighbours noticed the smell.'

'Don't worry though,' Charlie says. 'Yours isn't the only haunted house on the street.'

'Yeh, plus they come in and clean the places up real nice, so they don't stink like dead fellas no more. New paint and carpet and everything. Hope they changed the toilet seat for ya too.'

I hold my stomach.

Charlie, noticing my concern, punches Sean in the side of the leg. 'That's enough. She's turning even more white than she already is.'

'Maybe she's the ghost.' Sean laughs.

I look down at my arms. Nanna calls the colour of my skin 'porcelain'. Charlie is tanned, with cute freckles on her nose. Sean is darker.

'You going to Rosemeadow Public School?' Charlie asks.

I nod. 'Is that where you go?'

'Yeh,' she says. 'We're both in Year 4 there. What about you?'

'Same.'

'Maybe we'll be in the same class.'

Westminster Way is slightly less uniform than Kikori Place. There's a mixture of single- and double-storey homes. The places on my side of the street are built further back and have larger front yards than those opposite. Carports hidden behind metal gates, heavily chained and padlocked shut, separate our homes from those next door. Across the way, they're all stuck together, sharing walls, carports taking up half the front lawn. But all the façades are made of the same materials: a dreary mix of brown brick and beige cladding, dotted with small windows. The street is empty, except for the three of us and a couple of stray cats. The sun has started to set. Some streetlights flicker on, others fizzle out.

'So, what are you guys doing out here?'

'Waiting,' Sean says. His hazel eyes shine in the evening light, like the gold-flaked vodka that Mildred let me shake up when she pulled it out of the freezer for special occasions.

'For what?'

'For that to stop.'

I tune in to the background noise. A door slams. A man shouts. A woman screams back. Something glass smashes. A baby cries. 'What is that?'

125

'My parents,' Charlie says. 'And my baby sister, Bobby.'

'Are they okay?'

'They will be.'

'Does this happen a lot?'

'Yeh,' Charlie says. 'All the time.'

'Why?'

'Dad blames Vietnam. Mum says he came back from the war a broken man.'

'Not as broken as my dad,' Sean chimes in. 'He's only got one leg!'

'War too?'

'Nah, workplace accident. Had to amputate his leg at the knee.'

I pause, listening. 'Should we call the police?'

'No!' Sean and Charlie say together.

'So what do we do then?'

Charlie shrugs. 'Just wait.'

I sit in the gutter next to them. Lights start to come on in people's kitchens and bathrooms. The glow of TV screens begins to filter through bedsheets stretched across lounge-room windows. I scan the street and take note of which other bin people have put out. Yellow lid.

The sound of Charlie's parents fighting stops and the house falls into silence. Sean and Charlie look past me, towards the house. I follow their gaze. Is it over? I look back at my new friends. Their eyes are wide. They look like they've stopped breathing. My heart hammers. Oh no. Is it *really* over?

A light comes on down the street, followed by a woman's voice: 'Sean – dinner!'

'Coming!' But he doesn't move.

'It's getting cold!'

'I said I'm coming!'

The fight starts up again and we all breathe a strange sigh of relief.

'Okay,' Sean says. 'I gotta go. You gonna be alright?'

Charlie nods.

'I'll see ya at school tomorrow. Both of you.'

'See ya.'

'Bye.'

I stay with Charlie. She teaches me the string game she was playing with Sean. I teach her clapping games and the songs that go with them. We sing in whispers under the dim streetlights. *Your mother, my mother, down the street … A sailor went to sea, sea, sea … My boyfriend gave me an apple, my boyfriend gave me a pear, my boyfriend gave me a kiss on the lips and then he threw me down the stairs …* The smells and sounds of people having dinner drift into the street. I've already eaten – Rob picked up some garlic bread and a super supreme from Pizza Hut after he took the moving truck back to work – but Charlie's tummy grumbles loudly.

'Wait here.' I stand up, brush dirt off my bum. 'I'll be right back.'

I come back down the driveway, dragging the recycling bin behind me, orange Popper Juice in my pocket, lunchbox tucked under my arm. Mum's packed it full for my first day. Fruit Roll-Up. Le Snak. Little bags of chocolate Tiny Teddys and pizza Shapes. The sandwich, made with Singles cheese, has been a little dented by a Red Delicious apple, but I hand it all over. 'Here, you can have this,' I tell Charlie.

Then I sit down beside her and wait for the fight to finish.

13

I sit across from the principal of Rosemeadow Public School in my new uniform. It's a blue-and-maroon check dress with a pleated skirt. The curved collar of the dress sits nicely over the neck of the jumper, which is maroon with a white emblem. *With friendship we grow.* That's the school motto. Mum diffused my hair for the occasion. I brush blonde curls away from my face as Mr Bennett gives me the history of letter openers. He kind of looks like Santa Claus with his long white beard, except his hair is thinning on top. I can see scalp through his comb-over.

'Such a charming gift,' Mr Bennett says, elbows on the desk, turning over a small sword in his hands.

'What's the occasion?' Mum asks. Her nails are painted hot pink and match her lipstick. She wears a puffy black bomber jacket. The shirt underneath has the word 'Blondie' scrawled across the front in pink with an image of Debbie Harry. Black jeans are tucked loosely into stiletto ankle boots, and there's a studded belt around her hips.

'It's an early birthday present.' Mr Bennett looks over his glasses, then back at his gift. 'It arrived in the post today.'

The silver is so highly polished I can see his fingerprints on the blade.

'When's the big day?'

'Sunday.'

'Ah, you're a Pisces like me.' Mum nods like she knows him now.

'Am I?' Mr Bennett says. 'Well, there you go.' He wipes his fingerprints from the tiny sword with a small piece of velvety cloth and returns the opener to its display case. His desk is covered in paper and photo frames. In the corner is a touch lamp that looks like it's only been touched once today. It shines a dim light on a manila folder with my name on it. A cup of black tea or coffee is stuck to the cover. Mr Bennett peels it off, sets it down to the right and rubs his knobbly hand over the circular mark left behind. He opens the folder and shuffles paper around with one hand, while the other drifts back to his mug. 'So, Shayla Young, it looks like Glenfield has a different last name for you.'

'That's because Shayla is taking my maiden name,' Mum says. 'She doesn't see her father anymore. I have sole custody and her father isn't to have any contact with her.'

'You have the relevant paperwork?'

'I do.' Mum hands over a plastic sleeve.

'And your licence?' Mr Bennett holds out his hand while he examines the contents of the plastic sleeve.

Mum leans over the side of the chair to grab her handbag off the floor. The chunky silver chain handles clink against each other as she plops the bag in her lap and rustles through its contents. Keys rattle against the side of her musk-scented Impulse spray can. 'Here we go,' she says, sliding a small plastic card into his open hand.

Mr Bennett compares the two documents. He crosses something out, scribbles something else and closes my folder. 'Wonderful,' he says. 'Everything appears to be in order.'

'Thank you.' Mum collects her paperwork.

Mr Bennett takes his glasses off and folds his arms on the desk. Paper crinkles beneath them. 'Tell me, Shayla, do you know what you want to be when you grow up?'

I look to Mum. 'Maybe a hairdresser.'

Mum smiles. She says that being a hairdresser is a good job, pays good money, and that if I ever have kids, I can always work for myself, from home. But Mr Bennett doesn't look convinced.

'What do *you* enjoy doing? Sports? Gardening? Reading?'

'I like gardening with my pop.'

'Well then, you must consider joining the Green Gang.'

Mr Bennett searches through the papers on his desk.

'And I love reading.'

'Always has her head in a book, this one,' Mum says.

'Ah, better to have your nose in a book than in other people's business. You stay out of trouble that way,' Mr Bennett says. 'Well, I'm glad to hear you love reading, Shayla, because that means you're going to enjoy being in 4W. That's Mr Wand's class.'

'Wand as in wand?' I point and wave my arm.

'Yes, as in a magical wand, which is perfect actually, because he's Irish. Ireland's meant to be a very magical place.'

'Does he have the accent?' Mum asks.

'He does indeed. Very exotic for these parts. It pleases the office ladies very much.'

'I bet it does.' Mum laughs.

'But as an avid reader, Shayla, you'll appreciate that he's a bit of a bookworm too. Reads to his class every day. Takes them for regular visits to the library. And speaking of the library, have you learnt how to use a computer yet? Are you surfing the World Wide Web?'

I shake my head.

'You will now.' Mr Bennett pushes his chair away from his desk, stands up. 'Every student goes to the computer lab in our library once a week and has computer and internet classes.'

We stand up and follow him to the door. I'm surprised by how tall he is. Long legs. Very long legs. Reminds me of a daddy-long-legs spider, but Christmassy.

'We just need the ladies at the front desk to photocopy that.' Mr Bennett points to the plastic sleeve. 'And we'll make sure Shayla's teachers are aware she's only to leave with you.'

'Thank you.' Mum shakes his hand.

'And you, young lady' – Mr Bennett bends down, puts his hands on his knees – 'you know that you're only allowed to leave school with your mother?'

'Yes, sir.'

Mr Bennett holds his hand out for me to shake. My little hand disappears inside his big one. I hold tight, like Pop taught me.

'Welcome to Rosemeadow Public School, Shayla Young.'

The classroom is a demountable at the back of the school, near the playing fields. Office lady runs her hands down the front of her floral dress and adjusts her neckline, so it shows a little of the crease between her boobs. She points at the door, puts a finger over her lips and raises her eyebrows at me. I nod and smile. The door opens at the front of the classroom. Backpacks of all different sizes and colours hang on hooks along the wall to my right. To my left, a sea of new faces turn to see who just walked in. Mr Wand looks up, smiles, keeps reading.

Office lady helps with my Barbie backpack. I straighten my arms, down and back, so she can slide it off. She hangs it on a hook. Three rows of tables face the front of the classroom. They're wooden, sit two students each. Beige plastic chairs are tucked underneath. Office lady takes me to the first row on the right. She taps her finger on the side of the desk closest to the window and raises her eyebrows at me. I put my pencil case down.

Mr Wand sits on a low vinyl lounge chair. He has blond hair, but darker blond than mine. It's wavy and looks a little wet with gel. Office lady straightens up, pushes her shoulders back, chest out, and walks in towards Mr Wand. I follow her and stand behind the group sitting cross-legged on the floor. She looks at a space on the floor and I sit down.

'And that's the end of chapter three.' Mr Wand closes the book.

'Aww,' the group complains.

Mr Wand glances at his wristwatch. 'Okay, there's almost ten minutes until recess. Who wants me to read one more chapter?'

'Me, me, me!' everyone sings together, hands shooting up in the air.

'Alright, alright.' Mr Wand chuckles. 'But first, we have a new student. Shayla, give us a wave hello.'

Mr Wand waves. Everyone turns to look. I wave back.

'Shayla, we're just reading *The Magic Faraway Tree* by Enid Blyton. It was one of my favourites when I was about your age. Do you know it?'

I shake my head.

'Things are just starting to get exciting, so you've arrived at exactly the right time.' Mr Wand reopens the book. 'Thank you, Denise.'

Office lady's cheeks turn pink. So does the patch of skin between her boobs and neck. She smiles and scurries off.

'Chapter four,' Mr Wand reads. 'The Land of Spells.'

And it only takes the one chapter for me to fall in love with Moon-Face, Silky, the Saucepan Man and Mister Watzisname.

A new library bag bounces against my leg as I make my way to the school gate. Mum waves, cigarette in hand, smoke circling above her head. She's swapped her high heels for thongs.

'How was your first day?' She takes my backpack and heads towards the car.

'Good.'

'Did you make any friends?'

'Mr Wand took me to the library at lunch and helped me find a copy of a book he's reading the class. I'd missed the first few chapters. Now I can catch up.'

'What about your classmates? Did you make friends with any of them?'

'Charlie's my buddy for the week.'

'Is he nice?'

'Charlie's a girl. She lives up the road from us. I met her last night when I was putting the bins out.'

'That's nice. And what about that gardening thing Mr Bennett was talking about?'

'The Green Gang?'

'Yeh.' Mum stamps her cigarette out on the road, hops in the car and promptly lights another.

'Mr Wand helped me fill in my form today. I just need you to sign it.'

Mum grabs the piece of paper and puts it on the dashboard above the steering wheel. The windscreen is so clean I can see the form reflected on it.

It only takes a few minutes to drive home from school along Copperfield Drive. Cigarette in hand, Mum taps her thumb on the steering wheel in time with 'Wuthering Heights' by Kate Bush. I look out the window, take in my new neighbourhood, notice how much things change when we pass through the roundabout outside Rosemeadow Marketplace. People on the Rosemeadow Public School side of the roundabout live in bigger homes on wider streets. Each house looks different to the next. Most have nice, neat front yards. It feels like there's more air and space and sun. On the Ambarvale High School side of the roundabout, where we live, houses don't face the main road, only their back fences do. Our homes are hidden, crammed into dark little dead-end streets, lawns either dry and full of bindies or jungles of tall, itchy paspalum. Ours is dead and full of bindies.

Mum turns the music down and pulls into Westminster Way. Kids playing cricket on the street drag the garbage bins to the side so Mum's car can pass. Their parents sit around the white plastic outdoor setting, drinking, watching. Sean kicks his footy up and down the street.

'What's he doing home so early?' Mum nods towards Rob's black four-wheel drive parked in the driveway. 'He's meant to be at work.'

'Maybe he got an early mark.'

Mum unlocks the front door and steps inside. 'Honey, I'm home,' she calls, impersonating Earl Sinclair from *Dinosaurs*. 'I was hoping to have dinner on the table for you when you got home. Why are you back so early?'

'Got fired.' Rob cracks open a longneck of VB in the kitchen, throws the bottle top in the sink.

Mum drops her keys and a grocery bag on the bench. 'What? Why? How?'

I continue past the dining room into the lounge room, furnished while I was at school with all our stuff from Kikori Place, including Mum's shiny disco ball, which is now hanging from the ceiling. Afternoon sun streams through the sliding doors to my right. I pull *The Magic Faraway Tree* out of my backpack and plop myself down in the corner piece of the grey fabric lounge, my back to the dining room and kitchen.

'What does it matter?'

'Well, it matters to me.'

Mum follows Rob into the lounge room. His work shirt isn't tucked into his trackies like it was when he left for work this morning.

'Apparently I didn't have permission to borrow the moving truck the other day.'

'So you stole it?'

'No, I borrowed it.'

Mum rolls her eyes.

'What? I took it back, didn't I?

'You're lucky they didn't call the cops.'

'They weren't using it. I don't know what the big deal is.'

'How are we going to support our family?'

'Not *our* family.' Rob points at me with the beer bottle. '*Your* family.'

'You know I'm pregnant, Rob. It's not like I can just go out and get a job.'

'Yeh, well, let's just see how long that lasts.'

'How long what lasts? My pregnancy?' Mum's jaw juts out, mouth hangs open. Her eyes are wide and wild, her forehead creased.

'Wouldn't be the first time it hasn't lasted.' Rob brings the longneck to his lips, keeps his eyes on Mum. 'Or the second.'

Mum's and Rob's eyes burn into each other's. Mum looks away first, shakes her head.

'You're drunk,' she says, voice tired and sad.

'You're pregnant?' I ask.

Mum seems surprised to see me. 'Yes, honey.' She sits down beside me. 'I was going to tell you over dinner. Sorry. I didn't mean for you to find out like this.' She glares at Rob.

'Move,' he says.

I point to myself. 'Me?'

'Yeh, you.'

'What? Why?'

'I want to sit down.'

'But the rest of the lounge is free.'

'Yeh, well, I want to sit *there*.' He stands over me, stabs his finger down.

'But this is my spot.'

'Not anymore, it's not.'

'Honey,' Mum says, reaching for my hand.

I pull it away in protest. 'But I just got this spot back.'

Rob moves closer, his chin practically on his chest as he stares down at me. 'Get up and go to your room,' he says, voice low, firm, threatening. 'Now.'

'But I haven't done anything wrong.'

'I know.' Mum holds me, smooths back my hair. 'I know.' She looks up at Rob, arms still wrapped around my head. 'Come on, Rob. Leave her alone. She's just a kid.'

'She'll do as she's bloody well told,' he shouts in Mum's face.

Beer breath wafts past his chipped tooth. Veins bulge on the side of his head. My body trembles, like it did at Casula Fruit Market. Mum holds me tighter.

Rob bends down and points his finger right in my face. 'You need to remember who the adult is and who the child is here.'

'She's *my* child.' Mum pushes his hand away from my face. 'Not yours.'

'So she doesn't have to do what I say, is that it, *Lauren*?' Rob stands up straight, spits Mum's name out. He turns back to me, kicks my foot. 'I'm not going to ask again. Move or I will move you.'

'You won't touch her.' Mum stands up.

Rob looks at her and kicks my foot again. A cold tear finally escapes my right eye.

'Move!'

But I'm frozen, like I was when the broken glass rained down on me at Kikori Place. Rob rips *The Magic Faraway Tree* out of my hands and throws it across the dining room towards the kitchen. It hits the wall and then the floor.

'Fuckin' cut it out!' Mum's voice breaks as she tries to pull him away.

'I'm the man of this house now! And I'll sit where I bloody well want!'

'Oh, are you? The man of this house? What a provider! You can't even keep a job. And what were you before, then? At your mother's? Castrating bitch she was.'

Rob's face is such a dark red it almost looks purple. He sculls the rest of his beer, throws the empty bottle on the lounge and reaches for me. His grip on my arm is so tight it stings like a Chinese burn. Mum screams, slaps at his back. Rob yanks me up out of the seat so forcefully, my elbow snaps straight. It feels like he might rip my arm right out of its socket. I dangle, knees scraping across the carpet, trying to find my feet. They're dragged along behind me as I'm swung across the lounge room. Rob opens his fist, dumps me on the floor. The carpet burns my knees and palms.

Mum and Rob circle each other like boxers in the ring. I try to stand, but my legs fail. I crawl instead, on my stinging hands and knees, out of the lounge room, towards *The Magic Faraway Tree*, away from the screaming and shouting, to escape into the Enchanted Woods with Dick, Jo, Fanny and Bessie.

14

We've transformed our front yard into a second-hand shop for the weekend. Mum stuck handwritten signs up all over the neighbourhood to advertise our garage sale. Rob's dumped everything in a heap on the lawn. I'm doing the best I can to neatly arrange it into categories, like a proper department store.

'Where should the tarot cards go?' I ask Mum. 'Toys and games, or books and movies?'

She's sitting on the front steps, legs apart, pregnant belly round between them.

'I not sure they fit into either,' she says. 'But I don't want to mess with your system. Put them wherever you like.'

She turns up the portable cassette player next to her and sings along to 'Joey' by Concrete Blonde. I put her tarot cards alongside the Uno cards and stick a reduced-price tag on the back of a Pop-O-Matic Trouble board game.

'Loz, can I borrow your car?' Rob calls from inside.

'You know I hate how you drive my car.'

'Mine's got no petrol and I've gotta go pick up that thing from Pennant Hills for you.'

'Keys are on the kitchen bench.'

'What are we getting?' I ask Mum.

'I found a bassinet for free in the *Trading Post*,' Mum says. 'Brand new. Never been used.'

Rob comes out the front door in blue Dunlop joggers. Mum looks up at him.

'When I spoke to the woman on the phone this morning, she said they thought they were having a girl, so they bought something floral and frilly. Then they had a boy, so they've bought something different.'

'Got more money than sense, them folk out there.'

'Works out well for us though,' Mum says. 'And it's nice they're giving it away. I'd have sold it. Anyway, I told her we were keeping the sex of our baby a surprise too, but either way it'd be fine. We're not fussy as long as it's clean.'

'Don't matter what colour it is, long as it does the job, am I right?'

Mum nods and they kiss goodbye. 'Please drive safely,' she calls after him.

He doesn't say goodbye to me. We don't speak unless we have to. I've tried. Mum's asked me to, so I have, but he either ignores me or calls me names. I wonder if the name-calling is payback for my father bullying him in high school.

Rob jingles the car keys down the driveway and Mum counts the money we've made from the garage sale so far. It was Rob's idea. He and Mum had emptied the spare room to make way for a nursery like they'd seen on *Better Homes and Gardens* one night and Rob, still without work, said that we should try to make some 'moolah' before we put it all out on a council clean-up and everyone took it for free. The idea grew from there and became a bit of a pre-spring clean. He went through the shed. She went through our cupboards. I went through my wardrobe.

'We're doing well,' Mum says. 'See? This *is* the best time to have a garage sale. No-one wants to haggle with a woman in my condition. It makes them feel bad.'

I fuss with some of the clothes I've put out. Beautiful shoes and dresses I've outgrown, some long ago, but found too pretty to part with, maybe because Mum hasn't taken me shopping for new clothes since we moved here.

'Why don't you put out some of the books you've already read? Don might buy some for his granddaughters.'

She's put out her books on astrology and numerology, even sold some of her dream dictionaries, but I shake my head.

'What are you going to spend your money on?'

I play with the peplums of the dress I arrived here in and think on it. I've had a bit of a growth spurt since we arrived and pants that used to reach my feet are now cropped around my calves. I look at my bare ankles. 'Maybe some new clothes.'

'Really?' Mum ruffles my curls. 'I thought you'd say books.'

I *want* to buy books, but ... 'I can just borrow those,' I tell her.

'What are you reading at the moment?'

'*The Hobbit.*'

'Enjoying it?'

'Yep.'

'Well, I think we'll pack this up in about an hour.' She looks up and down the street. 'I don't think anyone will show up after three o'clock, do you?'

Don arrives just as Mum and I start to pack things away. He lives behind us, alone since his wife died of breast cancer. He's been my best customer. Yesterday he bought half of my clothes for his twin granddaughters, Brandy and Bailey. He said he'd be back for the rest today after he'd been to the bank.

'He's in such good shape for his age.' Mum sucks on her cigarette as she watches him walk up the street. 'You can tell he was athletic in his day. Tennis, maybe.'

'You two talking about me?' he asks as he comes closer.

'I was just saying to Shayla, you look like a retired tennis coach coming up the road. I'm used to seeing you over the back fence. You're so tall and trim. Did you play sport when you were younger?'

'Probably has more to do with that time I was a Japanese prisoner of war.' He chuckles.

Mum almost swallows her cigarette.

'Haven't I told you that before?'

'No.'

'Changi. That's how I got the house. Department of Veterans' Affairs.'

'I had no idea,' Mum says.

'I went in a young man and I came out an old one.' Don's voice sounds far away. 'Although it was lucky that I managed to escape at all.'

I look to Mum. She looks to me. We don't know what to say, so we say nothing. She just hands me my twenty dollars from yesterday's sales in fives.

'Speaking of which, terrible news today.'

'What news?' Mum asks, packing bits and bobs back into boxes.

'About Princess Di.'

Mum stands up straight and holds her lower back. 'Yeh, I heard this morning that she'd been involved in a car accident. I hope she's okay.'

'You haven't heard?'

Mum closes the lid of a box. 'Has there been more news? We've been out here all day.'

'She's dead.'

'No, she's not. She can't be.'

'I'm afraid she is,' Don says. 'That's why I was late getting here.'

Mum drops her cigarette on the driveway.

'It's been all over the news.'

Mum blinks and tears drip down her cheeks onto her Mötley Crüe T-shirt.

'Are you alright, love?'

'I have to go. Shayla, can you pack this up?'

I don't get a chance to respond before she waddle-runs towards the house.

'She really liked Princess Diana,' I tell Don. 'Said she felt sorry for her.'

'It's a very sad day. One we'll always remember.'

I look around at the mess strewn across the front lawn and wonder if I can rope Charlie and Sean into helping me clean up, but they're not around. Maybe they're watching the news too.

'Well, I'm glad I caught you before you shut up shop, anyway,'

Don says. 'You don't see dresses like that around here. The girls are going to love them.'

'I wasn't sure you were coming.'

'I'm a man of my word.' Don puts his hand over his heart.

'Me too. That's why I put them away for you, so no-one else could take them.'

'Thank you, milady,' Don says with a slight bow. 'How much would you like for them?'

'Five dollars each?'

'Sold!' Don hands me a crisp twenty-dollar note, fresh from the ATM.

I take the four five-dollar notes Mum gave me out of my bum bag and hold them in my palm with the twenty Don gave me. Forty dollars is a lot lighter in the hand than I expected, but I still feel rich, grown-up. I watch Don walk to the end of the street, where he turns and waves, arm over his head. I wave back, cash still in hand, as a taxi enters the street. Don and I both stop and stare. I've never seen a cab come into Westminster Way before. It pulls into our driveway and Rob gets out. He strides over to me and rips the forty dollars out of my hand, shoves it through the driver's window and grabs a box out of the back seat. There's a bloody gash above his eyebrow.

'Are you alright? Where's Mum's car?'

'Yeh, won't be seeing that again.' Rob wobbles a bit, takes a big step to the right.

'Why not? Was it stolen?'

The taxi reverses out of the driveway.

'Why would I be bleeding if it got stolen, moron? Nah, I crashed it.'

'Into another car?'

Rob rubs his face, like maybe he's sleepy. 'Nah, into a power pole.'

'Do you need to go to hospital?'

'No,' he almost shouts.

'Can the car be fixed?'

His head lolls forward and he shakes it at his feet. A string of spit drifts from his mouth through the air. It shines in the sun like the thread of a cobweb. 'Nah,' he slurps. 'It's a write-off.'

This is the longest conversation we've ever had and I don't know where to take it next.

'Princess Diana had a car accident today,' I say. 'She died.'

His head bobs up and down, as if he's asleep in a moving car on a bumpy road. 'I heard in the taxi.'

'Mum's really upset.'

Rob cranes his neck to the sky while his bloodshot eyes scan the front yard for her.

'She's inside. Crying.'

'Ah, fuck.' Rob scratches his head. 'Of all the fucking days to total her car.'

I nod.

'But I got the bloody bassinet.' He picks the box up and holds it like a trophy.

'Here, let me take that.'

He drops the box. The contents rattle. 'And clean this shit up, will ya?' He waves his arm at the garage sale.

'Yep.'

He staggers up the driveway and I wonder if he's in shock or if he's drunk. Either way, it isn't long until I can hear their screaming match from the street.

15

The shopping trolley, empty except for beer, rattles up Westminster Way. The air is hot and heavy with humidity. It makes the job of pushing a slab of VB up the hill and over the speed bump that much harder.

'Wait,' Mum says. 'Stop for a minute.'

I hold the front of the trolley, stopping it from rolling backwards down the street into oncoming traffic on Copperfield Drive. Mum pants like a dog, one hand holding her belly, the other supporting her lower back. Her black V-neck shirt, with the cover of the CD single *What's Up?* by 4 Non Blondes printed on front, is too short for her stomach now, so she has a longer singlet top underneath. Perspiration drips down her cleavage. She's so pink and sweaty she looks as if she's just stepped out of a scalding hot shower and dressed without drying herself. Wet clothes cling to her. She peels them away. They stick again.

'Talk about a hard-earned thirst,' she says.

'You shouldn't be doing this.'

She's four weeks from her due date. The cashier at the bottle-o gave her a weird look when she asked him to lift the carton into the trolley.

'I can't drive that car of his,' Mum says.

'That's not what I mean.'

Fresh sweat beads across the top of Mum's lip. 'He was watching *Gladiators*.'

'On tape,' I almost shout. 'He could have paused it and gone up to the shops himself.'

Mum wipes the sweat moustache away with the back of her hand. 'Not now, Shayla, please.'

I shake my head, look away. The late October sun bites through my T-shirt. 'When are you getting a new car?'

'When the insurance money comes through.'

'Why's it taking so long?'

'Rob complicated things by leaving the scene of the accident.'

'Was he drinking?'

Mum puts her hands back on the handle of the trolley. She keeps her head down as she speaks. 'A dog ran in front of the car and he swerved not to hit it.'

'Why did he leave if he didn't do anything wrong?'

'He was in shock.'

'That's what you told the insurance company?'

'No, I had to tell them I was driving because he wasn't listed on my policy.'

'So, you swerved to avoid the dog, hit a telegraph pole and then went home without seeing a doctor, even though you're pregnant, because you were in shock?'

'I know how it sounds, Shayla, but I had to say it otherwise we wouldn't be getting any money at all. Can we please change the subject? I'm upset about it, okay. It was the last thing that was mine alone, and now it's gone, and I don't want to talk about it.'

'I'm yours alone.'

'You know what I mean.' Mum swipes at her cheek and I'm not sure if it's sweat or tears.

'Do you know what car you're going to get?'

'Something cheap. Rob wants to keep some of the insurance payout as a bit of a safety net while he's between jobs.'

'Isn't that your money though?'

'It doesn't work that way when you've got kids, Shayla. Anyway, I've already said I don't want to talk about it, so change the subject, alright? Tell me about your school excursion tomorrow.'

I pull the front wheels of the trolley up over the gutter. Mum pushes from behind. The rattle of the trolley gets louder as we come up the pebblecrete driveway.

*

'Mr Wand says I need new sports shoes.'

'What's wrong with the ones you've got?' Rob glares down at them, longneck of VB in hand.

There are holes in the tops where my toenails have pushed through. I've cut my nails so short they've bled, but they still poke through. There's not even enough space for socks. In class, when my feet are hidden under the desk, I push the heels of my shoes down and slide my feet out, so I can stretch my toes. But there was nowhere to hide with all of Year 4 on a school excursion to Campbelltown Bicycle Education Centre. I tried to scrunch my toes up, so Mr Wand couldn't see them, but there was no room to move. My feet had throbbed from all the extra attention.

'Nothing. That's what. You tell that fucking magician, *Mr Wand*' – Rob wobbles his head – 'if he's unhappy with your shoes, he can buy you a new pair himself.'

Spilt beer drips off Rob's beard onto his bleach-stained blue Bonds singlet. I hang my head. I don't want Rob to see me get teary. He stands over me, barefoot. There's hair on the top of his feet and his toes. Particularly his big toe. And tan lines from the thick fabric straps of his Surfer Joe thongs.

'Otherwise he can build a fucking bridge and get over it.' His feet move out of sight, heels digging into the carpet and floorboards. 'None of his bloody business anyway.' He flops down in the corner piece of the lounge that he's claimed for himself, farts and turns up *Russell Coight's All Aussie Adventures*.

'Don't say that to Mr Wand,' Mum says.

As if I would.

'Put your foot up here for me.' She pulls out a dining chair. 'Where's your toe?'

I wince at her thumb pushing on the top of my shoe.

'It hurts?'

'My toenails feel, like, tender.'

Mum straightens up, holds her back with her left hand, rests the right on her stomach. She looks like a big balloon. 'How long till sports day?'

'Two days.'

'What about your black school shoes? Wear those this week and I'll write you a letter.'

'We threw those out ages ago, remember? The buckle snapped. You already wrote me a letter.'

I've been out of uniform for months, but thankfully Mr Wand has never made a big deal about it.

'I don't get paid until next week. We'll have to go shopping then.'

The TV gets louder. We look to the lounge room. Rob is making a big show of holding the remote control up high, so we can see it over the back of the lounge. The volume bar at the bottom of the telly gets longer and longer – his way of telling us to shut up. I feel my temper flare, like it did when he snuck up on me practising 'Dad' in the bathroom mirror, and look to Mum. She rolls her eyes and shakes her head, but there's a small smile on her lips that annoys me.

'Remember I want to watch *Nash Bridges* tonight,' she says.

'What?'

'Turn the TV down.'

'What?'

'Turn the bloody TV down!' Mum throws back the last of her coffee as the TV returns to a normal volume.

'What did you say?' Rob twists awkwardly, looks over the back of the lounge.

'I want to watch *Nash Bridges* tonight.' Mum opens a box of cigarettes, frowns and tosses the empty packet onto the dining table.

'Yeh, alright.'

'I'm just going up the shop to get some smokes and popcorn. You need anything?'

'Nup.'

I look from my shoes to Mum. She rolls her eyes and huffs.

'I'm just running up to Woolies, Shayla. I'm not going to Macarthur Square today. The shops will be closing soon anyway.'

'It's late-night shopping tomorrow. We could go after school. That way I'll have them in time for sport.'

'I already told you, it'll have to wait till next pay.' Mum kicks off her white joggers. 'Here, take these for now.'

'These are two sizes too big.' And they stink because she never wears socks.

'Don't be such an ungrateful little bitch.' I see Rob's head pop up out of the corner of my eye. 'Your mother has just given you the shoes off her feet. What do you say to her?'

'Thank you.'

'What do you say?'

'I *said* thank you.'

'Say it to her, not me.'

I look at Mum. 'Thank you.'

'I can't hear you,' he calls.

My throat threatens to close around the words. 'Thank you, Mum.'

The commercial break ends, Rob settles back down. Mum picks up her handbag, slings it over her shoulder.

'Are you getting something for dinner?' I ask, quietly.

'There's food in the pantry,' Mum says. 'It's catch and kill your own tonight. I don't want to cook. My back hurts.'

She leaves, and I head to the pantry. White melamine. Double-doored. Mostly empty. For the past few weeks there's been Maggi 2 Minute Noodles, yellow-and-green packets with red writing. Now there's Homebrand instant noodles. And only one packet. I reach for them, but Rob snatches them from the shelf first.

'I was going to make those for dinner,' I say.

'Yeh, well, you snooze, you lose.'

'I don't know how to make anything else.'

'Survival of the fittest, mate.' Rob crushes the instant noodles up in their bag, picks out the chicken flavour sachet and mixes the ingredients with water in a saucepan on the stove. He untwists the top of the Homebrand loaf of bread and puts the last two non-crust pieces down in the toaster. 'Here.' He throws the crusts at me in the bag.

The colours of brand-name products have been disappearing from our house since Rob got fired. They've been replaced with the red, black and white packaging of their Homebrand equivalent. We've been rolling the toothpaste tube up and running our toothbrush handles along it, trying to squeeze the last of it out. The next step is to cut the tube open, scrape out the insides and cling-wrap it, so we can get through to next payday.

I stand in front of the open fridge door and consider my options. There are more than a dozen VB cans lined up on the shelf, plus an additional two VB longnecks in the fridge door, next to some Homebrand milk and cola. There's still some real Vegemite left. I can see its bright-yellow lid up the back of the shelf. That will probably be lunch tomorrow. That and my crusts.

Toast pops out of the toaster. Rob pushes in front of me and grabs the Homebrand margarine. He smothers it across the warm, golden bread. I watch the margarine melt into yellow puddles. God, it smells good. I swallow an excess of saliva and reach for the almost-empty container of French onion dip. I spoon some into the middle of a small plate and circle it with a handful of real Jatz crackers.

'Oi, don't eat all of that.' Rob snatches the Jatz out of my hands. 'I want some of those for when your mother's watching her show.' He stuffs the silver bag back inside the red-and-white box and sets it down on the bench.

'Can I have a glass of Coke?'

'You can have half a glass.' Rob opens a kitchen cupboard, pulls out the smallest cup he can find, hands it to me, watches me pour. 'That's enough.' He grabs the bottle off me and pours himself a big, full glass.

I tuck the bread crusts under my arm and take them back to my room to keep them safe for tomorrow.

16

Charlie scrunches her nose up as I shove the last of my double-crust, semi-stale Vegemite sandwich into my mouth.

'I hate the crusts,' she says.

'Keeps my hair curly.'

Charlie's hair is pinned back from her face with glittery butterfly clips: six small plastic butterflies, all different colours, arranged like a band across the top of her head. We're using our jumpers as picnic blankets, sitting on them under a gum tree, watching Sean kick a footy around the playing fields behind the school.

'I'm not playing sport today,' Charlie says.

'Why not?'

'I have period pain and my boobs are sore.' Charlie pushes her boobs up with her forearms. 'Mum's given me a letter.'

We're both in sports uniforms: white polo shirts with maroon emblems that match our shorts. The fabric stretches so tightly across Charlie's chest that I can see the pattern of her sports bra underneath. My clothes hang off me.

'I don't want to play sport either. Maybe I'll tell them I have period pain too.'

Charlie looks at my flat body. No boobs. No sign of them coming. Certainly no bra. I'm still wearing singlets under my school clothes.

'I'm not sure they'll believe you, but we should get snacks in case they do. Wanna come to the canteen with me?'

'I don't have any money.'

'That's okay because I've got this.' Charlie reaches inside the top of her bra and whips out a shiny purple five-dollar note.

'Where'd you get that?'

'Found it outside the school gate this morning. Must've fallen out of someone's pocket.'

I hoist my backpack up onto my shoulders. It's heavy with *Goosebumps* books I've borrowed from the library.

'Come on. We don't have much time before the bell rings.' Charlie stops, looks back at me, scrunches up her nose again. 'Ah, why are you walking like you're wearing flippers?'

'Need new shoes. Borrowed Mum's. They're a bit big.'

'Just wait here then. I'll come back with snacks.'

'Period pain?' Ms Jones raises a sharp black eyebrow at me.

'Yes, Ms Jones.'

She folds her arms across her chest. 'Does your mother know? Or did this just happen?'

My heart picks up pace. I don't want them to call Mum. I look down at her big, dumb size nines – the real reason I don't want to play sport. 'Mum knows.'

'And she didn't write you a letter?'

'No. I didn't feel unwell when I left home this morning. That's why.'

'Do you need to go to the sick bay?'

'No.' I glance over at Charlie, setting up our snacks under the gum tree. 'I just need to sit down.'

Ms Jones frowns, clipboard dug into her left side. 'If you don't have a letter from your mother and you don't want to go to the sick bay, you must be well enough to play.'

'But, Ms Jones …'

She holds her hand up, turns her face away.

'Ms Jones, please.'

Hand down, frown gone, Ms Jones raises both brows at me. There's a shimmer in her narrow, black eyes. 'You'll be our first batter.' She says it slowly, sounding pleased with herself. 'Let's get it over and done with, if you're in so much pain.'

I waddle back to Charlie while Ms Jones helps finish setting up the field. A white FADS Fun Stick hangs from her lips like a cigarette. Five dollars at the school canteen goes a long way. She's lined up her lollies: Ovalteenies, Nerds, Pink Fizzers, little white paper bags of red frogs and freckles.

'You look so funny walking in those shoes. Like a duck.'

Charlie pulls a bag of Cheetos Cheese & Bacon Balls from her backpack. The ones with Tazos in them. I grab a Milko.

'You were right. They didn't believe me.'

'Yeh, I saw her get all "talk-to-the-hand".' Charlie holds up her hand, wobbles her head. 'Think she knew you were trying to pull the wool over her eyes. Shoulda told her 'bout your shoes.'

I shrug and point to a packet of Tasty Toobs. 'Save me some of those. They're my favourite.'

Charlie sticks a Redskin in her gob and nods.

Ms Jones explains the rules of the game. Hit the ball and run to the base.

'Batter up!' Ms Jones blows a whistle.

I don't move.

'Shayla, that's you,' Ms Jones says in her sing-song voice.

Should've gone to sick bay.

I look out at the field, where classmates are scattered around. There are three bases, a rubber tee with a ball on top and a bat on the ground. I try not to waddle, but the big grin on Charlie's face says I've failed. She pokes a black Ghost Drop tongue out at me.

'Hurry up, please,' Ms Jones says.

I slowly pick up the bat, considering my options. Three strikes and you're out, right? And if you don't hit the ball, you don't have to run. So, there's the plan. Miss it three times, go straight to the end of the line and hope they don't get back to me before sports day is done.

The players closest to me are crouched down, wrists together, hands open before them. Others, further away, stand around, looking bored and distracted. I take a swing at the ball and miss, as per the plan. Players in the field cheer and high-five.

151

'Strike!' Ms Jones shouts, and blows her whistle.

Players in the field resume their positions. My team, half of them friends from the Green Gang, start to chant in support: 'Let's go, Shayla, let's go.' Clap, clap. 'Let's go, Shayla, let's go.' Clap, clap. Charlie in the distance claps along too. I feel bad that I'm deliberately letting my team down. I want to at least look like I'm trying, so I swing at the ball extra hard and grunt loudly, like I've heard Monica Seles do when Mum watches the tennis.

'Strike!' Ms Jones shouts, and blows her whistle again.

My team groans. Players in the field laugh.

'One more strike and you're out, Shayla,' Ms Jones says.

'I know,' I say in a sing-song voice.

Ms Jones raises her eyebrows at me. I take my position. Players in the field look relaxed now, even if they're up front, but I can feel the tension of my teammates behind me, whispering quietly so as to not distract me from this last chance. I swing aimlessly and close my eyes as the force of it spins my body in a full circle.

When I open my eyes, the ball is gone. Gone quite far, apparently. Field players scramble away. My team jump up, clap and cheer: 'Run, run, run!'

I drop the bat on the dirt and run, clumsily, knees and feet high, towards the first base. The shoes slip off and on, off and on. I try to grip them with my toes. Blisters burn. I trip but don't fall, trip but don't fall. The team behind me gasp and cheer, gasp and cheer. Each trip seems to thrust me towards the first base, until the front of my too-big shoe catches on a tuft of grass. I feel myself fall. I throw my hands out and reach for first base as I land. My forearms burn. My knees burn. My ribs hurt. Air is forced from my lungs. But I can feel the fabric of first base under my fingertips, so I don't move. I keep my hand on the base. My team cheer. The ball whizzes past.

'Shayla, are you alright?' Ms Jones runs over.

'Did I make it?'

'Yes.' Ms Jones blows the whistle.

I roll over and hold my ribs. Fallen gumnuts stab me in the back.

Charlie runs towards me, boobs bouncing, despite the best efforts of her sports bra. She and Ms Jones help me up. I look at my badly grazed arms and legs.

'Can I sit down now, please?'

'I'm making you pancakes.' Mum holds a Green's Pancake Mix shaker bottle under the tap and fills it up to the line. 'Can you grab the strawberry jam and whipped cream out of the fridge and put them on the table?'

She must have popped up to the shop early this morning. None of this was in the fridge or pantry last night.

'I thought we could take the bus to Campbelltown today. Go and get your new sports shoes and then maybe see a movie at Dumaresq Street Cinema. They have those five-dollar movie tickets. And you know how much I've been craving popcorn lately.'

It's true. Once a week, when *Nash Bridges* is on the telly, Mum settles in to the lounge with a bag of microwave popcorn. The triple-butter variety. She tips the hot, freshly popped corn into an olive-green mixing bowl, sits it on top of her pregnant belly and adds salt. Lots of it. Plain salt. Chicken salt. Sometimes she adds 'all seasoning'. Excess granules are scraped along the bottom of the bowl, licked from her fingers, washed down with a big glass of icy cola. She even sucks the flavour off un-popped corn kernels before she chucks them out.

'I craved prawns with you.' Mum points with the spatula. 'Could sit down and eat a whole kilo of them myself. Did once, actually. Got such bad fluid retention that my fingers swelled up and I had to have my wedding ring cut off. What a shame *that* was. Not.'

We don't talk about him, so I ignore the remark about my father and stare into the frypan. All this talk of food has made my mouth water.

'I'm really sorry about what happened yesterday.' Mum flops a yellowy pancake onto my plate. 'I want to make it up to you. Are you feeling any better?'

Everything hurts. Especially my feet, where blisters have been rubbed until they've burst and bled. 'I'm fine.' I hug my ribs. 'Where's Rob?'

'He's gone to help that bitch mother of his with something.'

Margarine melts, batter sizzles, the pancake bubbles and Mum flips it. The second pancake is perfect, golden. 'Go sit down while they're hot and I'll bring the next one out to you. Here, take the margarine. You want a cup of tea?'

'Yes please.'

'I think I used the last of the milk in my coffee though, sorry.'

'I like black tea better anyway.'

I sit at the end of the table, back to the yard. Mum toddles into the dining room with a cup of black tea. A big pancake, perfectly cooked, hangs over the spatula. She flips it onto my plate. Rob usually sits opposite me, Mum next to him. It leaves me up the end of the table, all alone. But today Mum sits next to me. She sets the tea down and lights up a cigarette. I butter my pancakes with the back of the hot teaspoon, spoon on some jam and spread it out. It kind of feels like my birthday: pancakes for breakfast, being taken shopping, going to the movies. I feel my throat tighten.

'Thanks, Mum.'

'Why are you crying, honey?' Mum reaches out, holds my hand.

'I dunno.' I swallow pancakes and tea over the ache in my chest. 'I think I'm just happy. This is really nice.'

'It is nice, isn't it? We haven't had breakfast together for a while, have we?'

'No, we don't get much time together anymore. Just us.'

'Well, enjoy it.' Mum takes a puff of her cigarette and rubs her belly. 'Because once this little one comes along, we'll have even less.'

Whipped cream melts into the hot pancakes. I eat them in the order they were cooked. The yellow pancake is gone first.

'So, I have a favour to ask you.' Mum looks closely at her fingernails.

'Mhmm.'

'I need you to move into the front bedroom.'

'Why? I thought you were putting the nursery in there?'

'Yeh, we were, but now Rob wants to put it in your room.'

I drop my cutlery onto the plate. Mum holds her hand up to stop me.

'I really need you not to fight me on this one,' Mum says. 'You two fight enough already. I'm sick of being stuck in the middle. I really need you guys to try to get along.'

I point at Rob's empty chair with a butter knife. 'Well, tell him that.'

'I have, but I need you to make an effort too.'

I want to push my pancakes away, but I also don't know when I'll get to eat this well again, so I shovel them down before they go cold.

'He's not a bad man, Shayla.'

'He's not a nice one either.'

'He doesn't hurt us.'

'Yes, he does. He hurts my feelings all the time. He's always shouting and calling me nasty names. And he hurt my arm. Remember? I got carpet burn and everything.'

'He was upset, Shayla.'

'He was drunk.'

'He'd lost his job and we'd just found out we were pregnant.'

'That doesn't make it okay.'

Mum talks over the top of me. 'There was a lot going on. I know he's not perfect, no-one is. Even I'm not. But he'd never hurt us like your father did.'

'Being less bad doesn't make him any good!'

Mum waves my words away. 'Anyway, this isn't about either of you. It's about this baby.' She stubs out her smoke and rubs her belly. 'The room is bigger—'

'Why does a baby need a bigger room?'

'Let me finish,' she says. 'It's warmer in winter and cooler in summer. We'll be able to hear the baby cry from the lounge room and the backyard.'

Mum lights up another cigarette, rattles off her list of reasons. I tune out, eat my pancakes, wait for her to stop.

'When do you want me to move?'

'Before the baby arrives, which could be any day now.'

'But won't it sleep in your room for a while?'

'Yes, but ... Shayla, do you know how long Rob and I have been trying to have a baby? It hasn't been easy, for either of us.'

I think of Bonnie Vale. The screaming crab. Mum vomiting on her feet. Learning about a dead baby brother or sister.

'It's his first child, and you know he's had his heart set on putting together a nursery. It's, like, some weird male nesting thing or something. I don't know. But it's important to him, so, please, just let him do something nice for the baby, will you?'

'Fine.'

Cigarette in hand, Mum pushes down on the table to lever herself up out of the dining chair. She groans. The table groans. I stand up, arms out, ready to support her back and elbow. She holds her stomach and spine, forcing herself into a fully upright position. When she's straight, she kisses me on the top of the head.

'Thank you,' she says, picking up the empty plate.

'No, let me take it.'

Cutlery slides across the plate as I grab it. Mum inhales sharply.

'Are you okay?' I ask. 'What's wrong?'

Something goes *splat*, like a water bomb hitting the pavement.

'Ahh ... did you just wee on my foot?'

'I think my waters just broke.' Mum releases the plate. 'I don't know. The doctors had to break them manually with you.'

'If they did just break, what does it mean?'

'It means the baby's on its way.'

I put the plate down. 'Should I call an ambulance?'

'Hmmm.' Mum inhales her cigarette calmly. 'No.'

'Are you in pain?'

'No.' Mum exhales. 'That part comes later. Honestly, *so* much

156

later. This will take hours. It took, like, forty hours with you. So, let's just get dressed and go to the movies.'

I hold my arms out to the puddle on the floor. 'You can't go to the movies with all of this stuff coming out of you.'

'Let me change my pants.' Mum pushes hair out of her face. 'They give you these big nappies that soak up all of this shit. I'll sort it out. Just go and get dressed.'

'I think you should go to the hospital.'

'It'll be fine.' Mum pushes the dining chair in under the table, picks up the plate again. 'We'll see the movie, quickly grab your shoes, swing by the hospital on the way home and the baby will still probably be hours off. Trust me.'

'Give that to me.' I grab the plate. 'I'm calling Mildred's. Go and get dressed.'

Mum tilts her head back, opens her mouth and applies mascara. Blackest black. Mildred peers at Mum through round, thick-framed glasses, the smell of rotgut on her breath, the stain on her lips and teeth. Her short grey hair is freshly, tightly permed. She wears her usual earthy colours. Beige pants with a sharp crease in the front and back. A dark-brown blouse with some light floral detail in pink and white. Flat brown leather shoes. Matching handbag.

'Where's your overnight bag?'

Mum looks around, holds her hands out in a shrug, compact mirror in the left, mascara in the right. 'What overnight bag?'

'Well, what have you been doing all this time? Putting on make-up?'

'No,' Mum scoffs. 'This is just the finishing touch.'

In the time it took Rob and Mildred to get from Ingleburn to Rosemeadow, Mum's showered, dressed, blow-dried her hair and strapped herself in to the adult diaper.

'Don't stress,' Mum says. 'I've got everything I need in my handbag.'

'Don't be ridiculous,' Mildred chastises. 'Rob?'

'Yeh?' Rob appears covered in dirt and cobwebs from fixing a pipe under her house.

'I'm going to drive Lauren to the hospital.'

'I'll just shower all this shit off me and meet you up there.'

'Bring an overnight bag for her,' Mildred shouts after him as she ushers Mum out the front door.

The handles of the only bag big enough to be an 'overnight bag' hang over the edge of the top shelf in the linen press. I stand on the first shelf, stretch up, wiggle the bag free and put it on the end of Mum and Rob's bed. Their quilt is covered in yellow crescent moons, stars and swirly-rayed suns. Twirls of light and dark blues are meant to represent day and night. Next to the bed is the floral bassinet Rob brought home the day Princess Diana died and he crashed Mum's car. It has a white frill, a white frame and four little black wheels. Two of the wheels have brakes on them.

'What the fuck do you put in an overnight bag?' Rob mumbles.

'Here, let me help you.'

I reach for the bag and he rips it away. It hits the wall behind him.

'I don't want your help.'

I pull back, hold my hands up near my shoulders, retreat to my room.

The white melamine wardrobe and chest of drawers I had at Kikori Place didn't make it out of storage in great shape. The wood is a bit warped in some places now and expanded in others. Doors and drawers don't open or close properly. Nanna and Pop have ordered me a new wardrobe as a combined Christmas and birthday present, but that's still weeks away. The mirror on top of the chest of drawers shakes when I pull on the gold handles, and my favourite Polly Pockets, the pink clam shell and purple starfish, rattle across the dresser as I try to open the underwear drawer. I pull harder. Too hard. The front of the drawer comes off in my hand. It swings down and the sharp corner clips the top of my foot. Skin is removed. I suck air through my teeth and step on the pain with the other foot, trying to contain it. My eyes water, but there's no time for tears. I shove my hand in the front of my broken underwear drawer, pull out some clean undies, then flick through the coathangers in my wardrobe and feel up the back for a box of shoes that Nanna bought a while ago.

'They're meant to be a size eight, but they're a small make. Chinese,' she said. 'If you like them, keep them. You'll grow into them eventually.'

I unwrap them, pull out the tissue paper that's helped them keep their shape, and gently slide my bloody and bandaid-covered feet inside. They fit perfectly. If not for the little heel, on which I struggle to balance, I would have worn them to sport yesterday.

I'm dressed in a black dress with pink and blue flowers. It has short sleeves, a long skirt and buttons all the way down. I open my bedroom door just as Rob opens the bathroom door, dressed in his signature blue Stubbies, overnight bag in hand.

'Don't know what you're dressed up for,' he scowls.

'The hospital.' I spin back to my bed, throw one of Nanna's black Glomesh handbags over my shoulder, pop a strawberry Lip Smacker inside and grab one of the *National Geographic Kids* magazines that Pop got me a subscription to. 'Are we ready to go?'

'I'm ready.' Rob does his nose-lip sniff-twitch. 'But you're not going anywhere.'

'But—'

'Man, are you thick or what?' Rob runs his hands through the sides of his hair and hooks them together at the back of his head, so his elbows poke out from behind his ears. His cheeks turn red. There are purply lines under his nose. The more he drinks or the angrier he gets, the darker those spidery face veins become. 'Just don't get it, do you?'

I take a step back, further into my bedroom. There's a line on the floor at the door where the carpet was cut. Rob steps over it, digs the heels of his blue Dunlop joggers into the floor. I look at my feet and shake my head. No, I don't get it.

'Your mother has a new family now. The family she always wanted.'

He moves towards me, slowly, deliberately, like he's playing with his food. I make myself as small and still as possible.

'She loves me. Always has. Ever since we were kids.'

His feet come into my vision. He stands over me. I keep my head down, eyes on my damaged feet, which are frozen in place, becoming blurrier by the second.

'She *hated* your father. Do you know what that means?'

I shake my head and hot tears fall on my sore feet.

Rob hooks his finger under my chin, wrenches my head back, looks me in the face. His eyes glint like a blade catching the light, like the icepick shining in the sun at Kikori Place as my father leant in close, ready to stab. 'It means she didn't want you.' His spit sprinkles my face.

'No. She wanted me. She's told me so herself.'

Rob's lip curls like he's disgusted by me. 'That's what she has to say. But I can tell you the truth. And the truth is that you were an accident. A mistake. And now she's stuck with you. *We're* stuck with you.' He watches the words sink in, then snatches his finger away from my face.

I let my head fall.

'What are you, Shayla?

I shake my head.

'What are ya?' He shouts, so loud and so close I can feel his breath on my hair, my scalp.

'An accident,' I slobber. 'A mistake.'

'A leftover from a life she never wanted to live. A constant, rotten reminder of a time she wishes she could forget. But she can't, 'cause you even look like him.' Rob flicks a strand of blonde hair away from my face.

I shudder, even though I'm trying to stay still.

'Well, this is as close to a fresh start as we're getting, so – look at me. Look at me!'

I lift my head up and catch my face in the mirror behind him. Blonde curls around my face have straightened, darkened, stuck to my cheeks, wet with tears. I open my mouth, try to catch a breath. There are strings of saliva between my lips.

Rob bends down and sticks a finger in my face. 'You are not part of this family.'

17

Mum isn't at the school gates like she normally is to pick me up when the bell rings. I wait for her until it gets dark, then walk home alone. Rob's car is gone; his tyres have dug up clumps of wet lawn, left muddy tread down the gutter, skid marks on the street. The house is quiet and dark. No lights, not even the glow of the television screen through the window. No noise. Not the sound of Mum making dinner or Nash crying. Nothing. I turn the key in the lock, open the front door, switch on the lights and find my family sitting in the lounge room. Mum, Nanna, Pop and Nash. Their white skeletons are picked clean and propped up in Mildred's brown leather lounge chairs.

Black mould creeps across the ceiling of my new bedroom at the front of the house. My eyes sting from lack of sleep. I lie in bed, wrist on forehead, listening to the sounds of the morning. The Wiggles sing 'Wake Up Jeff!' in the lounge room. Kookaburras laugh. Magpies caw. Sean kicks his footy up the street, runs after it, kicks it down the street, runs after it.

There isn't enough air circulating through my windows to keep the damp room from becoming mouldy – sometimes I have to press my face up against the flyscreen to try to get a breath of fresh air. The windows are small, and open at an angle, manually wound out using a little brown handle inside. Rob calls them 'awning' windows. He says they're better for security. Harder for people to get through. What does get in, though, even if the awning windows are wound tightly shut, is noise. Through the thin glass I can hear all the sounds of the street, but it's the night noises that make me jump. They're the ones that keep me awake, heart booming in my ears. When I do finally fall asleep, it's to nightmares: the kind that leave a bad feeling that lingers all day. Maybe because the days are nightmarish too. Weekends are particularly shit, but school holidays are the absolute worst, when everyone is stuck here, in this house, all day, every day, together. And today's a double whammy. Easter. Saturday.

I drag myself out of bed and into the kitchen. There's only a trickle of milk left in the carton for my bowl of Homebrand fruit loops. I take them into the lounge room where Mum sits on the grey fabric lounge, Nash attached to her breast. He suckles in his sleep. I give her a hug, careful not to wake him. Mum hugs me back as best she can from that position, head on my shoulder, hand on my arm, breath in my hair.

'What's this for?'

'I'm just glad you're okay. I had a bad dream last night.'

'Another one?'

I pull away. 'Yeh.'

'About me?'

I nod, eyes on my fruit loops. There's just enough milk to wet a spoonful before I shovel it into my mouth.

'I feel like that's been happening to you a lot lately.'

I tip the bowl on its side and focus on scooping the wettest fruit loops up out of the milk.

'Ugh, I'm so sick of watching *The Wiggles*. Give me some real music!' Mum picks up the remote, flicks through the channels, settles on *Video Hits*. 'Oh, I love this song. You remember the Divinyls, don't you? You should. Or were you too young?'

'I remember.'

We used to dance to 'Make Out Alright' at Kikori Place, pretend we were part of the band. It was one of our favourite games. We'd stand in the lounge room, under the shiny disco ball, and imagine we were on stage. Mum would play air guitar, I'd play drums and we'd both be on vocals, singing into hairbrushes. Mum would pout, flick her hair and we'd wave at people on the telly like they were in the stalls. Nanna said Christine Amphlett wasn't a good role model for a young girl. Mum said 'bullshit', she was 'Australia's first woman of rock'.

'I saw Chrissy at a club in La Perouse once.' Mum pulls Nash off the breast. 'What a voice!'

Even though I've had months to get used to her breastfeeding, I'm still surprised by how big her nipples are.

'See him?' Mum puts her boob away and points at the guitarist. 'Mark McEntee. She loved him. I guess he loved her too. He did leave his wife for her. There was so much electricity between them on stage,' Mum says. 'Apparently things could get pretty heated off stage too.'

Mum wriggles her butt towards the front of the lounge, sits on the firm edge and groans quietly as she pushes herself up into a standing position with only her legs, Nash cradled in her arms. She puts him down in the frilly bassinet and straightens up, both hands pressed into her lower back.

'People said they fought a lot. Nothing that caused any lasting damage, obviously.' Mum waves her hand dismissively. 'They were no Sid and Nancy. But maybe that's how they kept that fire burning, that passion alive.'

Video Hits cuts to an extra-loud commercial break. Lowes screams about their specials. I turn the volume down so it doesn't wake Nash. Mum pops a dummy in his mouth, takes the brakes off the bassinet with her big toe and wheels him towards his bedroom. I follow her to the kitchen.

'Speaking of Sid and Nancy, check this out.' Mum stops by the back door, an amused smile playing on her lips. 'Those vegetable patches Rob's been working on look like a little family burial plot, right?'

The milk turns sour in my mouth. 'Yeh, they do.'

Mum shakes her head and has a little chuckle as she wheels Nash away.

'Oh, and can you grab the ladder and clean that mould off your ceiling, please?' she calls over her shoulder. 'Nanna and Pop are coming over for dinner tonight.'

A wave of nausea rises inside me. Maybe it wasn't a nightmare. Maybe it was a premonition.

There's one road into Rosemeadow and one road out. That road is called Copperfield Drive. Mr Wand told me it's named after the Dickens novel *David Copperfield*, because it originates in Ambarvale where street names recall the characters of Charles Dickens. The streets that shoot off it in Rosemeadow come from Shakespeare. Westminster Way was named after his history play *Richard II* – not Westminster Abbey, like Pop guessed. And just like Shakespearean stories, the streets of Rosemeadow are filled with drama.

'It's early days, but I wanted you to be the first to know,' Mum says.

She's pregnant again.

'You silly girl.' Nanna places her knife next to her fork and pushes her plate away. 'You never learn, do you?'

I stare at the table. Dark-brown wood with a secret compartment in the middle where extra table is stored away for special occasions. It kind of feels like Christmas. Mum has really gone all out with the food. Roast chicken with crispy skin and stuffing. Baked pumpkin, potatoes and onion. Cauliflower and broccoli, boiled until soft. Carrots, green beans and peas, out of the can. Everything covered in the homemade gravy that Nanna mixed in the baking tray when she arrived. There are even fancy little dinner rolls, cut and buttered, to sop up extra gravy.

'I didn't think you could get pregnant while breastfeeding.' Mum shrugs. 'But apparently that's an old wives' tale.'

She sits at the head of the table in a black Bad Religion T-shirt. Rob sits to her left, opposite Nanna and Pop. No-one sits next to Rob. He wears the same outfit he did when we first met: blue flanno tucked into blue jeans and blue Dunlop joggers. I now know that this is what he wears when he thinks he has to dress up a bit.

165

'Oh, grow up,' Nanna snaps. 'Take some responsibility for yourself. You're not a child. You *have* children. Stop behaving like you don't know any better.'

Me and Pop keep eating. I eat because this is the best meal I've had in … I can't even remember how long. Pop cuts the skin off his pumpkin. I'm so hungry I ate mine and now I'm eyeing his leftovers.

'Why can't you just be happy for me?' Mum asks.

'You're embarrassing yourself,' Nanna says. 'And you continue to embarrass your father and me.'

'How am I embarrassing you?'

Nanna looks at her antique engagement ring, straightens it with her thumb. Twenty small diamonds embedded in a high white-gold setting on a yellow-gold band. She wears it with a simple wedding band. The skin on her hands has lost some of its elasticity, but it's soft and smooth because she moisturises daily. There are some age spots, but they're light, like freckles. Her long natural nails are painted with a pearly pink polish.

'How am I embarrassing you?' Mum asks again.

'Unmarried. Living in sin. Another child out of wedlock. In fact, all children out of wedlock. None of them christened. We're sick of lying for you.'

'Wait, I thought you were married when you got pregnant with me,' I say.

Mum and Nanna glare at each other.

'No, she got married *because* she was pregnant with you,' Nanna says.

Mum drops her cutlery on her plate.

'Five months pregnant when she eventually realised.' Nanna looks around the table. 'Too late to do anything about it.' Her eyes finally settle on me. 'Married your father at a registry office in disgrace.'

'I was bad at taking my pill.' Mum throws her hands up. 'What? I forgot to take it sometimes, okay? And then I'd take several days all at once. I had no idea I was pregnant. I didn't look pregnant. I was still getting my period.'

'So, you didn't want me?'

Rob looks at me. His eyes glint with 'I told you so'.

'Of course I wanted you,' Mum says.

'But I wasn't planned?'

'Neither was this baby.' Mum touches her stomach. 'But I want them now.'

Rob turns away.

'I want all of my children,' Mum says.

'Your mother doesn't plan anything.' Nanna looks to Pop. 'Does she, Walter?'

He stuffs a perfectly timed potato in his mouth, shakes his head.

'Just acts on impulse,' Nanna says. 'Does whatever she wants without any care or consideration for the consequences.'

'The consequences being my children?' Mum narrows her eyes at Nanna. 'Your grandchildren?'

Nanna purses her lips, raps her long pink nails on the table, pinkie to forefinger.

'And what do you mean you're sick of lying for me?' Mum points her butter knife at Nanna. 'I've never asked you to lie for me. Not once.'

'Not everything is about you,' Nanna says. 'You've never once considered how this life you're living reflects on us.'

'Well, tell people we're married then, if that makes you feel better,' Mum says. 'We're getting married anyway.'

'*Really?*' Nanna looks to Rob.

Pop looks up at him too, knife and fork poised to cut into the next piece of chicken.

'Yeh, we're going to pick out the ring tomorrow.' Rob squeezes Mum's hand. 'We've just been waiting to get paid. That's part of what we invited you over to say.'

'Little difference that makes now.' Nanna shakes her head, waves her hand. 'I've been telling our family and friends you eloped years ago.'

'Tell them whatever you want,' Mum says, sounding over it.

'And you' – Nanna points at Rob – 'how do you plan on supporting all these children when you don't even have a job? Who's paying for this ring?'

Rob opens his mouth to speak, but Mum's voice comes out.

'Oh, get off his back, would you? He's been looking for a job. And we never go without, as you can see.' Mum spreads her arms, gestures at the unusual amount of food on the table. 'He even spent all day slaving away in the backyard, digging us vegetable patches so we can grow food and provide for ourselves, in case times get tough.'

Rob squeezes Mum's hand, nods at Nanna and Pop.

Nanna throws the tea towel she had draped across her lap like a napkin on the table and stands up. 'Walter, take me home. I've heard enough of this rubbish.'

Nash screams in the next room.

'It's time for his feed,' Mum tells Rob and disappears up the hallway.

Rob puts his hands in the back pockets of his jeans like an awkward teenager left alone at his girlfriend's parents' house. 'Well' – he shrugs – 'thanks for the dinner rolls.'

Nanna ignores him, looks in her handbag.

'And the gravy.'

Pop nods silently.

I walk them to the door. Nanna doesn't say anything when she hugs me goodbye.

'Don't worry,' Pop says. 'She's just upset.'

I place my head against his chest and breathe in the smell of his Brut Original deodorant.

Mum's and Rob's plates are empty like mine. All that remains is gravy, smeared by dinner rolls, drying in streaks.

'I need you to shut that kid up.'

'What does it look like I'm trying to do?'

There are muffled cries as Nash attempts to scream and Mum shoves her boob in his face.

'Shut up!' Rob shouts.

I turn the tap on, but the water isn't loud enough to drown out their argument.

'Don't shout at him. He's just a baby.'

'Shut him up then, will ya? You're his mother.'

'*You* shut up. You're the one making him cry.'

'He was crying before I came in here.'

There's a gurgled cough-cry, followed by teary hiccups.

'He's hungry, Rob.'

'Don't blame me.'

'You're making it worse.'

'Blame those parents of yours.'

'I know, okay. I know.'

'Even after all the shit that went down with her father, I'm still not good enough for their little princess. You've gotta be fucking kidding me.'

'Just go away, please.'

'Don't fucking tell me to go away. I'm speaking to you.'

'Please, Rob. Just let me get him down and we'll talk about this later, okay? There's no point us screaming at each other over the top of him. That's exactly what they wanted. And look how scared he is, poor baby. It doesn't matter what they think. They're not worth it. Just let me get him settled and I'll be out.'

I drop our plates into a sink full of hot, soapy water and let them soak while I eat Nanna and Pop's cold leftovers.

Billy Idol booms down the driveway. Mum is inside listening to 'White Wedding'. I sit in the gutter and hold the silver-plated crucifix Nanna gave me to my lips. It has a diamanté in the middle of the cross and dangles from an adjustable black cord tied around my neck.

'Hey, Shayla.' Sean's sports shoes scuff to a stop on the street in front of me.

I squint up into the sun, pendant still pressed between my thumb and forefinger. 'Hey.'

'Why aren't you reading your book?'

The Lion, the Witch and the Wardrobe lies unopened on the grass next to me. I drop my gaze, let my head hang. 'Just thinking.'

''Bout what?'

'Nothing.'

'Nah.' Sean moves so he's blocking most of the sun with his body. 'Come on. Tell me.'

Sean is surrounded by a halo of sunshine so bright I still need to shade my eyes. The crucifix drops to my chest, pendant warm against my skin.

'Do you believe in God?'

Sean looks down the street. An unmarked police car is parked on Copperfield Drive, directly opposite Westminster Way. We've seen it before. It's stopped in an unusual spot for any car, but particularly a nice one. The white paint is clean. The windows are darkly tinted. And the tint doesn't bubble. Sean looks to the sky. It's clear and blue. There's not a cloud in sight. Just bright, yellow sunshine. He takes a deep breath and sits down next to me, footy between his feet, forearms on his knees, fingers dangling over the road. He kind of shrugs and looks over at me, chin on his arm. 'Do you?'

'Yeh.'

'Why?'

'I dunno. I guess I wanna believe that someone's watching out for me. That everything happens for a reason.'

'Even the bad stuff?'

I pick at a blade of grass, mull it over. 'Do you think I'm a bad person?'

'No. Why?'

'You know how they say bad things happen to bad people? Bad things have happened to me.'

'Doesn't mean you deserved it. I've seen bad things happen to good people.'

'So maybe bad people go to hell eventually, and the good people go to heaven?'

'I dunno.'

'I guess we just have to trust that He has a plan.'

Sean looks up the street. A group of kids have cottoned on to the cop car. They point and run home to tell their parents. Mum changes her tune and 'Chapel of Love' comes blaring down the driveway.

I think it over some more. 'If God made the world and everyone in it, He must have a plan for all of us, right? So, wherever we are, whatever has happened to us, even if it's bad, it's meant to be. Like it's destiny or fate.'

Sean nods slowly at his footy, lips turned down. Then he looks at me out of the corner of his eye, forehead creased. He speaks gently. 'What if He doesn't have a plan?'

'What? No. He must. Otherwise, what's the point?'

Thin, tattooed men assemble at the top of the dead-end street with tyre irons, crowbars and baseball bats. One guy has pulled his kid's Orbit backyard tennis set out of the ground and is wielding the pole in the air like a spear. A yellow-green tennis ball on a string bounces off his head before he rips it off and throws it away.

I breathe in sharply and grab Sean's arm. 'What if He can't see me?'

Sean's distracted by the man with the Orbit set. 'Huh?'

'God. What if He can't see me?' I pull a photo out of the book beside me.

'Who's that?'

'It's me, as a baby. See this white dress?'

Sean nods.

'It's a christening dress. But I was never christened. I always thought I was, until the other day.'

'Does it matter?'

'What if it means God doesn't know I'm even here?'

'What do you mean?'

The group of bald heads with rat's tails and hooked crosses tattooed on their bare shoulders point their weapons at the car like they're about to march into battle. They advance past us, taking long, exaggerated strides down the road, yelling: 'I smell bacon' and 'fucking pigs'.

'I dunno.' I wrap my arms around my knees, hold them tight against my chest. 'I just need Him to see me, Sean. I just need to know that I'm not alone and that everything's gonna be okay because He's watching out for me and He has a plan and even though things are hard they'll get better cause He's gonna look after me.'

The unmarked cop car casually pulls away. The wannabe warriors of Westminster Way throw their weapons up in the air and cheer victoriously.

Mum blasts 'I Got You Babe', probably playing the roles of both Sonny and Cher. Sean slings his skinny arm over my bony shoulders and pulls me close, so the sides of our heads touch. He shakes his head and my blonde curls rub against his straight black-brown hair.

'God ain't coming to Rosemeadow, Shayla,' Sean says. 'Even the coppers don't wanna come here.'

18

Mum's passed out on the lounge, exhausted by the heat and a brand-new baby. She's breastfeeding both Joe and Nash. Each baby has its own breast and she says it feels like they're sucking the life out of her. She's in front of the pedestal fan, head back, mouth open, Metallica T-shirt pulled up, Joe attached to her left breast.

Mum says Joe is named after Nash's trusty sidekick Joe Dominguez in *Nash Bridges*. Also, the actor Joe Penny who she loved in *Jake and the Fatman*. And Joe Camilleri from the band Jo Jo Zep & The Falcons, now known as The Black Sorrows. Joe was born by elective caesarean at Campbelltown Hospital. Mum tried to convince the doctor to schedule the surgery for Nash's birthday, but the doctor said, 'No, that's not how these things happen. The baby needs to come earlier.' Their birthdays are now twelve days apart, which Mum says makes Joe a Scorpio and Nash a Sagittarius.

'Help your mother, will you?' Rob says as he ties up his boots, ready for work.

Rob had a brief stint as a courier between his engagement to Mum and Joe being born, but somehow twelve whole bottles of wine 'just vanished into thin air'. Twice. The first time the company gave Rob the benefit of the doubt and accepted that the box must have gotten lost on its way to the lady with the wine subscription. The second time they fired him for stealing. Rob said it was 'bullshit'. Now he's working at the rubbish tip. I'm not sure what he does there. We still don't talk. But sometimes he brings things home and says, 'One man's trash is another man's treasure.' Most recently it was a bag of jewellery. Some of it was real gold, silver and stones, so he took the bag to the hock shop, but he didn't get much for it.

Rob leaves and I close the door after him, bouncing Nash on my hip. Outside the kitchen window, trees swish and sway in the wind, signalling a storm is on the way.

'Well, that means we can't play outside.' I prise Nash's sticky fingers out of my curls. 'So, what are we gonna do? First, we're gonna change that dirty nappy. Yeh, you've got a stinky bum. Pooh-cy!'

Nash giggles like a tiny madman, kicking his feet. He knows the routine now. I lay him down on a towel spread across the dining table and carefully remove my hand from under his head. He kicks his chubby little legs while I peel open the tabs on his nappy, and squeals when I capture both his ankles in one hand to lift his bum up off the table. When he's cleaned up, I plop him down in front of *Bananas in Pyjamas*, fresh dummy in his mouth. He smiles up at me and claps his pudgy hands.

'Wait here. I'll be right back.'

Today's his first birthday, so I go in search of something, anything, that I can use to make this day a little different from the rest. I step outside and the white hairs on my forearms stand at attention, like they do when I'm cleaning the TV screen. Storm clouds roll across the sky, pushed by gale-force winds. Wind chimes jangle, frantic, until they're muted, strangled by tangled rods. I blink through the sting of the wind and the grit of dirt in my eyes. I tuck my hair behind my ears, put my head down and push forward. Wind rips at my clothes, pushes me back, sideways.

Eyes watering, arms full of old Christmas decorations in black garbage bags, I make it inside just before the electrical storm really lets loose. Flashes of dry lightning shake the windows. Thunder rumbles the walls. Wind howls around the house. It sounds like God is angry. Shouting. Slamming doors. Throwing things around. A domestic, without the tears, rages outside of the house instead of inside it.

Mum and Joe sleep through the racket. Nash bounces on his padded bum to the theme of *Barney & Friends*. I work at assembling the Christmas tree. When all the branches have been separated, when I've untangled the lights from the tinsel and sorted the baubles by colour, I tap Nash on the shoulder and present him with his birthday gift.

'What made you put up the Christmas tree?' Mum lifts Nash up so he can help put the star on the top of the tree.

'I just wanted to do something nice for his birthday.'

Mum kisses Nash on the cheek. 'Happy birthday, baby. I'm sorry I've been so tired. But, guess what? Daddy's going to bring home some ice-cream cake for you tonight. Won't that be nice? Yes, it will.'

Her regrowth blends with his hair perfectly. She hasn't dyed it since we got here. The red has grown out past her shoulders and the colour has lost its lustre. Her ends are dry and split. Her roots are oily. So is her T-zone. A couple of hard, red pimples have come up along her chin and on her neck. Nash pulls at her top.

'Hungry, are you?' Mum rolls her eyes. 'Of course you are.' She sighs, eases herself back onto the lounge and flops out a boob. 'I feel like a dairy cow. All I do is feed and change shitty nappies. Speaking of which' – she gestures towards Joe – 'do you think you can change him before you put him down?'

I nod, Joe's head on my shoulder. I pat him gently on the back and wait for him to burp or spit up on the tea towel over my shoulder.

'Thanks for helping me with this,' Mum says when she hears Joe's wet little burp. 'It's really hard for me when you're at school through the week and Rob is at work. God, I wish we could use the formula.'

'Why can't we?'

'This is free.' Mum points at her boobs. 'And it's better for them.'

I lay Joe on the towel over the dining table, one hand on his tummy so he doesn't roll away. I wipe the spit up from his mouth and pop a fresh dummy in. His eyes close and he drifts off to sleep while I change him.

Mum stares blindly at *The Little Rascals* on the telly, blinks as I gently put Joe down in his bassinet. 'Do you mind making me something to eat?' she asks. 'I haven't eaten all day. Can't seem to be able to get out of this chair. If it's not one, it's the other. Everyone's eating but me!'

She inhales her toasted ham and cheese sandwich before I've even made a start on mine, so I hand her half.

'Are you sure?' she asks, stuffing the whole thing in her mouth before I can answer.

I nod and yawn, hand over my mouth.

'So, what do you think of your new baby brother?' Mum asks, mouth full.

'I'm glad I don't have to share my room with a sister.'

'You don't look any less tired for it though.'

'It's so bloody hot in there at night I can't get any sleep.'

'Hey, language.'

'Well, sorry, but it is.'

'Why don't you just move the pedestal fan in there at night?'

'Rob said I'm not allowed to, that I'm wasting electricity.'

'Just take it in there. I'll talk to him.'

'Really?'

Mum nods.

'Thanks.' I lean in for a hug but settle for a quick pat on the back.

'What's wrong?' Mum asks as I pull away.

'Nothing.'

'What? Tell me.'

I shake my head, try not to laugh.

'I smell, don't I?'

'I didn't say that.'

'Oh, the look said it all, don't worry.'

I shrug and collect the empty plates.

Mum sniffs her shirt and makes a vomit face. 'God, I'm gross. I smell like dried breastmilk, spit up and baby wipes.'

'Go have a shower when you're done. I can put him down for you.'

Mum nods at me, then frowns at Nash. 'Hey, buddy' – she taps him on the cheek – 'no biting.'

There's a milk-gurgled giggle.

'Yeh, it's not funny, little man.'

Mum's still asleep when Joe wakes up for his next feed. I dog-ear the page I'm up to in *Animorphs*, heat some bottled breast milk and test the temperature on the inside of my wrist. When Joe goes back down, Nash gets up. I park the bassinet in front of the bathroom door so I can keep an eye on Joe while I bathe Nash and get him ready for his birthday cake surprise. To make the day a little more special I squirt some Johnson's Baby Shampoo under the tap and swish it around the bottom of the bath to make some bubbles. It came in a hamper that Nanna and Pop brought to the hospital. Nash's hamper had come in a white plastic baby bath, now passed down to Joe. Joe's hamper came in a blue plastic toy box with some bath toys. I throw a rubber tugboat in the water for good measure. Nash squeals at the bubbles and smiles up at me, cheeks pink with teething. His eyes are emerald green, just like Mum's, but they started out blue, just like Joe's are now. I remember how freaked out Rob was about it.

'I don't have blue eyes. You don't have blue eyes. You know who has? Her. Like him. Not like us. We don't have blue eyes. So, how the fuck did this happen?'

'All babies are born with blue eyes. Just relax. It takes a few weeks. They'll go green. Or brown like yours. You just have to give it some time. Trust me. It's fine.'

Rob blows in with the wind and the front door slams shut behind him. I hold my breath, body tense, and wait for Joe to wake, but he doesn't stir. Neither does Mum. The seals on the fridge door peel away from each other, glass beer bottles clattering in the side of the door. There's the pop and fizz of a screw-top being removed, the hollow tinkle of an aluminium lid tossed on the kitchen bench, spinning, spinning, then stopping flat. Heavy heels dig into the carpet. The lounge squeaks and the telly comes to life.

'Bit early for Christmas decorations, ain't it?'

Mum would flip if she saw his stinky KingGee work pants on the lounge. We don't have much and what we have is old, but there's a reason it's lasted this long. Mum does her very best to keep everything nice and clean and in good nick, especially since we can't just go out and replace it.

'It's the first of December tomorrow.'

'Shit, is too.' He does his nose-lip sniff-twitch and scratches his beer belly. It's grown bigger since we first moved in and it looks hard like Mum's stomach when she was pregnant.

'How'd you go getting Nash's birthday cake?'

'What?'

'The ice-cream cake Mum asked you to get on the way home.'

'Ah, fuck. I went straight from work to the hospital. Forgot all about it.'

Mildred has been in hospital for a few weeks. She was in there when Joe was born. The same hospital, just a different ward. Rob pushed her along the squeaky blue floor in a wheelchair, intravenous drip attached, to meet her new grandson. Her skin and the whites of her eyes had turned yellowish, her hands bruised, needles and tubes taped into them.

'Is your mum going to be okay?'

'It's not looking good.'

'I'm sorry.'

'Why? She ain't your mother.'

'I'm just sorry she's sick, that's all.'

Rob takes a big swig, the beer glug, glug, glugging down his gullet. He burps and crosses his ankles, like he isn't going anywhere. The bottoms of his socks are grey and fluff-bally. There's a hole in one of the heels.

'Mum's having a lie-down if you want to run up to the shop and grab the cake before she gets up.'

'He's one. He doesn't know it's his birthday. He doesn't know his arse from his elbow.' Rob looks to Nash, switches to drunk baby talk. 'Do ya buddy? No, you don't.'

Nash starts to whinge. Rob turns away, back to *Who Dares Wins*, and sucks on his own bottle. I sit down, legs crossed, and pull Nash into my lap.

'I think it might upset Mum if we don't have a cake for him.'

'Then she can go and bloody well get it herself. I've been at work all day.'

'She can't drive at the moment. She's still got staples in her stomach.'

'I can't drive now either.' Rob holds his beer up as if to toast. 'Always fucking coppers sitting off our street. If she wants it so bad, she can walk.'

'Not in this storm, she can't.'

'Well, then you go.' Rob throws a blue ten-dollar note at me. 'If you're so fucking worried 'bout him not having a cake, go get it then. Just stop fucking talking 'cause I don't wanna hear it, okay?'

A couple of gold coins land on the floor. Nash grabs for them. I prise them out of his fingers before they go in his mouth and he ends up in hospital as well.

'And bring me back the receipt too,' Rob says. 'Gotta make sure you ain't ripping me off.'

Rob turns back to the TV. I look out at the storm, then into Nash's beautiful green eyes, the same colour as Mum's, and sigh. I know there'll be a big fight if she wakes up and there's no birthday cake, so I shove the money in my pocket and give Nash a kiss goodbye.

'Be a good boy for me, okay? I'll be home soon with some yummy cake.'

19

The bookcase Nanna and Pop bought me was delivered today. I stand back, arms crossed, and marvel at my early Christmas present. Real wood. Five shelves. Already lacquered. A proper home for my books, which until now have been stacked up in piles on the floor. The card is written in Pop's scrawly, shaky handwriting. Hard to read, like doctors' notes. It wishes me a merry Christmas and a happy New Year, and congratulates me on winning the 1998 School Reading Competition. I tuck it away inside my copy of *The Magic Faraway Tree*, put the book on the shelf and catch a glimpse of myself in the mirror – there's a smile on my lips.

I feel warm and full inside, like I'm Violet Beauregarde in *Charlie and the Chocolate Factory*, and I've just chewed the gum that's meant to double as a three-course meal. Light, like a balloon, I drift around the room, stacking shelves with books, until the bedroom door is flung open with such force that the doorknob hits the wall behind it and swings back, revealing a dent in the gyprock, bursting my happy little bubble.

Rob stands in the doorway, tan lines in place of his usual singlet. He holds the swinging door back and points with his beer at the pedestal fan, blades spinning on the highest setting.

'What've I told ya 'bout that?'

'Mum said I could use it. She said she was gonna talk to you about it.'

'Oh, did she now?'

There's a glint in his eye that makes me worry for her.

'I asked her to.'

'Now ya going behind my back, are ya?' He puts his VB can

down on one of my books, wipes the condensation off his hand onto his Stubbies, and cracks his knuckles. 'Trying to undermine me? Trying to drive a wedge between ya mother and me?'

The cold can sweats in my hot room. Water drips down the side, like rain on a windshield. It leaves a wet ring on the paper cover.

'That's not it.' I move the can onto the wood of the shelf and wipe the cover of the book. 'It's just so hot. No air gets in here. I can't sleep at night. I'm so tired, I can't focus at school.'

He narrows his eyes and looks from me to the beer can. His beer that I just dared touch. His can that I just dared move. Stupid, stupid Shayla. He looks back to me and I feel the helium balloon inside my chest deflate and sink to the pit of my stomach.

'You know what? You're right. I shouldn't have asked Mum. I shouldn't have disobeyed you, and I shouldn't have put her in that position. It's not her fault. I'm sorry. I'll turn it off. Here. I'll put it back in the lounge room now.'

The left side of his top lip twitches towards his nose. He stares at my collection of books – re-homed from council clean-ups, second-hand shops, market stalls and garage sales, lovingly repaired and neatly lined up in the new bookcase – with disgust and contempt. He drunkenly grabs at them. Two fall on the floor. Another falls open in his hand. It's an old one, with yellow pages and a cracked spine that I've carefully sticky-taped together. *The Sword in the Stone.* He licks the tip of his finger, touches it to the corner of a page and slowly tears it out, watching me for a response. I try not to give him one, so he rips another and another, getting faster and faster, until my eyes start to prickle with tears.

'Please, don't.'

There's a satisfied smirk on his face as he grabs a fistful of pages and rips them from the frail spine, like a kid pulling the wings off a fly. He throws them over me, like confetti, tosses the empty cover at my feet and reaches for his next victim.

'That's a brand-new library book,' I cry, hands out. 'If you ruin it, we'll have to replace it.'

181

He flicks through the fresh white pages of *Harry Potter and the Philosopher's Stone*, until he gets to the front where there's a library card. He pulls the white card with blue lines out of the yellow pocket in the front cover and checks to see if I'm lying. Some of the second-hand books I've bought have library cards too, but there's only one stamp on this one. I'm the first to borrow it.

'Lucky.' Rob flings the book at me like a frisbee.

The book hits my chin, then the floor. Rob slams the door behind him, so hard the window rattles. The beer can is gone. He stomps down the hallway. I wipe the circle of condensation off my new bookshelf with my hand and press the cold water against my chin. It stings a bit. In the mirror I can see there's a small welt and a little blood.

I move quickly, as if the book he tore apart might bleed out and die if I don't get to it soon enough, carefully piecing the pages back together until the book is whole once more.

Santa's been pretty practical this year. It looks like there's a lot under the Christmas tree, but it's mostly clothes for me and Nash, each piece wrapped individually and a little too big so we 'can get the wear out of it'. I try on new school shoes: black Slazenger joggers, which Mum says I can wear with my normal uniform *and* sports uniform.

Mum points at the label. 'They're genuine leather.' Her T-shirt is stretched tight across her boobs, so swollen with milk that the white print of INXS has started to split.

'But I'm meant to wear white joggers for sport.'

'Point is, ya not going to fall arse over turkey like last time,' Rob says.

He's already opened his Christmas present, a bottle of Baileys Irish Cream liqueur, and tipped some of it into his morning coffee.

'Santa's done the best he can,' Mum says. 'Be grateful, please, Shayla.'

'I am grateful. I needed all of this.'

'Good, because, honestly, I can't get over how fast your feet grow.'

Mum puts her new The Living End album on and bops along to 'Prisoner of Society'. I rip the wrapping off some new socks and undies with the price tags still on. Mum rolls her eyes at Rob, plucks the socks out of my hands and removes the tags.

'Santa doesn't make everything himself,' she explains. 'He buys some things too, like clothes. But I'm sure he wouldn't have wanted you to see the price tags. He was probably just so busy last night that he forgot to take them off, isn't that right, Rob?'

'Yeh, busy. Or drunk.'

'Rob!'

'What? Some people leave Santa a beer.'

'So, let me get this straight. What you're telling our children on Christmas morning is that Santa's drink driving a sleigh now, is it?'

'Technically he ain't driving.'

Mum shakes her head, rubs her face.

'What? He's flying. Who's gonna pull him over up there, huh?'

'You have to ruin everything, don't you?'

Rob shrugs, pours himself another Irish coffee. 'How do you know it's not the little beer bubbles that keep him floating up there, huh?'

'Well ...' Mum slaps her hands down on her thighs and stands up. 'I think that's all from Santa. Now you can open your presents from us.'

'But Santa didn't bring Joe any clothes,' I say. Just a big box of nappies.

'Joe doesn't need them.' Mum picks him up out of the bassinet, ready to give him a feed. 'He's growing into all of Nash's old stuff.'

There's a gift bag with Joe's name on it. I hand it to Mum.

'Merry Christmas, little man,' she says. 'Look what Mummy and Daddy got for you.'

She unpacks the bag with one hand while Joe suckles. It's full of fresh bottles and dummies, Johnson's baby shampoo and talcum powder, baby wipes and nappy-rash cream. Nash pulls himself up on the side of the lounge and tries to pull Joe from Mum's breast.

'Ooh, your little nails are sharp.' Mum snatches her arm away. 'We'll have to cut those later. Yes, it's your turn soon. Open your present up first.' She points Nash back in the direction of the tree.

I help pull the paper off the Tonka truck I picked out for him. Nash loves trucks. When the garbos come, I take him down the driveway so he can watch. I've taught him how to wave, and when the drivers wave back Nash smiles and squeals and bounces on my hip. Sometimes he gets shy, pops his hand in his mouth, buries his face in my shoulder and peeks through my hair at the truck as we head back up the driveway.

'Now you can be like Bob the Builder.'

Nash claps his hands together, stamps his feet, flops down on his nappy-padded bum and crawls off, pushing the dump truck around the lounge room.

The tag on my present is bigger than the box it's in. A jewellery box. The insert has holes for earrings, but there's a small gold ring inside. The face of the ring is a heart with a small red ruby.

'It's a signet ring,' Mum says.

'What's that?'

'You have your initials engraved in it.'

I look closer at the ring. 'But these aren't my initials.'

'Oi, that's nine-carat yellow gold in your hand right there.' Rob slams his empty coffee cup down on the table and points. 'See inside the band? *And* a ruby.'

I bite my tongue and slide the ring onto my pinkie. 'It's lovely. Thank you.'

Soapy water trickles down the gutter into the stormwater drain at the end of our driveway. It's clogged with leaves that have been torn from their homes in summer storms.

'Nice top.' Sean shakes shaggy hair out of his eyes. 'Get it for Christmas?'

He looks long and lanky in a loose jersey and baggy shorts, footy on his hip held in place with a relaxed wrist. I look down at my new, slightly too big bubble-gum-blue top that has 'Girls with attitude' written on the front in pink glitter.

'Yeh. What about you?'

'Got some tickets to the footy.'

Charlie's parents' rusty white sedan rolls down the street. I stand up and we watch the car approach like a couple of meerkats. All the windows are wound down because the air-conditioning is broken. The front bumper is held together with gaffer tape. Faded tinsel decorates the dashboard, pressed up against the windscreen. A sun-bleached air freshener in the shape of a marijuana leaf hangs from the rear-vision mirror. Charlie waves from the back seat, battery-operated Christmas earrings flashing red and green.

'Merry Christmas!'

'Happy Boxing Day!'

'Where you off to?'

'Grandparents'.'

We wave until Charlie's arm, hanging out the window, disappears around the corner. The unmarked police car pulls up across the road. We sink down into the gutter.

'Can I ask you something?' I say.

'Shoot.'

'Do you believe in Santa?'

'Only 'cause it means I get more presents,' Sean says. 'Not many more, but, ya know.'

I nod.

Sean looks at me sidelong. 'Still believe in Santa, huh?'

'Yeh.'

'I bet ya believe in the Tooth Fairy too.'

'Why? Don't you?'

'No.' Sean smirks, shakes his head.

'I feel like the Tooth Fairy's been a bit cheap lately.' I wiggle a loose tooth with my tongue. 'Maybe my teeth aren't as good anymore.'

Sean picks up *Harry Potter* and flicks through the pages. 'Maybe you need to stop reading about witches and wizards and magic.' He tosses the book back on the lawn.

I grab it, hug it to my chest. 'Why?'

''Cause it's not real, Shayla. It's all make-believe.'

'I know it's not *all* real.'

'No, none of it is real.'

Sean's face is serious. I can see myself and the street behind me reflected in his dark eyes so clearly I have to look away, not yet ready to see the world in the same way.

'How do you know?'

Sean opens his arms to the street, flings them out wide. I lean back so I don't get a smack in the gob. 'Because this is what's real. You've got to stop waiting for God, or Harry Potter, or whoever, to come rescue you. This is where you are.'

I push his arm away from my face. 'For now.'

'Forever.'

'Don't say that. You don't know that for sure.'

Sean shakes his shaggy head at his bare feet. My bare feet next to his begin to wobble. I choke-sob and tears hit the concrete gutter like raindrops in a sun shower. It's so hot they dry and disappear almost as quickly as they appeared.

'I'm sorry. But it's true. Can't you see there's no magic here?'

'I see magic.'

'Where?'

'In little things.'

'Like what?'

'Like black cats.' I point to the black kitten hiding under the car with the illegal bull bar across the road. Me and Charlie have named him Midnight.

'They're just strays.'

'In fairy rings.'

'What are fairy rings?'

'You know when you get toadstools in a ring?' I draw a circle in the air.

'That's fungus.'

'Well, how do you explain them being in a circle except for magic?'

'I dunno.'

Sean looks down the street, at the cop car. I look up the street, towards the source of the soapy water in the gutter. One of the skinheads – that's what Mum and Rob call them – hoses soap off his car. The water mist catches the sun, making a beautiful rainbow. Kids playing limbo with a broom handle squeal and shout.

'You know, a lot of writers have been poor like us.'

'Bet they ain't poor no more.'

'I dunno. I guess they must make some money.'

'Gotta be more that what we got.'

'Probably.'

'Is that the plan then?' Sean turns to me.

'What?'

'You want to write books, get rich and get outta here?'

'Maybe not get rich, but yeh. Isn't that your plan?' I point at the footy sandwiched between his feet.

'Nah, I wanna get rich too.' Sean bumps his shoulder into mine, smiles and winks, back to his normal self. 'Talking 'bout rich, when'd you get this?' Sean grabs my hand, squints at the engraving on the signet ring. 'Wait. Whose ring is this? Maybe those cops are here for you after all, huh?'

'Dunno. Got it for Christmas. Think Rob found it at the tip. It's probably stolen.'

'What does "MIR" stand for?'

'No idea.' I twirl the ring around on my finger. 'I was told to *make* it mean something.'

Sean scans the street, from the unmarked police car, to the stray black kitten, to the tattooed skinhead making pretty water rainbows at the top of the cul-de-sac. The gold flecks in his eyes shine like hidden treasure. 'What about Magic Is Real?' he says.

I throw my arms around Sean and squeeze.

20

Mum waits until Rob's left for his mother's place – as he does every second Saturday, to mow the lawns and clean the pool – before she does her hair and make-up.

'Shayla, can you get a move on, please?'

'Where are we going?'

The boys are dressed in their best. I flick through the hangers in my wardrobe and try to find something on par. Mum pulls a black T-shirt over her head. Today's band is The Cure.

'I have a doctor's appointment,' she says.

Once I'm ready, she locks the door behind us and pushes the double stroller down the street; Nash sits up front, while Joe lies in the back. When she turns left at the bottom of Westminster Way, I pause, confused.

'I thought you said we were going to the doctor's?'

'We're going to a different doctor today.'

'Why?'

'Because I don't want them knowing *all* of my business. Is that alright?'

She doesn't wait for an answer but turns and walks away. I jog a few steps to catch up with her.

'So where are we going then?'

'The one just up from the shops in Ambarvale.'

'Are we going to catch the bus?'

'No.'

'What about on the way back? It's a big hill.'

'I don't have the cash, Shayla.'

'What about the card Rob left you? We could get some cash out.'

'No.' Mum shakes her head. 'We'll just have to take turns pushing the pram.'

The doctor's surgery is on Woodhouse Drive. Mum stubs out her cigarette when we reach the driveway, turns the double stroller around and pulls it backwards up the stairs while I hold the front door open for her. Jolted awake, Joe and Nash both start to cry.

'I'm Lauren,' Mum shouts over their screams. 'I have an appointment with Dr Lou.'

The woman behind the desk stands up, skin sickly white like maybe she's anaemic. 'Have you been here before?' she asks.

'No.'

The receptionist slides a clipboard across the top of her desk. 'Can I get you to take a seat and fill this out for me?' Her elbow-length blouse reveals furry forearms. Thick dark hairs stand out against the paleness beneath.

'Can I just confirm you bulk bill?' Mum asks.

The receptionist points at a sign on the desk. 'We do if you have your Medicare card and pension or Health Care card.'

'I do.' Mum takes the clipboard. 'So you don't need my bank details?'

'No.'

'And this file will be the only record of me being here?'

The receptionist looks Mum over, then me and the boys. 'The doctor will also take notes, which will be added to your medical record.'

'And where does that go?'

'Nowhere. We keep it here.'

'And everything I say in there …'

'Is completely confidential unless you consent to its release in writing.'

'Great. Thanks.'

Mum steers the pram into the dimly lit waiting room. The blinds are drawn but dust-light filters through the gaps and shines on rickety patients. They huff and their chairs creak as they grumpily rearrange themselves, disturbed by the boys' cries. Mum gives an apologetic wince-smile and whips out two bottles of breast milk. I reach for the indoor plant that's perished by the window and it crinkles, dead leaves crispy.

'Can you give them these?' Mum hands the bottles to me. 'Just try to keep them quiet for me, please.'

I feed the boys. Mum does her paperwork. The doctor calls her in.

'Do you want us to come in with you?'

Mum looks around the waiting room warily. A wilted old woman, one brittle leg folded over the other, crosses her arms, looks away and sighs loudly. She shakes her head and tuts.

'You better, in case they start crying again.'

Dr Lou, round and wrinkled like a sultana, sits behind a big wooden desk. His office is bigger and brighter than the waiting room, but just as dusty. The dried-out maidenhair fern atop the filing cabinet looks decrepit, like his other patients.

'Please' – he gestures at the seats opposite him – 'sit down.'

'I'm just going to burp him,' I tell Mum quietly.

She nods.

I unbuckle Joe and put him over my shoulder. Mum slides an old flannel under his chin to catch any spit up. Dr Lou waits until we're all set up before he speaks.

'How can I help you today' – he lifts his glasses to read the name on the file – 'Lauren?'

Mum wraps her arms around her waist and leans forward, as if into the conversation, but a nervous laugh comes out instead of words. She rocks back in her seat and bounces her right leg.

'Are you feeling unwell?' Dr Lou prompts.

'I'm, ah, I'm not feeling myself,' she says.

'How are you feeling different?'

'I'm exhausted.' Mum picks at her thumb nails, head down. 'All I want to do is sleep. I'm crying a lot.'

'Are you unhappy?'

'About what?' Mum looks up and around the room, surprise on her face. 'Why would I be unhappy?'

'You said you're crying a lot.'

'I think I'm just tired.'

'Do you need help sleeping?' Dr Lou opens a white-and-yellow script pad.

'God, no. I could fall asleep standing up some days.'

'Something to keep you awake then?'

'I've got two kids under two. Trust me, that's plenty.'

'So, you've come because you're feeling unhappy?'

Mum shakes her head, smile plastered to her face. 'I wouldn't say unhappy.'

'What would you say then?'

'I don't know. Anxious.'

'Can you elaborate?'

'Like all the simple, little things suddenly got really big and hard.'

'Go on.'

'I feel very indecisive about everything. Even if I do make a decision, I don't have the energy to follow through. Every day is a struggle. It's actually easier to do nothing. But then I know I have to do something, so I'm just in a constant state of, like, crippling anxiety.'

Dr Lou nods and scribbles. Mum sits up straight, eyes on his notes, a worried frown on her face. She swallows nervously, smiles and gives a small, coy laugh.

'But I'm sure this is all because of how tired I am.' Mum waves her hand, dismissively. 'Maybe I *should* get something to help me sleep, like you suggested? I just feel like I'm basically doing all of this on my own, you know? And I'm not feeling great right now. That's why I made this appointment. I thought there might be something wrong with my hormones or something.'

'How old are your children?'

'Joe is seventeen weeks. Nash is almost sixteen months. And Shayla's eleven.'

'Are you breastfeeding both the boys?'

'Yes.'

'I can see you've got a helping hand here.' Dr Lou gestures at me. 'Is there anyone else?'

'Their dad. But he's at work during the day.'

'So, you're at home alone with two babies when she's at school?'

'Yes.'

'What about family?'

Mum shakes her head.

'Friends?'

Mum shakes her head again.

'No visitors?' Dr Lou raises his eyebrows.

'No.'

Dr Lou sighs, rests his forearms on his desk and leans forward. Neck fat bulges over his white shirt collar. 'Well, look,' he says, peering at Mum over his glasses. 'It's normal to feel tired when you have a newborn. *And* you have a toddler as well. Unfortunately, there's not too much we can do about that, particularly while you're breastfeeding, so it's just going to be rough for a few months while you get into a routine.'

Mum nods.

'But you shouldn't feel sad.'

'I didn't say I was sad.'

'Exhausted. Anxious. Overwhelmed. Indecisive. Isolated.'

Mum nods as Dr Lou checks them off his list.

'None of those are happy feelings, are they?'

'Not really, no. But I don't think it's as simple as happy or sad.'

Dr Lou stares at his notepad. 'Are you feeling disconnected from your baby?'

'It's a bit hard to feel disconnected from them when they're crawling all over me all day.' Mum kind of laughs. 'I wouldn't mind feeling a bit of disconnection right about now.'

Mum's attempt at humour falls flat. Dr Lou looks up from his notepad, face stern.

'Wait, are you asking if I love my children?' Mum tilts her head to the side. 'Because I do. Of course, I do.'

'I'm simply asking if you're feeling happy and settled.'

'Because, what?' Mum tosses her head. 'Because, if I'm not happy I'm failing as a mother, is that it?'

'Is that how you feel? Like you're failing as a mother?'

Mum looks ready to attack: eyes wide, chin forward. Dr Lou gives her a gentle smile.

'I love my children.' Mum's voice breaks a bit.

'I can see that.'

'Good.'

'It's you I'm worried about.'

'Well …' Mum throws her hands up and bursts into tears. 'You're the only one.'

'It's okay.' Dr Lou pushes a box of tissues across his desk.

'No, it's not.' Mum plucks a few from the box. 'You're right. I'm not happy.' She drops her hands into her lap, full of crinkled white paper. 'There, I said it. I'm not happy, okay? But' – she clenches one fist around the tissues and holds her finger up like an exclamation mark – 'that doesn't make me an unfit mother or anything.'

'Of course not.'

'I've always wanted children. I love them and I look after them. It's just hard, you know, having them so close together.'

'Sounds like you've got the baby blues.'

'But I bounced back so well after having Nash.'

'Yes, but your body had a big break between baby one and baby two, not so much with baby three.'

Mum wipes her nose. 'Nash was around three months when I fell pregnant again.'

'It sounds like you could do with a little time out, just for you.'

'Does that make me a bad mother?' Mum asks. 'For wanting some time alone?'

Dr Lou shakes his head. 'Can you take some time away, go somewhere nice?'

194

'Like a holiday?'

'Like a quick getaway. Just for a couple of days?'

'No,' Mum scoffs.

Joe burps. I put him back in the pram. Dr Lou rustles around in his top drawer and brings out some little boxes.

'These feelings you're having, they usually resolve themselves, but sometimes they need a little push. This ought to do it.' He slides the boxes across his desk.

'What are they?'

'They're sample boxes. Antidepressants.'

Mum pulls her hand away. 'I'm not depressed,' she says.

'That's what the baby blues is. Postpartum depression.'

Mum shakes her head.

'Well, just keep them in case you need them in the future.' Dr Lou taps the top of the boxes and sits back. 'In the meantime, try to practise a little self-care.'

'What do you mean by that?'

'Take yourself shopping. Get a massage. Have a facial.'

'That sounds expensive,' Mum says.

'Go for a walk. Have a soak in the bath. Try meditation.'

'That's easier said than done when you have two kids under two.'

Dr Lou pushes the sample boxes further towards Mum. 'That's why I gave you these.'

I'm across the street with Sean and Charlie when Rob comes home from Mildred's. We're sitting in the rusted-out car that's disintegrating on Charlie's front lawn like an oversized garden ornament. Grass grows through the bottomless wreck, and the seats are full of fleas from the stray cats that hole up there at night.

Rob's diesel engine roars up the road, sounding the usual alarm that alerts Mum and me to the fact that he's just pulled up. Usually he's blasting his post-work song, 'I'm Gonna Be' by The Proclaimers. But today he turns the music off as he enters the street, kills the ignition and lets his car roll quietly towards the house where I've left Mum crying on the phone to Nanna.

Sean leans forward between me and Charlie sitting in the front seats. 'That's weird,' he says.

We all watch Rob get out of the car and close the door softly, so soft he has to press his bum against it to get the interior light to switch off.

'Looks like he's snooping.' Charlie scratches at the insect bites on her ankles. 'You gonna go check it out?'

Sean puts his hand out to stop me but keeps watch of Rob. 'Wait.'

'Why?'

'He doesn't know you're here.'

'So?'

'Wait till he's gone behind those trees.' Sean points to the row of conifer trees that hides our front porch from the street. 'Then you can sneak up on him like he thinks he's sneaking up on you.'

'Just be careful,' Charlie warns as Rob disappears from sight.

I slip out of the car and slink up the driveway, fast and light on the balls of my bare feet. I can hear Mum's voice, but I can't make out the words as I peer around the conifers. Rob stands at the front door, hunched at the shoulders, ear tilted towards Mum's conversation. I stop at the base of the steps and cough. Rob jumps and grabs at his chest.

'Fucking scared the shit outta me, ya fucking retard!'

'Sorry. Didn't mean to.'

Rob takes a few steps towards me and I take a few steps back. 'Why the fuck ya sneaking up on me like that then? Bloody idiot.'

'Why were *you* sneaking up on Mum?'

Rob balls his fists, stabs his finger down at me and shouts. 'Don't talk back to me, ya smart-arse little bitch!'

The tone of his voice makes my legs tremble. This is where I'd usually shut up.

Mum's advice when it comes to bullies is to just walk away. Don's advice, when he's shared war stories over the back fence, is to stand and fight the enemy. I once asked him if he was scared that he would be killed when he escaped from the prisoner-of-war camp, and he said, 'Better to die on your feet than to live on your knees.' Mum's high road hasn't got me far with Rob, so I decide to take a page out of Don's book.

I straighten my shaky legs, anger pushing against fear, and scream back at him, as loud as I can, words burning up my throat like gravel rash. 'No, you're the little bitch!'

Rob's brow twitches with surprise. 'Gonna cry are ya?' he teases.

My eyes are hot with tears, but I don't let them spill. I hate how satisfied he looks to see me so upset. But it also feels good to let go of everything I've kept locked up, so I open my mouth and empty the bucket. 'Stop calling me names, you big bully!'

'Stop bullying me,' he mimics me. 'Spastic.'

'What have I ever done to you, huh?'

Mum flings the front door open. 'What the hell is going on out here?' She seems surprised to see Rob. 'When did you get in? I didn't hear you come home.'

Anger and righteousness fizz inside me, a whole packet of Mentos dumped inside a bottle of Coca-Cola. I lift my arm and aim my finger at Rob, like a dart at a bullseye. 'That's because he turned his engine off before he came up the driveway.'

The smug look disappears from Rob's face. 'Bloody little dobber, ain't ya?'

'Why would you do that?' Mum asks.

Rob stands between Mum and me. His head swings back and forth.

'Were you spying on me?' Mum asks. 'Listening to me on the phone to my mother, were you? What do you think I'm talking about? *You?*'

He glares at her, thrusts his chin up. 'Where were you earlier today?'

'Here.' Mum opens her arms as if she has nothing to hide. 'Where else would I have been? I don't even have a car anymore.'

'I tried calling and no-one picked up.'

'I was breastfeeding the boys and couldn't get to it.'

He turns away from Mum and jabs a hairy, fat finger in my direction. 'So why didn't she pick up?'

I shake my head and huff, like I can't believe I'm being dragged into this, so I can get a quick read of Mum's face. She gives me a look. It's microscopic, but I know not to mention the visit to the doctor's surgery.

I look back to him. 'I've been playing outside with my friends all day.'

'You were meant to be helping your mother with the boys.'

'Give her a break,' Mum interjects. 'And if you don't believe me, check the bank accounts. I'd have to spend money to get anywhere or do anything and I don't have any cash. You've got it all.'

'You've got the card for emergencies.'

'So, check it,' Mum says, turning on her heel. 'Because you're being paranoid.'

21

Nanna runs into Rob as he's heading out the back door, Dunlop joggers in his hand.

'Won't you be joining us for lunch?' Nanna asks.

'Nah, thanks anyway.'

'It'll be ready soon. I'm just heating it up.'

'I'm not hungry, thanks. Already ate.'

'You ate?'

Rob nods.

'When you knew we were coming over for lunch?'

'Yeh, sorry. Was hungry. Couldn't wait.'

'Well then, don't let us keep you.' Nanna holds her arm out like an usher.

Rob goes outside to tinker in his shed.

I don't know what Mum said to Nanna the day I caught Rob spying on her, but the next weekend, here she is with Pop. They haven't visited since Mum told them she was pregnant with Joe. They came to see him at the hospital, but that was it.

'What are we having for lunch?' I ask Nanna.

'Shepherd's pie.'

'Yum.'

Nanna ruffles my curls, wrists smelling like Tabu perfume. 'Walter, do you want to take Shayla outside for a bit while I catch up with Lauren?'

I close *Alice in Wonderland* and push the chair in.

Mum sets two coffees down on the dining table. 'We'll call you when the food is ready.'

Pop and I head out to the side yard that runs past the laundry and bathroom and ends at the border of Pat's driveway next door. It's a narrow fenced nook with a long, thin clothesline that never gets used because of how little sunshine reaches it. A row of dense red bottlebrush trees grow along the outside of the fence.

'Nanna cut some slips for you to strike.' Pop looks around the damp, dark yard. 'I don't know what they are, but hopefully they like the shade.'

'I don't have anything to put them in.'

'I thought that might be the case, so I came prepared,' Pop says. 'I just need to go to the car. Can I go out this gate?'

'Yep.'

He opens the metal gate at the front and disappears down the driveway. A few minutes later, he comes back with a bag of potting mix with some plastic garden pots stacked on top. Inside are two pairs of garden gloves and shiny new spades.

'How's school?'

'Good. I came second in the speaking competition last week.'

'Yes, congratulations! Mum told me when we spoke on the phone. She said you would have come first if not for that wildcard at the end about sport. I celebrated by adding a little extra to your Happy Dragon bank account.'

'Thanks, Pop.'

'My pleasure.' Pop pulls cuttings from a bag and sorts them into piles on the stairs. He stands back to assess their potting requirements. 'I think we'll need five by the looks of this.'

I unstack the pots, which are nestled together like the babushka dolls on Pop's bookcase, and he scoops soil into them.

'Pop, can I ask you something?'

'Anything.'

He holds the stem of the first cutting and I shovel soil in around it.

'What does "postpartum depression" mean?'

He peers at me sideways. I push the soil down around the shoot, so it stays standing.

'It's when a woman is sad after she's had a baby. Why do you ask?'

'Oh, one of the girls at school said her mother has it.'

'That must be very difficult.' Pop sits back on his heels.

I nod. 'She cries a lot, and my friend is wondering if she'll ever get better.'

'I'm sure she will.'

'How? Like, with medicine?'

'Maybe. If that's what the doctor says.'

'What if the doctor gave her pills but she won't take them?'

'I can't imagine that would be good,' Pop says. 'When things are left untreated they can get worse. That's why I have to take cholesterol pills, so I don't end up having a heart attack.'

Nanna packs up her baking dish. Pop takes the garden supplies back to the car. Mum and I stand on the driveway, each of us holding one of the boys.

'Should we find Rob and say goodbye to him?' Pop asks Mum.

'Don't bother him.' Nanna flaps her hand. 'Just say goodbye for us.'

Pop gives me a kiss goodbye. 'Make sure you water those cuttings,' he says.

'I will.'

Mum and I wave goodbye as they reverse out of the driveway. Joe snuggles into my shoulder. Nash is already drooling down the back of Mum's shirt.

'They're tired,' I tell Mum.

'I know how they feel. Can you help me put them down for a nap? I might have one too.'

I nod. 'But then I need to water the plants Nanna gave me.'

But when I go outside, the pots Pop and I filled are empty. I turn in circles, scan the yard, look up and around for the cuttings. Finally, I find them, dangling from the bottlebrush branches, limp and wilted. Rob has tipped them out over the fence.

22

Mum finds an ad in the *Trading Post*. 'Free to a good home,' it says. Lovers of free things, Mum and Rob pile the boys and me into the rusty white Ford station wagon she finally bought with the insurance payout for her Corolla.

Free dog now secured in the rear, Rob turns up 'Cat's in the Cradle' and sings along with Harry Chapin, longneck of VB masquerading as a microphone.

'Do you remember Socks?' Mum asks me, twisting around from the passenger seat. Her black T-shirt has a gold heart in the middle and the name 'Neil Young' scrawled underneath, as if autographed.

'Not really.' My only memory is of playing with her in the backyard at Holsworthy one weekend when I was visiting my father. There was a big thick gum tree and a small wading pool in the backyard. My father came outside with a bottle of Tooheys in hand, slamming the door, shouting her name, and she ran; jumped straight over the fence to get away from him. He wouldn't go looking for her, even when I asked, and I never saw her again, except in photos.

'She was a boxer too,' Mum says. 'A different colour, though. Red fawn with white feet. That's why I called her Socks. This one's brindle.'

I twist in my seat and pat the dog panting behind me. Her ribs jut out and fly bites weep along the edges of her ears. Nash's and Joe's sleepy little heads loll around in their car seats, lips loosely holding dummies, fat cheeks flushed from the early spring heat.

'Didn't we have another red dog?'

'Yeh, Ginger. She was a cattle dog. We had her before Socks.'

'What happened to her?'

'Your prick of a father used to come home and beat her with his army belt, shove live electrical wires down her throat to punish her for getting under the house. Poor thing went under there to get away from him. Anyway, one day when he was at work, I took Ginger to the pound and surrendered her. I told him that Ginger got out, and of course he didn't look for her, just like he didn't look for Socks.'

'Why did we get Socks after we'd had to give away Ginger?'

She twists further around. 'What do you mean, *why*?'

I want to know why she'd bring another dog into a home where there'd already been so much cruelty. Even now, it makes no sense to me why we'd get a dog when we can barely afford to feed ourselves. But the look on Mum's face stops me. Her mouth hangs open a little and smoke pours out from between her parted lips, like maybe there's dry ice inside. Or a fire-breathing dragon. So, I say nothing and open my book, *The Twits*.

Mum continues with her tradition of naming dogs after their colour and markings. This one's called Brindy, due to her brindle coat. She has big brown eyes, a single white blaze down the centre of her squishy face and floppy jowls that drip with drool whenever she watches Mum eat toast on the back steps. Sometimes, when Rob's not around to see, Mum makes Brindy her very own piece of toast, smothered with Homebrand margarine and Peck's Salmon and Lobster Spread.

On the weekends, when Rob's in a good mood, usually around the two-VB mark, he tips some beer in her bowl. Brindy laps it up and bounds around clumsily, drunk maybe. Mum laughs and they call her an 'old lush'. Things start to turn sour around Rob's fourth VB, and at five, they're pretty bad for Brindy if she's been digging in the yard again, burying the bones that Mum picks up free for her at the butcher's. Rob corners her on the verandah. She cowers. He shouts, wielding a wooden garden stake in his right hand, crushing the green stubby in his left. Low down, like a commando, she tries to scooch away. He brings the stake down across her lower back, so hard she yelps, loses control of her bladder, and then gets in trouble for pissing on the verandah.

It only takes a couple of months for Brindy to start chewing Rob's shoes, pulling his clothes off the line. She doesn't touch anyone else's stuff, just his. And the more he beats her, the more destructive she becomes.

'Oi!' Rob slams the back door open.

I jump and drop *A Wrinkle in Time* in the dirt, body flush with fear, hot then cold.

'What the fuck do ya think ya doing?'

I turn towards the sound of the sliding door coming off its tracks but am blinded by the early summer sun.

'Don't make me come down there!' he shouts, louder.

I scramble to my feet, legs shaking. I can't see him, only hear him.

'What have I done now?' I shade my eyes, blink away tears and squint into the sun.

'Not you, ya idiot. Her!' Rob stands on the verandah and glares at Brindy, sixth can of VB in hand.

She stops mid-dig.

'Yeh, you know better now, don't ya?'

Head down, her ears twitch.

'Taught you a lesson or two, haven't I?'

He puts his beer down, returns the door to its tracks and is about to step inside when Brindy starts to dig again, harder and faster. She flings soil between her legs, up in the air, against the wooden fence palings behind her. Rob crushes the empty VB can in his hand and moves towards the steps. Brindy lowers her chest to the ground and sticks her butt up in the air. Her tail slowly swishes side to side. He throws his can at her and misses. She tosses her head and huffs out of her nose, jowls flapping. He picks up the wooden garden stake by the door and she rolls over on her back.

'That's right.' Rob smirks. 'Dumb bitch.'

But she hasn't rolled over in submission. She starts to wiggle on her back in the dirt, crushing what little remains of the veggie patch, delivering what I imagine is her equivalent of a middle finger. Rob gives chase and corners her under the carport. She tries to get past him, but he hits her so hard across the back that the wooden garden stake snaps in half. Her nails scrape across the cement floor as her back legs give out for a second. He lifts his steel-capped boot.

'Brindy!'

Rob looks back and stumbles. It gives Brindy just enough time to scramble away. She runs to me and curls up at my feet. I drop to my knees and throw my body over hers, gently, so I don't hurt her where she's already been hit. Rob throws the piece of garden stake that broke off in his hand after her and it whirls through the air. Brindy growls deep in her throat as it hits my shoulder.

'Shhh, girl. You're okay. I've got you. You're okay.'

'Get up!' Rob shouts.

I shake my head, face buried in Brindy's fur.

His voice drops to almost a whisper. 'Get up now.' He nudges me with his boot.

'No!' I scream into the dirt. It blows back in my face, gets in my eyes.

Rob grabs the back of my singlet top, rough, just as I hear Mum's voice, soft.

'Rob, just go inside and sit down, will you? I'll take care of it.'

He releases his grip on my shirt. 'You wanted this dumb bitch of a dog, so you better take care of it,' he says to Mum. 'Because if you don't, I will.'

'You don't need to point in my face,' Mum says sharply. 'I said I'd take care of it, didn't I?'

Brindy whines. I hold my breath.

Mum speaks again, low and slow. 'I'll take care of it.'

Rob's footsteps disappear. Mum touches my shoulder and it stings.

'The skin's broken,' she says. 'I'll clean it with some Betadine in a minute.'

I wait until the back door is slammed shut before I look up.

'Come on,' Mum says. 'I need you to give me a hand before the council rangers show up.'

'What?'

'Brindy's got to go. I've already called the pound. Told them I found a stray. They're on their way.'

'Won't they know she's ours?'

Mum throws Brindy's food and water bowl in the bin under the carport. 'Nope. Never told council we had her. And that guy we got her from said she wasn't microchipped.'

Heat moves through my body, out my mouth. 'Why do you keep doing this?'

'Keep your voice down,' Mum snaps, looking over the fence towards the neighbour's back door. 'Don't draw the crabs to it, alright? And what are you talking about? Keep doing what?'

'Getting dogs we shouldn't have, then chucking them away.'

Mum's eyes narrow and she tilts her head to the side, like Brindy does, trying to be certain of what she's heard before barking at it. 'I got her out of that puppy farm shitshow she was in, didn't I?'

'Yeh, out of the frying pan, into the fire.'

'I thought I was doing the right thing.'

'You don't think. That's the problem.'

'God, you sound like my mother.'

'Well, someone has to be the adult around here.'

'You need to remember who you're talking to, kid.' Mum points the two fingers holding her cigarette at me. 'You think you're so smart, always reading all the time. Always asking questions and making snide comments, judging me and my life, just like my parents do. Well, let me tell you something. There's a difference between being book smart and street smart, love, and I know which one I'd rather be. You wouldn't even be here without me. I saved you, just like I saved Brindy.'

'And now?'

'And now I'm saving her again.'

'From who?'

Mum throws Brindy's leash in the bin

'Who are you saving us from now?'

'Lower your voice,' Mum warns.

'Who?'

Mum shakes her head, avoids the question. 'Trust me,' she says. 'It's better this way. If we give her up, get her out, she has a chance. Someone will adopt her. A family that will treat her right.'

'And what if they don't? What if she isn't adopted?'

Mum takes a deep shaky breath. 'There are some fates worse than death.' She throws her cigarette butt on the ground and scrapes it across the concrete with the bottom of her shoe. 'Just take her collar off and go inside before they get here.'

23

I spent all day saving computer files onto floppy disks to protect them from the millennium bug. The news has been going on about this Y2K problem for a year now and I'm still not entirely sure what it is. All I know is that it's got something to do with computers failing as the clock ticks over from 1999 to 2000 and, given we won't be at home when that happens, I wanted to be prepared. Now we're here at Rob's aunt's place in Bexley North and the nine o'clock fireworks are long gone, I'm not so worried. This is the first time I've ever done something to celebrate New Year's Eve and it's got me feeling a little careless. The boys are with Nanna and Pop for the night, and I have a new party dress from Best&Less that's shiny and silver like the disco ball back home.

'What did Santa bring you for Christmas?' Aunty Barb slurs at me, fingering her short, tightly curled dark-brown hair, crisp with hairspray.

'Santa didn't come to me this year.'

'Oh, why not?'

I'd asked exactly the same question on Christmas morning. Up early, I'd waited behind Nash and Joe, picking paper off the floor as they ripped wrapping off their presents, heart hurting a little as the pile got smaller. Finally, right up the back of the tree, there was a package that had my name on it. It was from Mum and Rob. Inside were two sets of Shirley Barber bed sheets covered in fairies. One warm flannelette set for winter and one lighter cotton set for summer. They'd come at the perfect time too, with the only other set of sheets I owned so worn I'd ripped a hole in them recently just by rolling over.

'Been a bad girl?' Barb leans in awkwardly, so close I can see every wrinkle.

'No. I'm just too old for Santa now.'

'Really? How old are you?'

'I'll be twelve at the end of January.'

Barb shakes her head at Rob, slaps him on the arm with the back of her hand. 'Well, I think Santa should have let you enjoy at least one Christmas with your baby brothers.'

'I was sad about that too.'

'She had last Christmas with them.'

'Yeh, but it wasn't the same 'cause Joe was too small to know what it was all about,' I say.

'What happened to only speaking when spoken to, hey?'

'Aunty Barb *was* talking to me.'

'Seen and not heard tonight, remember?'

'Leave her alone, Rob,' Barb says, then leans in closer to him. 'Come. Tell me. How's your mother?'

'Back in hospital.'

'How much longer do you think it will be?'

'Not long now.'

Barb spills a bit of her drink on me as she and Rob disappear into the crowd, still talking. Mum scowls after them, stabs at cabanossi and cheese cubes with a toothpick, throws a Ritz cracker in her mouth. Crumbs trickle down the front of her new Red Hot Chili Peppers T-shirt. It came with *Californication*, the CD that Nanna and Pop gave her for Christmas – the one I'd helped them pick out at Sanity when they took me shopping. She pours herself a red drink from a silver bag in a box.

'Wait, isn't that the same stuff that made you sick at Bonnie Vale?'

'You know, you don't have to be so grown-up all the time.' Mum takes a sip from a plastic cup. 'Give me your book.'

I hand over *Around the World in Eighty Days*, and she stuffs it into her handbag.

'Go have fun. Be a kid for a change, yeh?'

I haven't been to a party in longer than I can remember. It means taking a present, and I haven't wanted to ask Mum for the money. The invitations stopped coming a while ago because my answer was always the same. But apparently you don't need to take a present to a New Year's Eve party, just some food and drink.

I turn back to Mum. 'What do I do?' I ask.

'Eat. Drink fizzy drinks. Make some friends. Watch the fireworks. Go!'

Aunty Barb's house buzzes with people I don't know. They swallow jelly out of shot glasses, sing karaoke and dance to 'Nutbush City Limits'. I move through the house, feasting from Tupperware containers full of rainbow popcorn and chocolate crackles. There are bowls of lollies and chips, trays of sausage rolls and party pies, even plates of fairy bread. There's so much food it feels like I've finally made it to the Land of Goodies at the top of *The Magic Faraway Tree*.

'Excuse me.'

The girl behind me has silver glitter spray in her blonde hair. She's older than me; I can tell because she's taller. Also because she wears her baggy hipster jeans and white midriff boob tube with the confidence of Christina Aguilera in the 'Genie in a Bottle' music video. There's a silver chain around her stomach that Charlie would just love. A butterfly dangles above her belly button, which is encircled by a temporary tattoo I recognise from the latest *Smash Hits* magazine. Pink shells hang around her neck, and the white skater shoes half hidden beneath her denim bell-bottoms give her a surfer-Barbie look.

I step aside. 'Sorry.'

'All good.' She takes the top off a cake carrier and picks up a knife. 'Did you want a slice of pavlova?'

'No thanks. I've had some already.'

She tips a slice of pavlova off the knife into a disposable bowl.

'Actually,' I say, 'do you mind if I ask you a dumb question?'

Surfer Barbie loads a plastic fork up with meringue. 'Go for it.'

'What's this?' I point at a big crusty bread roll that's been hollowed out.

'You've never seen cob loaf before?'

I shake my head. 'I don't go to many parties.'

'It's cheese and bacon cob loaf. You just rip some of the bread off the side and dip it in.'

I copy her demonstration. 'It's delicious.'

'Yeh.' She shifts her weight to the other foot. 'I'm kinda over it.'

I brush breadcrumbs off my fingers and hold out my hand like Pop's taught me. 'I'm Shayla.'

She laugh-smiles at me but shakes my hand anyway. Her hand is floppy, like she's only doing it to be polite. Pop's told me not to trust people with a weak handshake, but I have a good feeling about this girl. Her eyes are happy when she smiles.

'I'm Jess. Cute dress.'

'Thanks.' I wipe my hands down the skirt and my cheeks burn. I feel like a little kid next to this girl. She looks like she's just stepped out of *Dolly* or *Girlfriend* magazine. 'Are you family or friends?'

'Friends. How about you?' she asks.

'My brothers' father is family.'

Jess traces my family tree back a couple of steps with her finger. 'So, your stepdad?'

'He's my brothers' father, yeh.' I pick at the cob loaf. 'Are you in high school?'

'I'm starting Year 9 when I go back.'

'I'm starting Year 7.'

'My little brother is starting high school next year too.' Jess scans the room. 'Where are you going?'

'Ambarvale High.'

'I don't know it.'

'Yeh, it's not around here.'

'So do you know anyone here tonight then?' Jess asks.

'Not really. Just my mum and Rob and Barb.'

'Did you want to hang out?'

I nod.

'Cool,' Jess says. 'Should we get some dinner?'

Outside, the air smells like frangipani and barbecued meat. Women pour wine from bottles instead of boxes and line up on the grass to dance to the 'Macarena'. Men gather around the grill in short-sleeved collared shirts and cargo shorts. They talk loudly over each other, but not like they're angry. They smile, laugh, pat each other on the back. And their beer bottles aren't brown like the ones I see at home. Some are clear, with slices of lemon or lime stuck down the neck; others are green. The man doing the barbecuing wears a long apron with a woman's bikini-clad body printed on the front. He flips bacon and turns sausages. I rip open two crusty bread rolls.

'What would you like?'

'Can I have one burger with bacon and egg please. And one hot dog?'

He drops a rissole on the round bun. 'Caramelised onion?'

'Yes, please. On both.'

Jess picks at salad spinners and acacia bowls on the fold-out trestle table. I add iceberg lettuce, tomato, beetroot and pineapple to my burger until it towers like Mum's platform shoes.

'Is that all for you?' Jess raises her eyebrows.

I add barbecue sauce to both rolls and nod.

'You must be starving!'

'Yeh, I'm always hungry.'

'But you're so skinny.' She frowns, then tilts her head to the side. 'Maybe you're getting, like, a growth spurt or something.'

'Maybe.'

'Let's go inside. You're gonna need a table.'

'Evan!' Jess waves her brother over. 'Come meet Shayla.'

He straightens his black blazer as he walks towards the dining table, like he's a school prefect about to get on stage for assembly.

'Evan's starting high school at Trinity Grammar next year.'

My hands are sticky with egg yolk and barbecue sauce. Beetroot and pineapple juice drip down my forearms and puddle on the plastic tablecloth at my elbows. I smile hello, lips tight, mouth full.

'It's a very good school,' he says, looking around the room with an air of snobby dismissiveness, unlike anyone I've ever met my own age. 'Our father went there too.' His eyes pass over everything but settle on nothing. 'Bit of a tradition for the boys in our family.'

Jess points at me with the salad on her fork. 'Shayla's starting high school next year too.'

Evan glances up. 'Where at?'

I've stuffed my face so full of food, I can hardly chew. I try to give an apologetic smile as I cover my mouth with one hand and raise a finger with the other to indicate that I need a moment, please. Evan folds his arms across his chest, carefully, so as to not crease his white Tommy Hilfiger T-shirt, and taps his foot. Black-and-white check Vans shoes match his belt, the end of which hangs fashionably down the front of his jeans. I chew quickly, but not properly, and the food hurts as it goes down. I press the clean side of my wrist against the ache expanding in my chest.

'Ambarvale High,' I say from behind my hand, because my mouth is still full.

'Never heard of it,' Evan says. 'Is it private?'

I shake my head, chew my food, swallow a little more.

'Our school motto is "Detur Gloria Soli Deo", let glory be given to God alone. What's yours?'

I put my hand over my mouth again. '"New horizons".'

'Not much of a motto, is it?'

I shrug. I like it. It makes me feel like I have something to look forward to.

'Co-ed?'

I nod.

'Fancy.'

But the way he says it makes me feel like a dung beetle.

'What game were you playing, Evan?' Jess's voice sounds phony, but I'm grateful for the change of subject and for a chance to finish my dinner without an audience.

'Pokémon Red.'

'Don't you have that at home?'

'Yeh, it's old news now.' Evan flicks his wrist. 'I've had it since it was first released in Oz. Late 1998.'

'He's a bit of a nerd,' Jess tells me. 'He's, like, memorised a timeline of video games and consoles. Apparently, it's his shtick.'

'You know what else I have at home?' Evan doesn't wait for a response. 'The Dreamcast. It just came out here.' Evan finally looks interested in something, maybe even excited. 'I got it for Christmas. It's *so* cool.'

My plate and my mouth are finally empty, so I join in the conversation. 'What is it?'

'It's a video game console.'

'Like a Game Boy?'

'What is this – 1989? No.' Evan puts one hand on his hip and points with the other, side to side. 'Also, Game Boy is Nintendo. Dreamcast is Sega.'

'See? Told you he's a nerd. Did you get anything nice for Christmas?'

'My grandparents got me a Tamagotchi.'

Evan scoffs. 'They're *so* old.'

My underarms prickle with sweat, the way they do when the richer, cooler kids at school pick on me because I don't have the latest fashions.

Evan makes a phone shape with his hand and holds it to his ear. 'Shayla, 1997 is calling. They want their toy back.'

My cheeks burn so hot my eyes start to water. I look away, focus on the napkin holder, wipe my hands and forearms. The paper towel rips and sticks.

'Stop being such a little bitch-nerd, Evan,' Jess says. 'I'm trying to, like, balance my chakras and stuff, and you keep ruining it.'

'I'm going to tell Mum and Dad you called me that.'

Jess makes an L with her thumb and forefinger, holds it up to her forehead. 'Loser,' she says. 'You're gonna get your arse kicked at high school next year. Snitches get stitches, you little dibber dobber.'

Evan shakes his head and opens his mouth to say something, but someone turns up the music and 'Mambo No. 5' drowns him out. People start to move outside, like bees leaving the hive.

'It's almost midnight.' Jess holds her hands out to me, dances backwards, hips swishing side to side.

Barb is by the back door handing out whistles, party poppers and white party castanets with *2000* printed on them in gold.

'Have you seen Mum and Rob?' I ask her as I go past.

Barb closes her eyes and shakes her head, sways with the music and the drink.

'Find them later,' Jess says. 'We don't wanna miss the fireworks.'

'Head up there.' Barb points to the roof. 'Best seats in the house.'

I follow Jess up the extendable ladder at the side of the house and stand on the roof.

Someone in the backyard starts to count down with the television. 'Ten, nine, eight, seven, six ...'

People on the roof join in. 'Five, four, three, two, one!'

'Happy New Year!' Jess screams.

I raise my party castanets and look towards the horizon, happy and hopeful. Fireworks explode, lighting up the dark night, signalling the start of the new millennium.

'Anthem for the Year 2000' blares on the radio. Mum screams over the top of Silverchair. Rob yells back. His car flies down the M5, swaying in and out of lanes.

'You were flirting with her – your own aunty!'

'How was I flirting?'

Mum heightens her voice to imitate Barb. '"Oh, Robbie, look, there's a little bug in my flower."' She deepens her voice to mimic Rob. '"Gee, I wouldn't mind crawling in there with it." Are you fucking kidding me?' she screams, herself again. 'You're both as disgusting as each other. She's a drunk old lush and so are you.'

Rob's car comes up fast behind another one. He holds his hand on the horn, bears down on them and swerves at the last second, tyres screeching. I hold on to my plastic castanets so tight that it hurts.

'Slow down before you fucking kill us, you arsehole.' Mum slaps at him.

He pushes the side of her head and it smacks into the window.

There's some dried blood above Mum's eyebrow from where her head hit the car window. Rob's right up in her face. He stands over her in the dining room, shouting at the top of his lungs. She slaps him. He slaps her back. She slaps him again.

'I've survived worse than you,' she screams.

He throws her against the dining room wall, grabs her hair, pulls her head back, points his finger in her face and yells, 'Don't you ever fucking compare me to him!'

The photo I took of them with the boys, the one that hangs above his seat at the head of the table so whenever we sit down to eat I can see that I'm not a part of their family, falls off the wall behind her. Glass smashes inside the plastic frame. Mum starts to cry. So do I.

'Let go of me!' Mum tries to prise his fingers out of her hair.

I want to help her, but I can't move. I'm frozen.

'Or what?'

'I'll call the police.'

'Oh, you're gonna call the police, are ya?' Rob gives her hair one last tug before he lets go, rips the phone off the hook and thrusts it in her face. 'Here ya are then. Call them.'

Mum snatches the phone. 'You need to leave.'

'Call the police.'

'You don't want me to do that.'

'Call the police.'

'Just leave.' Mum tries to step around him, but he grabs her by the throat and pins her against the wall. 'Get out!'

216

Rob tightens his grip until Mum gasps. He rips the phone from her hand and shoves it in her face. 'Call the police. Go on. Call them.'

Mum's eyes bulge. She claws at Rob's hand. Mascara streams down her face and neck. She cries, silent tears that pool in the crevice between his fist and her throat. She opens her mouth, spit bubbling, and draws in a raspy breath. This is it. I see the skeletons propped up in the lounge room, the veggie burial plots in the backyard, and I lose all feeling in my legs. I crumble and sink down to the floor like I did when she took me to see my father at Casula Fruit Market.

Mum's voice is a choked whisper. 'Let go.'

'If you want me to leave, call the police. Do it. Call them. Call them!'

I'm crouched in the corner, back against the wall, still in my finest party dress and shoes, when Mum puts the phone down.

Rob punches the melamine pantry. 'Fucking pissed yourself, did ya?' he says to me on his way past.

He slams the screen door behind him. I look at the carpet and feel like I'm three years old again, wetting the bed and waiting for my father to burn our house down in the night.

Mum takes off her three-piece set – engagement, wedding and eternity ring, even though they're not officially married – and throws them out the back door. She opens a packet of baby wipes and cleans her face. Her body trembles and her voice shakes when she speaks.

'The police are going to be here any minute now, Shayla. Please just do me a favour: go to your room, keep the lights off and don't come out, no matter what you hear.'

Rob hurls a bottle at me as I pass the front door on the way to my bedroom at the end of the hall. The screen protects me from the shattered glass, but I'm covered in beer.

When the sirens come, they stop a couple of streets away and I wonder if the police are going somewhere else. I watch from my bedroom window as they enter the street and slowly approach the house. This is the first time they've come here for us. I move to the bedroom door, lie on the floor and press my ear against the crack underneath, but I can't hear much over the sound of my own heartbeat. I open the door, just a sliver, so I can hear better.

'Is there anyone else in the house?'

'No. My kids are staying with their grandparents tonight.'

'Do you want to press charges?'

'No.'

The police make it clear that Rob shouldn't be allowed back inside the house tonight. He offers to sleep it off in the car. They take his keys and give them to Mum, telling her to keep them safe and make sure he doesn't drive. She agrees.

As soon as they leave, she lets him inside. I crawl up the hallway holding my breath. There's a familiar sound coming from the dining room. It reminds me of going to Spotlight with Nanna, watching them snip and rip fabric from the roll. This sounds the same, just slower. I put my head on the floor and peer around the corner. Mum's sitting in my dining chair. Rob has hold of her top. It's torn. I can see her black bra beneath.

'If you ever take my sons away from me, I will fucking kill you.' He speaks to her in an angry whisper. 'Do you understand?'

Mum nods.

'Do you understand, or do I need to make you understand?' He raises his other hand towards her face.

'No.' Mum shakes her head. 'I understand.'

I crawl back to my bedroom and stare at the indent the castanets have left in my hand.

The dreamcatcher Charlie made me for Christmas twirls above my bed, but I'm not convinced it's working. I wake up from the skeleton nightmare. This time Joe's baby skeleton was in Mum's lap too.

I think of her going to bed with Rob last night. I think of her by his side, rubbing his back as he vomited, after he threatened to kill her. It makes me want to vomit too.

218

I smell of piss, both alcohol and actual urine, so I shower, strip my sheets and stick them in the washing machine before I start the search for Mum's engagement, wedding and eternity rings. She and Rob are still asleep when I scrub wee out of the carpet with soapy water and a nail brush, when I sweep up the broken glass in the dining room and on the front verandah, when I hang my sheets out to dry and hose the stickiness of stale beer off the front door.

When they finally emerge, Mum tells me she's taking Rob for an X-ray on his hand. 'I'm going to pick up your brothers while he waits to see a doctor. Are you happy to stay here while I do that?'

She puts her rings back on as if she never threw them out, and it makes my stomach turn.

Pebblecrete digs into my soft soles. I see Sean and Charlie in my peripheral vision. I stand in the gutter. Magic isn't real. God ain't coming to Rosemeadow. Fairy rings are fungus. I take the nine-carat-gold signet ring off my finger and drop it down the stormwater drain. Santa is a lie. And black cats are just strays. I turn, march back up the driveway, and this time it doesn't hurt as much. Back inside, I switch on the computer, pop in my floppy disks and realise nothing has changed. Just everything.

24

Mildred's furniture is in the lounge room. All of it. And it's not a nightmare. There are no skeletons. It's for real. Because she's dead. Her funeral is tomorrow. So is Valentine's Day.

I thought the way she died – cancer of the liver and lungs – would put Rob off drinking and Mum off smoking, but it hasn't. Mum's smoking has stayed steady. Rob's drinking has increased, and so have their fights.

Rob's lost his job. Mum's lost another baby. I've lost Mum. She seems dead inside, like the babies she's lost. Slow. Sleepy. Forgetful. She's either stopped noticing things or stopped caring. She feeds, burps and changes nappies like a robot; watches *The Sopranos* in a daze. Empty, like the skeletons from my bad dreams.

Rob's trying on the new suit he bought from Lowes. Small hairy Hobbit feet poke out from beneath his black pants. The fabric's tight around his thighs but cuffed at the bottom because he's short and stocky, like a wombat. He turns the TV off.

'What did you do that for?' Mum sounds like a whingy teenager, slumped on the lounge, stained and smelly. She hasn't showered or changed her clothes in about three days now.

'Got ya shit ready for tomorrow?'

'Yes.' Mum rolls her eyes.

Rob looks down his nose at her as he takes a big swig of beer. His grey collared shirt is more suited to a schoolboy than a grown-up. Tucked into the waistband of his cheap pants, it accentuates his billowing beer gut. Mum keeps her eyes on the blank screen, matted pillow perm at the rear of her head pushed up against the back of the lounge.

'Well?' Rob kicks her foot.

'Well, what?' Mum's tone switches from bored to annoyed. She straightens up, crosses her arms over her black Sex Pistols T-shirt and frowns at him.

'What are ya wearing?'

Mum closes her eyes, sighs and slightly shakes her head. 'Well, everything in my wardrobe is black, Rob, so it's not going to be a problem, is it?'

Rob's voice becomes quieter yet firmer. 'I *asked* what you're wearing.'

'A black dress.'

'You've got a lot of black dresses.'

'See why it won't be a problem?'

'I've asked which one, Lauren. Don't make me ask again.'

When he calls her Lauren, rather than Loz or Lozza, she's in trouble.

'The long one.'

'The sleeveless one?'

'It's called a cap sleeve.'

Rob points from his jacket to his pants and back again. 'You can see me here in a suit, right?'

'Yes, I'm not blind.'

'So, if I have to wear a jacket, the least you can do is wear some fucking sleeves.'

'It's summer, Rob. In Australia. It's hot. There will be other people with their arms out, trust me. Not everyone is going to come in long sleeves. It's too uncomfortable in this heat.'

'I don't give a shit what *they're* doing.'

'Fine.' Mum throws her hands up. 'I'll wear a cardigan over the top, okay?'

She goes to turn the telly back on, but he snatches the remote away.

'What about ya hair?' He points at her with the hand holding his VB longneck.

221

'What about it?'

'Got regrowth down to ya bloody armpits. You look fucking homeless.'

'Gee, thanks.' Mum stands up, sprinkling crumbs on the floor. 'Well, I haven't exactly had the time or the money to go to the hairdresser's lately, have I?'

'What do you need to go the hairdresser's for?'

'To get it coloured.'

'Just chop it off.'

'What? I'm not cutting it off.'

Mum turns away, but Rob grabs the top of her arm and yanks her back.

'Well, ya not going to my mother's funeral looking like that.'

'I'll put it in a bun.' Mum's voice breaks a little as she tries to prise Rob's fingers off her arm. 'It will look like it's meant to be that way.'

He lets go of her arm and flicks at her dry, frizzy ends. 'It'll look like a bloody bird's nest. I won't have you embarrass me in front of my family, Lauren.'

'Well, there's nothing I can do about it now, at ten o'clock at night when everything's closed, is there?'

'Get it cut.'

Mum shakes her head, pushes her hair out of her eyes. 'Why didn't you say something sooner if you had such a problem with it? Even if I go first thing tomorrow, I'll be late for the service.'

'Cut it tonight.'

Mum scoffs. 'I can't cut my own hair, Rob.'

'Get her to do it.' He points at me.

'No,' Mum says.

Rob gets up in her face. 'You will,' he says.

Mum looks at her feet. Her chin trembles. Rob grabs the back of her hair and yanks so her chin points to the ceiling. The skin tightens around her jaw and neck.

'If you don't get her to cut it, I'll fucking shave it off myself. Do you understand?'

Silent tears roll into the hairline above Mum's ears as she tries to nod.

Mum swipes at her runny nose with the back of a shaky hand. Her eyes are red-rimmed and her face is blotchy. She closes the door and sits on the floor between my legs, against the side of my bed. I gently comb her hair. When I close my eyes, I can still see the deep-red waves of her magnificent mane shining in the sun at Kikori Place, when it was just the two of us and she reminded me of Barbie, Ariel, a L'Oréal model.

Mum's voice wakes me from my daydream. 'Can you put it in a plait?' she asks, passing scissors and hairbands back over her shoulder.

I stare at the back of her head like I did when she acted as my toilet door on that last day at Puff 'n' Billie Preschool, dark roots showing. I recall how her lush hair seemed to lose some of its lustre after I told her about the bad secret *he*'d asked me to keep.

'I want to save it. It's all I have left.'

'No, it's not.'

'It is, Shayla. I don't have anything left that's just mine and mine alone. Not my car, not my furniture ...'

'You still have me.' I put my hand softly on her shoulder. 'I'm yours and yours alone.'

She reaches back over her shoulder and squeezes my hand. 'I'm sorry you have to do this.'

My throat is tight, my voice husky. 'Better me than him.'

'That's true.' She pats my hand. 'That's very true.'

I sweep her hair into a loose ponytail and pull the elastic down to the line of colour just past her shoulders. Mum leans forward and hugs her knees. She cries lightly at first. I comb out the ends and divide them into three sections, criss-crossing them all the way down her back before tying off the split ends where they get scraggly.

'Are you ready?'

'No,' she says, slobbering. Her crying becomes more violent. She takes short, sharp, shuddery breaths, ribs billowing in and out like sails on a stormy sea. I look to the ceiling, blink back my own tears and wait for the waters to calm. When the shaking stops, she pulls the plait around to her lips and kisses it goodbye.

'I'm ready now.'

I lean forward, wrap my arms around her neck in a hug and kiss the back of her head. 'I love you.'

'I love you too.'

The scissors squeak open and I slide them through the hair above the elastic band. I take a deep breath and hold it. Mum does too. The scissors snip shut. Mum emits a low, guttural cry. Cold tears escape down my cheeks.

'I'm sorry.'

The hair attached to Mum's head is severed from the plait down her back, one snip at a time. Her groan stretches so thin, it becomes nothing more than a silent sob.

'I'm so, so sorry.'

Mum's hair is buried in a shoebox at the bottom of my wardrobe, hidden with the sample boxes of antidepressants that Dr Lou gave her. She says if Rob ever finds out that she's crazy he'll take the boys off her.

We sit in the pews at Rookwood Memorial Gardens and Crematorium, dressed in black, arms covered: the perfect picture of respectability, according to the rules imposed upon us by Rob. Or so we think, until Aunty Barb gasps when she sees Nash and Joe.

'What are they doing here? They're far too young to be at a funeral, Lauren. What were you thinking?'

Mum doesn't respond. She bounces Nash on her knee. Her hair is the exact same colour as the boys' now, but curly like mine because it's shorter.

Barb tuts and turns to me. 'You look very calm,' she says. 'Do you understand what's happened here?'

I bow my head.

'Mildred is dead, Shayla. She's never coming back.'

224

'I know. I'm sorry for your loss.'

'Sorry for *my* loss? What about *your* loss? Why aren't *you* crying?'

'I have cried. A lot. I've cried so much I don't think I have any tears left.' I don't mention that those tears weren't for Mildred.

Barb wraps her arm around me, rests her chin on the top of my head and rubs my shoulder. Her black sequinned top scratches my cheek. 'Oh, I know, sweetie, I know. It dragged on for so long, didn't it? It's very, very sad, but she's in a better place now. At least she's not in pain anymore.'

'Her dying has probably ended quite a few people's suffering,' Mum mumbles, as Barb twirls away from me towards Rob.

'Mum!'

'What? I won't shed a tear for that bitter old bitch. And I'm not alone. Take a look around. Not a single person here is crying; even her kids, even Barb. Look at her make-up. She's dolled up like bloody Dame Edna Everage. All she's missing is the glasses.'

I shake my head.

'Well, I thought it was funny.' Mum shrugs.

'I don't think we should be telling jokes right now.'

'Oh, why not?'

I glance over at Rob. He glowers at Mum like an angry storm cloud, all black and grey in his funeral attire. I try to warn her without moving my lips, like a ventriloquist. 'Behave.'

The music starts and Mum gives Rob a sympathetic smile. He turns away, sits down in the front row, his back to Mum, me and the boys.

Mildred's funeral has an Elvis Presley soundtrack. 'Always on My Mind' plays as the curtain closes around the coffin. I listen closely to the lyrics, concentrate on the words, and the song feels more like an apology from Mildred than a tribute to her. I try to make tears come, but it's like someone has turned the tap off so tight that I can't turn it back on. I bow my head, so my hair falls around my face and hides my dry eyes.

*

'What the hell?'

Rob slows the car. Mum turns down 'The Horses' by Daryl Braithwaite. I look up from *The Catcher in the Rye*. Copperfield Drive is full of people.

'Do you think something's happening in our street?' I ask.

Mum blows smoke out the window. 'Probably.'

She's shed her cardigan. There are fingerprint bruises on her arm from where Rob grabbed her last night.

'Better bloody not be,' Rob says. 'I just wanna go home, watch some telly and have an ice-cold beer.'

'I bet you ten bucks it's Steve-o from next door.' Mum ashes her cigarette out the window.

I lean forward, between the two front seats, and peer out the windscreen. 'Didn't he just get out of hospital?'

'Probably slit his wrists again,' Rob says.

'Poor Pat,' Mum says. 'Imagine seeing your son like that. There was blood everywhere, she said. He's lucky he didn't die.'

'Does he want to die?' I ask.

'I think it was either a cry for help or emotional blackmail.' Mum shrugs. 'If he really wanted to get the job done, he would have cut down, not across.'

'Who was he trying to blackmail?'

'That junkie girlfriend of his,' Rob says.

'She has a daughter, you know?' Mum says. 'Pat showed me a photo. Pretty little girl, she is.'

Rob punches the steering wheel. Westminster Way is cordoned off. I've never seen so many men and women in uniform, so many red and blue lights, so much police tape. Kikori Place came pretty close when that man murdered his wife with a shovel, but this time there are fire trucks too. People from our street have joined with others from the 3Ms to stand on Copperfield Drive and watch. Charlie and Sean wave from the crowd as Rob's car is stopped from entering the street. Charlie's dressed for Valentine's Day in a red T-shirt with a pink love heart.

The size of the audience gathered for this evening's entertainment seems to make the police uncomfortable. They look over their shoulders while they speak into radios attached to the front of their bulletproof vests, firearms holstered on their hips and thighs.

Rob winds down the window and asks one of them what's going on.

'Bad break-up. Looks like Cupid only shot one arrow, not two, if you catch my drift.' The police officer rests his forearm against the top of the door and bends down to look inside.

Mum folds her arms across her chest, hand hiding the bruises on her arm.

'You live here?' he asks.

'Number twenty.'

'Well, apparently your neighbour has doused himself and his house in petrol.'

'Is his mother out?' Mum asks.

'She's out. We've had to evacuate the whole street. Everyone's out except him. The negotiator tells me he's just sitting inside having a ciggie.' The movements of the police officer's eyebrows match the inflections in his speech. 'It's a wonder he hasn't gone up in flames already, if what he's telling us is true, but we just can't take the risk.'

'Talk about My Bloody Valentine,' Mum says.

The officer chuckles.

'How long do you think it'll last?' Rob asks.

'Your guess is as good as mine, mate. We could be here all night.'

25

Screaming. Shouting. Crying. I wake to it.

Mum. Rob. The boys.

I hurry down the hallway, past the kitchen, into the combined living-dining area. But it's empty. I go back up the hallway and open the boys' bedroom door. It's dark inside, Mildred's old block-out curtains still drawn against the first light of the day. I rest my hands on the boys' chests and feel them breathe. They're asleep.

But I can still hear crying. It sounds like them.

I close their door quietly, then check in on Mum and Rob. I hold my breath while I watch theirs: bodies rising on inhale, falling on exhale. They're asleep too. I wrap myself in Mum's dressing-gown and walk around the house, listening to the upset, trying to follow it, to figure out where it's coming from, but it's everywhere, all the time. It feels like a bad dream, but I'm definitely awake.

I stick my neck out the back door, follow my feet down the stairs, stickybeak over the fence. Don's already up, putting a tea bag in the compost like I told him to during my Green Gang days. His blue eyes always look a little watery, as if he's on the verge of tears.

'Everything alright?' he asks.

'Can you hear that?'

'What?'

'Nothing.'

I step off the splintery fence stringer, make my way down the driveway and stand barefoot in the middle of the street. Sean's up early too. He kicks his footy over to me.

'Can you hear that?'

'What?'

'The screaming.'

'What screaming?'

I put my hands over my ears, try to block the noise out, but it doesn't get any quieter. It must be coming from inside me.

Sean frowns. His lips move, ask, *Are you okay?*

I shake my head. My chest heaves, heart pounds. Rapid breaths roll in like the tide when we stayed at Bonnie Vale. Sean drops his footy. It rolls down Westminster Way. He pulls my hands away from the sides of my head.

'Come on, man.' Sean holds my shoulders, gives me a little shake. 'Ya scaring me. What's going on?'

Over his shoulder, I see his footy bounce across Copperfield Drive. 'Sean, your ball!'

Sean spins, breathes in sharply and runs at full speed down the road. The bottoms of his bare feet slap against the cement. I shake my head, trying to dislodge the echo of last night's fight. And, in the distance, I hear the saddest sound of all. Sean's footy goes *pop*.

And finally the screams stop.

I eject the movie Mum sat up to watch after Rob passed out. *Fear.* I slide it back inside the cover with a photo of Mark Wahlberg and Reese Witherspoon on the front. Last night when I came out to grab a glass of water, I caught the scene where the bloody, severed head of a German shepherd is being shoved through a doggy door.

Mum and Rob are still asleep when I step outside with Nash and Joe, both fed and dressed. The air is crisp, there's dew on the grass and our breath turns to fog as we search for the Easter eggs that Mum would have put out last night, like she always does.

Last year, Joe was only four months old for Easter. Mum ate the ears off my bunny and joked that he was going to get a chocolate milkshake. This time both boys are old enough to go on an Easter egg hunt with me and I've been looking forward to it since December, when Santa suddenly stopped coming. Rob's since told me it was a matter of 'steal from Shayla to pay for Joe', so I don't expect there to be Easter eggs for me either, but that's fine. I'm not big on chocolate. The best part is the hunt.

'Laa-Laa!' Nash has named me after one of the Teletubbies. 'Choc?' He proudly holds a dart above his head. His green eyes shine, and he beams. White baby teeth show in a pink, gummy smile.

'I don't know. Is it?' I approach with caution. Nash has a tendency to waddle-run away, cackling hysterically, when he knows he has something he shouldn't, and he's not particularly steady on his feet. 'Let me look.'

Nash opens his hand and I take the dart.

'No, honey, it's not an Easter egg.'

The dart board, which Rob must have missed in his drunken stupor last night, hangs on the wooden door of the storage cupboard at the end of the verandah. The door is dotted with little holes, signalling countless misses. I stick the dart in the bullseye, open the door and look inside for Easter eggs.

Empty-handed, we head down the back steps. Joe on my hip, Nash holding my hand, we poke around the swimming pool that Rob picked up from the *Trading Post*, free to whoever was willing to remove it. Rob's brother, Peter, drives an excavator, so he helped dig it out of the ground in Blacktown. Then they dug a big hole in the right-hand corner of our yard and plugged it up with the semi in-ground pool. It's the only real swimming pool in the whole street, but there are no Easter eggs within its gates.

I manoeuvre Joe across my body, hoisting him up onto my other hip as we wander around the backyard, out of the carport gates and onto the driveway. There's no way Mum and Rob would have put chocolates out on the front lawn for all the street to steal, so we take the hunt into the side yard instead. I cast my eye over the chipped plastic pots and spot something shiny in one.

'Nash! What's that?'

He waddle-runs over to the pot, picks out an empty Cadbury Roses wrapper and holds it up for me to see. 'Egg?'

I shake my head. Nash tosses the dirty wrapper on the ground, stomps his fat little foot and stumbles back.

'How about we go inside and watch *Baby's Day Out*?' I hold out my hand.

Nash folds his arms across his chest and pouts.

'I'll make you a hot chocolate.'

In the dining room Mum looks up from her morning coffee and cigarette. 'Where have you been?'

I set Joe down next to Nash. He grabs my leg to keep himself steady. I pull their beanies off by the pompoms on top. 'Easter egg hunt.'

'Why no choc?' Nash holds his hands up, as if he's trying to grasp an explanation in his pudgy little palms.

'Been too naughty, haven't ya?' Rob stabs his heels into the floorboards as he makes his way to the lounge room. 'Easter Bunny doesn't come if you've been bad little boys.'

Nash's lip curls. His crying always makes Joe cry. Soon both of them are holding my legs, heads thrown back, howling.

'Come on. Don't cry. I'll make you both some hot chocolate.'

'There's no milk,' Mum says. 'Just used the last of it for my coffee.'

'Okay, well, let's go put your show on.'

Rob turns the TV on and up. I look to Mum for a little help. She just exhales and stares into her smoke.

'Get out of the way!' Rob slams his hand down on the horn as he weaves in and out of traffic. 'Fucking gook!'

I hate the way he drives. Nash and Joe cry in their car seats next to me. They hate it too. My head throbs from his screaming and theirs, which hasn't stopped since this morning's failed Easter egg hunt. Rob takes a swig of beer and puts the bottle back between his thighs.

'You shouldn't drink drive.'

'What would you know?'

'It know it's illegal.'

'Okay, smartarse. You tell me then, what's the difference between me drinking the bottle before I get in the car and drinking the bottle in the car?'

'I don't think you're meant to do either.'

'I'll tell ya the difference. My blood alcohol reading will probably be lower.'

'And what if you get pulled over?'

'We'll say ya mother was drinking it.'

Mum sits silently in the passenger seat, routinely lifting a cigarette to her lips, unfazed by the erratic driving and screaming children.

'But it will still be on your breath and in your blood, not hers.'

Rob turns the music up and sings 'Bad to the Bone' by George Thorogood & The Destroyers on repeat all the way to Preston's Trash and Treasure Market. I try to put a dummy in each of my brothers' mouths, but they spit them out. I open *Z for Zachariah* then close it, submitting to Rob's singing, Mum's silence and the boys' screaming.

We turn off Camden Valley Way. Sandstone and gravel crunch beneath the tyres as Rob circles the car park, waiting for someone close to the entrance to leave. 'Grand Bazaar' is painted in blue on a soft-yellow wall.

Rob stands at the exotically shaped entrance arches, hands on his hips. The buttons on his blue flanno look like they might pop, stretched across an ever-expanding beer gut. Side-on, flanno tucked into trackies – his nice black trackies, not the fluff-bally grey ones he wears around the house – he looks like a pregnant, bearded woman. He does his nose-lip sniff-twitch and rubs his beard in frustration, watching Mum struggle with the double stroller. Fed up, he turns on his Dunlop heels and disappears into the crowd. There are rows of gazebos, trestle tables and tarps. People are buying and selling new and used goods. Shoppers swarm around us, ice creams and fairy floss in hand. I move slowly, running on empty. The smell of hot chips makes my stomach grumble. I swallow, hoping the saliva will fill me up a bit.

'You know what I've just realised?' Mum stops pushing the stroller and turns towards me, holding a cigarette. 'You wear the same red jumper everywhere we go.'

I look down at my old jumper, too short to cover my wrists. I've paired it with my fake Adidas pants, black with double white stripes down the side. They're as close as I've come to being fashionable for a few years, though I'm too tall for them now and they graze my ankles instead of resting on my shoes – school shoes, even though it's not a school day, because they're the only closed-toe pair I have to wear when it's cold.

'It looks dreadful. Like you've been sleeping in it.' Mum picks at the arm of the jumper. 'Have you? Been sleeping in it?'

'Sometimes.'

'God, Shayla. Anyone who didn't know better would think you have nothing else to wear.'

'I don't. This is the only jumper I have.'

'No, it's not.' Mum flicks the butt of her cigarette dismissively, ashing on the gravel.

'When was the last time you took me shopping for clothes?'

Smoke spirals into the air and disappears.

'It's so long ago you don't even remember, do you?'

She's got a crazy look on her face, like she might laugh.

'It's so long ago, even I don't remember.' I drop my hands to the sides of my thighs, tired, hungry, head splitting.

Mum waves her cigarette hand, batting my words aside. 'I probably lost track because your grandparents are always buying you clothes.'

'Nope. I hardly see them anymore.'

'And, what? That's my fault?'

'I can't even call them because the phone's been cut off.'

'They can still dial in.'

'Yeh, but they ask why I don't call them, and you've told me I can't tell them that we haven't paid the phone bill.'

'Well, if you think they're so great, go and live with them then.'

'And who will help look after the boys?'

'What do you think happens when you're at school all day? Do you think the world just stops spinning until you're home?'

I try to pull the too-short sleeves down to my wrists.

'The boys don't need you, Shayla. You're not their mother. I am. That's what they have parents for. That's why they have Rob and me.'

'Is that what you want? For me to leave?'

'Well, you obviously don't want to be part of this family.'

'I was told I *wasn't* part of this family.'

'Oh, by who?'

'Your Romeo. Your Heathcliff. Your Robbie.'

'Don't call him Robbie. *She* used to call him that.'

'You know what? I don't even care about that.'

'Then, what? What's your problem?' Mum adopts her battle stance, the one I've seen her assume in countless fights with Rob. It makes me ache. The only thing we've really ever had a disagreement about was sending Brindy to the pound. Other than that, it's always felt like us against the world – and Rob. But I'm also sick of it. All of it. And this morning, with the boys, that was just the icing on the cake.

'You ruined Easter.'

'Oh, for Christ's sake, don't tell me you still believe in the Easter Bunny.'

'No, I don't, but they do. They believe in the Easter Bunny. And I made the mistake of believing in you. You didn't ruin Easter for me. You ruined it for the boys.'

'They're babies, Shayla. They don't know what day of the week it is.'

'Exactly, which is why you could have said it was Easter tomorrow. That I had my days mixed up. But instead, you let Rob tell them they'd been bad, so they got nothing. Did you see how much that upset them?'

Mum shakes her head. 'I don't have any money, okay?'

I look at her T-shirt. The Pretenders. Fitting, given she's lying to me. 'If there's no money, why are we at the markets?'

'Rob wants an electric drill. He just got word that they've sold his mother's house.'

'So, there is money.'

'Not my money.'

'Well, they are *his* children, so why can't he buy them chocolate, "for Christ's sake"?'

I spin away from her before she can respond and get swept into the crowd.

I wash up at a stall, staring at a Styrofoam box of books. The pages are open, yellowing, turning in my hand. A woman's squeaky voice snaps me out of fiction, back to reality.

'Everything in that box is fifty cents.'

I look up to say thank you, but something else catches my eye. A Magpies footy.

'Excuse me, please. How much is this?'

'Two dollars.'

I dig into my pockets, even into the hole at the bottom of one, and pull out seventy-five cents. I look around, search the ground for coins that might have been dropped and camouflaged in the gravel, but there's nothing.

I hold out my palm. 'This is all I have.'

The car pulls into the driveway. Mum stops singing along with GANGgajang, turns down 'Sounds of Then' and spins around in her seat. 'Just give me a second to open the front door and I'll help you get the boys out of the car.'

She leaves the passenger door open, so as not to wake the boys, but Rob slams his shut and they jump out of their sleep.

'We're home,' I soothe with a quiet, happy voice.

Mum comes back and grabs Joe, I pop Nash on my hip, and we make our way up the front steps.

'Oh,' Mum gasps and points. 'Look.'

On a log in the middle of the garden bed by the front door, surrounded by impatiens, is a bag of Cadbury Creme Eggs. She must have grabbed them when Rob stopped at the servo on the way home.

'You've both been very good boys,' Mum says. 'The Easter Bunny must have just been running late.'

I look at Nash's sleepy face and see him smile behind his dummy. His green eyes shine. He rests his head on my shoulder and I rest my cheek on his head, and my heart feels like it's soaring and plummeting all at once.

After the boys have had an Easter egg each, I put Nash in his cot, push hair out of his face and pull the dummy out of his mouth. Mum does the same with Joe. Then she follows me into my bedroom, opens my wardrobe and cries.

Charlie and Sean sit in the gutter, huddled together for warmth. Charlie has her scrawny tan arm thrown over Sean's bony brown shoulders, a black-plastic tattoo choker stretched around her neck.

'You alright? We heard your folks fighting on Thursday.'

I nod.

'Did you hear us knock?'

'Was that you?'

'Yeh. We've started playing knock and run whenever we hear someone fighting. Helps break it up. Distracts them for a few minutes, at least. Did it work?'

'Yeh. They thought someone had called the cops.'

'Hear that, Sean? They thought we were cops.'

Sean grunts, head hung low. It's been two days since he lost his football.

'Sean said you were acting strange on Friday. He was worried you'd lost your marbles or something, like the crazy cat lady in number nine.'

'Nah, I'm okay.'

'I'm glad *you're* okay,' Sean says.

'I'm so sorry about your footy, Sean. I really am.'

He looks down the street at where his footy met its fate. 'It's not ya fault.' He shakes his head at the gutter. 'It's mine. I just dropped it. Just let it roll away and get run over. And now I've lost my chance.'

'At what?'

'Getting out of here.'

'What are you talking about?' Charlie asks.

But I know what he means.

'How will I ever become a footy star if I don't have a ball to practise with?'

'You haven't lost your chance,' I say.

'Oh, yeh? How would you know?' He frowns at me, the gold flecks in his hazel eyes the colour of autumn leaves on rain-soaked soil.

'Because I got you something.' I pull the football out of my library bag.

Sean jumps to his feet. 'Where'd ya get this?' He turns the ball over in his hands. 'It's even better than my old one.'

'I think it's pretty new. The lady at the markets said she bought it for her son a while ago, but he never used it. She got Magpies instead of Tigers by accident or something.' I turn to Charlie. 'Got something for you too.'

I reach back into the bag and pull out my Cadbury Creme Egg.

26

Mist hangs in the air like a shroud. It smudges and softens sharp edges like steam from a hot shower. Except it's cold. And there's a light sprinkling of rain. So light I can't see it fall through the grey haze, but I can feel the icy droplets on my skin. My forearms are covered in little white hairs and every one of them stands at attention.

It's winter, but I'm dressed in a light-blue polo T-shirt and navy shorts. Charlie doesn't have a jumper either. She wears her polo with fluff-bally blue trackpants. Everyone else has long pants and jumpers over their polos. My legs look purple, like wee girl's at Glenfield Public School, and I think about how different things were then, when I had warm pants and a bag of stockings to give her.

It's sports day and our Year 7 class is walking to the sports centre on Woodhouse Drive to play indoor soccer. Normally we go straight down Copperfield Drive, but today we have a relief teacher, Mrs Penn. She's a bigger lady, a little wheezy, like maybe she has asthma. And she decides to take us on a shortcut through the reserves.

'Watch your step!' Mrs Penn points at the ground in front of me. There's broken glass and a used syringe with some blood inside.

'And *that's* why we don't go this way,' I mumble under my breath.

She's not from around here. I can tell when people aren't from around here. They look neater. Their hair is washed and styled. Their clothes are nearer to new; colours are brighter, blacks are blacker. They smell like perfume or cologne. They hold themselves differently; walk quickly, heads up, shoulders back. They have light-hearted conversations, talk about what restaurant they went to on the weekend, what movie they're going to see tonight, where they'll go on their next holiday.

Charlie loops her skinny arm through mine and pulls me close, to share body heat and gossip. 'I heard her telling one of the other teachers that she's on a diet, but it's really hard to stick to because her husband keeps buying all this food and leaving it around the house.'

I roll my eyes.

'God, Shayla.' Charlie squeezes my arm. 'Imagine having so much food it's making you fat! She was saying she doesn't eat things like bread and cereal or rice and potato anymore.'

My mouth waters. 'Oh, man, if you're not gonna eat it, give it to me.'

'I know, right?' Charlie giggles.

'Imagine having so much choice you can actually cut out an entire food group and *still* not lose any weight!'

'Remember that time I wanted to be a vegetarian?' Charlie asks.

'Yeh. How long did that last?'

'A day.'

I laugh.

'I was hungry!'

Mrs Penn leads our class directly across Rosemeadow Reserve, from Ambarvale High School towards Dickens Road. It's wide, open and mostly flat; vacant, except for the occasional upside-down shopping trolley and a big stormwater drain that can't be seen through the fog today. To the right, cars swoosh by on a wet Appin Road, blurry red tail-lights disappearing into the distance. To the left are the back gates of the 3Ms: chained, padlocked and tagged with spray paint.

'Fucking housos,' Murray shouts.

He lives on the good side of the roundabout, in Rosemeadow Gardens, and he's got the sports pants I want from Lowes. They're boys' pants, but I don't care. They have elastic around the ankles so the bottom of the pants don't get wet in the rain. The outside layer is a soft quick-dry fabric. The inside is a nice, warm white fleece.

A couple of Murray's friends join in the 'housos' chant.

'They pay their rent just like your parents pay their mortgage,'

I call after them. It's similar to what Mum says when she drives past nice houses on the way to Nanna and Pop's.

Charlie tightens her grip on my arm and pulls me back against her, as the three of them turn on me, circling like a pack of dogs.

'Aren't you cold? Fuckin' houso.'

'Got the wrong shoes for sports day again, huh?'

'Ya dole-bludger parents junkies or something? That why ya so skinny?'

Charlie steps forward, skinny everywhere except for her boobs. I remember in primary school thinking they couldn't get any bigger, but they did. And I'm still wearing singlets. Not a bra in sight.

'Her parents aren't junkies,' she says. 'You're just little prats.'

Someone from the 3Ms beats their fists on the metal gate, making a loud boom, boom, boom. The latch opens and a man's voice spills out. 'Oi, you little shits! If you don't shut the fuck up, I'm gonna come out there and make you shut the fuck up. Permanently.'

Mrs Penn hears the threat. 'Boys!' she calls. 'Children!'

Murray skips off with his cronies to catch up with the rest of the class, but he trips and lands flat on the field. No-one laughs. Everyone holds their breath, even me. Murray gets up slowly, careful not to stick himself with something that hasn't already stuck him.

'Did anything get you?' Mrs Penn hovers, hand supportively on his shoulder.

'I don't think so.' He brushes dirt and grass off his stomach. 'I think I'm okay.'

Everyone scans the ground under him. Clear. Everyone scans his clothes. Clear. Everyone resumes breathing.

'Please be careful,' Mrs Penn says. 'No running. No lagging behind. No mucking around. And watch your step. Okay? Okay. Let's go.'

Mrs Penn waits for stragglers in the small car park on Dickens Road before we carry on along Birunji Creek. The people who live opposite sit on their verandah, watching. Some of the brick under their verandah is lighter than the rest, where graffiti has been scrubbed off.

I get why they're watching. It's unusual to see people in the reserves around Rosemeadow. Most locals, even kids, know to avoid them and the people who frequent them, so I understand the novelty of suddenly seeing a group of school kids in this out-of-bounds area. Mrs Penn tries to look at them without looking like she's looking at them. The whole 'it's rude to stare' thing doesn't apply here. Residents are naturally suspicious and unashamedly watchful. I'm used to it now, but it unnerves Mrs Penn. Her eyes dart around the onlookers quickly, like they make her nervous but she's embarrassed to feel that way.

We follow the creek; it's always dry unless there's a flood. Sean's told me 'birunji' is the Aboriginal word for 'attractive'. Maybe it was once, but not anymore. We pass behind and between the huge housing commission estates that stem off Copperfield Drive and Dickens Road. Classmates walk with their heads down, watching their step. Mrs Penn's head bobbles from side to side as she takes in the hundreds of homes crammed into dead-end offshoots like a root-bound pot plant. All the houses look the same. Single-storey with a common wall. Light brick with some beige cladding. Brown roof tiles, brown window frames, brown security doors – the kind that'll take a chunk out of the back of your heel if you don't move fast enough.

Nurra Reserve becomes Sheil Reserve and there's a look of stressed perseverance on Mrs Penn's face, like she regrets the shortcut but knows it's too late to turn back. Big black rubbish bags have been dumped behind fences and under trees. The one closest to me rustles and a litter of kittens spills out. I try to get Mrs Penn's attention, but she's distracted by the sound of an escalating domestic dispute.

'Hurry up,' she scream-whispers at the group. 'We're almost there.'

We pop out on Woodhouse Drive, opposite the indoor sports

centre, and Mrs Penn does a headcount. She looks relieved to be on a main road. Visible, but without any weirdos staring at us. Class fully assembled, her shoulders relax. She breathes out a heavy sigh, like she's been holding her breath the whole time.

The relief only lasts a second.

A rusty white Ford Fairmont accelerates loudly towards a mangy black cat crossing the road towards us. It has a saggy stomach, a dead noisy miner in its mouth and is heading in the direction of the garbage-bag kittens, probably taking food to its babies. Mrs Penn's arms suddenly spring from her sides, signalling that no-one should cross, and our class takes a collective step back from the kerb as the car veers towards the gutter. We all watch as the cat leaps towards safety, but the corner of the bumper bar catches her midair. The dead noisy miner falls from her mouth and lands on the verge. The driver speeds off, honking victoriously.

Mrs Penn clamps her hands over her mouth, stifling a scream as she spins away from the cat writhing in the gutter. Her teary eyes are so wide that her forehead is creased into little rolls.

Our class watches the cat disappear down a stormwater drain to die.

I sit outside the school gate reading *Animal Farm*, waiting for Sean so we can walk home together. He's sweaty from playing footy, grass stains on his knees.

'How was it?' he asks.

'Good. Well, someone hit a cat on the way to sport. Like, deliberately. And that upset our relief teacher so much she went home. They had to send another one to come get us. So, you know, not great, I guess. How 'bout you?'

'Man of the match.' Sean thrusts his thumb towards his chest. 'Got a Macca's Award.'

'With the free cheeseburger?'

'Yep. And I'm starving.'

Sean shares his cheeseburger with me, standing on the

corner of Thomas Rose Drive – named after the free settler or convict, depending on which history teacher I speak to. I eat my half so fast it feels like it gets stuck and expands in my chest.

'Man, I hate pickles,' Sean says.

'Same, but I eat them anyway.'

'Me too.'

I pick the melted cheese off the wrapper and eat it. Sean licks sauce and crumbs off his fingers, wipes his hands down the side of his sports shorts and picks up the Magpies footy he's wedged between his feet.

'Ready?'

'Yeh.'

I'm careful to step over ants as we walk up Copperfield Drive. Black. Black-blue. Black-orange.

Sean watches me and shakes his head. 'Couldn't even hurt an ant, could ya?'

'I try not to.'

'So, how ya gonna do it then?'

'What?'

'Poison him.'

I stop dead in my tracks. Sean takes a few more steps, turns around and fixes his eyes on me, tossing his footy from hand to hand.

'I don't know what you're talking about.'

'Yeh, ya do.' Sean's voice is flat, unlike his eyebrows, raised and accusing. 'I heard all the questions you were asking in science this morning. About mercury poisoning.'

'So?'

'So, you've got a big mouth. If he suddenly dies of mercury poisoning, ya know who they're gonna come looking for now, right?'

'People get mercury poisoning all the time from, like, eating too much tuna and stuff.'

Sean holds his hand out. 'Give it to me.'

'What?'

'The thermometer. I know ya took one, Shayla. I had to count them all up at the end of class and one was missing.'

'Why didn't you say anything?'

'I didn't want you to get in trouble. What are ya gonna do with it anyway? Break it open and put it in his food or some shit?'

'Or his beer.'

'Fuck, Shayla. No.'

I look down at my shoes, at the ants. 'You know, once, two bull ants got into my jeans and they bit me all up and down my legs. I killed them.'

'I know he's hurt ya,' Sean says, head bowed.

'I read somewhere that when you kill an ant it gives off this smell that warns all the other ants that there's a threat.'

Sean looks up at me from under his sweaty flop of hair. 'Ya really think ya could do it?'

'No. I just thought it would make me feel better, knowing I had something up my sleeve if things got really bad.'

Sean puts his footy between his feet, his hands on my shoulders and squeezes. 'Remember when ya asked me if I thought ya were a bad person? You're not.'

I nod.

'But ya would be if ya did that.'

I nod again.

'Even worse than him. Even if things were real bad. Ya know that, don't ya?'

I nod and recite a line that stuck with me: '"And remember also that in fighting against man we must not come to resemble him."'

'Huh?'

'It's a line from the book I'm reading.' I hold it out.

Sean glances at the cover. 'Give me the thermometer. We both know ya never gonna use it. And we both know having it isn't gonna keep ya safe either. I can put it back tomorrow.'

244

The thermometer changes hands. Sean heads off and I follow.

'You know when we talked about good people going to heaven and bad people going to hell?' I ask.

'Yeh.'

'What if this is limbo?'

'I dunno what ya mean.'

'Maybe in a past life or something, we weren't good enough for heaven or bad enough for hell. So, if heaven's up there and hell's down there ...'

'You think we're stuck in between?'

'I know it sounds crazy.'

Sean bobs his head up and down in agreement.

'I've just been trying to figure out what I've done to deserve this, that's all.'

'In a past life?'

'When you say it like that, it sounds even more crazy.'

More furious nodding.

'Well, I can't think of anything I've done in this life to bring it on.'

'Maybe it's those two bull ants ya killed.'

We both laugh.

'So, you don't think this is limbo?'

'Nah.' Sean looks at me with sad eyes. 'Just life.'

'Well, that sucks.'

'Yeh, but think of it this way: limbo or real life, God or not, ya not gonna end up in a good place if ya planning shit like that, yeh? I know things are bad now, but they're gonna get better.'

'You promise?'

Sean gazes at me warily. 'You know I can't promise,' he says. 'But I don't think things can get much worse.'

Mum's music blares down the street. 'Back to the Wall' by the Divinyls on full blast. The outdoor setting across the road is littered with empty beer bottles, goon bags and cigarette boxes. The neighbours slumped around it slip into a collective coma while their kids play on the street in stained school uniforms and saggy nappies.

Charlie waves from the gutter; a stray kitten hugging her calf with its scraggy white tail. 'What took you so long?' Her voice booms down the street and the cat scampers away, back to the rusted-out car on Charlie's front lawn where the litter was recently born. 'You better not have gone to Macca's without me.' She stands up, brushes herself off and meets us at the bottom of Pat's driveway. 'You okay?' she asks.

I point to the house, the source of Mum's music.

'Oh, yeh. I saw Rob leave a while ago. That started up pretty much straight away.'

'Great.'

'Sorry,' Charlie says.

'Nah, it's not your fault. Things have just been bad since his mother died. Like, worse than normal.'

'Looks like Steve-o's having a tough time too,' Charlie says.

'What makes you say that?'

She points up Pat's driveway. There's a noose hanging under the carport, next to my bedroom window.

I look to Sean. 'Thought you said things couldn't get worse?'

Sean holds his hands up, as if at gun point. 'Didn't make any promises, did I?'

'Well, hopefully this time the whole street doesn't need to be evacuated,' Charlie says.

The grey sky begins to sprinkle. Kids squeal and run home. The drowsy day-drinkers stir and start to head inside, slow and sluggish.

I feel my shoulders sag. 'I better go check on her and my brothers.'

'Good luck,' Charlie says.

Sean nods.

I cut across the lawn and turn back when I reach the driveway. Sean and Charlie look after me from the gutter, arms looped around each other, waiting in the rain. I wave and step behind the conifer trees.

Inside the house, Nash and Joe cry, hands over their ears. Mum has the music turned up so loud their bedroom window vibrates with the bass. She spins in a circle, surrounded by the brown of Mildred's furniture, and I remember how her long red hair used to fan out around her. Now it's short and brown too. Mum screams and sings, cries and dances, and it looks like the fight of a wild bird trapped within the walls of a small cage. I'd ask her to turn the music down, but this desperate dance for escape is the most alive she's looked in months, so I take the boys into my bedroom and we take a trip to Treasure Island with the Famous Five.

The pool has turned green. New dead bugs float on the surface. Older ones have already sunk to the bottom. Yesterday there was a water strider skimming across the top like a leggy, ice-skating spider, but it looks like Rob fished it out – or perhaps it died and sank too. Only the mosquito larvae thrive, wrigglers rippling the water because Rob won't waste money on chlorine and filtration when it's too cold to swim.

It's the winter school holidays but I sit outside in the cold, on the deck Rob built with his brother next to the watery bug cemetery, because being eaten alive by mozzies while freezing my arse off is better than being stuck inside with all of them. Back against the wooden fence palings that separate Pat's backyard from ours, I open *Rita Hayworth and Shawshank Redemption* by Stephen King. Behind me, Pat's son Steve-o mows the lawn. Every time he mows, he goes a different way, vertically then horizontally. He's told me that's the secret to a healthy lawn, and theirs does look much better than ours.

Today he mows vertically. He starts by the fence we share. The smell of freshly cut grass and petrol fills the air. The noise becomes slightly fainter as the lawnmower moves further away, towards the other side of the yard. Soon the mower stops, the back door opens and I hear Pat's voice. She's brought him a cold drink and tells him she's going to Macarthur Square to do some shopping. It's Thursday.

Thursday is payday. Everyone around here does their shopping on Thursday.

'Need me to bring you anything?' she asks.

I imagine he shakes his head because I don't hear him reply.

'I'll see you when I get back.'

There's some movement under their carport; the car door opens and closes, the ignition starts and I go back to my book.

An hour or so later, the smell of sizzle steak and boiled veggies reaches my nostrils just as the sound of the smoke alarm reaches my ears, signalling that the meat is more than well done; it's basically cremated. Like Mildred.

Through the back door I see Mum, too short to reach the smoke alarm, waving a tea towel. The sound stops momentarily then starts back up again, competing with 'Black Velvet' by Alannah Myles. Mum disappears for a few seconds, reappears with a broom and pokes at the fire alarm with the handle.

I'm about to stand up when I pause at the hum of the car engine next door. I can't remember hearing the car leave, and something about that makes me feel sick in the stomach. I stay half sitting, half standing, holding my breath. I strain my ears, hoping to hear something that will either make me feel brave enough to have a stickybeak over the fence or silly for imagining the worst. The thud of a car door brings a wave of relief. Keys jingle and clunk against the screen door. It creaks open and full plastic bags bang into it. I pick up my book, ready to head inside, but the hum of the car engine keeps on.

'Steve, can I get a hand bringing the groceries in, please? Steve?'

I peek over the fence at the freshly cut lawn. Lush buffalo grass, emerald green, cushions Pat's footfalls as she steps out the back door and wanders around the corner, towards the carport where the engine is still running. She inhales sharply, right hand flying to her mouth. 'No, no, no, no.'

I follow with my eyes to where her son sits behind the wheel. He looks asleep. Peaceful. When she swings open the driver's door,

I half expect him to jump awake. Instead his body slumps, slides out of the car, sinks onto the oil-stained concrete floor of the carport. His dead weight drags Pat down too. I can't see her anymore, but I can hear her.

'My baby. My boy. My poor, sweet baby boy.'

27

Rob fancies himself a bit of a builder. He has three sheds, now full of tools and work benches. The biggest two were brought across from Mildred's place after it was sold. He's told Mum there's no money left from the sale. That it all went back to the bank. Home loan repayment and credit card debt. But I notice he's bought a portable CD player for his shed. He drinks in there now and sings along to 'Down Under' by Men at Work while he tinkers away with his hand tools and maybe clamps something in the vice. It's alright for me to be in the backyard at this point, hitting a tennis ball against the back wall of the house. I hear the occasional expletive when Rob misses a nail and hits his thumb, but that's about it.

After a few more drinks, Rob thinks he looks like Ned Kelly in his welding helmet, and blue sparks start to fly. Sometimes he opts for the electric sander or saw instead. But, essentially, as soon as he's 'brave' enough to start up the power tools, that's my cue to leave.

Inside, Mum is watching *The Burning Bed* with Farrah Fawcett again. She let me watch it with her once, told me it was based on a true story: a battered housewife who waits for her husband to fall asleep one night, then pours gasoline around the bed and sets it alight. She turns it off when there's a knock at the front door and leaves the Sydney 2000 Olympic Games on the telly instead.

Pat from next door sits at our dining table. She holds her coffee cup with both hands. They're shaking. Thick veins poke through thin skin sprinkled with age spots. She brings a hanky to her round and wrinkled face. There are silver bristles along her thin upper lip.

A few stray hairs sprout from her chin. I can see comb lines in the hair on her head, which is thin and shows her scalp.

'I've lost all the men in my life,' she says. 'My husband, Bernard. He was an engineer. I was seventeen when we got married. He was twenty-one. We had nine children, pretty much one after the other. Eleven, actually, if you count the stillborn twins. They were boys too. We stopped trying after that.'

Mum gives Pat a sad smile at the mention of lost babies.

'We had a nice double-brick home in Strathfield. Not our own, of course. Can't afford a home of your own when you have so many kids running around that you have to tie them to the clothesline just to get some housework done.' Pat stares into her mug, as if at memories reflected in the milky instant coffee. 'But we rented from a nice old couple, and the kids never went without. We always had a roof over our heads, clothes on our backs, food on the table.'

Mum sits at the head of the table in a black Nirvana T-shirt with a dead smiley face on the front. She opens a packet of Arnott's Milk Arrowroot biscuits. The rip and tear of the packaging perforates the hush that Pat's voice has draped over us.

'Sorry,' Mum says, her face a grimace.

But Pat doesn't seem to have noticed the interruption. 'We'd grown up together, and I thought we'd grow old together,' she continues. 'One day he was fixing a fence paling out back and he stepped on a rusty nail. Neither of us thought too much of it. He was busy with work and the yard. I was busy with the house and the kids. Then he died. Septicaemia. He wasn't quite forty.'

I take off my Sydney 2000 Olympic Games baseball cap from Macca's and set it aside, along with my thoughts of Cathy Freeman and Nikki Webster.

'Steven looked so much like his father.' Pat dabs the corners of her eyes with the hanky. 'He was the youngest. Only seven when his father died.'

'Oh, Pat, I'm so sorry,' Mum says.

I use the pause in Pat's story as an opportunity to reach for the biscuits.

'I didn't realise you lost Bernie so early on,' Mum says.

Pat twists her wedding band around her finger, her eyes deep set and watery.

'I didn't realise you had nine kids!' I say.

Mum frowns, gives me a sharp shake of the head. I shove the biscuit in my mouth.

Pat smiles. 'Seven girls and two boys.'

'That must have been so hard for you.' Mum crosses her arms under her boobs, puts her elbows on the table and leans forward into the story.

'Bernard didn't leave me anything. There was nothing to leave, really.' Pat shrugs, shakes her head. 'He had a good job, but we had a big family. Like I said, we never went without, but at the end of the week there wasn't very much left, you know?'

Mum nods.

'Thankfully, the old couple we rented from, she helped me get a pension and put my name down for a government house; he let me live there rent-free until we got given a place, so that I could feed and look after the kids with what little we had coming in.' Pat takes a sip of hot coffee and steam fogs up her glasses. She waits for it to clear before she continues. 'We ended up in what's now known as Riverwood, but back in 1956 it was called Herne Bay Housing Settlement. The US Army had set it up as a military hospital barracks during World War II. It was the largest one in Australia.'

'Is that why Riverwood has streets called Washington and Kentucky and stuff?' Mum asks. 'Yanks built it?'

Pat nods. 'And when they left, the Housing Commission took it over.'

I grab another Milk Arrowroot biscuit, shove it in my mouth, wish for margarine, spread on thick.

'I grew up in Punchbowl, just around the corner from there.' Mum looks pleased with her local insights into the United Streets of

252

Riverwood. She stubs out her smoke and scrapes the bent cigarette butt across the bottom of the ashtray with a yellow middle finger, all the ash and butts now in one neat little pile.

Pat puts her wrinkled elbow on the table, knobbly fingers on her face. 'My poor kids.' She takes a deep, shaky breath. 'They lost everything. They lost their father, they lost their home, they …' Her voice breaks.

'They had you.' Mum rests her hand on Pat's forearm, rubs it with her thumb.

Pat drops her hand from her face, squeezes Mum's fingers. 'Our whole world was turned upside down,' she says. 'They placed us in an old wooden army hut. There were no walls inside. Instead they divided the space into four rooms using partitions that didn't even reach the ceiling. There were three small bedrooms and a combined kitchen-living area. There was no privacy. Clotheslines were strung up off the back of the huts, toilets were tin sheds outside and each laundry was shared by four families. The roads and footpaths were all dirt, and when it rained, they turned to mud. The kids would play outside in it. It was loud and crowded and dirty. We were only there a few years before they decided to demolish it.'

'You did the best you could with what you had.' Mum takes Pat's hand in both of hers. 'You kept them together. You kept them safe.'

A tear rolls down Pat's nose, splashes on the table. 'No,' she says. 'My eldest, Phillip, he got in with the wrong crowd. Even after we moved to Liverpool, where we had a nice home with carpeted floors and its own laundry, he couldn't leave Herne Bay behind. He kept getting sucked back in.'

Pat wipes the tear off the table with her hanky. It isn't floral like the ones she puts in my birthday cards with a five-dollar note. This one is brown-and-white check. It's a man's hanky. Steve-o's.

'One night he said he was going to a party.' Pat wrings the hanky in her hands. 'I asked him not to go. I just had this bad feeling. But he wasn't a child anymore. He was a twenty-one-year-old man. He wanted to do what he wanted to do, so I told him I loved him and kissed him goodbye. Later that night, he was robbed and beaten to death.'

Mum's hand flies to her face, covers her mouth, the way Pat's did when she found Steve-o's body in the car.

'He was found on the side of the road.' Pat stares at the hanky in her hands. 'The police never worked out who killed him.'

I let the Milk Arrowroot biscuit I've bitten into dissolve in my mouth, so I can swallow it silently.

'One by one the kids left home, started lives and families of their own. Anne moved overseas, a few moved interstate, and I didn't need that many bedrooms anymore, so Housing moved me here. Steven was doing really well. He'd married, bought a home, had some kids. Everything was going good for him, until he discovered his wife was having an affair.'

My mind drifts to Kikori Place and the man who split his wife's head open with a shovel after he found her in bed with his mate.

'They came to an arrangement,' Pat says. 'She'd keep the house in place of child-support payments, and he'd see the kids every second weekend. But after he signed over the deed, she sold it and took off to Queensland with her lover and the kids.'

Mum shakes her head, lights a cigarette.

'It was all downhill from there,' Pat says. 'He missed being a dad, kept getting in with these troubled single mothers, tried to be the husband and father he was robbed of being to his own wife and kids. I've never met anyone as unlucky in love as my Steve.' Pat's lip curls so I can see her worn bottom teeth. Her weathered face collapses. She presses her palm to her forehead and her frail shoulders heave. 'Oh, Lauren, I miss him so much.'

Mum stands up, moves behind Pat, rubs her back.

'I don't want to be here anymore.'

Mum stops rubbing Pat's back. 'Don't talk like that.'

'No, I don't mean like *that*. I mean I don't want to live *here* anymore. I can't live in the house where my son killed himself. I can't. I just can't.'

'That's understandable.' Mum resumes the back rub. 'Have you put in for a transfer?'

'Yes, but they said it's not high priority and that I could be waiting years.' Pat looks up at Mum and tears roll down her face. 'I'm almost eighty. By the time I make it to the top of the list, I'll probably have died in that house too.'

'Tell them you can't get up the stairs anymore, that you can't maintain the land,' Mum says. 'Get your doctor to write you a letter to say you have arthritis or something and you need a single-storey home, maybe one closer to one of your daughters so they can care for you.'

'That's a good idea.' Pat taps Mum's hand on her shoulder. 'Thank you. I'll call them tomorrow.'

Mum returns to her cigarette and Pat, armed with a new plan of attack, pulls herself together like a drawstring pouch. She dries her face with Steve-o's hanky and puts her glasses back on. She sits up straight, smooths her skirt and shakes her head, as if clearing it. I watch her reassemble herself over my mug of International Roast, and when she catches me staring, she waves a knobbly finger at me.

'You shouldn't be drinking coffee at your age,' she says.

'She'll be right,' Mum says. 'She had her first coffee when she was still drinking out of a bottle. That's how we weaned her.'

28

Mum's budgie, a birthday present, sits on her shoulder, like she's a pirate. He fluffs out his blue feathers and nibbles on Mum's earring.

'Should've called you Casanova,' Mum says, laughing. But in keeping with the tradition of naming animals after their colour, Mum has named him Bluey. He's a chirpy little guy with a white head and black flecks on his wings, which have been clipped so he can't fly away.

'Gets more bloody attention than I do,' Rob sulks.

'Eat your heart out,' Mum teases.

I look up from the pages of *Lord of the Flies* and watch Rob crack open his fourth VB using the corner of his shirt. His beer belly is so big now he has to wear his favourite blue flanno open over a singlet. Today he's paired them with his grey 'round the house' trackies. He frowns at Mum, shakes his head at Bluey.

'You're a beautiful boy, aren't you?' Mum coos, running her fingers down Bluey's back. 'Yes, you are.'

Rob skulks off to the shed to tinker and brood.

Charlie made me a God's eye from paddle pop sticks and wool. She says it will watch over me while I sleep, but I don't think it's working, maybe because I don't believe in anything anymore.

I shuffle up the hallway, heavy and slow, unsure if last night's fight was real or imagined. They're so frequent, the fights and the nightmares, that they've started to muddy in my mind. Awake or asleep, it all just feels like one long bad dream.

The boys are up and out of their cots, but the house is quiet. There's no *Rugrats* on the telly. Mum isn't on the phone to Nanna. I can't hear the kettle boil, the toaster pop, the scrape of a teaspoon along the bottom of a coffee cup, not even the flick of a cigarette lighter.

The photo frame in the hallway is crooked. I straighten it. The bathroom mat that usually hugs the toilet is skew-whiff. I fix it with my feet. There's an empty beer can on the bathroom vanity. I take it to the kitchen where an empty beer carton is doubling as a recycling bin. It's chock-a-block and the extra can sends the overflow spilling onto the floor.

Mum sweeps into the kitchen, wearing the flowing black-satin robe that Nanna and Pop bought for her birthday. 'Be quiet, will you?' she scream-whispers at me.

I look up at her from the old laminate floor, chipped and lifting in some places, hands full of empty cans.

'Just leave it till later.' She waves her arms and the wide sleeves of her robe slide back to her elbows, revealing fresh bruises on her forearms. She pulls the sleeves down, glances at me quickly, then spins away out of the kitchen. The bottom of her floor-length robe flares out in a dramatic full circle around her, like a Disney princess's ball gown.

I follow Mum through the dining room into the lounge room, where Nash and Joe have started to whine at *Dennis the Menace*. The volume on the telly is down so low the boys are standing right in front of it to hear. Nash taps on the TV screen as if knocking on a door. Mum turns the volume up, just one bar. 'Come on now. Be good boys for Mummy. Daddy's still sleeping and we need to be very quiet so we don't wake him up.'

There's a blanket on the lounge. Mum's black mascara is smudged across the white pillowcase. Her eyes are red-rimmed and puffy. She avoids eye contact with me while she slides the movie she must have watched last night back into its case. It has a photo of Julia Roberts with wet hair in a bath on the cover. *Sleeping with the Enemy*. She let me watch it with her once. It's about a woman who fakes her own drowning to escape her violent husband, and what happens when he finds her.

I step outside. War drums sound in my ears. They beat loud in my head, my chest, and reverberate through my body, making everything tremble. I want to slam the back door, pull it off its rails with my bare hands, put my fist through the glass, tear this place down to the ground, bury it.

Instead, I close the door quietly. Chipped white paint flakes off the rusted metal back-stairs handrail. The paint catches on my clothes and sticks to my hands as I press my belly against the rail. My stomach churns. The emotions I have swallowed boil beneath the surface. I double over the railing, fold myself in half, emit a strangled sob. I stare at the seedlings beneath me, vision blurred by tears. Rob's veggie patch has been restored. Baby plants poke through the soil, stretching towards the sun, bright-green spots against the brown dirt. I want to rip them up, like Brindy did. Instead I take a deep breath, look to the sky and watch as one of Bluey's little white head feathers is carried through the air. It floats over the roof, away from here, and when it's out of sight, I feel something lighten and lift within.

I head down the back steps and around the corner to check on Bluey, make sure he has feed and fresh water. I can't see him in the aviary Rob built and attached to the back wall of the house, but I check the door and it's locked, so he must be in there somewhere. I scan every branch, every mirror with a bell, every stick of bird feed. If the door is locked – I check again and it is – he can't be anywhere else. An ant bites my foot. I give a little stomp, hoping to dislodge it from between my toes, and look again over the walls and floor of the cage. The ant bites again, harder. I balance on one foot to brush it away. Something is stuck to the bottom of my foot, so I peel it off.

A blue feather covered in dry blood.

I scream until Mum clamps her hand over my mouth. 'What the hell's going on?'

I point to the unmistakable blue feathers at my feet, meaty and covered in ants.

'Oh, shit.' Mum lets go of me and steps back. Her robe has fallen open. There's a black Cold Chisel T-shirt underneath.

I point to the feathers. 'How did this happen?'

Mum pulls a packet of cigarettes from the pocket of her robe and lights one. 'Looks like those feral cats got to him.' She sniffs the air and curls her lip. 'Smells like cat piss out here.'

'No, I mean, how could he have got out?'

Mum inspects the latch on the aviary door and points at it with the cigarette wedged between her fingers. 'Did you close this?'

'No.'

The cigarette hangs loosely between her lips while she inspects the walls of the aviary, as if looking for a hole in the wire. 'You didn't close this door just now?'

'I triple checked. It was locked when I came out.'

Mum steps back. 'Maybe someone got into our backyard last night.'

I swing my arms out wide to the rest of the yard, untouched. 'And, what, just let our budgie out?'

'Well, I don't know, Shayla. Don't yell at me. I didn't have anything to do with it.'

'If they were going to take anything, they would have taken Rob's tools. Wouldn't take much to open the shed with boltcutters.'

'What? Where do you learn this stuff?'

'School.' I shrug. 'Took a metalwork class last year. Point is, if they came to rob us, they would have been prepared. Nothing else is missing.'

Mum frowns at the cage. I watch her face, the lines that form around her lips and how her cheeks concave when she takes a drag of her smoke. Her frown slowly deepens.

'What?' I ask.

Mum moves closer. The satin sleeve of her robe touches my arm. I can smell cigarette and coffee on her breath. She speaks in a low, shaky voice, eyes on the aviary. 'What if it was Rob?'

'Rob?'

Mum shushes me, grabs my wrist, holds it down by her side, as if it's a lever that controls my volume. 'He was jealous.'

'Of what?'

'Bluey,' Mum says. 'Do you remember what he said yesterday? About the bird getting more attention than him?'

I think of Bluey, tiny and lost in the big, dark backyard, trying to fly but unable to escape as he was hunted by feral cats.

'He's a jealous man. Once when we were dating, before I met your father, we were out and I was dancing with someone else. Harmless fun. This guy's girlfriend was there and she was a friend of mine. Rob just walked up, grabbed him by the shirt and threw him straight down the stairs.'

'And you didn't think that was a bad sign?'

'It was the eighties, Shayla.'

'So?'

'So, it was different back then. Men were real men. They were masculine. They had moustaches. They fought for their women. It was romantic.'

'Doesn't sound romantic.'

'Well, we didn't know any better at the time, did we?'

'And now?'

'Now I guess it's too late.'

29

The school hall has brick walls and a wooden floor. Mrs Johnson stands on the stage above a sea of Year 8 students dressed in sky blue and navy. She hunches forward, hands behind her back, and peers through her glasses at kids in the front row, waiting for them to be quiet. Row after row, the chatter dies down. Charlie continues to fidget and talk. I tap her on the shoulder, point to Mrs Johnson and she sits up straight. Mrs Johnson gives a sharp nod and marches towards the microphone stand. The short square heels on her shoes clip-clop across the stage. She clears her throat, taps the mic and smiles.

'Good morning, Year 8,' she says. 'You all took a test in March called the English Language and Literacy Assessment, the ELLA exam. Today you will receive your results.'

Mrs Johnson opens her arms to the hall. Teachers start to hand out pieces of purple paper to their students.

'There's a graph that shows four levels of achievement: low, elementary, proficient and high. And a black dot placed somewhere along that spectrum indicates your personal performance. This helps us compare your results with that of your peers to see if there's anything we can do to help you improve your skills.'

Mrs Martin hands me my piece of purple paper. 'Well done,' she whispers.

I read the first paragraph: *In the Year 8 literacy test, Shayla's score placed her in the high achievement level for Writing, high achievement level for Reading, and high achievement level for Language.*

'Overall, the results were pleasing,' Mrs Johnson says. 'You can all give yourselves a pat on the back. But there were a few students who performed exceptionally well.' Mrs Johnson reaches into the pocket of her jacket and pulls out a piece of paper. Her glasses slip down her nose a bit as she unfolds it. 'If you hear your name called, please come up on stage to collect your principal's award.' Mrs Johnson looks over her glasses and reads out the names. 'Brody Baxter, Shayla Young and Luke Williams.'

Sean gives me a little shove. The gold flecks in his eyes sparkle. 'That's you!'

I look to Charlie and her smile is so big, her cheeks almost swallow her eyes. 'Go, go!'

My legs shake a little as I climb the stairs at the side of the stage. Mrs Johnson holds out her hand and I shake it. Both of our hands are nice and firm. Pop would be proud. I hope the phone has been reconnected so I can call him and Nanna when I get home.

'Congratulations, Shayla,' Mrs Johnson says. 'If you keep this up, the sky's the limit.'

Mum wakes me screaming that America has been attacked. Two planes have crashed into the World Trade Centre in New York. She keeps me home from school and we huddle together in front of the telly. Normal programs have been suspended. In some cases, so have commercials. Every channel is showing the same thing. Planes slice into the sides of big, tall buildings. They look like they explode from the impact, showering glass and concrete and steel over neighbouring buildings before they catch alight and begin to collapse. Mum cries as people jump from the windows to their deaths. Others run for their lives below, chased by great big billowing plumes of grey smoke tunnelling through the streets, rubble raining down like an avalanche.

Mum finally conks out on the lounge while the boys are down for their afternoon naps. Somehow it feels wrong to turn the telly off, so I put it on mute. Over the pop-pop-pop noise that comes out of Mum's mouth when she's very tired, I can hear the sound of Sean's footy being kicked up and down the road. I head out the front, and it appears Mum wasn't the only one tuned into the news all day. Across the road, neighbours have congregated around the plastic outdoor setting. They drink in silence, listening to the latest on a portable radio.

'Shayla! Up here.'

Across the road from Pat's place, on the corner of Mowbray Way, Sean is halfway up a tree, spindly like a stick insect.

'What are you doing up there?'

'My footy's stuck.' Sean points.

The branches of this tree are covered with light papery bark that spiders and other bugs hide in, camouflaged.

'Can you shake the branch?' I shade my eyes, looking up as I get closer. 'Maybe it will come loose.'

'Can ya catch it if it does? Don't wanna lose it like the last one.'

'I'll try.' I squint into the sun, arms out in front, ready to catch the footy.

'Hey,' Charlie calls from her driveway. 'What are you guys doing?'

'His football's stuck.'

'Did you see the news?' Charlie starts towards us, thongs slapping with every step. 'They had TVs on in every classroom today and in the library at lunchtime. I didn't even know the school had that many TVs!'

I nod, eyes on the ball, not wanting a repeat of the last football fiasco.

'What do you think will happen next?' Charlie asks.

'Dunno. War?'

'Do you think that means we'll go to war too?'

'Maybe.'

'Shayla, ya ready?' Sean calls.

'Yep.'

Sean shakes the branch. Leaves fall. The ball moves. Eyes up, hands out, I step onto the grass and something sharp stabs me in the foot. I wince, reminded of my first day in Rosemeadow and copping a bindi in the big toe. The football falls out of the tree and bounces down the street.

'Shayla!' Sean shouts.

Charlie's thongs flip-flop frantically down the street as she chases after it. 'Got it!' she calls.

'Thanks, Charlie. Shayla? Shayla, ya right?'

I stare at my feet. Charlie's hand is on my shoulder. I hear a sharp intake of breath.

'Shayla?' Sean's voice comes again.

'Just give us a second,' Charlie calls back.

'Why? What's going on? Is everything okay?'

'I'll go get your Mum,' Charlie says quietly.

I listen to her thongs scuff up the street, fast. Sean scrambles down the tree and stands by my side. We stare at the used syringe.

'Oh, shit,' he says.

'Yep.'

I pinch my big toe and push blood out of the puncture wound, while Mum calls the doctor. They tell her they're just finishing up for the day.

'Come in first thing tomorrow.'

Rosemeadow Medical Centre is on the corner of Fitzgibbon Lane, across the road from Rosemeadow Marketplace. According to my high school history teacher, Fitzgibbon Lane is the oldest street in Rosemeadow. Once it was a farm track that went all the way to Menangle Road. Now only the portion between Appin Road and Copperfield Drive exists. Rizal Park and Demetrius Road have been built over the rest.

The doctor's surgery is a two-storey red-brick building, long and rectangular, with customer parking behind and in front. We approach on foot because Mum is almost out of petrol. Upstairs has an enclosed balcony that makes it look like a residence. Downstairs, all the doors and windows have bars on them. Sensor lights and a security alarm are wired into the wall by the entrance. A big sign above the door tells us Rosemeadow Medical Centre is open seven days. A smaller sign above the window says they have a lady doctor. A note on the front door advises no drugs or cash are kept on the premises.

The waiting room is full, and the lady at reception says all doctors are running behind schedule due to an earlier medical emergency, 'Take a seat'. Mum and I sit in plastic chairs connected at the sides. She picks up a glossy magazine from 1991.

'Have you ever wondered why this place is called Rosemeadow?' I ask.

'Not really, no.'

'It's named after a guy called Thomas Rose. He used to own all this land. Bought it when it was part of Mount Gilead farm.'

'Oh, yeh?'

'Yeh.'

Mum turns back to the dated, glossy magazine, completely uninterested. I open *The Handmaid's Tale*.

'You know, there's a country in this book I'm reading called Gilead.'

'Oh, yeh? Is it nice?'

'No.'

Mum nods into the shiny pages.

Dr Dwyer wears glasses, black Gucci frames. I saw that brand in the *Harper's Bazaar* magazine in the waiting room. It's very expensive. Behind the glasses, there's brown eyes. His square jaw is clean shaven, his teeth so straight and white he could be a Colgate model. He tightens a tourniquet around my right arm and feels for a vein. His hands are soft and smooth, his rounded nails buffed. I look down at my callused palm and close my fingers to hide it, unintentionally revealing the dirt under my nails, so deep I can't reach it with a nail brush or file.

'This is to check for HIV, hepatitis B and hepatitis C.' Dr Dwyer swipes the inside of my elbow with an antiseptic wipe and releases the tourniquet. 'Little sting,' he warns.

I watch the needle slide in under my skin, piercing my vein, and blood pour into one, two, three vials. A cottonwool bud obscures my view of the needle being removed.

'Hold it there,' Dr Dwyer says.

I press it in place with my least dirty finger. He rolls back to his desk, pushing his ergonomic chair across the floor with brown leather loafers. The clasp on his shiny silver wristwatch scrapes against the desk as he scribbles my details on the sticky labels of the three small glass vials before returning with a round skin-coloured bandaid.

'I need to give you a tetanus shot and a booster for hepatitis B.' He rubs another antiseptic wipe over my upper arm. We're both wearing white shirts, but his is whiter than mine. 'Try to relax.'

There's a sharp sting. Two of them. I squeeze my eyes shut, clench my teeth. A dull muscle ache follows.

Dr Dwyer issues two more bandaids. 'Your arm might feel sore for a few days.' He spins back to his desk, moves the mouse, brings his computer screen back to life and pokes at the keyboard with his two forefingers.

'When do we get the results of the blood tests?' Mum asks.

'We'll need to re-check HIV status in three months and hepatitis serology in three and six months.'

I stare at the university degrees that hang on the wall above his desk, feeling even more out of reach now. The closest anyone in our family has come to university is Mum and me driving past the University of Western Sydney Campbelltown Campus on the way to Nanna and Pop's place.

'That's a long time to go without knowing.' Mum folds her arms across the front of her Midnight Oil T-shirt.

'We see this happen with kids a lot around here and, in most cases, everything turns out to be just fine,' Dr Dwyer says.

I know he's probably just trying to ease her fears in the

detached, statistical way that doctors do, but he says it so casually, so dismissively – like it's nothing, like it's expected, like it doesn't even matter. Like I don't matter. Just another day in Rosemeadow, he probably thinks. But it's not. Not for me.

30

Charlie has recorded 'Barbie Girl' by Aqua on her pink plastic battery-operated stereo. The song's a few years old now, but it's still her favourite. We rewind the cassette and listen to it on repeat, practising dance steps on the dry and mostly dead front lawn.

I hear the screen door slam shut, see Rob appear on the driveway. He sticks his fingers in his mouth and whistles at me. That's the command for me to come. I'm no dog, so I ignore him. He whistles again and I keep dancing, pretending I can't hear him over the music. Charlie looks at me. Worry widens her eyes and wrinkles her forehead, but she follows my lead.

'Oi!' He shouts so loud that the drunks passed out at the outdoor setting across the road are startled awake.

'What?' I spin around.

'Don't fuckin' "what?" me, you little ingrate. You come when I call you.'

Charlie presses pause. I walk up the driveway. Rob stands with his hand on his hip, foot jutted out. His face does its sniff-twitch.

'What have I done now?' I ask.

'More like what you haven't done.'

'What haven't I done, then?'

'What'd I say about playing out here before all your chores were done?'

'I got up early and did all my chores before I went to school today.'

'Well, the dishes need to be done.'

'The sink was empty when I left this morning.'

'Yeh, well, now it's not.'

'I'll clean it again after dinner.'

I turn to walk away, but he grabs me by the arm, hard.

'Are you deaf, dumb or stupid?'

'Let go of me.' I try to shake him off.

'What part of what I just said didn't you understand?'

'I'm not playing. We're rehearsing for the school talent show tomorrow. Our teacher nominated us to perform. It's to celebrate the end of the year. I don't know all my steps yet. Charlie is teaching me.'

'Bullshit.'

'It's not. It's for school. I can show you the flyer.'

'Go and do the dishes like I asked and then you can come back out.'

'I can't. This is the only time Charlie has. Then she has to go and visit her Mum in hospital.' I look to Charlie and she nods. 'See? I can do them as soon as I come inside. I promise.'

'I've told you to get your arse inside and clean the kitchen.'

'No.'

'What did you just say to me?' Rob raises his eyebrows, eyes narrow.

'I said no. This is my homework. I'm going to get up there tomorrow and look like an idiot. My teachers are going to be angry. Everyone is going to laugh at me.'

Rob leans in and points a fat, hairy finger in my face. A stubbie of VB is clenched in his fist. I feel his spittle on my skin. 'I said get your arse inside, right fucking now.'

'No.' I take a step back. 'You're not my dad. You can't tell me what to do.'

We glare at each other. I watch Rob's face turn from red to purple. A vein pulses in the side of his head. He looks up and around the street. Realising all eyes are on us, he nods, does his sniff-twitch and heads back up the driveway. I wince as the front door slams shut behind him.

*

'Is Shayla home?' I hear Charlie ask at the front door.

'Yeh, darl, she is,' Mum says. 'But she can't come out. She's grounded.'

'Again?'

Yes. Again. For the whole school holidays. I was only allowed out of my bedroom for three hours on Christmas Day. And those three hours, which included cleaning up after everyone, could only be taken in half and whole hours, so Rob could keep count while drinking.

'Can you give her this for me then?'

'What is it?'

'It's the *Xena* tape she's been after. The last-ever episode. I taped it for her, but Bobby put it in the wrong cover and I couldn't find it anywhere until last night when I was helping her clean her room.'

Because even when I wasn't grounded, Rob always took over the telly when I wanted to watch *Xena: Warrior princess*. Even if there was nothing else on, he'd just flick through the channels to upset me.

'I'll make sure she gets it.'

'Cool. I'll come back and get it in a couple of days.'

'You need it back so soon?'

'Dad said he wanted it back in time to tape a movie on Saturday night. Is that alright?'

'It's just that Shayla may not be able to watch it before then.'

I'm not allowed to watch TV. In fact, I'm not even allowed to be in the vicinity of the TV if it's on, which is basically all the time. In an open-plan house, where I can see the TV from the kitchen and dining room, this essentially means I'm banished to my bedroom, unless I'm doing chores. And the list of chores has grown to include almost all of the housework. Mum does the washing and cooking. Rob mows the lawn and cleans the pool. I do the rest. That means I have to be up to clean the kitchen and living areas while everyone's still asleep. Once they're plonked in front of the telly, I move on to the bedrooms and bathroom. I've started to feel like Sara Crewe in

A Little Princess after her father dies and she's exiled to the attic to live and work as a servant girl.

'Being grounded, she's not really allowed to watch TV at the moment,' Mum says.

I'm also not allowed to hang out with Charlie and Sean. I'm not allowed to swim in the pool. I'm not even allowed to sit in the backyard to read my books. I'm worried that, with nothing else to do but read in my room, I don't have enough material to last me until school is back. At the end of term, I discovered the horror section of the library and borrowed as many Diane Hoh books as the librarian would allow, but I'm quickly running out.

'Oh, okay,' Charlie says. 'I just don't have another empty tape to give Dad for his show and I don't want to upset him, that's all.'

I fan myself with *Funhouse*, pulling my shirt away from my skin. It's stinking hot in here. The heat gets trapped in my tiny box of a room, suffocating me. The windows are so small there's no way for me to climb out or for fresh air to get in. All that gets in is the light and heat and noise.

'How about you keep this one then?'

'But then Shayla will never know how the show ends.'

Every night I'm expected to be in bed by eight o'clock and not a minute later, even though the sun is still high in the sky. It's important to time my last trip to the toilet perfectly, because for every minute I'm late to bed, Rob adds more time to my sentence. I don't have a blind, so light streams through the lace curtains. I read until it gets too dark to see, because I'm not allowed to put the light on. When it finally does get dark it's still too hot to sleep. I used to get up and lie on the bathroom tiles to cool down sometimes, but Rob caught on to that and now I'm penalised for every trip to the bathroom after eight o'clock, regardless of the circumstances. Once, I had to vomit, and not only did he add the time on, he rounded it up.

'Well, she's done the wrong thing, so she might just have to miss out,' Mum says. 'Otherwise, she'll never learn.'

★

I watch from the window as Charlie knocks on Sean's front door. He comes out, footy in hand. They talk and look towards my house. I knock on the glass and wave to get their attention, winding the window out while they jog over. Sean gives Charlie a leg up from Pat's driveway. I pull the flyscreen out of the window.

'Here, take this.' She hands me the VHS. 'Watch it when they're asleep or something.'

'Wait a sec.' I open the wardrobe, find an old tape with *Harriet the Spy* and *Matilda* scribbled on the label. 'Take this so you don't get in trouble with your dad.'

Charlie passes it down to Sean. 'Are you okay?' she asks.

I squeeze her hand and nod.

'What the fuck do you think you're doing?' Rob slams my bedroom door into the wall. Again.

My hand slips from Charlie's. I spin towards the sound of his voice and crouch down, making myself small. I can hear Sean and Charlie legging it home, joggers on the driveway; none of us wander around barefoot or in thongs since I stepped on that syringe.

'I was just looking out the window.'

'Oh, yeh. That why the flyscreen's on the floor?'

'I'm trying to get some air. It's so hot in here.'

'And who were you talking to?'

'Myself.'

'Bullshit. Where is it?'

'What?'

'Don't play dumb with me, ya little smartarse. Those little shits were giving ya something. Where is it?'

My eyes betray me, straying to the VHS half under the bed. Rob puts his beer down. There's condensation on the bottle, fresh from the fridge. He wipes his hand down the front of his singlet and snatches the video up.

'That's not ours.' I hold my hands out. 'It's Charlie's. I can go give it back to her.'

'Should've thought 'bout that earlier.' Rob opens the back of the case, rips the black tape from the white spools, scrunches it up in his hand and dumps it on the floor.

Mum and Rob splash around in the pool with the boys, who screech and squeal in delight. I breathe in the smell of chlorine and sunscreen, jealous as I shuffle lethargically around the kitchen, washing dishes, drying them, putting them away. I throw the wet green-and-white-check tea towel in the washing machine and look at my fingers, wrinkled from water and cleaning products. Chores done for the day, I stand in the kitchen and stare sleepily into the middle distance, waiting for the kettle to boil so I can make a coffee and try to wake myself up a bit. The *TV Guide* slips off one of the shelves in Mildred's full-wall entertainment unit and draws my eyes to a small red flashing light that was hidden beneath it. Rob's new video camera.

Bubbles in the kettle grow louder. Steam rises from the spout. The on switch clicks into the off position. And all the energy sapped from me by hot and sleepless nights seeps back in.

I stare at the little red light, watching me, surveilling me in my own house. My house. My house with Mum and the boys. Not his house. He shouldn't even be here. I pour hot water into my coffee cup, heat and steam rising. I want to throw the camcorder on the ground and stamp on it. I want to pull the cabinet doors off their hinges, slam them so hard the glass shatters. I want to swipe my arms across the shelves and watch all of Mildred's brown and beige ornaments smash on the floor, broken to smithereens.

Instead, I stick both middle fingers up in front of the lens. 'Fuck you, Rob.' Then I turn the camera off and slap the *TV Guide* down on the dining table, right in the middle, so he can see it as soon as he comes through the back door.

I take my coffee down the front steps just as I hear Mum coming inside to put some music on. She turns up Icehouse, 'Great Southern Land', as I sit in the gutter, watching black ash fall from the sky.

Some of it still has an orange glow as it descends upon

Rosemeadow. What the news is calling the Black Christmas bushfires are still burning, gusty winds fanning the flames and smudging the blue sky with hazy grey. I look to my left and see a stretcher being rolled out of the house three doors down by two paramedics, the body on it completely covered and unmoving.

There's no sign of rainfall. Grass is yellow, so dry it crunches beneath my feet. Birds wander around parched, beaks open, in search of water. I watch the stretcher being placed in the back of the ambulance. The wheels fold up under the bed and double doors close behind it.

Another police car silently arrives. The air is hot and smoky and dry. A bright ember, carried on the wind, floats and flutters. It lands at my feet and fizzles out like a faulty streetlight as soon as it touches the concrete of Westminster Way. I reach out to touch it. Cold and dead, it leaves marks on my fingertips, lead-pencil grey.

No lights, no sirens, no rush. I watch the ambulance indicator blink, slowly, before it turns left onto Copperfield Drive and disappears towards Campbelltown Hospital. Sean sits down next to me and stares through his arms, rested on his knees, at the footy between his feet.

I point my thumb over my shoulder. 'Another one bites the dust.'

'I heard them having a big fight last night,' Sean says.

'I think I did too. I mean, I must've, right?'

'It was pretty loud.'

'Why didn't you call the police?'

'I dunno.' Sean's head snaps up. 'Why didn't *you* call the police?'

'I'm not sure I heard it. It all just fades into the background for me now. And when I do hear it, I'm not even sure it's real. Sometimes I think they've just screamed so loud and so long it's gotten stuck in my ears, like an echo. You notice these things more because your parents don't fight.'

Sean swallows and his sharp Adam's apple, becoming more prominent in his thin neck, bobs up and down. Then he says to his feet, 'Do ya think he killed her?'

'Maybe.' I look over my shoulder, count the cars, the cops. 'There's more cops than usual.'

'I heard my folks talking 'bout it.' Sean leans in close, speaks quietly. 'Mum said he smothered her in her sleep with a pillow. Dad said he went back to sleep afterwards and called triple-0 this morning, pretended he woke up and found her dead in the bed beside him.'

I squint at the street, try to remember if I did actually hear them fighting last night, but my memory is as hazy as the sky.

'Sometimes it's hard to know when to call the cops, ya know?' Sean continues. 'Like, ya don't know if ya helping someone, or just pissing them off. That's why we knock and run.'

'Did you knock and run last night?'

Sean shakes his head. 'Ain't nowhere to hide with his place. He can see the whole street from his front door. Then, when he dobs me in to my parents, what help am I to you or Charlie or anyone?' Sean holds his head in his hands.

'It's not your fault. You're just a kid. No-one called the cops. They never do. It's like the law around here, isn't it?'

'I know, but I still feel shit about it.'

'I still feel shit about Steve-o.'

'He wanted to die though.'

'Yeh, but maybe I could have stopped him.'

'He would have done it eventually.'

I nod, eyes on the blue-and-white crime scene tape strung up around the house. 'You know, sometimes I feel like that's the only way we're getting outta here.'

'How?' Sean asks.

'In a body bag.'

'Aren't you still grounded?' Charlie asks.

'Yep.'

'So, what are you doing out here?'

I shrug.

Charlie raises her eyebrows at Sean and sits down next to me. The cops have gone. Kids throw water bombs and shoot water pistols, run shirtless and shoeless around the street.

'I feel like you're grounded all the time,' she says.

'Every single school holiday the past year,' I say. 'And most weekends too.'

'Why?'

'Think he just wants to play happy families with Mum and my brothers and pretend I don't exist.'

Charlie holds my hand and squeezes it. There are black jelly bracelets on her wrists, two of them linked together on each arm. 'What's he grounding you for, anyway? Reading too much?'

'Talking back. Apparently I'm not allowed to speak anymore.'

'What does your mum say?'

'Once she told me that I was too smart for my own good.'

'Did you get in more trouble yesterday?'

'He pulled the insides of your tape out. I'm sorry.'

'Don't worry about it.'

'You can keep the other one.'

'Thanks,' Charlie says. 'Are you okay?'

'Yeh, I'm just upset I'll never get to see how my favourite show ends now, that's all.'

Charlie does her best to catch me up on the episode I've missed, complete with hilarious re-enactments of horses galloping, Gabrielle's high kicks and Xena's war cries. She's almost finished when I hear his voice.

'Shayla, get your arse inside now!'

Rob's waiting for me when I open the front door. He grabs me by the back of my T-shirt and throws me through the air, past the kitchen. The wind is knocked out of me as I land in the dining room, where the *TV Guide* is torn into pieces. I scramble under the dining table. He pulls the chairs out, grabs my foot, pulls me out too. Carpet burns down the side of my body. He yanks me up and pins me against the wall. The whites of his eyes are bloodshot.

His chipped teeth are yellow. Those purple spider veins around his crooked nose have started to cobweb across his cheeks. There's grey in his beard.

'Think you're a smart little bitch, don't ya?' He screams right in my face. His hot breath stinks of beer and stings my eyes, makes them water. 'Gonna cry, are ya?'

I know he won't stop until he gets a reaction. I'm the new Brindy; he wants to break me the way he broke her, making me cry the equivalent of making her piss herself. He keeps repeating himself, maybe because that's the result he's going for, maybe because he has nothing else to say. I feel my throat tighten, jaw lock. *Don't cry, don't cry, that's what he wants.* I lift my eyes to his. I flinch every time he shouts, right up in my face, but I don't look away. He gets louder, closer, as if sensing my resistance. He's so loud and so close I feel the muscles between my mouth and nose begin to twitch. If I was a dog like Brindy, I imagine this is how my face would feel just before I bared my teeth and ripped his fucking face off.

I'm about to break when Mum appears, wide-eyed. Hair, wet from the shower, hangs over the shoulders of her black Placebo T-shirt.

'What the hell is this?' she says.

Rob releases his fist hold on the front of my shirt, so tight the fabric stays peaked, moulded by his grip. My heels suddenly hit the floor. I stumble back into the wall.

'Did you know he was recording me?'

Mum flinches, face folding into a frown. 'What? No. Where? When?'

I don't get time to answer. Her expression quickly shifts from confused and annoyed to disgusted and accusing. Brows raised, lips firm and downturned, her eyes sharpen on Rob. I've never seen her look at him this way. I haven't seen this look on her face since she protected me from Granny in the car park of Casula Fruit Market, since she defended our home from my father at Kikori Place. She straightens up and steps forward. Her voice shakes when she speaks, but not because she's scared – she's fuming.

'What were you doing, recording my daughter?'

Fear chokeholds me against the wall. I hold my breath, waiting for Rob to assert his dominance over Mum and me and the whole situation, but he appears affronted by the question.

He pulls back, head retracting into his neck. 'What the hell do you think I was doing?'

'I don't know,' Mum says. 'But it seems really fucking creepy, if you ask me.'

Rob's eyes widen with disbelief. 'You've gotta be kidding.' He half turns away, then back, points at Mum, then me. 'You saying you think I'm some kinda sicko like her father, are ya?'

'I've asked you a question, Rob, and I want an answer.'

He throws his head back, both hands on his hips. 'Fuckin' bullshit.'

'Now!'

Rob shakes his head, casts his eyes and his hand towards the dining room. 'I wanted to make sure she wasn't damaging my property and blaming Joe for it.'

The lack of conviction in his voice releases me from the angst pressing me against the gyprock.

'What the hell are you talking about?' Mum almost screams.

And her rage fuels mine, gives me courage, gives me strength, because I know she's fighting for me again, so I can fight for me too.

'The heater,' Rob says. 'You can watch the video if you don't believe me.'

The fucking heater. The one he brought over from his dead mother's house and sat behind his chair at the head of the dining table, so he was nice and toasty while he watched the rest of us freeze at dinner during winter. The one Joe has been pulling the front grille off for the past few weeks. Completely re-attachable, mind you. Total fucking non-event.

'You're insane,' I say. 'If I was going to break anything, it would have been that fucking video camera.'

'Don't you speak to me like that, ya little bitch.' He points a hairy finger in my face, so close he almost touches my cheek.

'No, don't you speak to *her* like that.' Mum grabs me, pulls me towards her. 'Get out!'

Her firmness surprises me. It surprises Rob too.

He steps forward, reaches out to her. 'Loz ...'

'Just get out, Rob. Now.'

31

Charlie and Sean tell me they saw him leave. That he slammed the car door and almost ran them over as he sped out of the driveway. That his car looked like it was going to flip over sideways as he screeched out of the street.

Mum tells me she's been on the Housing transfer list since before Steve-o died, and we're almost at the top of the list. 'Pat's getting out too. She got the call a few weeks ago, but I didn't want to say anything in front of him.'

I hear Mum speak to Rob on the phone. 'It's not working, Rob. It hasn't been working for a long time. Ever, really. And as much as you may not like to hear it, I have three kids to think about, not just your two. Shayla's been through enough. And I want to get the boys out of here before they grow up thinking this is normal. So we're leaving this place and you're not coming with us.'

I don't know where Rob is. Maybe he sleeps in his car or stays with his brother for a few days — because that's as long as Mum's resolve lasts. She spends most of that time listening to 'Nothing Compares 2 U' by Sinéad O'Connor, which does my head in, and then he's back.

'Don't shake your head at me like that, Shayla,' Mum says. 'We're not getting back together. He's just got to pack all of his stuff up. And then we need to rip all that shit up out of the backyard so we don't get fined, because none of it was approved by council. It won't be long before we move, and when we do, I won't even let him set foot inside the house. I promise.'

Sweat beads on the bridge of my nose and soaks into the armpits of my shirt. I've stocked up on books from the library and shift the weight of my backpack from one leg to the other. Sean, Charlie and I stand at the bottom of Pat's driveway, each with a thirty-cent soft serve from Macca's. Ice cream runs down the cones onto our fingers, tips stained brown by melted chocolate. We share one Flake between us; bite the end off and pass it on. *When You Grow Up* is sandwiched between my elbow and waist. Connie Nungulla McDonald, the lady who lives next door to Nanna and Pop, wrote it and gave me a signed copy as a gift.

Neighbours have congregated around the white plastic outdoor setting across the street to watch the moving truck pull out of Pat's driveway. It's been more than eighteen months since Steve-o died and since Pat applied to Housing for a transfer. But finally, her day has come. Pat smiles and waves as she pulls out of the driveway and follows the truck. We watch and wave as she turns left out of Westminster Way, onto Copperfield Drive, leaving Rosemeadow behind.

'See?' Sean wipes his hands on his shorts, bounces his footy on the road, catches it. 'Not everyone leaves in a body bag.'

Rob wakes me up early and tasks me with helping fill the enormous hole left behind from the swimming pool. The pool wall, floor and fence have been pulled out and packed up. So have the three sheds. Yesterday, we smashed up the concrete around the pool with a mallet and shovelled it into the hole with Bluey's weathered aviary. The concrete was thin, yellow and crumbly because Rob had mixed in too much sand, but my lower back still hurts. Rob says there's no time for breakfast. Today my job is to help bring soil and sandstone from the front yard to the back: soil in a wheelbarrow, sandstone by hand. He thinks the more rubbish and rock we chuck in, the less he'll have to spend on soil to fill the hole.

'Don't you buy soil by the tonne?'

'What's ya point?'

I gesture at the items being buried in our backyard. 'I just don't think this is going to make a big difference to the amount you have to order, that's all.'

'Well, no-one asked you, did they?'

'What about a council clean-up?'

'We've used them all.'

'What if we take it to the tip?'

'You gonna pay the tip fees? No? Then you have no say. Get back to work.'

Rob's still ripping out the rotten wooden pool deck when I plop down on the back steps around lunchtime, elbows on my knees, hands holding my head. His steel-capped boots come into vision as the hot February sun beats down on my slouched shoulders. My head throbs, my legs feel weak.

'Oi, what do you think ya doing?'

'I just need to get out of the heat for a bit, have something to eat and drink.'

'The faster you finish, the faster you get food.' Rob takes a swig of his VB.

'I'm shaking.' I hold out a dirty hand, covered in scrapes and grazes, to show him. 'I haven't eaten anything since yesterday.'

Rob grabs my arm and roughly pulls me to my feet. It feels like I've been hanging upside down on monkey bars and suddenly stood up. I squeeze my eyes, stumble and sway. Rob tightens his grip until the skin on my arm stings. I can feel my heart beating in my brain, thrumming through my body.

'It's your fault all this is happening anyway. So get back to work.'

He releases his grip, thrusts me forward and I go limp, like a ragdoll. I don't know if my eyes are closed or if I've lost sight, but everything goes dark. There's nothing but blackness and the cool of the ground on my skin as I collapse.

Charlie and Sean are in the gutter when I get home from the five-hour blood test for diabetes that Mum insisted on. That's despite the doctor telling her it was probably a mixture of low blood sugar, sunstroke and dehydration that took me down.

'How come ya weren't at school today?' Sean asks

'Yeh, we were worried,' Charlie says.

'I had to get some blood tests.'

'For the syringe thing?'

'Nah. Gotta get those ones in a few weeks though.'

'For what then?'

'Mum thinks I have diabetes.'

'Why?'

'I fainted yesterday.'

Charlie looks at the bruises on the inside of my elbow.

'They took fourteen vials of blood.'

'You feel okay now?' she asks.

'Yeh.'

Sean looks from the fingerprint marks on my forearm to the sky and shakes his head, as if at God. The gold flecks in his hazel eyes shimmer in the dying sun. His jaw is clenched. Veins strain in his neck.

I fold my arms, putting all my bruises away, and shrug. 'I think it was just because of the heat.'

Sean nods. Slowly. His lips are down-turned, eyes on the footy wedged between his feet.

I sit, squishing in between them, hold my hands out for theirs and squeeze. 'I have to tell you guys something.'

'You're moving,' Charlie says quietly, head down, voice disappearing into her cleavage.

'How'd you know?'

'Well, it sure looks like ya moving.' Sean nods his head towards the house.

I look up the driveway. The carport gate is open. Tools and toys have been packed into recycled boxes and stored under the awning. Rob moves some into the back of his car.

'Where are you going?' Charlie asks.

'I don't know yet. I think Mum's asked for somewhere closer to my grandparents. They're getting on in years.'

'When?'

'Two weeks.'

'I was worried you were leaving today, while we were at school. I wasn't sure I'd get a chance to say goodbye.'

'I'd never leave without saying goodbye. And we'll stay in touch.'

I squeeze Charlie's hand and she squeezes back. I look at the colour of the mood ring on her finger. Black means she's stressed.

'I know,' she says. 'I just panicked.'

'Is he going with you?' Sean asks, eyes on the road.

'No.'

'Good.'

I rest my head on Charlie's shoulder. A spikey bone stabs me in the temple as she takes a deep, shaky breath. Her voice cuts in and out when she speaks. 'Well, I hope you end up some place better than this.'

'She will.' Sean nods like a doggy on a dashboard. 'I mean, how could she not?'

I think of the move from Kikori Place to Mildred's and then Rosemeadow. It makes me laugh out loud.

'What?' Charlie looks worried.

'Let's just say, given our track record so far, I'm not getting my hopes up.'

'As long as you're away from him, it'll be better,' Sean says, as if he's trying to reassure himself.

We lace our arms over each other's shoulders and pull each other close, heads together, like we're in a scrum.

'I'm really going to miss you guys.'

'Remember us when you become a famous author, alright?'

'How could I ever forget you? You've been my best friends through everything.'

Cars pass on Copperfield Drive. Kids ride their bikes up and down Westminster Way. The smell of barbecued meat wafts through the air.

Eventually Charlie sniffle-chuckles. 'Hey, Sean, remember when Shayla first arrived, how white she was?'

'Like a ghost.' Sean laughs.

'Hey, I'm pretty tanned now.'

'Not as tanned as me.' Sean holds his forearm out, against mine.

'That's not a fair comparison. You're naturally dark.'

'Put ya arm against Charlie's then. Yeh. See?'

'It's 'cause she was stuck inside, grounded the whole bloody time.'

I roll my eyes. Charlie laughs. Sean slaps his knee.

'Oh, oh, do ya remember the time ...'

We sit in the gutter and reminisce about the past five years, until stars sparkle above the street.

I walk down the centre of the driveway, shoes in hand. I go slowly, carefully watching every single step, because I've learnt my lesson about being barefoot, but I want to feel the pebblecrete dig into my soles one last time. It doesn't hurt anymore. Nothing much hurts anymore. This place has made me tough, and not just the bottoms of my feet.

It's a sunny yet crisp autumn morning. The perfect day for a fresh start. Dew drops shine like diamonds on the front lawn. The sun is golden. The air is cold. It burns a little when I breathe in deep, but it feels cleansing. The telephone rings in the house, but I keep walking. I watch my feet move forward, one step at a time, one foot in front of the other, until I reach the end of the driveway.

'Hey,' Mum calls. 'The doctor just rang.'

I hold my breath. She slides a box into the tailgate.

'Your test results are all clear.'

I watch the breath leave my body in tiny puffs of smoke. Breath. I can see it. I'm getting out of here alive. There's no body bag for me. No diabetes. No HIV. No hepatitis. Nothing bad following me.

'Don't be long, okay?'

I slip my feet inside my shoes, walk up to Charlie's and down to Sean's. They've gone to school early for a Year 9 excursion, but I leave something for each of them on their front doorsteps. Nothing fancy. I don't have much to give. Charlie gets one of Mum's dream dictionaries that I saved from our garage sale and a pair of evil eye earrings that I made for her. Sean gets a Western Suburbs Magpies keyring and a copy of *The Merry Adventures of Robin Hood,* stealing from the rich to give to the poor. Each book has a short message from me on the title page, saying thank you and goodbye.

Mum starts to load the boys into the car, wings spread across the back of her black Eagles T-shirt. Her hair is freshly dyed dark red for the move. The removalist pulls down the roller door on the back of the truck. I take one last look around Westminster Way, taking it all in. The unmarked police car at the bottom of the street where Sean's footy got run over. The skinheads at the top. The rubbish dumped on the kerb. The tree on the corner of Mowbray Way where I stepped on the syringe. The rusted car full of stray cats. The dirty outdoor setting covered in empty goon bags. The carport where Steve-o died. The front lawn where Charlie and I made up dance moves to 'Barbie Girl'. The gutter where I read books, made friends, laughed and cried, looked to the sky and at the stars.

Some of the younger kids I go to school with walk past and wave goodbye. Their school shirts, stained and wrinkled, hang loose on their tiny bodies, always a bit too big, so they last longer, get grown into. I watch after them until they disappear, a pang in my chest because I know I'll probably never see them again. I hope they'll be alright.

The moving truck pulls out of the driveway and heads down the street. I close my eyes and think of Pat, smiling and waving goodbye. But this time, it'll be Mum's rusty white Ford station wagon turning left out of Westminster Way, onto Copperfield Drive, leaving Rosemeadow behind. And I'll be sitting in the passenger seat.

When we're on the M5 I put my hand out the window, roll my

wrist up and down, making waves. The air feels full of promise, possibility at my fingertips, opportunity waiting to be seized. I close my eyes, let the wind blow in my hair, feel hopeful and fresh and free, as Mum cruises towards Sydney.

The boys are asleep in the back seat when Mum takes the Fairford Road exit and turns right at the lights. She sings along to 'You're the Voice' with John Farnham while I look out the window at the light industrial area. Factories and warehouses here aren't as big and modern as the ones out Campbelltown way, possibly because this is an older area.

We pass the sign to Padstow Shopping Village and the area quickly becomes more residential. The streets are wider here and they actually go somewhere, connecting with other streets, instead of all being dead-ends. The houses are bigger, further apart, and each of them looks different from the one next door. There's light and air and space. Fairford Road becomes Davies Road and Mum turns into Alma. She lowers the music and looks for number seventy-nine, somewhere on the left. I feel my heart flutter with anticipation as she pulls into the driveway of our new home.

I hop out of the car and look around, expecting spectators, but no-one watches us arrive. No-one is sitting out the front of their house to have a stickybeak. People walk, jog and drive by, but they don't even look our way, too busy with their own lives to bother themselves with us.

The house is green fibro with a brick chimney. In the backyard, there's a big, bare jacaranda tree that promises to flower beautifully in late spring. By the front door, there's a yellow frangipani tree nearing the end of its blooming season, and fallen flowers carpet the front lawn. I bring one of the waxy, slightly bruised flowers to my nose, and it still smells sweet. The back of the moving truck rolls up and the ramp lowers. I ignore the beep, beep, beep ringing in my ears, the sound of Mum trying the wrong keys in the lock of the screen door, the cries of Nash and Joe still stuck in the back seat. I close my eyes and breathe in deeply, imagining a tropical island getaway, like on *Sydney Weekender*, letting the idea fill me up. Escape, I think. This is the smell of escape.

'Oi, Loz!' A familiar voice shakes me from my daydream. 'Where'd ya want this?' Rob slams his car door and strides across the front lawn, flanno over trackies, shiny disco ball in hand.

'Just in here.' Mum holds the front door open, and he steps inside.

32

It's not until my first class at Picnic Point High School that I realise they've changed the uniform slightly since my dress was donated to the school office. The pinstripe is thicker now, a slightly darker shade of green. The collar is a little less pointy, a little more Peter Pan.

Someone kicks the back of my chair. 'How come the new girl has an old dress?'

I turn in my seat. There's a row of three behind me. Two girls, one boy. The girl asking the question has multicoloured braces and mousy brown hair. It hangs limply past her shoulders, oily at the roots, not unlike the skin on her face, dotted with yellow pus-filled pimples. I quickly scan the classroom. All the other girls are wearing the new dress. Their uniforms are clean and ironed. Their shoes are black and shiny. Bright-white socks poke out around their ankles. I don't want to be the Picnic Point High School equivalent of the Glenfield Public School wee girl, so I lie.

'My mum's friend gave it to her for me.'

I turn back to the English teacher. Short, round and dressed in black, she shakes her bouffant hair, stiff with hairspray, at the rowdy Year 9 class. A Russian accent floats from her pouty red lips as she instructs the class to be quiet. There's a beauty spot above her lips, like Marilyn Monroe. The girl behind kicks my chair again. I tuck it in tighter.

'Where'd she get it?'

'Her daughter must have come here,' I say over my shoulder.

I hear her slide down in the plastic chair behind me. 'Who's her daughter?' She kicks the back of my chair again.

I spin around, arm out, hand up. 'Stop.'

She stares at me, a blank yet insolent look on her face, and asks again. 'Who's her daughter?'

'I don't know.' I stare back, eyebrows raised. 'Her mum worked with my mum. I don't know either of them.'

She opens her mouth to say something, transparent rubber bands hooked on to her braces covered in spit. The dark-haired boy sitting next to her shuts his book, puts it on the desk and shakes his head. I notice he has an eyebrow piercing.

'No-one cares, Larissa,' he says. 'Stop being a bully.'

Larissa closes her mouth like a goldfish and swallows. A blotchy red rash works its way up her neck to her acne-scarred cheeks. She tilts her head towards the girl sitting next to her but doesn't look away. Instead she scrunches up her face, as if in distaste. 'What's wrong with her eyes?'

I feel myself blench, but Larissa doesn't notice. She's too busy sneering and sniggering, making her face uglier with every mean expression. I want to tell her if the wind changes she'll be stuck like that. Instead, I feign nonchalance and intellectual superiority. 'It's actually called *heterochromia iridis*, if you must know.'

'What?' Larissa scrunches her face up even more. 'Speak English, loser.'

'Don't worry, new girl.' The boy to the right lifts his backpack onto his lap, slides his book inside. 'Larissa doesn't understand Latin. She barely even understands Shakespeare.' He winks at me with chocolate-brown eyes. A cheeky smile slips across his face and a dimple appears in one cheek. He stands, taller than me, and puts his backpack on the table. 'Ignore her,' he says. 'She's just insecure.'

Larissa scoffs, folds her arms across her chest, red rash now up to her hairline. Dimple boy keeps his head down, focusing on zipping up his backpack. His olive-skinned hands are veiny, but in a nice way. I'm surprised by how my attention is drawn to them.

'There's nothing wrong with your eyes.' Dimple boy smiles up at me from under a flop of brown hair. 'I think they're beautiful.'

*

I walk through the quad, head in a book. I haven't been given a buddy like I was on my first day at Rosemeadow Public School. I think of Charlie and Sean and feel sick about losing the piece of paper with their phone numbers on it in the move, about not leaving them a number to call me on because I didn't know what it would be. Mum said I can't write to them because she doesn't want anyone from there having our new address – or our deliberately silent phone number. I tried to look them up in the *White Pages*, but their parents weren't listed either.

I go down the stairs and past the canteen towards D-block, which the map tells me is the woodwork and metalwork demountable, and spot dimple boy outside the school gate. He's smoking, holding the cigarette between his thumb and forefinger. Our eyes meet and he smiles wide. I feel my heart lurch, like it's tripped over its own feet, and look back over my shoulder to see who he's smiling at. There's no-one there. My face burns with embarrassment and I give a small wave. He takes another puff of his cigarette, stamps it out and shakes his floppy-haired head while he has a quiet laugh.

'Yeh, new girl, I was smiling at you,' he says. 'What's your name, anyway?'

'Shayla.'

'Nice name. Matches your eyes. Unusual, but beautiful.'

I look at my feet, unsure of what to say.

'I'm Mirko.'

'That's an unusual name too.'

'Means peace and celebration.'

'Where's it from?'

'Malta. My parents were born there.' Mirko puts his hands in his pockets. 'What about you? Any special name story?'

'I was named after a Blondie song released in 1979, if that counts.'

'Yeh.' Mirko nods. 'I'd say it does.'

Mirko's eyes never leave my face, and even though I'm used to Rosemeadow where people just stare at you, this is something else, unlike anything I've ever experienced before. I don't know how to respond, so I just look over his shoulder.

'So, you like books.' Mirko points to *Firehead* by Venero Armanno. 'Do you like music?'

'I do.'

'What kind?'

'All kinds. I don't discriminate.'

'What *part* of the music do you enjoy the most?'

'Oh, now that's a good question.'

Mirko looks at me. One arm crosses his body, the other holding his chin while he studies my face. I try to avoid his gaze, but my eyes are drawn to his as if magnetised. The corners of his lips twitch and slowly, softly curve into a smile.

My face feels hot. I laugh nervously and run my hand through my hair, pushing it out of my face. 'I haven't been asked that question before.'

'Take your time.'

He reaches out and takes the book I'm carrying. I watch his hands hold the spine and open the cover. He flips through the pages, turning them gently, carefully, like they're precious, alive. And when I finally tear my eyes away, I realise his eyes have never once left my face. He's just been watching me watch him.

He's taller than me, but he doesn't stand over me. He doesn't break eye contact, but he doesn't try to stare me down. It just feels like I have his complete and undivided attention. Like there's no-one else in the world but me. It's so intense it's difficult to breathe or swallow. I have to look away to gather my thoughts, to answer his question. 'The lyrics.'

'Makes sense that as a lover of words you'd be drawn towards the lyrical component of music. You know what doesn't make sense?' He hands the book back.

'What?'

'Why you won't look at me. Am I that ugly?'

'No.'

'What is it then?'

'It's just … I dunno. The *way* you look at me.'

'I can stop, if it's making you uncomfortable.'

'No. It's just a bit … intense. I'm not used to being looked at the way you're looking at me.'

'And how's that?'

'For so long!'

'I like looking at you.'

'Well,' I say, waving my arms, feeling flustered. 'I don't know what to do with that.'

'Enjoy it.' Mirko shrugs.

I shake my head at his simple response and the stupid smile I can feel spread across my face, because I *am* enjoying it.

'You know what I think?' he asks.

'What?'

'I think you've got a little crush on me.'

'Oh, really?'

'Yeh, but don't worry. I'm okay with it.'

'Gee, thanks.'

'No worries.'

I stare at my school shoes, unsure of what to say next, but not wanting the conversation to end, because maybe he's right – maybe I do have a crush on him. 'So, Larissa. She's a bit of a cow.'

Mirko nods. 'Brave of you to stand up to her on your first day. She looked like a stunned mullet. I was impressed.'

'Well, personally, I'm a little disappointed I didn't even make it through my first class before making an enemy.'

'You also made a friend.' Mirko looks at me from under his fringe.

'That's true. Thanks for standing up for me in there. It *really* got her nose out of joint.'

'Well, that's probably because she's got a huge crush on me.'

'Mhmm. And why am I not surprised to hear that?'

Mirko shrugs. 'Because you have a huge crush on me too.'

I roll my eyes.

'Don't worry.' He smiles, dimple showing. 'I like you better.'

Mirko points me in the direction of the library. It's at the back of the school, above the science block, up two dark flights of stairs. This is what I've been waiting for. Each new school I've gone to has gifted me a bigger, better, more beautiful library. The libraries at Rosemeadow Public and Ambarvale High were modern, expansive and full of hidden treasures. My chest fills with anticipation and I clutch my book against it, as if that will help contain the excitement. Instead it bubbles up and spills onto my face. I can feel myself smiling like an idiot as I climb the stairs two at a time and fling the door open wide.

'Well, are you coming in or not?' a woman asks. She's wearing winkled linen and has hairy caterpillar eyebrows.

'Sorry,' I say from the doorway. 'Is this the library?'

She opens a book, stamps the inside cover, hands it to a student, eyebrows raised. 'First day?'

I nod.

'You're here to see the guidance counsellor?'

I look at the piece of paper I've been given. 'Miss Miller?'

'Back right corner.'

'Thanks.'

The library is small and dim. It smells like dust and mothballs, and reminds me of being locked inside Nanna's wardrobe on Mum's last day at Family Law Court. Miss Miller's office is hidden behind the last row of bookshelves. The windows are filled with book posters, probably to provide some extra privacy, but the door is open. I poke my head inside. 'Knock, knock.'

'Hi,' Miss Miller says, looking up from her desk. 'You must be Shayla. Come on in. Take a seat.'

A couple of padded chairs have been set up across from each other, a small coffee table with a box of tissues between them. Miss Miller stands up and closes the door behind me. She's barefoot, skin-coloured stilettos kicked off under the desk. She wears a sleeveless navy knit dress. Blonde hair reaches her shoulders and there are three chickenpox scars on her forehead. She plops down across from me.

'Welcome to Picnic Point High School.'

'Thank you.'

'I saw you're joining us from Ambarvale High.'

'I am.'

There's a file on the coffee table with my name on it. It makes me think back to starting at Rosemeadow Public School, sitting in the principal's office with Mum.

'So this is just a standard first-day meeting.' Miss Miller clasps her hands together. 'I like to meet all our new students. Some kids find it difficult to start at a new school. We want them to know they're supported.'

I open my hands in my lap. 'I've done this before. This is school number four for me.'

'So you've had practice.' Miss Miller smiles. 'Good! How are you finding it here so far?'

'Fine.'

She takes a sip of coffee, waits for me to elaborate.

'Different.'

'Different to Ambarvale or different to what you expected?'

'Both.'

'How?'

I look around and shrug. 'Well, I thought the library would be nicer.'

'Don't let Ms Anderson hear you say that.' Miss Miller laughs. 'What else?'

'Well, I assume you guys don't have an agricultural plot?'

'You had agricultural classes? What did you learn in them?'

'I know how to castrate a goat.'

'What?'

'Yeh, you just put a rubber band around—'

Miss Miller holds her hand up like a stop sign. 'So it's' – she nods – 'different. Have you made any friends?'

'I think so. I met someone nice in my English class.'

'Who's that?'

'Mirko.'

'Ah, the boy who smokes cigarettes outside the school gates.'

'He stood up for me, which I thought was nice.'

'Why did he have to stand up for you?'

'I'm not exactly wearing the latest school fashions, am I?' I uncross my arms, drop them down the sides of the chair. 'One of the girls noticed. She wanted to know why the new girl had an old dress.'

Miss Miller eyes my second-hand uniform.

I pick at the pleated skirt. 'The office lady failed to mention the uniform had been updated.'

'I think you're just ahead of your time,' Miss Miller says. 'There's a whole movement around environmentally and socially sustainable fashion.' Miss Miller flicks her hair back over her shoulder with an air of superiority that reminds me of Evan from the New Year's Eve party at Aunty Barb's, but in a good way. She opens my file, pulls out a copy of my latest report card. 'And speaking of being ahead of everyone else, your grades are amazing.'

'Thank you.'

Miss Miller flips the file shut, crosses her arms on her knees and leans forward. 'We spend a lot of our lives trying to fit in when we're actually meant to stand out,' she says. 'The stuff that matters to mean girls in high school doesn't translate to the real world. And that's going to be a very rude awakening for some of them when they leave here. You're smart, Shayla, and you've done this before, so you're resilient. If you've already mastered the art of banding a goat, there's nothing you can't do.'

33

The bell rings. I meet Mirko in the food tech rooms and he plates up lunch for the two of us in the empty classroom, as if it's a private dining room in a fancy restaurant. Black half-apron tied around his waist, tea towel over his shoulder, he lifts a spoon to my mouth and shakes his head when I try to take it from him. 'Na-uh. Open.' He cups one hand under the spoon as he brings it to my mouth. I close my eyes. The warm metal grazes my bottom lip and its contents spill into my mouth. 'What do you think?'

'My compliments to the chef.'

'Thank you.' Mirko takes a bow and I note a freckle on top of his ear with the piercings – stud in the lobe, bar through the top.

'So you want to be a chef?'

'I do.'

'Why?'

'What greater joy in life than sharing good food with great company?'

'How very hospitable of you.'

Mirko leans over the table, hands clasped, eyes intense as always. 'Speaking of hospitality, skip sport with me today. I want you to come over.'

'To your house?'

Mirko nods.

'Won't your parents be home?'

'They're at work till five.'

We've been together since that first day. But it's been little more than a school-based flirtation. Legs grazing under the desk as we share a book in English class. Bumping into each other in the school halls. Tickling. A friendly poke in the arm to say hello that I know will instigate a tight hug around the waist. Really, any excuse to touch each other, be close to each other, without being too close. There are still butterflies in my stomach when I see him. He's the first thing I think about when I wake up and the last thing I think about before I go to sleep. When I get home from school, he calls to check I got there safely, and we talk for hours. But we've never been to each other's houses.

'Don't worry, we won't be alone.' He winks as if he can read my thoughts. 'A couple of the guys are coming over to jam.'

Mirko doubles me home on his BMX. I stand on the pegs, stomach pressed against his back, arms wrapped around his neck, breasts – just starting to blossom – pressed against his shoulders. I wonder if he can feel my heart thump against his back as I breathe in the smell of him: minty chewing gum and Lynx deodorant. His back is hot and damp with sweat from pedalling in the early summer sun and the heat of our two bodies pushed together. He pulls up in front of a two-storey house on Gallipoli Street. It's brick and square with a big white fountain in the front yard and metal bars on the windows.

'Welcome to the wog box.' He looks at his watch. 'The guys will be here soon, so I better set up, and then I can give you the grand tour afterwards. That okay?'

'Who's coming?'

'My mates Christopher and Nicolas. We used to go to primary school together. Now they go to De La Salle Catholic College.'

Ambulance sirens, screeching on their way to and from Bankstown Hospital, melt away as we enter the cool of the house with its tiled floors, high ceilings and ducted air conditioning.

'Hello,' he calls from the foyer.

'I thought you said your family would be out.'

'Yeh, they should be,' he whispers back. 'Just got to check in case they've come home early.'

The only answer is that of Beethoven, the family's old Saint Bernard, named after the 1990s kids movie. His nails tap on the tiles as he pads through the foyer to sniff at my feet. I kneel to pat his head and rub behind his velvety-soft ears. We're at the bottom of a staircase that flares out into the foyer, dividing it in half. A large wrought-iron chandelier dangles from the ceiling. I point at the painting on the wall at the top of the stairs. 'That's beautiful.'

'Thanks. I painted it.'

'No, you didn't.'

'Yes, I did.'

I stand, head back, mouth open, marvelling at it. 'How did you get so talented?'

Mirko shrugs. 'My family's pretty creative.' He opens double doors on the left. 'This is our music room.'

There's a drum kit in the centre of the room, an upright piano against the wall, a guitar on the stand in the corner.

'So who taught you how to play?'

'Mum teaches piano. Dad plays guitar. That's how they met. Playing at a concert in a little village in Malta. My brother plays the drums.'

'Don't your neighbours get annoyed with all the noise?'

'Nah. This room is soundproof.'

I stand at the piano and tap out the opening notes of 'My Heart Will Go On' from the *Titanic* movie while he sets up.

'Want to see my party trick?'

'Sure.'

Mirko sits on the floor, back to the keys, hands over his shoulders, and plays 'Ode to Joy'.

'Show-off.'

He winks and holds his hand out to be helped up. I pull too hard, and we bump into each other. His hands gently squeeze the tops of my arms and I feel his warm breath in my hair.

'Sorry.'

'Don't be.'

Our voices are quiet, breathy. He lingers. My body tingles. I stare at his lips, full and soft and pink, and watch the lump in his throat bob up and down as he swallows. He slides his hands along my arms until our fingers are entwined. And the doorbell rings.

Mirko closes his eyes as he plays the opening instrumental of 'Bitter Sweet Symphony' solo on the piano. I set *Angela's Ashes* aside and watch his fingers dance across the keys, soft and slow to begin with. The notes, clear and defined, carry across the quiet room, filling the space as they become more layered. His fingers move faster, but with no less precision, as the music gains momentum, and I feel as if it grows stronger inside of me too. Nick and Chris join in on electric guitar and drums as the instrumental reaches the peak of its crescendo. And when I hear his voice, I'm transfixed.

He turns from the piano and I must look awestruck. I *feel* awestruck.

'What?'

He's so nonchalant.

'You can sing?'

'A little.'

'He's our lead vocalist,' Nick says.

'Good, huh?' Chris chimes in.

'Yeh, really good.' I turn back to Mirko. 'And what, you just kept this hidden from me for nine months?'

He shrugs and moves to the stool by the guitar stand in the corner of the room. 'I'm full of surprises.' He picks up the guitar and puts it over his knee.

'Any other hidden talents you're keeping from me?'

'Let me think about it and get back to you.'

He strums the opening chords to 'Wonderwall' and the band kick in after him. I can feel his eyes on my face, but I'm captivated by his hands, how they pluck and strum at the strings.

As the band concludes their cover of 'Iris', I finally begin to understand why Charlie had so many posters of the Hanson brothers on her bedroom wall. I think I'm in love.

'You guys are amazing!'

Nick and Chris have packed up and left. I'm following Mirko upstairs to finish off the grand tour of his house.

'You know what would have been more amazing?'

'What?'

'If they hadn't shown up exactly when then did.'

He opens the door to his bedroom and I look around. There's a built-in wardrobe, a single bed made with a blue doona, and a television on top of a chest of drawers. Mirko turns on the TV, flicks through the channels and settles on *Ready Steady Cook*, while I look at the visual arts diary left open on his computer desk.

'I've been working on adding a new song to our repertoire that I wouldn't mind audience testing with you in a couple of weeks, if that's okay? Before I tell the guys about it.'

'Sounds good.'

I sit on the floor, back against his bed, and check out his music collection. His bedside table has been converted into a CD stand, drawers replaced with black plastic racks.

'I made that in woodwork.'

'Is there anything you can't do?' I feign annoyance. 'I'm starting to feel like an underperformer.'

Mirko sits down next to me. 'I haven't been able to kiss you yet.'

I push the CDs in to pop them out. 'I didn't know you wanted to.'

Blink-182, Coldplay, Eminem.

'Yeh, you did.'

Good Charlotte, Linkin Park, Muse.

'Then why haven't you?'

They're all in alphabetical order.

'I guess I've felt nervous. This will be my first time.'

I pull out the CD single of 'Teenage Dirtbag' by Wheatus. 'Your first kiss?'

'Yeh. Why? What did you think I was talking about?'

I feel my face flush and put the CD back. 'It'll be my first kiss too.'

I'm too nervous to make eye contact, so I focus on the unbuttoned V-neck of his polo shirt, which doesn't make me any less flustered.

'Hey,' he says, putting his finger under my chin and gently lifting my face to his, my eyes to his. 'I really want to kiss you.' He traces his thumb along my bottom lip. 'And I think you want to kiss me too.' His eyes search mine for an answer, for permission.

My voice is almost a whisper, a vow. 'I do.'

He smiles, squeezes my hand, looks around the room. 'You know what I think might make this a little less scary?'

'What?'

He pulls the doona from the bed over our heads and kisses me in the dark.

34

'So, where are you guys going?'

'Bonnie Vale Campground,' Mum says. 'We took you there once when we were living at Rob's mother's place. I'm not sure if you remember it.'

'How could I forget?'

Mum rolls her eyes.

'But thanks for the invite.'

'Would you have come?'

'Not if he was going, no.'

'So, what's the point of asking?'

'Well, it's the polite thing to do since, you know, I am your daughter.'

'Really? Because you wouldn't know it from the way you talk to me.'

'Yeh, it's also kinda hard to tell when your mother says she's taking her kids away for a few days in the school holidays, and then tells you you'll be staying with your grandparents.'

'You said you wouldn't come, so what's the problem?'

'My problem is that when we moved here you said you weren't even going to let him in the house, but he's always here.'

'He's not *always* here.'

'He's here all weekend, every weekend. And sometimes through the week. You even let him sleep in your bed.'

'Well, where do you expect him to sleep? I can't kick the boys out of their beds.'

'He shouldn't be sleeping here at all!'

'I'm not having sex with him, if that's what you think.'

'That's not the point. You're not together. You said we moved here so you could get away from him, but he's still hanging around.'

'He's the boys' father, Shayla. What do you want me to do?'

'What all other parents who have separated do: let the boys visit him every second weekend. This situation you're in is completely dysfunctional and it's confusing them.'

'It's not.'

'It is. They don't know if you're together or not. I'm ten years older than them and even I don't understand it.'

'I'm not having this conversation, Shayla. I don't have to answer to you or anyone else.'

'You asked me what my problem was and I'm telling you.'

'No, I asked why you had a problem with this camping trip, not for your permission on who I can and can't have stay in my house.'

'My problem is you running off to play happy families together.'

'We're not.'

'Well, it looks like you are. Especially to the boys.'

'I can't just have them stuck at home all school holidays, Shayla.'

'Well, why couldn't *we* have taken them camping then?'

'Just you and me? Do you know how to put up a tent?'

'No, but we could have figured it out. We could have had a practice run in the backyard.'

'You expect me to believe you would have helped me put up a tent when you do nothing at all around here to help me?'

'That's not true. I help the boys with their homework. I do the dishes. I help wash and dry and fold the clothes. I keep my room clean.'

'Say what you will about Rob, but he helps me around here. He fixes things. He mows the lawn.'

'Pop could mow the lawn. He used to.'

'Look at the size of this yard. He's too old to do it. They just downsized so they could stop mowing the lawn, and theirs wasn't even half this size.'

'So buy your own lawnmower. Pay a handyman.'

'With what money?'

'Get a job.'

'You know what? I'm getting real tired of the way you speak to me.'

'Yeh, well, I'm getting real tired of this shit.'

'Go live with your grandparents then.'

'Fine, I will!'

'You did such a good job helping us pack. Not a single thing got broken in the move,' Nanna says, closing the oven.

They've only been in the new Revesby house for a couple of days, but it already smells like them. Tabu perfume, Brut cologne, freshly baked bread.

'I've had lots of practice.'

'I'll put some money in your Happy Dragon bank account for helping us,' Pop says.

'You really don't have to. I'm happy to help.'

'Nonsense,' Pop says over his shoulder, taking a box into the back room.

I pull newspaper from between the last of the dinner plates and stack them on the dining table. 'That's everything for the kitchen,' I tell Nanna.

'Fabulous, thank you!' Nanna opens the fridge. 'Do you think you can help your grandfather for a bit while I make us some lunch?'

'Sure.'

The second bedroom is behind the kitchen. It has a sliding door that leads to a paved courtyard with raised garden beds. Pop hangs his clothes in the wardrobe.

'Why aren't your clothes in the master bedroom with Nanna's?'

He turns and shakes his head, arms stretched towards the wardrobe, hands full of coathangers. 'Have you seen how full that wardrobe of hers is? She hasn't even finished unpacking and it's already bursting at the seams.'

'I can hear you,' Nanna calls.

'Nothing I wouldn't say to your face.' Pop puts the hangers on the rack and turns back to me. 'We've never shared a wardrobe,' he says. 'The secret to our long and happy marriage.'

'I thought it was my amazing culinary skills?'

'Yes, dear. That's certainly part of it,' Pop calls. 'It's all about give and take. I take the food and give her the wardrobe. She takes the wardrobe and gives me the food. Win-win.'

'What would you like me to help with?' I ask.

Pop points at the boxes labelled 'Books' and I open the top of it, look inside.

'What are you reading at the moment?' Pop asks.

'*'Tis* by Frank McCourt. It's a memoir.'

'You enjoying it?'

'I am.'

'I might borrow it after you.'

'I'll give you *Angela's Ashes* to read first.' I pull books from boxes and stack them on shelves, alphabetically. It reminds me of my days as a library monitor at Rosemeadow Public School. 'Did you know I wanted to be a librarian, once upon a time?'

Pop shakes his head. 'What do you want to be now?'

I shrug. 'Something with books.'

'Like a publisher or editor or literary agent?'

'Yeh, maybe. Or maybe like a writer or something. I dunno.'

'Good writing is art,' Pop says.

I nod.

'And I'd say it's a transferable skill too.'

'Yeh?'

'Not all great writers are authors,' Pop says. 'Some are journalists, others are playwrights. There are famous speechwriters. You think the President of the United States just gets up and knows what to say? No, someone's scripted him up. You need to be a good writer to work in marketing, communications, public relations. The list is endless. Plus, we have that internet thing now. Who's writing what goes on that?'

'So it's not silly?'

'It's not silly, but it might not be easy either,' Pop says. 'And you might not get exactly what you want, when you want it. I think the trick is to aim high and work hard, so that, even if you fall a little short, the distance between you and what you really want will be a whole lot shorter.'

'Hello?' Nanna answers the phone. 'Oh, you're home early. Is everything alright?'

Pop and I keep eating strawberry jelly with vanilla ice cream.

'I agree, it's far too hot to keep them out there,' Nanna says. 'Does that mean you're coming to get Shayla tonight or tomorrow? Not at all. Well, she's welcome to stay as long as she likes.'

Melted ice cream drips down the front of Pop's green polo shirt. He scrapes it off, spoons it into his mouth. Nanna shakes her head, hands him the tea towel she keeps across her lap like a napkin. Pop dips the corner in his glass of water and dabs at the stain on his shirt.

Nanna puts her hand over the receiver. 'Mum wants to know if you'd prefer to go home tonight or tomorrow?'

'Is *he* there?'

Nanna peers at her melted ice cream as if looking into Mum's eyes. 'She wants to know if Rob is there.' She looks back up. 'Yes, he is.'

'Is he staying?'

Nanna stares blindly into the dessert bowl. 'She'd like to know if he's staying.' She addresses me. 'She doesn't know.' Nanna holds the phone out. 'Here, she wants to speak to you.'

I shake my head. Nanna waves the phone. I shake my head again. She sighs. Pop starts to clear the table.

'Lauren? Yes, she's just stepped into the bathroom for a shower.' Nanna closes her eyes, rests her elbow on the table and holds her forehead like she has a migraine. Her pearly pink nail polish is chipped around the edges from the move. 'It sounds like you've had a long day,' Nanna says. 'Why don't you get the boys settled, have an early night and we'll just bring her home tomorrow? Okay. I'll ask her to call you in the morning. Yes, you too. Goodnight.' Nanna puts the phone down and straightens her plastic placemat. 'Did you and your mother have a fight before she went away?'

'Feels like we're always fighting at the moment.'

'Why?'

'I just don't *get* her, you know?'

Nanna scrapes crumbs off the placemat into her cupped hand under the edge of the table and sprinkles them on top of what's left of her melted dessert. 'I think you should go a bit easier on her,' she says.

'Why?'

'Because she's your mother.'

'So?'

'You only get one,' Nanna says. 'I wish I still had mine.'

'And she only has one daughter.'

'She's been through a lot for you,' Nanna says. 'You may not know it, but she has.'

They're magic words. Something rumbles awake inside me. A sleeping dragon, poked with a stick, casts off its chains. I feel its fiery breath creep up my back, like hot magma rising from the deep dark earth. The pressure builds in my chest and I open my mouth, ready to spew forth molten lava. My grandparents look at me with sad eyes and I swallow the explosion back down. Still, I can't help but blow off a little steam, volcanic gas escaping through small cracks on the surface.

'Do you think just because we never talk about it that I don't know what happened to her? To me? She wasn't the only one who got hurt. It would be nice if someone actually acknowledged that for a change, instead of ignoring it just because it's uncomfortable.'

Nanna purses her lips, pushes her chair out, steps away from the table. Pop keeps his head down, hands in the sink, busies himself with the dishes.

'Here, let me help with that,' Nanna offers.

'No, I'll do it,' Pop says. 'Can you just wrap that up and put it away?'

'Good idea. We can have it for lunch tomorrow. I always find these things taste better the day after, don't you?'

'Yes, it's like the flavours have had time to fully develop or something.'

They keep pretending like it never happened, and I push it back down, chain it back up.

Mirko picks me up and swings me around when I walk through the school gate. 'I've missed you!'

We haven't seen each other all school holidays because he spent the full six weeks with his family in Gerringong down the south coast, but we spoke on the phone almost every night.

'Me too.'

We give each other a quick kiss as the bell rings and our lips fit together perfectly, like the pieces of a puzzle.

We don't have many classes together this year. So, on sports day, we both jig and he doubles me back to his place.

From the prime position of his BMX pegs, I admire his tan. After all that time on the beach, his skin is golden. There's a new silver chain around his neck, a Christmas present from his parents. I can feel the muscles at work beneath his polo shirt as he pedals me towards Bankstown, and when there's a bump in the road, I take the opportunity to push my hips towards his lower back. His ears move up like he's smiling. There are patches of not-quite-yet stubble along his jaw. He's just started shaving.

In the music room, he straddles a stool, strums at the acoustic guitar and serenades me with the song he's been practising. 'Your Body Is a Wonderland' by John Mayer. I shift in my seat, lean forward, press against the heartbeat that has descended from my chest. Chris and Nick have perfect timing, as usual, and ring the doorbell just as Mirko finishes playing the final notes.

'Started without us?'

'Nah, mate.'

'Got a new tune for us?'

'Sure do. You guys get set up. I'll grab us some drinks.'

I follow Mirko into the kitchen and sit on the breakfast bench while he pours everyone glasses of Coca-Cola.

'Do you want some timpana for lunch?'

'What's that?'

'It's like a baked pasta pie.'

'Sure.'

Mirko puts a dish in the microwave, then moves in front of me, standing in the gap between my knees. He rests his forehead on mine. I keep my eyes on his lips. The microwave hums in the background.

'I liked having you on my bike today. I think you liked it too.'

I nod.

'I really missed you this summer.'

'Me too.'

'Can I do something?'

'What?'

'Hold you closer? Just for a moment? Before we start to play?'

I open my arms for a hug.

'No.' Mirko shakes his head. 'Not like that.'

He puts his hands behind my knees and pulls me towards him, until there's no space between us and everything feels like it's on fire. He puts his hands in my hair. The wet of his mouth is on the hot skin of my neck, his breath on my ear, his teeth on my bottom lip. There's a firmness pressed up against me, and I can't tell if the throbbing is coming from him or me or us both. I feel an impulse to press against it and Mirko must feel it too. He runs his hands down my back, digs his fingers into my hips and pulls me hard against it. I run my hands up the front of his sports shirt, his chest, feel the bump of the new nipple piercing he got during the school holidays under my palm, and push back against him. Mirko closes his eyes, bites his lip.

We rub up against each other, slow and firm, breath shallow and shaky. Saliva pools in my mouth, like I'm a starving woman looking at a slice of baked pasta pie. Nick and Chris start up their instruments in the music room. The microwave dings.

35

Mum looks up as I come in the front door from my last day of Year 10, her face full of poison. My diary is open on the dining room table, gold lock broken apart.

'You can take the girl out of Rosemeadow, but you can't take Rosemeadow out of the girl.' She slams my diary shut and stubs out her cigarette so hard I worry she'll snap her yellow finger. 'You're fifteen. I should have him arrested for statutory rape.'

'I'm almost sixteen, and it wasn't rape, but you'd know that from reading my diary, no doubt.'

Her eyes and lips narrow, powder foundation cracking around the edges, accentuating her crow's-feet and smoker's lines. She stabs her finger at my diary – the first bloody book she's ever read. 'This that sleazy little wop you've been talking to on the phone?'

'You mean my boyfriend of almost two years? The one who took me to the Year 10 formal?'

She flings the diary across the table at me. 'So how long has this shit been going on then?'

'The sex? Not long.'

She commences her tirade. I tune out.

It had been all hand holding, French kissing and dry humping until a couple of weeks ago, when his parents went away to celebrate their wedding anniversary and I told Mum I was staying at my friend Samantha's house for the night.

'Will her father be there?' she'd asked.

'No, he doesn't live with them.'

'I'll talk to her mother first, thank you.'

When the day came I told Sam that I wasn't feeling well, I would stay with her another night. And then I went home with Mirko.

The sex wasn't amazing. In fact, it wasn't even good. It was awkward, a little painful, brief, and happened just the once. In the morning, we both woke embarrassed, shy and sore. Since then, we haven't had a chance to be alone again.

And now this.

'I don't know where he's been or what he's got, but what I do know is that I don't want you bringing that filth back here,' Mum screams. 'From now on, do your own washing and do it separate to the rest of ours. Disinfect the bath after you've showered. Get your own towels. Get your own plates, cups and cutlery too.'

'Anything else?'

'Yeh, you're grounded. Give me your mobile phone and go to your room.'

I open the door that leads from the dining room to the hallway and turn to look at her.

'What?' she spits.

I want to tell her that I hate her. Hate her for ruining this moment, for shaming me, degrading me, for calling it rape when it was completely consensual sex with someone I love, who loves me back. I want to scream it in her face, push her, pull her hair. How the hell can she judge? She was fucking engaged to Rob at sixteen!

Instead, I keep my voice low, my words slow. 'This happened on my terms. And I haven't lost anything that hadn't already been taken from me.'

It's been ten days since she read my diary and eight days since my period was due. Every day the phone has rung. Each time my heart has skipped a beat. Whenever she's heard Mirko's voice, she's hung up. I tried to call him while she was asleep, but she's managed to put a password on the landline phone and I can't dial out without the pin. He showed up once, on his bike. She locked me inside, told him to get off her front lawn, threatened to call the police, have him charged with trespass and rape.

'Just tell me if she's okay and I'll go.'

'She's fine, no thanks to you. Now get lost before I knock your block off!'

So now I sit on the front steps every day, listening to the mixed CD Mirko burnt for me, hoping he might show up on his bike again and whisk me away.

I've heard that it's not unusual for a period to be late when stressed. Or pregnant. I hope it's stress, but I wonder what our baby would look like if I was pregnant. I imagine Mirko playing music to our growing baby, serenading my stomach, his hands, lips, breath on my pregnant belly, as if worshipping an unborn god. Would it look like me? Blonde hair and mismatched eyes, fair skin with a speckling of freckles across the nose and cheeks. Or would it look like Mirko? Olive skin and full lips, dark eyes and brown hair. Where would we live? His parents have a self-contained granny flat in their backyard. Maybe we could live there until we found our feet. His mum could give up volunteering at the aged-care home and help look after the baby while I finished school, maybe even went to university. Would they be angry with him, like Mum is with me? Or is that only because I'm the girl?

'Nash! Joe! Come and eat your dinner!' Mum screams, putting an end to my daydream.

I stare dead-eyed at the makeshift driveway on the front lawn. Two lines of compressed dirt, in the middle of the grass, killed by Rob's car tyres, despite there being a perfectly good concrete driveway to park in. He's here a lot, hence the destruction of the lawn, but he hasn't been here for this and I notice some fresh green sprigs poke through the dusty dirt as a result. Mum's kept him away, probably because she's embarrassed by me, the same way Nanna and Pop were embarrassed by her having three children to two different men. She probably doesn't want him here in case Mirko shows up again, or we have one of our almost daily blow-ups, or Mirko calls. Not that Rob should be answering the phone anyway. Not his bloody house. Although, since we moved it's often felt more like his than mine. Backyard full of his shit; no different to Rosemeadow at all, really.

The front door screeches open and Mum sits down next to me, instant coffee in a stainless-steel cappuccino cup on a matching saucer. She lights up a cigarette. I bring my designated cup, individually washed and sterilised with boiling water, to my lips. In my peripheral vision I see her staring at me.

'Your hair looks good today,' she says, hand reaching out to flick my curls.

I slide across the stairs, move away from her.

'So does your skin.'

'Thanks.'

'In fact, you've got a bit of a glow about you,' she says. 'Almost maternal.'

I open *Flowers in the Attic*, rest it across my knees, disappear into Foxworth Hall.

Rob has taught her well. Ten more days of isolation pass. The phone still needs a pin to call out. She disconnects all of Mirko's calls. I've seen no-one and done nothing, but finally I wake to a familiar dull ache in my abdomen and lower back. My light cotton pyjama pants are wet and I'm flooded with relief, until I throw the covers back and realise it's not my period. It's not blood at all. It's some kind of clear, gunky fluid I haven't seen before.

It leaks out of me into the pad lining my undies as I stand in the lounge room with a bundle of dirty clothes in my arms. The wet items are in the middle, hidden from her. She's listening to Roxette, and the lyrics to 'Spending My Time' feel like a cruel taunt.

'Is it alright if I do my washing?'

'Just let me get my stuff out of the machine.'

It's an effort to stand up straight. The cramps have become so severe I want to hunch over, curl up in the foetal position. While Mum hangs out her washing, I sneak a strip of the Prodeine Forte that she keeps in the medicine cupboard for her herniated discs and haemorrhoids, then hobble back up the hallway to my bedroom, a tight rectangle nestled between the bathroom and my brothers' bedroom.

Joe and Nash are five and six years old now and they enjoy their bunk beds, but Mum tells me frequently that it won't be long until they'll need their own rooms, so I'll have to get out. Right now, they're playing in the backyard, under my bedroom window. It's a big yard. Big enough to fit another two or three houses on it. For now, though, it's just a big ugly mess. Mum is still a lover of free things, and with 'Rob the Builder' still on the scene, the backyard resembles a shanty town. Two decent-sized sheds are full. The overflow is stored in a cubby house Rob built for the boys that's so packed a couple of the wooden panels have popped off. At this point, normal people would stop and have a big clean-up. But these guys have constructed another storage area, which is essentially a roof on stilts perched precariously over a concrete slab. To the right of that, to extend the hoarding even further, there's an old carport housing a trailer full of shit collected from the side of the road.

I pull the blind down and wonder if their lives are so empty they collect this junk just to fill the void.

Codeine isn't enough to keep me asleep through Mum's music. It's so loud the glass in my bedroom window shakes. She bangs on my bedroom door and screams at me to hang my washing out. I hold my stomach as I shuffle up the hallway and straighten before I step into the lounge room. Mum's wearing her black 'Dancing Queen' T-shirt. She turns away from me and bashes on imaginary drums under the silver disco ball. She doesn't want to see me. She's told me that. 'Get out of my sight. Don't come to me for anything.' That's what she said. 'I'm not your mother anymore. You're on your own.'

I empty washing out of the machine, leaning on the sink for support. I feel heavy and tired, maybe because of the pills I took. More stuff leaks out of me and my lower back aches when I pick up the basket. I take small steps, the plastic wings of the pad chafing my thighs. My legs feel like jelly going down the back steps, and I wonder if maybe I have low blood sugar again, like I did at Rosemeadow.

Outside, the blue sky is clear of clouds. The summer sun shines like liquid gold and the brightness of it hurts my head. I take the narrow concrete path, past where the jacaranda was on the right – before the borers got to it and Housing cut it down – to the clothesline. A light breeze twirls the squeaky Hills Hoist like a flower pinwheel on a stick. I put the basket down and for a moment the world spins. My heart feels like it's going to fall out of my mouth. I stumble and take a wide step to stop myself from falling. More stuff leaks out of my body.

Back in the bathroom, I sit on the toilet, bent over like somebody beaten across the back with a baseball bat, head over the bath in case I vomit. The gunky fluid now has a pinkish tinge and some red blood streaks through it. I don't know what it means, and I'm too sick and tired to care. I change my pad, pop a couple more Prodeine Forte and go back to bed.

Wisps of bright red look stark against the white ceramic of the bathtub.

'Hurry up and get out!' Mum bangs on the bathroom door.

Blood mixes with water, makes it look like I'll bleed to death. Was there this much when Steve-o slit his wrists?

'Hurry up!' Mum's voice fades back up the hallway. 'I need to wash your brothers.'

She must turn the tap on in the kitchen because the water turns ice cold, but I can't move. Big, thick globs of blood are sucked down the plug hole. I wrap my arms around myself, drop my head to my chest and watch little red rivers run down my legs.

'Hurry up!' She bangs on the door again. 'Hello?' Mum's tone changes; there's a hint of concern, and she knocks on the door like a reasonable person. 'Are you alright in there?' I hear her hand rest on the door handle.

'Yes. I just need a minute, please.'

317

'Well, hurry up!' The malice returns to her voice. 'And make sure you clean the bath out too.'

I kneel on the floor, lean over the tub and guide what remains down the drain, with a sprinkling of Ajax and tears.

I sit on the front steps, hunched over, legs pressing my arms against my stomach. There's an ache in my chest. It's been there since the day Mirko showed up and Mum sent him away. But now it feels worse. Bigger. Deeper. As if it might swallow me whole.

I remember Mildred saying 'Sometimes Mother Nature knows best.' I didn't know what she meant at the time. But now I do. And maybe it is better this way. For everyone. I wouldn't have been able to give a child the life they deserved. I know that. But knowing it doesn't make me feel any better.

The screen door opens. Mum sits down next to me, places her coffee cup on the step and lights up a cigarette. 'He didn't call today,' she says, smugly. 'Looks like he finally got the message.'

36

Mirko's at TAFE studying a Certificate III in Commercial Cookery. I haven't spoken to him, but I've heard that he has a new girlfriend. She's in his class and she plays the violin.

'Are you okay?' Sam asks after telling me.

'Yeh, why?'

'You're bleeding.' She points at my right knee. 'You were scratching.'

'Was I?'

'Ah, yeh.' Her eyebrows are raised. 'How can you not have noticed? You've removed layers of skin! Didn't it hurt?'

'Nup.' I look at the blood under my fingernails. 'Didn't even feel it.'

Probably because of the amount of codeine I've been chewing every day for the past three months.

Sam shakes her head. 'I'm worried about you,' she says.

The school bus pulls in to the kerb.

'Don't be. I'm fine.'

Sam rolls her eyes, picks up her backpack and waves goodbye.

At home, I imagine Mirko and his new girlfriend making food, making music, making love. I tie my hair back, fold a towel under my knees and turn the shower on so my mother can't hear me shove my fingers down my throat.

After the Easter break, I tell Sam I have a new boyfriend. I hope she tells Mirko. I want it to hurt him to hear that I've moved on just as it hurt me.

My mother doesn't like him, which isn't surprising. She doesn't like anyone. Not even me anymore. But she's only met him once, when he walked me to the front door and kissed me goodbye. I'd asked him not to, but he insisted. She saw the two of us from the lounge-room window and swung the front door open, forcing us to go through awkward introductions. The fact that she so strongly disapproves means I'm more inclined to date him, even though I don't really like him either. What I like is that he lives two hours away, which gives me an escape from Mum and Rob. I head to his place most weekends.

His parents aren't comfortable with us sleeping in the same room. 'You're only sixteen,' they say. So he vacates his room for me and sleeps on the futon in the lounge room. His mother knows that hasn't stopped us from experimenting, since she walked in on me going down on him late one night in the lounge room. I was sitting on the sofa, facing the television. He was standing in front of me. She rounded the corner and came face to face with her son being sucked off. But so far it hasn't been full-blown sex.

Not long after his parents go to bed, I hear his bedroom door creak open, then latch shut. He's snuck away from the futon before, so I don't think too much of it when he slides in under the sheets and starts to kiss me. But his grip on my arms, on my hips, feels different tonight.

'I think we should stop,' I whisper, because I don't want to wake his parents and get into trouble.

He rolls on top of me.

'Okay, that's enough.' I turn my head away from his kisses. 'Stop.' My voice isn't a whisper, but it's still not loud enough to wake anyone.

His body feels heavy on my chest. It makes it hard to breathe, let alone talk. One hand reaches down and pulls my nightie up, my underpants aside.

'No.' I sound like I'm chastising a dog.

He doesn't listen.

I say it again, firmer. 'No!' I try to wriggle away, but I'm trapped under the weight of him, breath and body caught. My heart beats fast and hard against my chest and his, as if it's trying to break free from both of us and save itself. 'Please, don't.'

He puts his hand over my mouth and bites me hard on the neck. It stings and feels wet. I'm not sure if the wet is his saliva or my blood. I tear my skin from his teeth and try to bite his hand. He clamps his hand down harder; my upper lip pressed back, up under my nose, his palm on my front teeth. He forces my knees apart with his.

I try to prise his hand off my face with one hand and push against his chest with the other, attempting to create a safe distance between us, but I'm not strong enough. My spit is smeared around my mouth and chin as I try to shake my head. He grabs his dick. My skin resists. He pushes past that. I inhale sharply. He pumps his hips. The friction between his skin and mine hurts, inside and out. The more I hurt, the more he sounds like he's enjoying it.

I try to position my hips in such a way that the full length of him doesn't enter me. I want to cry but I know I can't. I'll suffocate. And will he know how to revive me? Will it be over fast enough for him to be able to do that? Or will I be left with brain damage or something? Would he even bother to revive me, after this? Would I want him to? My breath catches as I choke back a sob and focus on breathing through my nose. I look at the glow-in-the-dark stars stuck to the ceiling. They look back. Together we wait for it to be over.

When it is, he cups me between the legs, kisses my wet face, rubs his cum over my stomach, then leaves. I reach for my phone. My thumb hovers over the buttons. I realise there's no-one to call. It's the wee hours of the morning. Trains aren't running and, even if they were, I don't have a way to the station. It's not within walking distance, I don't know the way and I don't have money for a taxi. I briefly contemplate catching a taxi all the way back to Padstow, but I know there won't be money to pay for it when I get home either.

*

The next morning, I wake to the weight of his body on my back. He digs his fingers in.

'You're wet already,' he whispers in my ear.

I'm not. It's just his mess from last night. I try to whip around, to roll over. 'Get off me!'

He pins my arms down and pushes my head into the pillow with his chin. 'I like it when you play hard to get.' He bites me hard on the neck again. His grip tightens on my wrists.

'I'm not playing. Stop it. You're hurting me.'

'Shhh.' He licks the side of my face. Stale cigarette smoke mixed with morning breath. It makes me want to gag.

I consider screaming, but there's no-one home to hear me – the clock on the wall tells me that his family has already left for church – so all that will do is increase the risk of asphyxiation when he tries to shut me up. I was lucky last night; I might not be lucky again.

He pushes my legs apart and crams his cock inside. There's not as much friction this time because of what he left behind last night, but the depth of his penetration seems greater. He pulls my body down as he pushes up. It hurts, feels like my insides are being pushed up under my ribs, but at least I can breathe. Out of my right eye I spot a fallen glow-in-the-dark star on the mattress, next to the pillow my face has been forced into. I look at it. It looks at me. Together we wait for it to be over.

When it is, I hear the sounds of his family returning from church float through the air; the sound of the car turning into the driveway, handbrake being pulled up, engine being turned off, doors being opened and closed. He goes to greet them and I grab my bags.

The train weaves back to Hurstville. The 948 bus winds its way around suburban streets – Forest Road, Henry Lawson Drive and Clancy Street – before I get off at Davies Road in Padstow. I put *The Color Purple* back into the overnight bag that bounces off my thigh as I walk up Alma Road and cross the street outside the house with the rusted white picket fence. Mum picked it up on a council clean-up. I imagine it's not quite the white picket fence she'd had in mind.

I try to let myself in quietly, but as soon as my key enters the lock of the screen door, she flings the wooden security door wide open. There's a big 'U2' printed in white on her black T-shirt and she looks disappointed to see me, although I'm not sure who else she was expecting, since Rob is already here and she doesn't have any friends. She unclips the door and, without even so much as a hello, walks away. I close the door, make my way to the kitchen and pull a packet of potato chips out of the pantry but, before I can open them, she snatches them out of my hands and tells me to finish off the other pack.

'These are stale,' I tell her, tasting them.

'Go buy your own freaking food then.'

I try to go to the bathroom, but nothing comes out except a tiny trickle of semen. I can't push because I'm so sore and swollen. I can't even wipe, so I dab myself and flush the toilet.

Nash and Joe watch *The Simpsons* and eat the fresh packet of chips. My tummy grumbles enviously. I haven't eaten all day. I had to spend the last of my Youth Allowance on the morning-after pill.

Mum catches my eye, follows me into the kitchen. 'You got something to say?'

I'm slightly taller than her, so she tilts her head back to look down her nose at me.

I shake my head. 'I just came out to get some Panadol. I'm not feeling well.' I try to step around her, but she moves to block me.

'What do you think this is? A pharmacy?'

'I'll replace them.'

'That's not the point.' Cheap pink lipstick bleeds into the smoker's lines around her lips.

'What is the point, then?'

She sticks a stained, cracked finger in my face. 'I'm sick of you treating this place like a hotel, coming and going as you please.'

'So, what? I'm never meant to leave this place, is that it? Because that's not a home, Mum, that's a prison. And I'm not the one treating this place like a hotel. I actually live here. Perhaps you're thinking of our other guest?'

Her breath is a mixture of Bushells instant coffee, Horizon Blue cigarettes and fresh Smith's chicken-flavoured potato chips. 'This is my house, not yours. I can have whoever I want here. And I don't want *you*.'

I feel her spittle on my face and wipe it off. 'Really, after all the shit he put you through, you ask *me* to leave?'

'And what about all the shit you've put me through too, huh?'

'Like what?'

'Oh, you don't even want to go there right now.'

'You're right. I don't.'

She stares at me, eyes wide and wild.

'Well, if you get out of my face, I can leave.'

She leans in closer, pulls at my strategically placed scarf and cranes her neck like a deranged cockatoo. 'Lover boy give you those, huh? If you think he's so good, go and live with him.'

My throat tightens as I fight tears. I grab her shoulders, try to move her aside.

'Don't push me, you little bitch!' She flails at me like an inflatable air dancer on a windy day. I put my arms up to shield my face.

Rob grabs me by the arm and pulls me out of the kitchen. 'Get your stuff and go,' he says, like it's his right to do so.

It's a cold and windy winter's day. I adjust my scarf, wrap my arms around myself and contemplate where to go next. I need something warm to eat and somewhere safe to sleep.

When the going gets tough, the tough go to Nanna's. I had a T-shirt that said that as a kid. It had a koala on the front with an Akubra on his head and a bindle stick slung over his shoulder. It's not a short walk to Revesby and it's slow going because every single step hurts.

324

I'm so swollen between my legs it feels like my insides are on the outside.

It starts to rain. Lightly at first and then more heavily. To people passing, nice and dry in their cars, I imagine I look pretty pathetic, if they even bothered to give me a second glace. But I surrender to the rain, and each drop takes a little of the sting out of the pain: dilutes it, washes it away, with the disgusting fluids he left on my body, quickly but tenderly. My clothes are heavy with water, my shoes squelch when I walk, raindrops drip off the end of my nose, but as I enter Blackall Street, I feel a renewed sense of strength.

I press the buzzer and take my shoes off while I wait. It hurts to bend over and unlace them, so I kick them off instead, move them aside with my wet and wrinkled feet. Even that hurts, but a little less. Nanna opens the door, short hair softly curled in its usual fashion. She has a tea towel in her hand and slippers on for pottering around. The smell of an oven-baked dinner wafts past her.

'Hi, Nanna.'

'Quick, come in. Let me get you a towel. Oh, you're drenched. You'll catch your death like that. Go have a hot shower and let me find you something warm to put on.'

'Do you mind if I stay here tonight?'

'Of course you can. Did you have another fight with your mother?'

I nod.

'Well, you know I have to let her know you're here safe, but you can stay as long as you like. Okay? Now go and get warm. And when you come out, we'll have a nice dinner.'

37

The one almost redeeming quality about this library is that it has an upstairs area. Arguably it should be filled with books. I'd like it better if that was the case. Instead it's cluttered with stands, shelves and desks full of flyers promoting universities, TAFE and private college courses. I wait outside the door for Mr Bell, the careers advisor. He never rushes anyone out, which is fine because I'm in no rush to go back to class. The bell rings. The students he was with leave for their next period. I stay put.

'Shayla, I've been expecting you. Come on in. Take a seat. Tell me why you're here.'

'I think you already know.'

Mr Bell has a soft face. Deep laughter lines curve around his mouth, and smile lines crinkle the corners of his eyes.

'In your own words,' he says, rolling his hand.

'I told our year advisor that I wanted to drop out of extension English and history, and he told me I needed to come and see you first.'

Mr Bell opens my file.

'I'd also like to withdraw from the reading-tutor training program.'

He looks at me quizzically, lined forehead creased into a surprised frown. 'You no longer wish to help students at Picnic Point Primary School with their reading?'

'No.'

'You know that means you'll have to go back to playing sport?'

I huff, cross my arms over my chest, slouch in the chair. 'Let me think about it then.'

Mr Bell smiles slightly.

'But I still want to drop my extension classes.'

The smile goes away. 'You were encouraged to take these classes because your Year 10 marks were exemplary.' He looks up from my grades. 'These classes are meant to challenge you.'

'Well, consider me challenged.'

'Sure,' he says. 'But I never considered you a quitter.'

'Please.' I hold up my hand and shake my head. 'That's not going to work on me. I'm done.'

Mr Bell flicks through my paperwork. 'You were able to meet the challenge at the start of the year,' Mr Bell says. 'These marks are ... outstanding, really. I know some of your friends had moved on. Perhaps you had some more free time?'

I shrug. Maybe I should have moved on too. My mother has already asked me why I'm still here when I could be out there in the real world, making money as an apprentice hairdresser. I could have gone to TAFE with Mirko. We'd still be together. He wouldn't be dating that violin-playing chef bitch.

'Have you taken on a part-time job or something?'

'No.'

'Well, things have gone a little downhill since July. Your grades have dropped. So has your attendance.'

'So?'

He closes my file, leans forward, elbows on his knees, hands clasped in front. 'So something's changed, Shayla. What is it?'

I close my eyes and in the darkness I see glow-in-the-dark stars. I feel my throat tighten with the threat of tears, my heart quicken with the fear of suffocation, the force of his hand over my mouth, on my teeth. The cold rain on my skin and the pain between my legs as I walked the streets, trying to get somewhere warm and safe.

'Is there something I can do to help?' Mr Bell asks gently. 'That the school can do? Because we'll do it.'

'I'm just having a rough time, alright? And I don't need the extra stress.'

'Is it school stressing you out or is it something else?'

I throw my hands up in the air, exasperated, and slap them down on my thighs. 'It's everything, okay? Everything! And I just need to lighten the load a bit. So are you gonna help me or not?'

Miss Miller holds her finger up like a weathervane, trying to detect a change in the wind. 'Did something happen in June that you'd like to talk about?'

'No.'

She looks down at my file and I can see regrowth at her roots. It's the same mousy brown as her eyebrows. I can't imagine her not being golden blonde, and she can't imagine me giving up my extension classes.

'He's right, there's a sudden change in your attendance and grades here.'

'I didn't say nothing happened; I just said I don't want to talk about it.'

'But here, at the start of Year 11' – she stabs her acrylic nail at my grades like a pin into a map – 'your grades were unexpectedly good, even for you.'

I throw my hands up. 'Now I'm in trouble for getting good grades as well?'

'No, I'm just saying it's unusual for grades to be *this* good so early on, even for our best students. Year 11 is harder than Year 10, and these extension classes are even harder. Not only is the work more difficult, the workload is increased, especially if you take extra units. It takes time to adjust. We expect to see good students slip a little at the start. It's normal.'

'So what are you saying? That I cheated? Because I didn't.'

'Not at all. What I'm saying is it's obvious to me that you really threw your whole self into this at the start of the year,' she says, making a circle with her hands. 'To the point where, I feel, it would have been unsustainable without complete and utter burnout further down the track. So the most important thing for me to understand right now is why you did that. What was the motivation? The trigger?'

'Why is that the most important question?'

'*Why* is always the most important question,' Miss Miller says. 'But in this case, because sometimes we over-perform in certain areas of our lives, like school, to prove to ourselves and others that we're doing alright when perhaps we aren't doing so well more broadly.'

I cross my arms and legs.

'Other times we throw ourselves into something as a distraction from a problem,' Miss Miller continues. 'But that also isn't sustainable. And based on this timeline, I'm wondering if something happened over the summer school holidays that we should talk about?'

I look at my hands in my lap and see clots of blood being sucked down the drain while I was held hostage all school holidays. I hear Sam tell me Mirko has a new girlfriend. I feel the numbness of Mum's codeine pills, of attempting to fill the void with extracurricular activities and a new boyfriend.

'Because this isn't just about your grades or wanting to quit classes. There have been other changes in you, Shayla. You've changed your look. You don't come in uniform. You appear to have lost a lot of weight. You take days off sick and then come to school looking tired. One teacher is concerned you may be drinking. Are you? Do we need to get you some help?'

'You know what would really help me?'

'What?'

'Get me out of these classes like I've asked. I feel like a bloody circus animal with all the hoops you're making me jump through, when I could literally just stop showing up or drop out altogether. I don't *have* to be here.' I stand up, grab my bag.

'Shayla, would you be comfortable if we called your mother to discuss this?' Miss Miller asks, looking up at me.

'Good luck with that. She's already told me she thinks the HSC

329

is a waste of time, that it would have been more practical to spend these two years doing an apprenticeship and earning a wage as a hairdresser.'

'Do you want to be a hairdresser?'

'You know what I'm learning from all of this? It really doesn't matter what I want.' I turn to leave, spit some venom over my shoulder. 'It's been a real fucking education. Thanks.'

'Shayla, wait.'

I pause outside her door.

'Before you make any decisions, make a list. Forget now. Look to the future. What do you want to achieve in this life of yours? Your own home? A good job? Travel? Family? Whatever it is, work backwards from that and write down what you need to make that dream become a reality. You are one of our best students. When you leave here, we want all the doors and windows of opportunity to be flung open for you. These classes are key to keeping your options open while you choose what you want to do next. We're not fighting with you, Shayla. We're fighting for you.'

White blouses with hot-pink bras underneath. Short tartan skirts with cute schoolgirl shoes. No visible panty lines under tight grey pants that hug the bum and thighs before they flare out from the knee. Year 11 girls walk in groups, pairs at least, and cars stop for them at the pedestrian crossing on Kennedy Street. I walk alone. It's spring, but I'm dressed for winter in boys' grey cargo pants and a baggy jumper. When I come to the pedestrian crossing, the first car doesn't stop for me. Nor does the second.

At the school gym there's an exercise bike directly opposite the join of two big mirrors on the wall. I always use that bike because my reflection disappears. All I am is bodiless arms. If I get skinny enough, maybe I'll disappear completely. Perhaps, side-on, I already have.

I'm back home after a longer than usual stay with Nanna and Pop, but my mother doesn't look up when I walk through the front door. It's as if I'm not even there. Like maybe I'm a ghost. And I wonder if I've died without knowing it and gotten trapped here.

In my bedroom, I pop the lid off my blue Ventolin inhaler and, when my lips peel apart like the seal of a zip-lock bag, I realise this is the first time I've opened my mouth since brushing my teeth this morning. I haven't had anything to eat, I haven't had anything to drink, I haven't spoken a word. I exhale before I close my lips around the mouthpiece and inhale slowly as I press down on the canister – one, two, three times. When my heart starts to race and my body starts to shake from the overdose I stop, because I know I'm still alive. I'm just not sure if that's a good thing.

The pre-recorded announcement at Revesby Station doesn't sound like a warning.

'The next train does not stop here.'

It feels like a warm hand on my lower back, guiding me towards the edge of platform one.

'Please stand clear.'

I flirt with the idea. Take a step forward as the train comes into view. Tease myself. Lean in for the kiss of death, with the intention of turning my lips away at the very last moment.

'Please stand behind the yellow line.'

But I feel the magnetic pull of the tracks. And it's so strong I have to use all my will to step away. I don't trust my body to obey my brain anymore. It feels like there's some weird disconnect between the two. Like I don't have full control. Like I'm out of my body, when, in fact, I'm probably just out of my mind.

My mouth waters as the train swooshes by, doors rattling. It leaves me to watch after it like a forlorn lover. I swallow a lump in my throat as it disappears into the distance.

'The next train to arrive on platform one goes to City Circle. First stop: Padstow.'

Back home, the boys start their dirt bikes under my bedroom window. I pull the blind down, latch my bedroom door and move in front of the mirror. I wonder if my hair has stopped growing, or if it's just breaking off. What used to be bouncy golden curls have become stringy, lifeless strands. Maybe it's the shitty straightener I use every day, but I'm sure my hair used to shine like the sun.

I pull my jumper off. My collar and hip bones protrude, but I could still be thinner. I turn to the side and suck my stomach in until I can see the bottom of my rib cage. There are bruises on my arms and legs, in places that can be hidden. Fresh ones look a little purple. Older ones fade to brown. I poke them, but they don't hurt anymore. Even when I punch myself, over and over in the same spot, I feel nothing. It stopped working a while ago. And now I need something new.

I retrieve a box from under the bed. Inside are bandaids from the medicine cupboard in the kitchen. A lighter I took from one of my mother's cigarette boxes. Razor blades stolen from Revesby shops earlier today.

I trace the delicate blue veins beneath the soft skin of my forearm with my thumb, black nail polish chipped and chewed. The steel of the razor blade is still warm when I gently press it into my flesh. It's almost comforting, like a hug. Blood beads through broken skin. My brain sees it and my body feels it and they reunite; whatever spell has been cast to make me feel so absent from my own body, so numb to my own experience, lifts. Albeit briefly.

Mum gets the boys ready for school while I read *The Bell Jar* by Sylvia Plath. I've decided not to go today. I've told my mother that I have horrendous period pain. She just nodded. It's a lie. I stopped having periods months ago. It's also the first time I've spoken to her – to anyone, actually – in more than a week. Even at school. The truth is, I feel like there's nothing left to say. I've tried writing, combed my mind for the perfect combination of words, but my brain is as empty as the page before me, which blurs as my eyes lose focus. All I want to do is sleep. I'm always tired, and dark circles have become a permanent fixture under my eyes, despite the fact that I sleep so much. Most days I come home from school, go straight to bed and don't wake up until the next day, to Mum screaming, 'You're going to be late if you don't get up now.' And I get up and I go to school, and I move through the day unseen, unheard, unfeeling, like I'm just observing life, not really participating. A spectator. A spectre. Already dead. At least on the inside. Maybe that's why I feel nothing. Maybe that's why my period has dried up.

The doctor says I'm not dead, even on the inside, but I will be; the reason I don't get a period anymore is because I'm so underweight my internal organs can't function properly. He says eventually they'll shut down altogether if I don't get this bulimia-turned-anorexia under control. But I have no appetite and the smell of food makes me gag, so I don't eat often. When I do, I feel both my mind and my body recoil. My mouth dries. I have to chew and chew and chew. My jaw aches. My throat tightens. Everything is so dry it just gets stuck in my diaphragm. And often it's to no avail. My body has become so accustomed to rejecting food that if I don't vomit it up, it just goes the other way.

I hear the security door shut, the screen door lock, and I stand up, the wooden slats beneath the mattress creaking – because I'm still too fat. Nanna and Pop bought me this bed when I was still living at Kikori Place. It has a white frame with round arches at the head and feet. Inside the arches are five white pillars topped with golden knobs. Some of the gold has been scratched off because I tried to make the bed fly after watching *Bedknobs and Broomsticks*.

Mum is dropping the boys at school, then taking Nanna shopping. Since I rarely come out of my bedroom these days, I take the opportunity to sit in the lounge room and enjoy the space while no-one is home. The room feels lighter, airier than mine. There's a big window that the breeze blows through. It gently lifts the side of the white lace curtain, its rise and fall simultaneous with that of my chest as I breathe in and out. I uncover my wrists, air the injured skin, remove the sweatbands that have become such a permanent fixture I observe a tan line. The black screen of the TV shows my reflection. I turn it on and hit mute, watch myself fade as the screen comes alive with colour, and write down all I have left to say.

Goodbye.

38

'Oh, thank Bowie! Finally! Where were you?'

'I was here.' I wrap the blue phone cord around my body, don't mention that I've spent the last half-hour drawing a bath, flirting with razor blades, remembering how she once said if Steve-o was serious about killing himself he would have cut down not across. 'Just figured it was for you and they'd leave a message. What's up?'

'Pop's had a heart attack.'

I hold the receiver tightly in both hands.

'Hello? Shayla? Are you still there?'

'Is he alive?'

'Yes. The ambulance came and got him. They took him to Bankstown Hospital. We're just waiting to see him now. Can you meet us here?'

'I'm on my way.'

I run down to Chamberlain Road so fast I have to hook a finger through the belt loop at the back of my Supré jeans to stop them from falling down. Keys bounce in the kangaroo-pouch pocket of my baggy Jay Jays hoodie. The 927 bus has pulled away from the kerb and rolls towards the corner, blinkering left. I run across the road without looking. A car comes around the corner and blasts their horn at me. It makes the bus driver look my way and I wave my arms at him. He pulls over and opens the door.

Mum paces outside the hospital entrance. One arm is tucked around her stomach, holding her elbow. Her smoking hand trembles.

'Is he okay?'

'They're putting him in a ward now.'

'Did you see him? How did he look?'

She tilts her head in a sort of shrug, cigarette flicked out to the side. Her lips are turned down and she wrinkles her forehead. 'Frail.'

'Are you okay?'

There are tears in Mum's eyes. She inhales slowly and exhales shakily, blowing grey clouds towards the sky. She presses her lips into a thin, firm line and nods, but her chin quivers. I look at her black T-shirt. The Beatles. 'Tomorrow Never Knows'. I've seen it before, but today there's something about the uncertainty of those words that makes me feel queasy.

'Is there anything I can do?'

Mum shakes her head, taps her foot, looks up and around, then back to me. Her body trembles as she tries to hold back a sob. It finally breaks free with such force a small spray of saliva escapes her mouth.

'Sorry.'

'Don't be sorry.'

She swipes at her mouth and chin with the back of her hand. I stand next to her, scared to touch. There hasn't been any physical contact between us for longer than I can remember. A single droplet of spit shines in the short, white hairs on her chin. I hand her a tissue.

'Thanks.'

'So what happens now?'

Mum's cigarette hand flutters up to her forehead. She brushes some hair off her wet face with the side of her thumb. 'Now I need to go and get the boys from school,' she says. 'I'll come back after. Rob is coming to mind them. He just can't get there in time for pick-up.'

Rooms shoot off wards shoot off hallways, like arteries. My white skater shoes squeak on the shiny plastic floor. Curtains on railings are whipped around beds on wheels to provide privacy and muffle whispered conversations. Medical-grade disinfectant burns my

336

nostrils and eyes, but it's better than the occasional wafts of piss, shit and vomit.

Pop has a private room with a small window and its own bathroom. I stand by the bed and listen to machines beep, studying his face. There's a blue-purple vein under his eye that I haven't noticed before, but he still smells as he always has, like Brut Original.

'Doris?' Pop's eyes flicker open. He looks at me groggily and smiles weakly. 'Where's Doris?'

'She's gone to get a vase. She brought you some flowers.'

Pop nods. His eyes roll back, close, open again.

'You don't look well. Should I get you a nurse?'

Pop shakes his head gently, pats the side of the bed. The crisp white sheets rustle as I sit down. I hold Pop's hand. It's cold, like a bag of frozen peas.

'You know, I see you, Shayla. And you don't look so well either.'

'Yeh, I know.'

'I'm worried about you.'

'I'm not the one in hospital.'

Shoes approach on the squeaky-clean floor outside. We both turn to the open doorway. A nurse passes at an unnatural pace, ponytail swooshing from side to side with a sense of purpose.

'You know I want the best for you.' Pop squeezes my hand. 'I always have.'

'I know.' I squeeze back. 'Thank you.'

'Are you doing what's best for you? And not just you as you are today. But you in ten, twenty, thirty years from now. Are you on the right path to get you where you want to be?'

'Probably not.'

'Do you know where you want to be?'

'I think so. I want to write.'

'You always have.'

'But is that stupid?'

'No. If that's your calling, stay true to it.'

I reach across Pop's body and take his right hand in my left, so I'm holding both.

'It's alright to have little detours, Shayla. We learn from our experiences. And in the past, you haven't had much control over where you've ended up. But that's different now. You're steering the ship.'

I look into Pop's eyes. There's a white growth on the side of one of his irises. The whites have turned yellow and there are little red veins that I haven't seen before.

'Think about what *you* want. What you *really* want. Because the decisions you make now will affect you — future you — more than they will affect anyone else.'

I look at Pop's left hand. Long fingers that he used to play the piano with. Perfectly rectangular nails. I know the right hand is full of metal, after a workplace accident that took the tops of two of his fingers. There's no nail left on the middle finger and just two little nubs on the index finger. 'Where's your wedding band?'

'I took it off him in the ambulance,' Nanna says as she enters the room. 'Things can go missing in these kinds of places.'

Pop's eyes follow Nanna and the bouquet of dark-red roses she puts on top of the drawers next to his bed. She cups his hollowed-out cheek and kisses him on the forehead, gently rubs the red lipstick from his grey skin. Usually his skin is tanned and pulled tight across a strong jaw and high cheekbones. Today it looks thin and slack, as if Nanna's nails might tear it open like tissue paper.

'Have you eaten?' Nanna digs around in her handbag, pulls out her purse. 'You look very thin, Shayla. You must be hungry.'

'I'm not.'

'Please go and get yourself something to eat. It will make me feel better.'

I head to the takeaway shop outside the hospital. A warm golden light is cast over hot food in the bain-marie. I search for something that will be easy to throw up later. The young girl behind the counter wears a hair net over a blonde bun and a black apron over a pregnant belly. She drops fresh hot chips out of a frying basket into a metal tray and looks to an old Italian lady using a walking frame.

'Chicken or plain salt?'

'Chicken.'

The girl shovels hot chips into a foil-lined bag. 'Who's next?' She looks at me.

'Can I get a small fried rice, please?' I hand her the five-dollar note Nanna gave me and step back to wait.

'Shayla?'

I turn towards the voice. Mirko stands in the doorway. Floppy brown hair falls over his face, and there's a small boy with big blue eyes and round pink cheeks on his hip.

'Hi! What are you doing here?' Oh God. Today of all days. When even my grandparents have said I look like shit.

'Big brother's in hospital. Came off his motorbike.'

'Oh no, is he okay?'

'Yeh, he'll be fine. What are you doing here?'

'My pop had a heart attack.'

'Fuck.'

'Yeh.'

'Does that mean your mother's around here somewhere?' He looks over his shoulder.

His jawline has become more pronounced since I last saw him, and the once-patchy hair along it has matured to become Calvin Klein model-esque stubble. He's taller too, his shoulders broader, his arms more muscular. And when he speaks, I notice a tongue ring.

'You're safe for the moment. She's gone to get the boys from school.'

'Good.'

I put my hands in my back pockets, rock on my heels and try to avoid his gaze, but I can't. He smiles knowingly, and I force myself to look away from his dimple, change the subject. 'So is this little guy your nephew?'

'Yep, this is Matthew.'

'He got your brother's hair.'

Floppy brown hair, not unlike Mirko's.

'Yep. And his mother's eyes.'

We glance at each other quickly, before we turn our attention back to Matthew, and I wonder for a second if he knows – even though I never told a soul.

'How old is he now?'

'Nine months.'

I step towards Mirko and wiggle my finger at Matthew in a little wave. He clamps his tiny hand around my finger and pulls it towards his mouth. A couple of white baby teeth push up under pink gums.

'Sorry, he's teething.' Mirko prises Matthew's fingers off mine and wipes drool from his chin with his bib. 'Wants to put everything in his mouth at the moment, don't you?'

'Small fried rice,' the girl behind the counter calls.

I turn and smile at her, grateful for the interruption, but she doesn't smile back. Mirko follows me to the counter. Matthew holds his hand out towards the bag being passed over the bain-marie and the girl smiles at him, even gives a little wave.

'Well, I guess, while you're here, I should probably introduce you to my fiancée too,' Mirko says.

I feel my eyebrows spring up so high they've probably disappeared into my hair line.

'Shayla, this is Rebecca.' Mirko gestures to the girl handing me my food. 'Rebecca, this is Shayla.'

I exhale loudly, like someone's punched me in the stomach, quickly reshaping the painful surprise into a gushing smile. 'It's nice to meet you.' I look from her to Mirko and back. 'We went to school together.'

'I know who you are,' she says. 'Your change is in the bag.'

'Well, congratulations on your engagement and, ah …' I glance at her pregnant belly before I hoist the plastic bag up in the air to gesture at the takeaway food. 'Thank you.'

I step backwards, bump into someone, apologise as I move around them and leave.

'Hey, wait up.' Mirko follows me outside. 'Could you have gotten out of there any faster? You almost took out the old guy with the walking stick.'

'How does she know who I am?'

'Maybe I talked about you. A bit. At the start.' Mirko shrugs. 'I rebounded pretty hard.'

'Yeh, I can see that.' I shake my head at the pavement.

There's gum on the concrete. It's been there so long it's turned black. I poke at it with my shoe.

'It's so nice to finally see you.'

I nod.

'You're looking good, Shayla. Really good.'

I'm not, but it's nice to not feel completely invisible for a change. I always felt like Mirko saw me. The best version of me. Maybe he was what brought it out. Maybe that's why it went away.

I look up, into this brown eyes. 'So are you.'

Mirko bites his lower lip and I feel my body respond involuntarily. The dark cloud that has hung over my head finally parts and the sun shines through. It makes my body feel nice and warm, inside and out, after being cold and numb for so long.

'Come back to mine,' he says. 'Let's catch up. I've missed you.'

My heart beats fast without the need for a Ventolin overdose to prove I'm a living, breathing thing. A heat grows inside of me. It reaches up, like a flower to the sun, so that even my breath feels warm. His lips are slightly parted. I salivate in anticipation of kissing them, of feeling his hot breath mingle with mine. I hear myself swallow. I wonder if he feels the same. I'm scared to speak in case I lose the moment. Finally, Matthew slaps Uncle Mirko in the face and his scream-laugh breaks the spell.

'You know I never stopped thinking about you, Shayla.'

'Really? Because it kinda looks like you did. And pretty quickly too.'

'You never answered my calls. Your mother told me you didn't want to talk to me anymore. You just vanished. And then Sam told me you had a new boyfriend. What was I meant to do?'

'It doesn't matter now. You have a fiancée. You're going to have a child.'

'It *does* matter.' Mirko wipes Matthew's drooly face. 'I think about you, about us, all the time. If you'd just answered my calls, our whole lives could have worked out differently.'

I turn away, catch my reflection in the window of the takeaway shop and, as my eyes refocus, I look past myself, through the glass, and I see Rebecca. She watches our interaction while she scoops creamy potato bake into a plastic container, and I know, whatever he's bringing out in me today, this isn't the best version of myself.

'Actually, you know what?' I look at Matthew, brown hair, blue eyes, chewing on his own fingers. 'They probably wouldn't have been all that different. This could just as easily have been our lives.'

'It would have been different with you.'

'No, it wouldn't have. Except, instead of having this conversation with me, maybe I would have been watching you have it with someone else.'

'I think about you all the time.'

'Well, no offence, but maybe you need to stop living in the past and start living in the present. With your future wife. The mother of your child.'

'What if things could be different?'

'How?'

'I'm going to be a dad. There's nothing I can do about that now. And that's fine. It's my responsibility. I was stupid. We were both stupid. And now I have to face the music.'

'Yeh, you do.'

'But what if we could still be together?'

'You're going to leave your pregnant fiancée for me, is that what you're saying?'

Mirko shrugs, glances inside the shop. 'If that's what you want.'

I hear Pop's voice in my head. *Is this what you want?*

'Well, what are the alternatives? You think I'm going to be the person you cheat on a pregnant woman with?'

'No, of course not. That's not what I meant. If you want to be with me, yes, I'll leave. I don't want to get married. Our families made us get engaged. I just want you. I always have. I always will. I never stopped wanting you.'

My body aches. My heart aches too, but I know that no matter how much I want things to go back to the way they were, they never will. Too much has changed. I've changed.

I step back from the flames, so I don't hurt myself or anyone else. 'Yeh, well, I don't want any of that. But I wish you well. I really do.'

And I throw the small fried rice in the bin as I walk away, because I don't want that either.

Yellow trumpet daffodils and blue Singapore orchids sit atop a shiny black coffin. Yellow and blue. They were his favourite colours. White church candles burn, and 'Unchained Melody' by The Righteous Brothers plays quietly in the background as people dressed in black, grey and navy sit in the chapel at Woronora crematorium.

'Pop was a gentleman with classic and immaculate style. He enjoyed the small, quiet things life had to offer, including a passion for reading.'

When the phone rings that early it's never good news. Mum took the call. None of us expected it. He'd made it through surgery and out of recovery – then had a massive heart attack during the night. Hospital staff said they worked on him for as long as they could, did everything they could to revive him, but he was gone.

'Pop and I were always very close. I'm very lucky to have a memory overflowing with happy and sometimes hilarious times spent with him.'

Mum broke the news to Nanna in person while I took the boys to school then caught the bus to Bankstown Hospital to collect his things. Staff gave me a big, pink plastic bag. His grey trackpants. His navy slippers. His dentures. A book by Tom Clancy that I gave him for Father's Day. I wondered if it would bother him that he never got to finish it and decided, just in case it did, I'd read *The Teeth of the Tiger* out loud each night, so his spirit could hear how it ended.

'We read together, watched cartoons together, fell down the steps together, and once, when I wanted to be a unicorn, he got a saucepan stuck on my head.'

I stood by the simple water feature at the entrance to the hospital and waited for Mum to pick me up. Coins caught the morning sun and shone through the water, each representing a wish. I looked to the sky, beautiful and bright and blue. The clouds looked like ripples of water and glowed golden with the yellow sun behind them.

'Pop was the best grandfather I ever could have asked for. He was also the closest thing I've ever had to a father.'

I scoffed at Mum when she told me she didn't have anything to wear to a funeral, even though every single item in her wardrobe is black. The three of us went shopping. Nanna swapped her signature knee-length skirt for black trousers and bought a new bottle of Tabu. Mum bought a black blouse with billowing, sheer sleeves to go underneath a conservative black pencil dress. I opted for a high-waisted skirt and a long-sleeved turtleneck.

'And today we lay to rest the most influential and important man of my life.'

The slideshow I put together plays to 'Yellow' by Coldplay. Each of us chose a song for Pop. This was mine. I sit in the pews, but it feels like I'm watching from above. This could have been my funeral. In fact, it probably would have been if that call hadn't come through.

The three of us stand behind the coffin, holding hands, as mourners place white and yellow daisies on top. Then we move into position. I'm worried I'm not strong enough for this part. I look across the coffin at Mum and take hold of the shiny silver handle. Nanna, standing behind Pop, gives a nod and 'The Last Farewell' by Roger Whittaker plays as Mum and I lead the pallbearers towards the hearse.

39

At the last parent-teacher conference, Ms Carr, the principal, told Mum that I wasn't 'university material'. Mr Bell, the careers advisor, says there's still time to turn that around. His warm brown eyes sparkle with hope, and there are flecks of grey in his brown hair, probably caused by problem students like me.

'Can I let you in on a little secret? Year 11 marks don't count towards your UAI. They do set the foundations for Year 12 though.' He flicks through my file. 'You're passing. Not with flying colours, but you're not failing.' He closes my file, leans forward. Elbows on his knees, hands clasped in front, he looks into my eyes. 'Tell me, Shayla, what do you want to do?'

'I want to be a writer.'

He eyes *The Complete Poems of Samuel Taylor Coleridge* atop the ring binders on my lap. 'What kind of writer?'

'I want to write books. Fiction.'

'Have you written a book?' Mr Bell sits back, rests his ankle on his knee.

'Not yet.'

'So it's fair to say you're not going to leave high school a bestselling author?'

'Yes.'

'It might even take a long time to write a bestseller.'

'True.'

'In fact, I think most authors are in their mid-thirties by the time they get their first book deal.'

I nod.

'So what do you want to do in between high school and writing your bestselling book? What's your back-up plan?'

I look around the room. 'Well, I've been thinking about newspapers.'

'Becoming a journalist?' Lines of surprise crease his forehead, but his eyes twinkle.

'Yeh.'

'I'm impressed,' he says. 'You'd need to get into uni.'

I hear the inflection of a question. He raises his brows further, making them question marks.

I nod and his whole face folds into a smile.

'Okay!' Mr Bell slaps his hands on his knees and jumps up, shuffles through some papers on his desk. 'Here's a list of universities that offer courses in journalism, media, communications and the like. You will need to up your game to get in, but I think you're ready. And what about if we try to set up some work experience for you at the local newspaper?'

I use my free period to review the materials Mr Bell gave me in the library, until Miss Miller taps me on the shoulder with French tips filed into sharp points.

'Got time for a quick chat?' She gestures towards her office.

I gather my papers and follow. She wears tight hot-pink pants and black open-toed stilettos.

'I just wanted to check in,' she says, closing the door. 'Last time I saw you, you weren't travelling so well. I understand since then you've lost someone close to you.'

'My pop,' I say. 'I only just came back to school this week.'

Miss Miller nods. 'I wanted to see how you're going and if there's anything I can do to support you, but it looks like you've jumped straight back into things.'

'Oh, this? This is about applying for uni.'

'Last time we spoke, it didn't sound like that was on the cards.'

'It wasn't.'

'What changed?' Miss Miller kicks off her heels and crosses her legs on the couch, like she's a schoolkid sitting on the classroom floor.

'I ran into someone. An old boyfriend.'

'Oh, yeh?' She leans in.

'Yeh. And he had a fiancée.'

Miss Miller shakes her head.

'And she was pregnant.'

Her eyes pop and she sighs loudly, lips fluttering like a horse. 'Now, that's a lot to process.'

'Yeh. Tell me about it.'

'I imagine that brought up quite a few feelings for you?'

'It did actually.'

Big blue eyes peer at me while she waits for me to elaborate.

'Like, all of the feelings, which was kinda interesting, since I don't think I've had any feelings in, like, a really long time.' I half laugh, half sob. Tears hit my knees.

'Oh, Shayla.'

I pull two tissues out of the box on the table. 'I mean, I was shocked, obviously. And then hurt.'

Miss Miller uncrosses her legs, leans forward.

'And then I felt relieved.' I take a big deep shaky breath. 'Relieved that it wasn't me, that it wasn't my life. But also guilty that I felt that way.'

'Why guilty?'

'Because it *could* have been me. It *really* could have been.'

'I understand.' Miss Miller looks at me pointedly through her own tears, which she blinks back. 'Well, maybe the universe is giving you a sign. A chance to do things differently. The most important thing is that we learn our lessons. And it sounds like you have.'

'I know. It's just that I came so close to fucking it all up, you know? And there have been a couple of near misses over the past year or so, where if things had gone any differently, I wouldn't be sitting here, talking to you, looking at university brochures.'

'Then maybe you're exactly where you're meant to be.'

There's the glug, glug, glug of the water cooler and Miss Miller puts a white plastic cup in front of me. 'Did you get to talk to your pop before he passed?'

'I did. And he knew I was sick or, like, struggling.' I fiddle with the Barbie sweatbands on my wrists. There aren't any fresh cuts beneath them, just scars. I've started applying Bio-Oil, hoping they'll fade.

'And how *are* you going with that?'

'Better.' I nod. 'Pop told me to choose something better for myself. To follow my calling. To start working towards the life I want for myself. Kinda like what you said to me.'

'And what's your calling?'

'I want to be a writer.'

'Do you have a story you want to tell?'

'I do.'

'What is it?'

'I'm not ready to talk about it yet. It's just an idea at the moment.'

'Ah, spoken like a true artist.' Miss Miller sits back. 'So, what are you thinking of studying at uni.'

'Journalism.'

'Great pivot!' Miss Miller's eyes brighten. 'You'll still be writing, still be getting paid, still be getting published. And lots of journalists go on to write books. I think that's a really great idea. Well done, you.'

'Thanks.' I look at the floor while an awkward smile bubbles up. This is the first time someone's spoken to me about my future with such enthusiasm. She sounds more excited than I do.

'And where are you thinking of studying?'

'I hadn't really thought about it. I assumed I'd stay here. But there are universities all over Australia offering these courses. Maybe I could move interstate, make a fresh start.'

'What's stopping you?'

'I don't know if I can afford it.'

'What? Uni? HECS will cover that.' Miss Miller waves that worry away. 'And then you don't pay it until your degree starts paying you.'

'And I'd have to get there, find a place to live — which means I need a plane ticket, rent, bond.'

'So, get a part-time job,' Miss Miller says. 'Start saving. You've got this.'

My feet ache. I sit on the lounge and rub my soles, bandage my blisters and slide my work shoes on for another night of waiting tables in Beverly Hills. I've picked up some extra work at the café because it's the school holidays. Double shifts on weekends, open to close, plus my usual evenings. There's also the walk to and from Padstow Station at the start and finish of each stint.

'You going to work?' Mum asks.

'Yep.'

'Again?'

'Yep.'

'I feel like you study all day and work all night.'

'That's because I do.' I pull my socks on. 'Trying to save up and catch up.'

It's a cash-in-hand job, so it doesn't increase Mum's rent or reduce my Youth Allowance. Mum's asked me to pay thirty dollars a week rent, but apart from that, schoolbooks, train tickets and driving lessons, I save everything.

'Save up for what?'

The stench of silverside wafts from the kitchen and activates my already sensitive gag reflex. I've stopped purging, but the smell of boiling meat makes me want to vomit anyway. I double over to tie up my shoelaces, breathing in the fresh scent of Radiant washing powder and sun-dried work pants.

'A car. Uni, hopefully,' I mumble into my thighs. 'Or whatever happens after I graduate.'

'But it's the holidays. How do you still have study?'

'Spoke to my year advisor. Organised to get my textbooks and reading list early.' I stand to button my blouse. 'I fell behind last year, so I'm trying to make up for it. Hopefully this frees up more time for extra study later on.'

Mum sits at the dining table, my two most recent report cards spread before her. She smokes her cigarette, drinks her coffee and compares my results, term on term. 'You're doing better,' she says.

'I was still getting sixty to seventy per cent in exams.' I point at the examination marks defensively.

'Hey, it's better than what I would have got.' Mum puts her hands up. 'But you're smarter than me. And they know it. That's why they said you could do better. And you have. All your marks are sitting between seventy and eighty per cent.'

'It's getting there.' I collect my report cards and put them back in my school bag. 'And they've given me some practice exams to do, so I'll be able to get some feedback on those when I go back too. I'm hoping all of that pushes me up into the nineties.'

'You're all work, no play,' Mum says. 'You should do something nice for yourself.'

'I'm going shopping next weekend, between shifts. I need to get some nice tops and pants for work experience at the newspaper.'

'When's that happening?'

'The week before I go back to school.' I tie my hair back.

'What about work?'

I check my weekly train ticket is in my purse. 'They know and they're fine with me starting my shifts an hour later that week, so I can get from A to B.'

'Then you really will be working all day and all night.'

'Yep.' I nod. 'Short-term pain, long-term gain.'

40

The bruises on my arms and legs have faded, but the scars on my wrists still turn purple in the cold: a reminder that the troubles aren't too far behind me. I must stay focused on the future. I rub Bio-Oil into the wounded skin, cover the scars with Barbie sweatbands and look in the mirror. My first newspaper by-line stares back, stuck to the glass so I can see it every single day, like an affirmation. I catch my reflection and smile at the memory of the *Canterbury-Bankstown Torch* being delivered to the front lawn, thrown from the window of a passing car. I sat outside in the ramshackle backyard and read my article on the Stallholders Expo to the sky, hoping Pop could hear me and that he'd be proud, even though it was significantly rewritten. And then I pored over the edits so I knew what I could do better next time.

There's a knock on the door.

'Come in.'

Mum holds the report card I left on the table when I got home from work last night with this week's rent. Things feel like they've improved between us. She's started letting me wash some of my clothes with hers and the boys' again. Except for my underwear, which is fine. And I still have my own towel. But at least I can use communal plates, bowls, cups and cutlery again.

'Just read your report card.'

'What do you think?'

'Well, this says it all, really: "Shayla is a perceptive and articulate student who has achieved a high standard in her work. With continued revision of all concepts and syllabus outcomes, success in the HSC will ensue."'

A little bud of hope starts to bloom in my chest. 'Did you see I finally managed to crack ninety per cent?' I point to my society and culture results. 'Only just: ninety-one.'

'Hey, it's moving in the right direction, and you're beating everyone else.' Mum points. 'Look, "Position in examination: one."'

'Yeh, that's the one I got the academic achievement award for. And I'm in the top ten for all my classes now.'

'That's great!'

'It's better,' I say. 'But I'm aiming for the top five.'

Mum drops the report on my dressing table. 'Well, I think Ms Carr will be singing a real different tune at the parent-teacher conference next week.'

'Knock, knock.' Noah taps on my locker door. He's my competition in extension English. A bit of a nerd. Uses big words. School tie. Shirt tucked in.

'Hi?'

'I just wanted to say congratulations on receiving your academic achievement award the other day.'

'Thanks.'

'Really well deserved.'

I give a polite smile before I return to the contents of my locker.

Noah shoves his hands in his pockets, rocks back on his heels. 'So have you submitted your university preferences yet?'

'I have. You?'

'Sure have.' His voice sounds perky.

'Good.'

Noah's shoulders sag at my flat response. I close my locker and head towards my next class. He follows.

'So where are you going?' Noah asks, tone sunny but strained.

'Wherever they take me, I guess.'

'Maybe we'll end up at the same uni.' He bumps his shoulder into mine, like we're mates.

'May-be.' But very unlikely.

I stop outside the classroom just as the bell rings. Noah rubs his face with his palm like I've seen him do in class when frustrated.

'Is everything alright?' I ask.

'Yeh. I just wanted to … You have very unusual eyes.'

'Yeh.' I eye him warily, shifting my weight onto my back foot. 'I've been told.'

'No,' he says, holding his hand out, as if trying to retract the comment. 'I didn't mean to offend you. I meant it in a nice way. They're beautiful.'

I give a small, awkward laugh.

'I like them,' he says.

'Yeh, I got that. Thanks.'

People start to line up for class behind me. Noah rubs his face again, shakes his head. 'Well, I've really stuffed this up,' he says.

'Stuffed what up?'

'I came over to tell you that I like you and to ask you out.' He opens his arms wide, lets them drop to his side, intentions laid bare. 'But then I lost my nerve.'

'Like boyfriend-girlfriend? Or like, let's get a coffee and chat?'

'Like boyfriend-girlfriend.'

I clutch my textbook to my chest. 'I'm really just focusing on study at the moment, with the HSC and everything.'

He peers at me like a timid puppy from under his blond fringe. 'A coffee then?'

'Sure. I'm always up for a coffee.'

His brown eyes shine and he beams his braces at me. 'Great!' He walks backwards, almost bowing out of the conversation. 'I'll call you.'

The door opens and I head into class wondering if I've agreed to coffee or a date.

41

Noah slides into the chair next to mine in extension English. He tries to kiss me on the mouth. I turn my head. He kisses me on the cheek instead. Classmates still look surprised we've hooked up. They've told him that he's 'punching above his weight'. He didn't like it to begin with, but since then his confidence has grown and he's become a bit of a nerdy Casanova. He's swapped his school shoes out for black high-top Converse All Stars. He's stopped going to church and started drinking at house parties. And, since he's already eighteen, he's swapped stacking shelves at Woolworths for shaking cocktails at Revesby Workers' Club. His parents think I'm a bad influence, but he's not spending his weekends with me.

'What have I done wrong now?' Noah asks.

'Forget something over the weekend?'

'No.'

'Me?'

'We didn't have plans,' Noah says.

'I tried calling you all weekend. You could at least have had the decency to call me back.'

'I was working.'

'So was I. And, what, you were so busy you couldn't even manage to send me *one* text all weekend?'

'Phone died.'

'Your phone was dead *all* weekend?'

'Yep.'

'Right.' I slam my pencil case down on the desk. 'Well, that explains why it was still ringing.'

'Gum?'

I roll my eyes at the change of subject. Noah empties his pockets onto the desk. Wrigley's Extra Peppermint chewing gum. Some spare change. And a piece of paper with a name and phone number on it. I snatch the paper.

'Who is Crystal and why do you have her phone number?'

'Some chick from the bar. I didn't ask for it. She gave it to me.' He takes the paper from me, scrunches it up and tosses it in the bin. 'There. Happy?'

'No.' I sulk back in my chair, arms crossed across my stomach. 'No, I'm not.'

It's our last week of classes. I've spread out at the library. Post-it notes, Spirax notebooks and assorted Stabilo highlighters are littered across a table big enough to seat four people. I plug in my earphones, pick up a fluffy pink pen and channel Elle Woods from *Legally Blonde*.

Miss Miller pulls out the chair opposite me, looking very summery: roots freshly bleached, spray tan, yellow sundress and heeled hot-pink sandals.

'That was a bit of a scene in the quad earlier,' she says. 'Are you alright?'

'Yeh.' I take my earphones out. 'Noah found a copy of my university preferences in one of my textbooks.'

'Why was that a drama?'

'We weren't dating when I lodged them, and now he knows I applied interstate.'

'And you don't want to change them?'

'I don't think so, but I don't know. Things are better with Mum now, you know?'

Miss Miller nods.

'But her ex is still around and she changes when he's there. Like, I can tell by the tone of her voice, even on the phone, if he's there. And I just want to get away from all that. I feel like this is my chance to finally start living my own life.'

'Have you explained that to Noah?'

356

'No.'

'Why not?'

'This probably sounds harsh, but I just don't think I trust him.'

'With that kind of personal information, or more broadly?'

'Both.'

'It sounds to me like you're trying to protect yourself,' Miss Miller says.

'From what?'

'Sometimes we try to put distance between ourselves and what we perceive as a threat, something that might hurt us. It's called a defence mechanism. So when you say you don't want to tell him about why you want to move interstate for uni, that says to me that you don't want to show him your vulnerable side. You've already said you're not sure you can trust him and, as always, the most important question to ask is: why?'

'I feel like he's just being super sketchy at the moment.'

'Like how?'

I throw my hands up, then let them fall back to the table. 'Like, he was meant to pick me up from work yesterday, but never did. Wasn't contactable either. It's not the only time he's basically fallen off the edge of the earth either, then shown up with some other girl's phone number.'

Miss Miller's eyebrows twitch, freshly tinted and waxed.

'I mean, it feels a bit rich of him to show up looking like he hasn't been home or slept all weekend, demanding I change my preferences. Why do I have to change mine? Why can't he change his?'

'Did you ask him that?'

'He said because his family is here in Sydney. And so is mine.'

'Yeh, but you'll be a plane or a train ride away. And it's not forever, if you don't want it to be.'

'I know. But he's got me thinking, like, how will my friends and family take the news?'

'Well, they might miss you, but if this is really what you want to do, they should be happy for you.'

'I don't know what to do anymore.'

'What does your gut tell you?' Miss Miller raps her white acrylic nails on the desk. 'If I could give my seventeen-year-old self three words of wisdom to live by, it would be: trust your intuition. Our gut instincts are usually right. Intuition evolved as a survival instinct. We spend a lot of time as young kids and young adults suppressing what we know instinctually. We try to be popular. We try to fit in with people, even when it feels wrong. But actually, that gut instinct is one of the oldest and, I would argue, most vital forms of human intelligence. So, go with your gut.' Miss Miller stands up. 'And if you decide otherwise later, you can always change your preferences in time for round-two offers. You've got options.'

42

Mum drives through Minto, east of Pembroke Road. Suburban streets are busy with tradies in hi-vis vests. They drive utes and slow-moving trucks loaded with heavy demolition machinery. Minto public-housing estate is being knocked down in stages for the Minto Renewal Project, also known as One Minto. News articles say more than a thousand dwellings will be levelled in total; they were poorly designed and constructed, are infested with termites – and rather than being segregated, public and private housing will be incoporated into a single development for the first time in New South Wales. The houses that still stand look dilapidated, ill-maintained. I watch them go by, reminded of Rosemeadow.

'I don't wanna go to his house,' Joe cries.

'Me either,' Nash says.

They sulk on opposite sides of the back seat, arms folded, heads against the car windows. Hot tears and sobby breaths fog up the glass. Joe draws a sad face in the condensation. They've just turned seven and eight and they look like Mum: dark-brown hair and bright-green eyes. I'm the odd one out in the pack, like Mowgli in *The Jungle Book*.

'You have to go and see your father,' Mum says.

'Why?'

Mum ashes her cigarette out the car window, turns up Joe Dolce and sings 'Shaddap Your Face' to the boys via the rear-view mirror. It's very theatrical. Lots of big gestures. Nash and Joe throw their heads back and groan.

'Because he's your father,' Mum finally answers. 'And you haven't been to see him for weeks.'

'He's been to ours,' Nash protests.

'That's not the same,' Mum says.

Mum pushes freshly dyed hair out of her face, smoke trailing along the roof of the car, threatening to singe the headliner.

'Is Shayla staying with us?' Joe asks.

'No,' I scoff.

'Why are you coming then?' Nash asks.

'I'm going to drive back. Need to get these last few hours done so I can go for my P-plates in a couple of weeks.'

Noah and Joe keep snivelling in the back seat. It takes me back to that trip to Casula Fruit Market in Mum's yellow-glow Toyota Corolla and my heart aches. I rub at the centre of my chest with my fist, as if trying to rub away indigestion, and turn around in the passenger seat. 'Why don't you want to go?'

'Because it's boring,' Nash says. 'He doesn't do anything with us.'

'Yeh, he just makes us work in the backyard,' Joe says.

'Ah, child slave labour. Rob's specialty.' I say it loud enough for Mum to hear as I twist my body back to face the front.

Mum rolls her eyes at me, before saying to the boys, 'Surely you can help your father for one weekend. It's not even the whole weekend. It's just one night.'

'But that's two whole days.'

'No, it's not. It's almost dinnertime now, and I'll pick you up early tomorrow.'

Joe flings his legs against the seat, like a toddler throwing a tantrum.

It's never as simple as just dropping the boys off. Mum always needs to go inside to 'help get them settled', which is probably more about getting Rob settled than the boys, given the process involves having a 'quick cuppa', which takes about an hour, while I wait outside in a sweltering car with a warm bottle of water. I wind the window down and watch the boys drag their feet. Mum's hair shines in the sun, along with the velour of her black Juicy trackpants.

Rob rents privately, although the house looks like it might be ex-Housing. It's the same design as the one on Alma Road, except this one is painted beige instead of green and has two bedrooms instead of three. Mum's told me it's like a mausoleum inside, full of his dead mother's old brown furniture and beige ornaments. When the door opens it looks dark from outside, and I imagine it being cold, like a tomb.

It's a quiet street. Some kids are playing with a bouncy ball at the end of the cul-de-sac while their parents unload groceries from a car. A middle-aged couple tend their lawn: she pushes the lawnmower; he whipper-snips the edges. An older lady in gardening gloves kneels on a blanket to pull out weeds, white Maltese terrier trustily by her side. Everyone has a nice neat front yard, except for Rob. There's a trailer full of junk under his carport. A couple of immobile cars rust out on the lawn. A small boat on another trailer weathers in the driveway, while the car he drives is parked out on the road, alongside a new motorbike. It's not completely dissimilar to the shit fight of our backyard at home, but there's a discrepancy in value.

I check my messages and there's still no reply from Noah. I call his phone and it's off. I open *Monkey Grip* by Helen Garner and disappear into the inner-city suburbs of Melbourne.

'Sorry, it took a while to get them to settle.'

'All good.'

Mum opens the passenger door. I slap the magnetic yellow L-plates on the bonnet and tailgate.

'Hardly seems worth all the trouble for them to stay one night.' I slide into the driver's seat and nod to the house. 'How can he afford all this?'

'He's living off the money his mother left him.'

'But she died when he was living with us. I remember him telling us there was no money.'

Mum nods.

'So, what, he was just squirrelling away money in some secret bank account while we were all living off instant noodles?'

'Apparently.' She looks out the window. 'Owns a block of land somewhere too.'

I shake my head as I adjust the seat and mirrors.

'Wasn't happy when Housing said he had too much money to go on the waiting list for a place.'

'Well, I'm not sure why he felt entitled to one.'

'Still doesn't pay child support either. I pay for everything.'

'How?'

Mum hasn't had a job since we lived at Kikori Place.

'With your child support.' Mum laughs.

'Hey, then why am I paying rent?'

'You live there, don't you?'

'Yeh, but, like, I pay for all my own stuff too. So shouldn't that cover some of it?'

'That's why you're only paying thirty dollars a week.'

I turn the key in the ignition and depress the footbrake, release the handbrake and push the indicator stick down.

'You try renting anywhere else for that,' Mum says.

I check the mirrors and my blind spot, move my foot across to the accelerator, edge away from the kerb and roll towards the intersection.

'Anyway, do we really need to get into this?' Mum lights a cigarette and sighs. 'It keeps a roof over our heads, it puts food on the table.'

'No, but it would've been nice to know it was there.'

'Why?'

'I don't know. Because it's *my* child support.'

'Nah-uh. That's not how it works. Otherwise the payment would go into *your* bank account.'

'It goes to you to cover the costs of raising *me*.'

'Yeh and I've raised you, haven't I?'

'Yes, but the amount of money you were getting was to raise one child, not three.'

'We made it work, didn't we?'

'Barely, and that's not the point.'

Mum throws her hands up. 'You get Youth Allowance and you have a job now, so what are you worried about?'

The change in the tone of her voice has been rapid. Disappointed and depleted to sassy and shrill before we've even made it out of Rob's street. She's never taken the mood stabilisers Dr Lou gave her. I found them hidden in her drawers, still unopened and very out of date, when I rifled through her room for codeine a few weeks before Pop died.

'Yeh, *now* I do.' I glance over at her while I wait for a break in the traffic.

There's a wry smile on her face. Her eyes have gone from tired to wired. It's taken having my own troubles with mental health to recognise the effects of trauma. The violence of my father. The miscarriages. Isolation. Poverty. Baby blues. And all of that untreated, due to the stigma of it, the fear of losing her children, the complete lack of access to support. We only ever had just enough to make ends meet and that meant Mum provided for us, as best she could, but never had the luxury of taking care of herself.

Keeping that in mind, I change my tone, try to de-escalate the situation, shift the focus. 'I'm just trying to save up for uni, that's all.'

'Well, the money we get from your father runs out when you turn eighteen, so what do you want me to do about it now?'

'Why don't you dob Rob in?'

Mum shakes her head and looks out the window. 'He'll only take it out on the boys.' She sighs. 'I'll figure something out. I always do.'

I sit at the computer desk with the roll-out keyboard shelf in the corner of Mum's bedroom. I want to review my preferences on the university admissions website, but the dial-up internet keeps disconnecting. I lean back in the dining chair and take a deep breath.

The phone rings and I spring up. 'Hello.'

'Is your mother there?'

I walk the cordless phone into the dining room and hand it over.

Mum looks up at me from painting her toenails purple. 'Who is it?'

'Who do you think?'

She rolls her eyes and takes the phone. 'Hello.'

I can hear Rob shout down the line.

Mum turns the volume down on the receiver. 'I didn't know you were calling, because Shayla's been on the internet.'

I throw my hands up, pissed off that the modem was disconnected by his persistent calling.

'Why didn't you call the mobile? Well, I don't know … Can't *you* bring them back? Been drinking, have you? Are they alright? Let me talk to Nash … Hi, honey. Why aren't you in bed? It's past your bedtime. Are you feeling unwell? … He being mean to you, is he? Is Joe okay? Can you just go to bed for Dad and I'll come and get you first thing tomorrow? Okay, put your father back on … Yeh, I'm leaving now. Make sure their bags are packed because I don't want to be hanging around. I'm tired, Rob. I was just about to get into bed. Okay, I'll be there soon. Tell them I'll be there soon. Okay. Bye.' Mum puts the phone down, throws back the last of her instant coffee and slips on her thongs. 'Can't even get one bloody night to myself.'

'What's wrong?'

'They don't want to stay. And he's had enough of them. I have to go get them.'

'Now? But it's almost midnight.'

'I know.' Mum yawns, rubs her eyes. 'But he's been drinking and I can hear them crying in the background. It's just not worth it. Do you have twenty bucks I can borrow for petrol?'

'Sure. Do you want me to come with you?'

'It's up to you.'

'I could use the extra driving hours.'

*

I steer the car down the M5 while Mum has a cigarette.

'Has he always been like this?'

'Who?'

'Rob. You've known him since he was a teenager. Has he always been ...?'

'As useless as tits on a bull?'

I shrug.

'Yeh. Pretty much.'

'Why'd you like him then?'

'Was young and dumb, I guess. What I would give to have known then what I know now.' Mum winds the window down, throws her cigarette butt out, winds it back up. 'I think I did know. Somewhere deep down inside I knew that he wasn't right for me.'

'Like a gut feeling?'

Mum nods. 'But I didn't listen. I kept trying to make it fit.'

'Why?'

'I guess I wanted it to work. Maybe I thought time would change him. Maybe I thought I could change him. Maybe I thought I'd change. But, really, I shouldn't have planned my life around anyone but me.'

'What would you do differently, if you could do it all again?'

'I wouldn't have dated Rob. I wouldn't have married your father. I wouldn't have had kids. I would have learnt everything I could and gotten a good job. Like a lawyer or something. Made lots of money. Travelled the world. Lived my own life.'

'You regret having us?'

'I don't regret having any of my children. I regret who I had them with. I'm just saying that if I could do it all over again, I'd do it differently. You only get one chance at life. You've got to live it for you. Make it what you want.'

After I park, I watch Mum approach Rob's, a list of tour dates and locations emblazoned in white down the back of her black Angels T-shirt. Noah should have just finished his shift so I give him a call.

It's disconnected. I call again and again and again. Eventually the call goes straight to voicemail. His phone is turned off.

Mum tosses a postcard on the end of my bed. 'This came for you.'

I put down *Promiscuities* by Naomi Wolf and Mum closes the door behind her. The postcard is an ad from the University of Sydney. There's a picture of the main quadrangle, looking very Hogwarts-esque, beneath a starry sky with a shooting star. *Shayla. No Limits.* is written in scrawly white text on the front.

It makes me think of Rosemeadow, of sitting in the gutter with Sean and Charlie, looking to the sky for some sort of sign that everything would be alright, only to have the street lights fizzle out, leaving us in darkness, listening to drunken domestics. I wonder how they're doing. I hope they're getting the same postcard.

43

'You know you could've had people over.' Mum comes down the back stairs in her black Deep Purple T-shirt.

I sit on a rickety wooden bench in the backyard with *Goodbye, Mr Chips*. There's just enough room on the side of the table for my coffee cup. The rest is covered with boxes.

'You don't like any of my friends.'

Finally, I'm eighteen. Old enough to drink. Legally. The pressure of the HSC is over. Noah and I have agreed we can make decisions about changing preferences or doing long distance or whatever later, but for now we're just going to try to enjoy each other's company while we anxiously await our letters of acceptance. Or rejection.

'I like Noah,' Mum says.

'Well, that's nice, but I have more than one friend.'

A series of celebrations are lined up. Tonight, I'll have a drink with Noah. Saturday will be dinner at the pub with schoolfriends. Sunday will be a roast lunch with the family, and Nanna will make her amazing gravy.

Mum chucks another black garbage bag on the table. My left eyebrow twitches. Mum sighs and rolls her eyes.

'I'm having a garage sale soon,' she says.

I sip my coffee. She's always having a garage sale.

'I know you don't believe me.'

I give a polite smile and return to my book. Nanna gave me this book for Christmas, continuing Pop's tradition. This was one of his favourites. I remember watching the film adaptation with him too. She included a photo of us as a bookmark. His scrawly shaky handwriting is on the back. 1994. The photo shows us both smiling proudly in front of the flowerbed we'd built in the corner of the backyard at Kikori Place. We'd filled the garden with clippings of Nanna's impatiens but, in the photo, it looks like we're just standing in front of a small patch of dirt with a semicircle of sandstone rocks around it.

'You know, there's enough space to have everyone over.' Mum gestures around the big backyard.

It's a shambles. Behind me, a trailer overflows under the carport, full of crap collected from council clean-ups. Under my bedroom window, the side of the cubby house has been ripped off to make it easier to stuff things inside, and rusty nails are exposed. In the back-left corner of the yard, two sheds are filled to the brim, padlocked shut, stained with rust. In the back-right corner, hundreds of red pavers are stacked up against the wooden fence. In the middle, two dirt bikes are parked on a lawn laden with bindis.

'And we have the pool,' Mum says.

The one from Rosemeadow. I watch the water ripple in the pool between the cubby house and the rusty sheds and shake my head at the memory of the five-hour diabetes blood test I was subjected to just so they could save a few bucks on soil by dumping rubbish in the hole left by the pool. Mum must think I'm shaking my head at her.

'Fine, don't have an eighteenth, but don't say I didn't offer.'

'I won't.'

Mum groans as she slowly eases herself into a low armchair. Her back is bad. Discs have popped out and they press on nerves that partially paralyse her legs sometimes. Every morning she shuffles into the kitchen to make her instant coffee, hunched over like Quasimodo, hand on her lower back, smoke hanging from her mouth. She's not yet forty but her hands are deeply wrinkled, darkly bruised and so dry the skin has cracked around the nails.

'Your hands look sore.'

'Years of hard work.' Mum holds her hands out like a badge of honour, even though she hasn't had a job in fourteen years.

'You need to drink more water and start using hand cream.'

'I moisturise.' Mum sucks on her cigarette, smoker's lines forming canyons around her lips. 'It comes off in the sink when I'm doing the dishes.'

'So wear washing-up gloves.'

Mum grunts.

I read to the end of the chapter. Mum stubs out her cigarette. She scrapes the butt along the bottom of the ashtray with her yellow middle finger and collects the ash in one corner. Then she lights another cigarette and tosses the lighter onto the table.

'Any news about uni?' she asks.

'Nope.'

'What are you going to do if you don't get in?' Mum leans forward, grabs the local newspaper off the table. The one I did work experience with. She licks her finger and pinches the corner of the page, flicking from the back cover towards the front.

I shrug. 'I'll figure something out.'

'Are you worried?'

I rub my palms up the legs of my jeans. 'A little.'

'There's lots of bar work being advertised.' Mum points at the classifieds section.

'Yeh, I've been looking into getting my RSA. The money is a lot better than what I'm earning now, even after tax. But I guess it depends on where I get into uni.'

'It's a New South Wales-wide accreditation, isn't it?'

A plane hums overhead. I watch the white body, red tail and iconic Qantas kangaroo glide across the summer sky towards Sydney Airport.

'Yeh, it is. But I might just see what happens with uni first.'

'Do you think you and Noah will get into the same uni?'

'Probably not.'

'Why?' Mum looks up from the paper. 'Where did he apply?'

'The University of Sydney, the University of NSW and, I think, the University of Technology Sydney.'

'They sound good,' Mum says. 'You didn't apply to go to any of those?'

'No.'

'Where did you apply?'

'Oh, a few different places. Can't even remember now. Guess I'll have to wait and see what comes in.'

I order a cosmopolitan and stand at the bar at Revesby Workers' Club feeling like Carrie Bradshaw from *Sex and the City* with my curly blonde hair and pastel-pink high heels. The DJ kicks off with 'My Humps' by the Black Eyed Peas and the dancefloor fills with awkward eighteen-year-olds, fresh out of high school. Girls who haven't yet mastered the art of walking in high heels cavort around as gracefully as emus performing a mating dance. Boys who don't know what kind of dress shoes to wear with jeans watch from the sidelines, hands in their pockets trying to hide their boners.

Noah's flirting with a girl at the bar when I come back from the bathroom. She takes the drink he's bought her and walks away. He watches her disappear into the crowd. I tap him on the shoulder and raise my eyebrows.

'What?'

I roll my eyes.

'What?'

I pick up my handbag, one of Nanna's vintage Glomesh ones, and shoulder my way through the crowd grinding to 'Don't Cha' by The Pussycat Dolls, teenage anxieties now drowned out by loud music and Smirnoff Ice Double Blacks. Noah trails behind, dragging his feet like a toddler who doesn't want to leave Toys 'R' Us.

'Why are we leaving?'

'*We* aren't doing anything.' I storm across the car park towards the train station.

'Why are you angry?'

I spin around and stab my finger at the club. 'If that's what you're game enough to do while I'm in the bathroom, I can only imagine what you've been up to while I've been sitting at home waiting to turn eighteen.'

'You're overreacting,' he says.

'Noah, it's my *birthday*.'

He rubs his hand over his face, frustrated. 'You always make me out to be such a bad guy.' He pushes his hair back, tries to focus his eyes, rubs his hand over his face again. 'But I've never hit you when I've been angry.'

'What a fucking hero.' I step forward. 'Take your best shot. I've faced up to bigger and badder than you.'

Those words sound so familiar. Mum said something to the same effect once. I still remember the party castanets, the imprint they left in my hand.

The sound of train doors closing brings me back from Rosemeadow to Revesby.

'We're done,' I say, and walk away.

44

The old Hills Hoist clothesline squeaks and groans as it spins. Mum's blacks catch the summer breeze and flap in the wind like a murder of crows. She puts the empty washing basket down on top of the bags, on top of the boxes, on top of the table. 'Do you think you made a mistake?'

'With what?'

'Breaking up with Noah. Do you think you made a mistake?'

'No.'

'Are you sad?'

Mum lowers herself into one of the armchairs, plops down at the last moment and sighs, back sore from yesterday's roadside scavenger hunt, which has resulted in even more shit being stashed under the carport.

'A little. But also, I'm angry. It's not just what he said to me but *how* he said it, as if he was entitled to hit me. Like he wanted to and I should be thankful he'd refrained because that made him a good guy or something.'

Mum stubs out her cigarette. 'I'm not saying he should have said what he said,' she starts.

'He shouldn't have even been thinking it.'

'But let me tell you, there's a whole lot worse than him out there.'

I stare at her 'Hurts So Good' T-shirt for a long moment. She's worn it enough for me to know there's a John Mellencamp portrait on the back. 'I don't think that's the point,' I say, finally. 'In fact, that sets the bar pretty low for what constitutes a good guy, if you ask me. And I think I can do a whole lot better than be spoken to like that.'

'You guys had an argument. You'd both been drinking. He said something he shouldn't have. True love hurts sometimes.'

I slam my book down on the table, loud enough to make us both jump. 'You need to stop romanticising that shit, Mum. Debbie Harry and Chris Stein. Chrissy Amphlett and Mark McEntee. Tina Turner and Ike. All of them. They all had toxic relationships. Some were deeply violent. That's nothing to aspire to for yourself, or to teach your daughter to aspire to, or your sons. Love actually *isn't* meant to hurt. And it's not more real the more it hurts. In fact, it's probably quite the opposite.'

'Lozza, ya want another coffee?' Rob shouts from the kitchen window.

'Yes, please.'

'And that's another toxic relationship right there.' I sit back. 'Why is he even here?'

'He came over to see the boys.'

'Yesterday.'

'Yeh, and he helped me pick something up.'

'And he needed to stay, because ...'

'Because he hardly got to see the boys yesterday.'

'So why have they been holed up in their room all day?'

'I don't know, Shayla. You'd have to ask them.'

'I'm asking *you*. You're the adult. It's your house. Why can't he take them to his place for the weekend? That's what normally happens when people are separated.'

'They won't go. You know that. You've seen it.'

'Yeh, because they hate him.'

Mum sighs deeply.

'Why can't he just take them out for the day and then drop them back? Why does he have to be here? And *stay* here?'

'He says it's too far to go.'

'Really? Campbelltown is too far to drive to and from in a day?'

She nods.

'You do realise there are people who live in Campbelltown and commute to and from the city every single day for work? If they can manage it, why can't he?'

'Well, he can't drive if he's been drinking.'

'Maybe he shouldn't be drinking here then.'

'Why does it bother you so much?'

'Are you serious? Because he's got you as trapped here as you were in Rosemeadow.'

'That's not true.'

'Why do you think he's here?'

'I already told you, to see the boys.'

'Oh, stop pretending he's here for the boys. He's not. He never does anything with them. That's why he's sitting in front of the TV alone with a bottle of beer. The boys don't want anything to do with him. That's why they don't come out when he's here. None of us want anything to do with him. He's here to control you.'

'Here's here to help me.'

'You say that all the time, but really he's just manipulating you. He knows you don't have the resources to do things yourself. He knows that because he doesn't pay any child support. And why do you think he doesn't? It's financial control. He wants you to need him, even if you're using him, so he can claw his way back into your life. You think he does this out of the goodness of his heart? You think it's free? It's not. He stays here. He eats our food. He uses our utilities. He stores his crap in our yard. And it's all to control you. As long as his shit is in your life, you'll never be free of him.'

'He doesn't control me anymore.'

'We moved here to get away from him. You promised me he would never set foot in this house. And he was the first one to walk through the door. He terrorised me as a child and every time you let him in this house, I feel like you've chosen him over me.'

Mum looks away, shakes her head.

'Imagine how you'd feel if I suddenly forgave my father and invited him over for dinner.'

'Not to my house you wouldn't.'

374

'No, not to any house. But hypothetically, if I did, wouldn't it feel like the ultimate betrayal? A big bloody slap in the face after everything that we went through together?'

Mum nods, and tears spill down her cheeks.

'That's how I feel about him coming here.'

'It's different.'

'Maybe it pales in comparison to what my father did, but that doesn't make it okay. He's still a bad man. He's just a different kinda bad.'

'Anyway, we're not talking about that.' Mum pats her cheeks dry. 'We're talking about you and Noah.'

'Yeh, another arsehole.'

Mum looks scolded again.

'Why are you taking this break-up worse than me?'

'I just want you to find someone nice, someone who loves you and looks after you,' Mum says.

'I'm fine. I can look after myself.'

'I know you can. I just want you to have a better life than me, that's all.'

'Well, no offence, but this is probably a step in the right direction, because if he's lying and cheating and threatening me now, how do you think it's gonna go in the future? It's a sign of things to come. And it's not a good one. It's a big red fucking flag.'

Mum's eyebrows rise. She takes a deep breath and nods slowly, more to herself than me. Her face and body soften, and she relaxes back in her seat, a wistful-looking smile on her face. 'You're right, Shayla. You're right. You've always been so smart. That's why you're going to go off to university.' She points at me with her cigarette. 'You'll be the first person in our family to do that, you know? Actually, you're the first one to even finish high school.'

'Well, we don't know about the uni bit yet.'

'You'll get in. I know you will.'

'Thanks.'

'You know I'm proud of you, right? I know I didn't always

get it right. I made mistakes with you, and I'm sorry. Sometimes I didn't know what to do. Especially with Mirko. After everything that happened with your father, I didn't want anyone else to take advantage of you. I was scared and I was angry, and I didn't know how to handle it. I thought I was protecting you. I didn't mean to hurt you in the process. But I am very proud of who you've become and what you've accomplished.'

Nanna opens her front door. She wears her signature black skirt, straight to the knee, with slippers on for pottering around. Her green eyes are framed by black mascara and there's rouge on her cheeks. She throws a tea towel over her shoulder and kisses me on the cheek, smelling of Tabu. 'Happy birthday!'

'Thank you.'

Nanna holds the door open while Mum, Nash and Joe file in after me, each of us branded with red lipstick as we enter.

'Can I get another?' Mum asks Nanna, pointing to the opposite cheek.

Nanna obliges. Mum looks into the mirrored back of the display cabinet, full of glass and porcelain, and rubs the red lipstick into her cheeks like blush. The boys scrub at their faces.

'Here,' Mum says, reaching for my face and rubbing the lippy off with her thumb. 'There you go.'

Nanna's oven radiates warmth. The hearty aromas of home cooking fill the house. A freshly baked vanilla sponge cake sits on a cooling rack. Mixing bowls of pink icing, strawberries and cream blanket the busy kitchen benches. Nash turns on the telly and Joe pops a DVD in the player. Nanna still has the same squeaky green velvet lounge she had at James Street. The soft fabric is patterned with fern fronds.

'Lunch won't be long,' Nanna tells the boys.

They're already transfixed by *The Goonies*.

'It smells amazing, as always,' Mum says.

'Thanks for cooking, Nanna,' I say.

'My pleasure.' Nanna puts some mixing bowls in the fridge. 'It's nice to have someone to cook for. I miss cooking for your grandfather. Good food and wine are meant for sharing with family and friends. There's very little joy in eating and drinking alone.'

She's lost weight since Pop died. Dropped five dress sizes in sixteen months.

'Speaking of wine, shall we sit outside for a bit? The chicken needs another ten minutes or so. Then all I need to do is make the gravy and put the icing on the cake.'

Mum and I follow Nanna into the second bedroom. Pop's books are still on the shelves, his slippers by the back door. The room leads out into a cosy courtyard, where I'd often find Pop reading. It's paved with terracotta.

They decided they didn't want to have to maintain a lawn and store a mower or whipper-snipper when they downsized. But they still wanted a garden and installed raised brick flowerbeds with edges thick enough to sit on, so they didn't have to get down on their hands and knees to weed. Hanging pot plants hover from scrolled outdoor wall brackets hooked over the fence. Nanna's herbs grow from a vertical garden attached to the back wall.

And in the middle of the courtyard is the white five-piece filigree outdoor setting they brought with them from Punchbowl. Today there's an ice bucket in the middle of the table, with a bottle of Moët & Chandon and four champagne flutes.

'Lauren, can you open that, please? I don't want to break my nails.'

Mum removes the foil collar around the neck of the bottle and the little cage over the cork. She wraps her hand around the top and looks to Nanna.

'Ready?'

Nanna nods. Mum twists the cork and it pops.

'Yay!' they chime together.

'What's that about?' I ask.

Mum pours the bubbles.

'You should always celebrate popping a cork,' Nanna says, like it's just common sense.

'Little family tradition,' Mum says.

'I've never seen you do it.'

'I haven't had anything to celebrate.' Mum picks up the fourth glass. 'Am I filling this one up too?'

'Just a splash,' Nanna says. 'He'd want to be here for this.'

Mum sets half a glass down in front of what would have been Pop's chair. Beads of bubbles trail to the top of the glass. Nanna raises her glass. Mum and I follow.

'Happy eighteenth birthday,' Nanna says. 'And congratulations on completing your High School Certificate.'

'We'll need another bottle for when she gets into uni,' Mum says.

'And when she graduates.' Nanna smiles.

We clink glasses.

'I've got some orange juice inside, if it's too much for you,' Nanna says to me.

'No, it's fine. I like it. Thank you.'

'Good.'

Nanna looks to Mum and raises her eyebrows.

'We have something for you.' Mum slides an envelope across the table.

Nanna taps the envelope with her nail. 'This is from the two of us.'

I put my glass down and pull the card out of the envelope.

'Careful,' Nanna says.

But it's too late. Ten green bills fall out into my lap.

'Ohmigod!' Tears spring to my eyes. 'What is this?'

'It's a thousand dollars.' Nanna sips from her glass, green eyes sparkling like the champagne.

'We know you've been saving up so you can buy a car,' Mum says. 'We thought this might help.'

'It will help enormously, but I feel bad taking it.'

'Don't,' Nanna says.

'It's too much.'

'It's really not.' Nanna pushes a book-shaped gift towards me.

'Are you sure?' I look to Mum.

She nods and her eyes glisten with tears too.

'Here,' Nanna says, giving the book another little poke towards me.

I put the money back in the card and rip the wrapping off *The Book Thief*. 'Thank you!' I stand up and hug Nanna around the shoulders. 'I've been wanting to read this.'

'I'd be looking at the bookmark if I were you,' she says.

I flip to the middle of the book and there's a photo that Mum took of Nanna, Pop and me in the front garden at James Street. Nanna in her black knee-length skirt. Pop in his polo shirt.

'Turn it over,' Nanna says.

I turn it around and there's a piece of paper folded and sticky-taped to the back. It's a cheque. A cheque for ten thousand dollars. My breath catches in my throat.

'It's from Pop,' Nanna says, tears on her cheeks.

'What? No. I can't. This is way too much! You've already given me enough. Honestly, I can't take this.' I hold the cheque out to Nanna, but she pushes my hand back towards me.

'It's not mine,' she says. 'It's yours.'

'How? And don't say "because I'm giving it to you", because you're not.'

Nanna shakes her head, wipes her tears. 'Remember that Happy Dragon bank account Pop started for you in kindergarten?'

'Yeh.'

'He kept it going. Every birthday, every Easter, every Christmas, he added to it. Every time you passed an exam. Every time you won an award. All his spare change. Almost every week he put something in the account and over time I guess it all just added up.'

'Probably earned some interest too,' Mum says.

We're all crying now.

'He wanted to be here to give it to you himself on your eighteenth birthday. He wanted you to have something to start your life with. He can't be here to do it, but he did want you to have this. It was his last wish. I can even show you his will if you don't believe me.'

I sit back down and sob. Nanna stands up, puts her hand on my shoulder.

'Don't squander it,' she says. 'Do something important with it. Make your grandfather proud.'

'I will. Thank you.'

'I'm just going to check on that chicken,' she says. 'Come in for lunch when you're ready.'

I look across to Mum and shake my head in disbelief.

'Is my mascara running?' she asks.

'Yep.'

'So much for being waterproof.'

I step out of my bedroom to go to the bathroom and hear them fighting in the lounge room. Not like they used to. More of a squabble by comparison, really.

'What have I done now?' Rob asks.

'Nothing,' Mum says.

'Then what's the problem?'

'I just don't want you staying here.'

'Why?'

'Because you've been here all weekend. You even waited here while the rest of us went to Mum's for Shayla's birthday. Now it's Monday night, you haven't done anything with the boys and there's no reason for you to be here.'

'I wish you'd told me that before I had a drink.'

'Well, stop drinking now so you can drive home later.'

There's the twist and fizz of a fresh beer bottle being opened.

'What's brought this on?'

'I just don't want you here. You've overstayed your welcome. It's not your place. It's mine. I shouldn't have to explain myself to you. You have a home to go to, so go.'

'It's *her* isn't it?' Rob slams the beer bottle down on the coffee table. The lounge creaks as he stands up. 'I saw her getting in your ear out there the other day.'

I move from the hallway into the dining room. 'I assume you mean me?'

'Hiding in the hallway listening, were you?'

I narrow my eyes. 'Oh, you recognise the behaviour, do you? Perhaps because you yourself have a nasty little habit of sneaking up on people.'

Rob puts his hands on his hips. 'What've ya been saying to ya mother about me?'

Mum sits at the dining table with a smoke and a steak knife doubling as a letter opener. I scan the mail and see a fat A3 envelope with the Australian National University logo under the pile of bills and Priceline rewards club vouchers.

'C'mon' – Rob steps forward – 'have the fucking balls to say it to my face.'

I walk across the dining room. 'I said you're a bad person. A bad man. I said the relationship between the two of you is toxic. It always has been, it always will be. And that I don't like you being here.'

'It's none of your fucking business if I'm here.'

'Actually, yeh it is. I pay rent. I pay bills. I buy food. I live here. You don't.'

He shifts his weight onto one foot. There's the nose-lip sniff-twitch. He scoffs and looks away. *The Footy Show* flashes on the telly behind him.

'Nobody wants you here, Rob.'

He gets up in my face. The drinking has aged him. His beard is fully grey now. His chipped tooth is stained and his face is red. His beer breath turns my stomach. When I was younger, he would stand over me. Now I realise he's actually pretty short for a man. He can't stand over me anymore.

'Mum has asked you to leave. And it smells like you've only had one beer, so you should be okay to drive.'

I try to turn away before my courage runs out, but he grabs me, pulls me back. I look at his hand on my arm. The 'Such is life' tattoo on his forearm has faded to grey, just as the Southern Cross has on his shoulder. His grip burns, my temper flares and a spark of adrenaline rushes through my body. I try to rip my arm away, but he tightens the vice around my bicep. My skin is twisted, wrinkled by his fist, but my eyes are bone dry. I stare down my nose at him.

'Go on. Make your mark,' I say. 'She mightn't press charges, but I sure as hell will. And when I've got that AVO in my hot little hand, you'll never be able to come near here again.'

He tries to stare me down like Brindy. But I don't break eye contact.

'Do it.' I thrust my chin forward and dare him.

Mum pushes her dining chair back from the table, across the carpet. Her back cracks as she stands up. 'Take your hands off my daughter,' she says, calmly. 'I've asked you to leave.' She picks up the phone and hits three buttons. I assume all zeros.

Rob looks past me and blinks a few times. 'You crazy bitch,' he says.

'Oh, honey,' Mum says, laughing. 'You don't know the half of it.'

Epilogue

Westminster Way is gone. I thought it would be here forever. I thought I would be too, once. And even though I left, it stayed with me. I shake my head, remembering how my heavily pregnant mother struggled to push slabs of VB up this street for a man who definitely didn't have a 'hard-earned' thirst. The street seemed so much longer, wider, steeper then. Now it could be mistaken for a driveway.

'Can I help you, lady?'

I turn towards the crunch and grind of dirt and rock under work boots. A man approaches slowly, grease-stained Macca's bag in hand. He's tall and athletic-looking, despite walking with a slight limp. There's swelling visible around his right knee, perhaps from a sports injury. It makes me think of Sean, makes me wonder if his dreams of footy fame ever came to fruition.

'You lost?'

I hold my arms out and gesture widely. 'Where is everything?'

He looks around. 'Gone.'

'Ha!' I drop my arms and turn in a small circle, taking in the emptiness behind the temporary fencing, excavator track marks in the dirt where houses once stood and neighbours sat around a grubby outdoor setting drinking, while their kids played cricket with rubbish bins on the street.

'Are you okay?'

I press my palm against my stomach, just below my ribs, trying to stop the hollow ache that's sprung up from moving into my chest. 'Sorry. I grew up here. I just can't believe it's gone.' My throat tightens, tears prickle in my eyes. I pluck sunnies off the top of my head and push them up the bridge of my nose. 'I actually hated living here, so I don't know why I'm so upset.'

He stares into the gutter, giving me a small amount of privacy while I compose myself.

'Do you know where number twenty was?'

'Just where that blue skip bin is.'

'Oh, I thought it was up further.'

'Nope, just there.'

'I used to live there.'

'This place must have made a lasting impression, huh? We've had a few people come back and take a look.'

I wonder if they felt the same as me – conflicted.

The man puts his lunch bag by his feet, zips up the grey fleece jacket under his orange vest.

'Are you building more of those fancy new houses here?' I ask.

'Nah, I'm just in the demolition side of things. Why, don't like them?'

'I know it sounds crazy, but I feel like seeing them here hurts my inner child a bit.'

'Nah, I get it. I grew up in a similar sorta place.'

'Where?'

'Housing estate in Villawood. They'll probably knock that down one day too.'

I nod. Demolition man puts his hands in his pockets and shifts most of his weight onto his left foot. We look towards the new houses on the horizon.

'Stand out like a sore thumb, don't they?'

'Yep. Like big, shiny beacons of economic disparity.'

'I feel sorry for the kids,' he says. 'I wouldn't have liked seeing this across the road from me when I was growing up. Would've made me feel like shit.'

'When I lived out here, this kinda thing was more contained to Glen Alpine or Rosemeadow Gardens, so it felt like most of us were stuck in the same shitty little boat.'

'Yeh, but now it's really obvious. It's, like, right under your nose.'

'Maybe when you're halfway through "rebuilding a community" it just kinda accidentally looks like the segregation has closed in for a bit.'

'I dunno.' He shrugs. 'Feels like salt in the wound to me.'

'I guess there's also the whole "you can't be what you can't see" argument.'

Demolition man tilts his head to the side, like he's considering whether or not he agrees.

'I'm just not sure if seeing like *this*' – I open my arms to my old neighbourbood, now seemingly divided into an upper and lower class by Copperfield Drive – 'helps close the gap by showing you what's possible, or widens it by showing you what's unattainable.' I hold my hands out, weighing the options. 'Probably depends on the time. And the place. And the person.'

'Well, you must have seen something pretty different.' Demolition man gestures towards my car. 'That's a fancy drive.'

I nod slowly, realising that I must stand out like one of those fancy new homes now too.

'So, what do you do with yourself?'

'I'm a journalist. I'm actually writing an article on new integrated developments like this.' I look around again. 'Maybe when they finish the project the differences won't look so … stark.'

'Maybe.' Demolition man picks up the Macca's bag and pulls out two cheeseburgers.

'Gosh they smell good.' My stomach grumbles. 'You know what? I don't think I've had Macca's since I lived here.'

'Take it.' Demolition man holds a burger out to me. 'Go on. May as well have the full trip down memory lane experience while you're here. I don't have enough time to eat them both before the crew get back from lunch anyway.'

'Oh, I'm sorry.'

'Don't be. It's been nice talking you. Interesting. And you're probably doing me a favour,' he says, patting his stomach. 'I'm Damien, by the way.'

'I'm Shayla.'

I hold my hand out to shake and he slaps the burger into my palm.

'Thanks.' I look at the greasy wrapper, thinking of Sean, both of us so hungry we'd even eat the pickles.

'No worries.' Damien plonks himself down on the edge of the gutter.

I sit down next to him and a shard of sandstone stabs me in the butt. I think of the artifacts of my life here, buried in that pool grave. 'Man, if this street could talk, the stories it would tell.'

Damien nods, mouth full of French fries.

'You know, I've lived in a lot of places. I've lived interstate and I've lived overseas, but no place ever shaped me the way this one did.' I look up the street, down the street. I feel kinda sad. Almost like I've lost something. 'Soon the whole area will be rebuilt and renamed, and it will be as if it never existed. As if we never existed.'

'Well, this place might not be standing, but you still are. You're a journalist. Write about it.'

'Yeah, but a newspaper article just doesn't feel like enough, you know?'

Damien shrugs. 'What more can you do?'

I smile to myself as I peel the pickle off my cheeseburger. 'I'm gonna write a book.'

Acknowledgements

First thanks go to my mentor, Kathryn Heyman. None of this would have been possible without you. You were the first person to see real potential in what I thought was just a pipe dream. Your unwavering confidence in this project gave me the courage to keep on believing in it. I feel no words will ever be able to fully capture just how grateful I am. You're an incredible writer, an amazing teacher, a remarkable person and I feel so blessed to have worked with you on this – thank you!

A huge thank you to my publisher, Aviva Tuffield, for championing my work and assembling a fantastic team to help release it into the world – editor Margot Lloyd, publicists Louise Cornegé and Sally Wilson, designer Amy Daoud, proofreader Lauren Mitchell, and everyone else behind the scenes at UQP. From the very first meeting, I knew this book would be in safe hands and that really meant a lot to me. I have appreciated your honest feedback and expert advice throughout this process. Together, I believe we've made this book the best it can be.

As a first-time author, asking for endorsements is, like, the most terrifying thing I've ever had to do. It's scary enough to let friends and family read your work, let alone published writers whose work you admire. Thankfully, authors are a friendly bunch, and everyone was very gentle with me and my exceptionally fragile ego. Big thanks go out to Venero Armanno, Tony Birch, Kathryn Heyman and Michelle Johnston – I'm just so deeply honoured (there were lots of happy tears).

Faber Writing Academy, class of 2018, you have been a tremendous support – especially the little writing group I was lucky enough to fall into with Alison, Christine, Felicity and Marianne. Writing can be so solitary, and the importance of a community like this one cannot be underestimated. Thank you for creating a safe space where I could share early (very rough!) drafts. Thanks also to Autumn and Jacqueline for your ongoing encouragement over big glasses of wine – much appreciated.

I'm so lucky and grateful to have such fabulous friends in my life. I adore you all and your support has meant so much to me. Very special mentions must be made of Sarah (who has listened to me talk about this book pretty much every single day for five years – I'm sorry!) and Rose (the first friend entrusted with reading the entire draft manuscript from cover to cover). I have such love, respect and admiration for you two wonderful women. My life is richer for having you both in it.

To my original cheerleader (and proofreader), Mum. I think you've been more excited about this than me, if that's even possible. There was never any doubt in your mind that this book would go places. When the offer came through, you weren't even surprised – you were like, 'See? What did I tell you?' Like all mothers and daughters, we have those moments when we could kill each other, figuratively speaking – but we'd also kill for each other. Thank you for always having my back.